# Where Lions Still Roar

## Joyce Baker Porte

Wavefront Publishing
P.O. Box 2965, Homer, Alaska 99603

Wavefront Publishing
P.O. Box 2965
Homer, Alaska 99603

www.joycebakerporte.com

Library of Congress control number: 2004116266

Porte, Joyce Baker
    Where Lions Still Roar/Joyce Baker Porte
    1. Africa 2. Tanzania 3. Massai 4. World War I
    I. Title

ISBN 0-9773252-1-0

This book is dedicated first of all to my parents, Russell and Helen Baker, who gave me the opportunity to grow up among the beautiful people of Tanganyika. Second, to my husband who tolerated so much neglect as I lived, ate, and breathed this book; and to my children, of course, who humored my forgetfulness and single-mindedness. Not least are the wonderful people of Invisible Ink, my writers group, who listened patiently as I read first drafts to them.

Parts of this novel have also appeared as short stories on Zoetrope Studio Short Story Workshop, and the critiques from my friends there have been invaluable. Several, especially, kept me writing when I doubted myself.

This book is a novel. The characters are fictional except for historical ones such as the German governors of German East Africa, and the generals in the Great War. In some places, I have kaleidoscoped events to make the plot flow smoothly. I have placed a hospital where none existed at the time in an effort to not recount the history of an existing hospital less than fifty miles away. The Maji Maji Revolt is historical fact, as are the effects of the War. The Huru Tribe does not exist because I do not wish to malign any existing tribe with events in this book and the following sequels in the trilogy.

I apologize if I offend anyone by my depictions of the Africans and Europeans, or by any inadvertent variation from facts. Attitudes, customs, and living conditions varied from clan to clan, and have changed drastically since the period of 1905-1920.

Some of the books I used for immersion in culture and history are:

*A Modern History of Tanganyika,* John Iliffe, Cambridge University Press 1979

*Africa Explored: Europeans in the Dark Continent 1769-1889,* Christopher Hibbert, W.W. Norton, 1982

*Road to Kilimanjaro,* Ruth T. Shaffer, Four Corners Press, 1985

*A Tale of a Maasai Girl,* Grace Mesopir Sicard, The Book Guild, Ltd., 1998

*Barefoot Across the Serengeti,* David Read, 1979

*In Darkest Africa,* Henry M. Stanley, Charles Scribner & Sons, 1891

And many other articles, travel books, personal communications, and internet research articles.

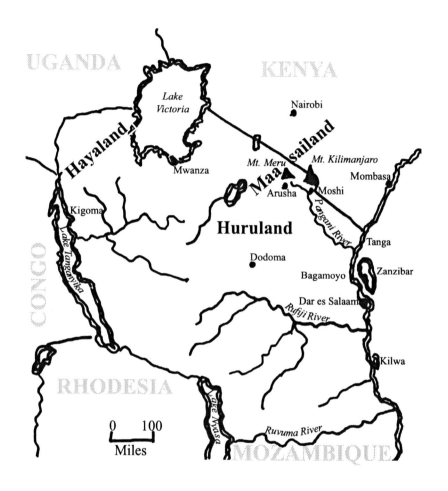

UGANDA

KENYA

Lake
Victoria

Nairobi

Hayaland

Mwanza

Mt. Meru

Mt. Kilimanjaro

Maasailand

Mombasa

Arusha

Moshi

Kigoma

Huruland

Pangani River

Tanga

Lake Tanganyika

Dodoma

Zanzibar

CONGO

Bagamoyo

Dar es Salaam

Rufiji River

Kilwa

RHODESIA

Lake Nyasa

0      100
Miles

Ruvuma River

MOZAMBIQUE

# German East Africa
## 1885 - 1918

# 1905

**In this year, three insignificant events occurred** that appeared to have no bearing on each other, yet these events changed the direction of several lives, bringing them together in an epic dance of shadows and light.

**In Arusha, German East Africa**, a German doctor and his wife took into their home a newborn girl orphaned by smallpox epidemic. They named her Rebeka.

**A hundred miles from Arusha**, Mpepo, a ten-year-old boy of the Huru tribe, observed the futility of a massive revolt against the Germans and discovered his life's purpose.

**In Torino Italy**, thugs hired by then-socialist Benito Mussolini assaulted Vito Fernaldi, a young law student, who then determined to spend his life seeking truth and justice wherever it might take him.

CHAPTER ONE

# German East Africa, 1905

**Mbae ole Kipchong stood in the deserted kraal and watched the herd of cattle,** along with the entire Maasai village, disappear north in a cloud of dust. Small boys scurried around the cattle wielding supple branches as whips. Mbae could no longer see his two wives, their belongings balanced on their heads and strapped to their backs. He knew he would never see them again. The pain in his soul equaled the pain in his injured foot, and he knew he would die when the two pains reached each other and united in one great sorrow too heavy to bear. He stood like a tree, tall and thin, his body covered only by a length of coarse cloth tied over one shoulder.

He had said goodbye, placing a hand on each head, giving them his blessing. Sitanga, his sister's son, would care for them. Sitanga had contracted the awful disease early, but survived it along with a handful of others. Both Mbae and his wives had survived the scourge twenty seasons before, and had not contracted it this time. But their three sons were not so fortunate and were among the recent dead.

Mbae might have gone with the survivors, but he could no more travel north with the clan than he could fly with the vultures that followed the band. He had soaked his wound in fresh cow urine and poulticed it with dung, but it continued to fester. His foot was swollen and any pressure caused a sharp pain to travel from his toes to his knees. He would only slow the traveling group and die of agony in the process. The wound oozed with the evil spirit that would continue up through his body until it reached his soul. Perhaps *Engai* planned this wound to keep him in this place, he thought with a bitterness that twisted in his stomach. He might have been tempted to go with the survivors, but no, he must sacrifice his life to ensure the survival of a child not yet born.

Behind him, in one of the huts that hadn't yet been torched, a young girl wrestled with the smallpox that ravaged her body. He prayed to Engai to keep him alive until the baby was safely born and he could be assured of its survival. Perhaps the girl would recover, since she was young and strong. In any case, the child's survival was more important than his or hers.

The disease had come with the boys who had shared a circumcision celebration with boys from other villages. Ten days after their return they came down with fevers and rashes all over their bodies, including the palms of their hands and the soles of their feet. Then they began to die, and other villagers sickened. The ones who lived were those few healthy enough to recover and the old who had survived the previous epidemic. More than half the people died.

The elders met and decided that *Engai* no longer blessed this location; they must move north to a place where he would smile on them again. Nareyu and Wambui, Mbae's wives wanted to stay with him, but he insisted that they go with the rest. If he should survive this infection he would join them. He gave them his cattle to care for them in their old age and instructed Sitanga to become the keeper of the legends at his death.

This child, soon to be born, would be the only living

descendant of *The One True Lion.* The young woman, Mbae's brother's only child, had been married to the only living person who carried the Lion's bloodline. Sadly, he had died in the recent epidemic, leaving no other children. And now she fought fever and incoherence. If he could find a way, he would keep her alive until she gave birth to her child.

Mbae glanced around the deserted village. Most of the *manyattas* were burned to the ground. Those remaining hunched down as though to hide their barrenness. Only one cow stood where many scores had milled around only moments before. She would supply nourishment for him until he died.

Beyond the thorn enclosure the yellow plains stretched out under the intense heat of the sun. Maribu storks stood portly guard and vultures huddled in the acacia trees; every now and then one would flap its wings and resettle in the branches to wait for another feast. He knew the lions were not far off. Their roars had filled the night air as they fought with the hyenas over the remains of the dead. Every day, for many days, those who remained strong carried the dying out to the plain for their final hours. This was the Maasai way. Those who exhibited bad manners and died in their *manyatta* had their hut burned down around them. It was taboo for a Maasai to touch a dead body.

For several hours Mbae stood in contemplation, his oozing, festering foot propped against the other knee. He found himself at peace with imminent death. His life had been good and he had held to the traditions and customs of his people. His body would nourish the lions that would defecate his remains onto the ground where they would nourish the grasses that fed the cows that gave the people milk to live. It was a cycle of human life, like rain and sun. It perpetuated the individual forever.

In the hut behind him the girl began to cry out as her disease-ridden body convulsed in too-early birth pangs. He bent double and, with the aid of his spear, limped through the low doorway to do what custom forbad a man to do—deliver a baby and sever the birth cord. As he drew it from the delirious mother's body he prayed, *let this be the manchild who was promised.*

The child was a girl. Mbae's disappointment twisted his stomach. *Not this generation,* he thought, and bowed his head to the will of *Engai.* The baby gave a healthy wail and he knew he must ensure her survival. She must carry on the lineage of *The One True Lion.*

He cut the cord with a sharp stone and knotted it close to the baby's navel. He wrapped her in a rag and placed her next to her mother's ravaged body, hoping that somehow the woman would find the strength to hold and nourish her child. He did not know what else to do.

The child lay in the semi-darkness of the windowless hut making little mewling sounds. Myriad flies clustered around her eyes, nose, and mouth. Mbae limped out of the stifling *manyatta* into the blinding sunlight to ponder his next move. The young mother, he knew, might not live.

For two days the child lay naked next to her mother, barely satisfied with the meager sustenance she found in her breasts. On the third day, her mother died and the baby's cries reached the ears of the waiting man. He pondered the situation for some time as he struggled to keep his mind clear through his own delirium. As her wails piled up in layers high enough to reach the ear of *Engai,* he knew he must find a source of food for the infant. Later, when her mother's body began to stink and he would have to set fire to the hut, he would think of what to do with the child.

The cow that remained in the kraal stood in the mind-numbing heat and tried to find something in her cud to chew. Her depleted hump sagged to one side; her ribs almost protruded through her skin. She stood there, patient and unmoving, as Mbae approached with a gourd in one hand, his spear in the other as a crutch. He leaned down and squeezed an udder between his leathery thumb and forefinger, sending a thin stream of milk into the gourd.

Next, he took the tip of his spear and stabbed the cow in the jugular. She flinched and tossed her head away but continued to stand still. Tiny scars across her neck testified to previous bloodlettings. Mbae caught the stream of hot blood in the gourd. He then pressed his thumb against the wound to staunch the flow and waited for several minutes until he was satisfied it stopped. He picked up a piece of fresh dung and plugged the wound.

The sun at its zenith melted the air into shimmery waves against the far hills as Mbae hobbled over to the hut, shaking the gourd to mix the blood and milk and hasten the clotting process. He would give the child a warrior's food of courage and strength.

The old man comforted her stomach and stopped her cries by forcing several clots of blood and milk into her mouth with his dirty fingers. Then she slept. He stood guard again outside the hut, his injured foot propped against the other knee. His mind blank, he leaned on his spear, certain that help would come.

The sun crossed the sky. A pride of lions slept on their backs, their distended stomachs gorged with human remains. As long as these lions lived, Mbae knew, human flesh would be their preferred diet. He stood motionless, dozing.

**Doctor Fritz Scheibel of the Leipzig Lutheran Mission wiped his forehead with his red handkerchief**. Tiredness filled his whole being, and the heat that bore down sucked out every bit of moisture. They would have to stop soon. His fifty-year-old legs did not want to keep pushing him forward.  They would have to turn back on the morrow to protect the remaining smallpox serum from spoiling. He closed his mind to the massive exhaustion. He would push on just a little further. Lives depended on his effort.

He knew that this smallpox epidemic would exact a huge toll. For fifteen years he and his wife had lived and doctored among the people of German East Africa and he knew by heart the progression of famine, pestilence, and disease. For two years the rains had held back and crops and grasslands suffered. Then came a rinderpest outbreak, an acute and contagious bovine virus that affected both wildlife and cattle when they became weakened by famine. The German governor estimated that ninety percent of the cattle died leaving the cultures that depended on them for survival at the mercy of disease.

Then, when a survey team came through Arusha and someone came to his hospital with smallpox, he knew it could not be contained. Contracted in the ports of Eastern Africa from the seamen who came and went like flotsam and jetsam, the disease had spread through the native villages like a grassfire in dry season. Fritz had ordered a large supply of vaccine because he knew the pox would come.

He first vaccinated the townspeople and then moved into the native villages around the foothills of Kilimanjaro and Meru. The Chagga people welcomed the help, but the Maasai distrusted anything introduced by outsiders.

Now he was headed north toward several villages he had heard about on the other side of Mount Meru. Along with him went Kuyoni, a town Maasai, to translate. The serum was packed in wet straw surrounded by canvas water bags to keep it as cool as possible. All this was loaded onto a mule-drawn cart along with their food and supplies.

They traveled most of the day and found one large Chagga village that hadn't yet received the vaccine. Then they continued on to the verge of a river where they set up camp. The river was a bed of sand now, with a few pools of stagnant water that slaked the thirst of beasts, and where they could re-soak the straw protecting the serum. After dark, as they sat around the campfire, they heard the coughs and roars of lions and the whooping laughter of hyenas.

"Don't be alarmed," Kuyoni said after he listened for a few minutes. "They go north to a big kill. They won't bother us."

They laid their bedrolls close to the fire and slept. In the morning when they woke there was no sign of predators. Herds of antelope and zebras grazed peacefully across the plain. They walked beside the cart all day without a sign of any village.

Now, as late afternoon approached and the sun's heat began to wane, Fritz decided to turn back to preserve the serum and his own health. The two men began to look about for a camping place. They came to an open area where many cattle had grazed the dry grass down to the dust beneath. Recent dung lay on the ground. A sickly sweet smell assaulted their noses as they approached and flies buzzed in their faces.

"Look." Kuyoni pointed. There, under a tree, a pride of lions slept like so many kittens in a pile, stretched out full length with distended bellies exposed. "We must go around," he said. Fritz had never seen lions so close and he felt the hairs on the back of his neck rise. One or two lions raised their heads to look at the men, but lay right back down.

They backed up and skirted the lions. As they entered the scrub they saw human bones scattered around. The putrid smell increased to where they had to place handkerchiefs over their noses. Many vultures pecked at the bones, and more perched in the trees. As the men came out of the bushes they saw what was left of the village—the circle of thorns that encompassed an empty cattle kraal, and the deserted and burned *manyatta*s.

*I'm too late,* Fritz thought. *Everyone is dead or gone.* They drew closer and saw one lone man standing in the kraal watching them. Without a word he went into the *manyatta* behind him, came out with a bundle in his hands, and held it toward Fritz.

Fritz took it from him. He looked down and saw that it was a baby, half-alive, its face dotted with flies. In all his medical experience, he had never failed to feel the joy and miracle of a newborn baby, and now a feeling of tenderness washed over him. But immediately another feeling replaced it, a strange premonition of trouble, a feeling of dread that squeezed his chest. He didn't want to take this baby. The old man, his intense eyes sunken into his skull, jabbered away in the Maa language.

"He says that *Engai* sent you," Kuyoni translated. "He waited for you to come. Now he can die in peace." Mbae looked at him for assent.

Fritz's German common sense stepped between his foreboding and his duty as a doctor to save this child. He nodded to Mbae, who let loose another stream of language. Kuyoni looked serious.

"What did he say?"

Kuyoni was quiet for a few moments and then said, "This child is special. You must treat her with care. She is a child of *The One True Lion.*"

"What do you mean, she's a child of *The One True Lion*?" But Kuyoni wouldn't answer. He only shook his head and shrugged. The premonition squeezed Fritz again, but he ignored it.

He noticed the man's foot, swollen with infection. "Ask him

what happened to his foot."

Kuyoni spoke a few moments with the man. "His name is Mbae ole Kipchong. He is *oloiboni* of the Engerot Clan. Many people have died and the rest have fled north with the cattle to escape the wrath of *Engai*. He stepped on a poisonous thorn in haste and he believes he will die."

"I should take a look at his foot and treat him. It's late. We might as well stay the night here in the kraal."

It was now late afternoon and the setting sun touched the world with a red-gold wash. They would camp inside the thorn-enclosed kraal for safety and leave in the morning. Kuyoni fed the baby some of the blood and milk curds while Mbae set fire to the *manyatta* that held the baby's dead mother. Fritz then washed Mbae's foot with antiseptic and bandaged it.

"Tell him he must come to Arusha with us," he told Kuyoni. "I can't leave him here to die."

**Ursula Scheibel stumbled to the door of the fieldstone mission house.** Her hair, usually braided and crossed over the top of her head, lay in damp, blonde strands on her shoulders and made her look younger than the stolid matron she was. Her malaria attack was over and the hospital needed her. But first she needed a bath, and that meant a call to the kitchen for hot water. For three days she had tossed on her bed with fever. As she squinted her eyes against the burning, bright sunlight on the dusty yard, she couldn't avoid the sight of the fresh mound under the bougainvillea that was all she had left of baby Marta. As her eyes brushed past that pain, she couldn't help but see the other two grass-covered mounds with little crosses. Peter and Katherine.

"*Gott,*" she whispered as a fresh stab of heart-pain shot

through her. "You have gone too far this time. I cannot bear it. Why have you done this? Why do you continue to test me?" She forced her eyes past the symbols of her pain and looked toward the kitchen, a small mud-brick building with a corrugated tin roof about ten yards from the house. She could hear the houseman in friendly argument with someone.

"Anderea, *leta hapa maji moto!* Bring me hot water!" The kitchen conversation ceased and Anderea stuck his head out of the doorway.

*"Eh, Mama!"*

Ursula returned to sit on the side of her bed feeling lightheaded after her first venture from the bedroom since Fritz left three days before. She was fine, she insisted to him as he kissed her goodbye. He said he hated to leave her right after Marta's burial, but he must take the smallpox vaccine north. She intended to work hard at the hospital, keep her breasts bound to dry up her milk, and try to forget. But as soon as he was out of sight she felt the familiar wave of nausea and fever that signaled a malaria attack. If it weren't for Songea, the *ayah* she hired four months before to help with the baby, and the kitchen boys who made tea and soups for her, she might not have survived.

Thank God her illness was only a touch of malaria, not the dreaded blackwater fever that took her four-month-old baby. That fatal disease caused the deaths of most of the Europeans who came to this stern country. Some people survived only a year or two before they succumbed. Those with stronger constitutions were able to live through the heat and disease. Everyone suffered from malaria.

She sat in a semi-stupor as she heard Anderea splash hot water into the galvanized metal tub in the washing alcove. She heard him set the five-gallon tin on the cement floor, pick up the cold-water tin and mix it slowly with the hot. Gratitude filled her heart. He had never done that before. He must have realized she didn't have the strength to lift it herself.

"All ready, *Mama!*" Anderea knocked on the closed inside door, and she heard him leave through the outside door. She waited a moment, got up slowly, picked a clean towel off the shelf, and went to her bath.

Cleansed, with a fresh dress on and her hair braided and pinned up on her head, Ursula sat in a chair on the covered porch and sipped tea with honey. Songea hummed an African tune inside the house as she changed the linens on the bed. Anderea whistled as he poured the used bathwater on the vegetable garden and sprinkled what remained over the yard to keep the dust down. Water had to be carried from a mile away, and every drop had a use. A few scrawny chickens pecked and fought over invisible tidbits. She nearly dozed in the peacefulness of the late afternoon. The hospital could wait until tomorrow. There were others to carry on.

"*Hodi, Mama.*" The voice came from close by and startled her. She jumped and looked to her right. Sawaya Mawala, the African *akida*, government agent, stood before her in his white full-length *kanzu,* his head bound in a white turban. He might have resembled a black angel except for his left eye, diseased and blinded, which stared at the sky as the good eye fixed itself on her.

"I hear you are sad, Mama," he said. "I have come to bring you cheer." He brushed off the lowest step on the porch and sat carefully so as not to dirty his clothing. His feet were thrust into laceless shoes of indeterminate age and color.

"I will tell you a story, Mama, to bring you happiness," he said, using Swahili, the trade language. "Close your eyes and listen with your heart." His lips spread in a twisted grin, distorted by scars that gave him a fierce appearance. But Ursula had no fear of him. Sawaya spoke five languages fluently, was a member of the coastal aristocracy, and possessed a gentle disposition along with a keen mind.

"This story was told me by my grandfather Tippu Tip, the most famous slaver of the days before the Germans. That was when Sayyid Said, the Sultan of Zanzibar, owned all the land along the coast from Mombasa to Lindi. Tippu Tip was a big man, half Arab and half African, and everyone from the coast to the Congo River shook with fear at his name. Yet he walked in his own way of honor, which is why he lived many years and died of old age."

Ursula knew she had no choice but to sit and listen to him, so she leaned her head against the chairback and closed her eyes.

"Many years ago, when my grandfather was a young man, there lived a beautiful Haya princess whose father was a great chief far away between the great lakes toward the sunset. He made war with the people beyond his lands, as well as with the Wanyamwezi, and brought in many captives to till his warriors' fields. One of these slaves, a tall Nyamwezi, fell in love with the princess and she with him.

"Unfortunately, the Haya chief had already promised her to a chieftain, never mind that the chieftain already had many wives and was old. It is the way of the people of Africa; the mixed blood lines mean that the young men will go to war alongside each other.

"The wedding preparations were made. Troops of dancers came from many days' journey away, and the young men practiced their drums while the women cooked food and made beer. On the day she was to be given to the chieftain, the princess disappeared—as did the young Nyamwezi slave.

"This, of course, angered the chief, and he swore he would kill the young man. He sent word to find them and bring them to him. But they could not be found, for they took refuge with my grandfather's slave caravan. They convinced him to allow the young man to join the strong Nyamwezi men who were porters. They hid the princess with a group of women slaves.

"Another slave trader would have cheated them and sold her with the others, but my grandfather kept his word. He gave them a house on his estate at Bagamoyo and made the young man overseer of the slaves who tilled the fields and cultivated the tobacco crop.

"As time went by they had a child—a son. Before the child could walk his father died of the pox and the Haya princess had no one to provide for her. A new, cruel overseer took charge of the workers. He took her house away from her and turned her and her son out to live in the bush like *mshenzi* barbarians.

"She turned to my grandfather for help, and the great Tippu Tip treated her with honor. He offered her a choice: either a place in his household as a concubine or, if she preferred, he would give her safe transport back home to her father in exchange for her healthy son. Either way, her son would be raised as Tippu Tip's son. She chose to go home, for she was sick for her mother as well as the fields and mountains of her childhood. She gave her son to Tippu Tip, never to see him again, to be called his son instead of hers.

"They say she died of a broken heart before she reached home. I do not know if that is true or not. But her son received an education befitting  the grandson of the greatest chief of the Haya people. He became influential in the house of Tippu Tip, with the Sayyids of Omani as well as the Portuguese, and finally the Germans." Sawaya fell silent. His blind eye now appeared to glare at the top of the flame tree where two hawks watched the chickens down below.

"Why do you tell me this story?" Ursula asked.

"No reason, *Mama*," he shrugged. "It is merely to amuse you."

"If Tippu Tip really was your grandfather, you must have known this princess or her son. Did you? And is this story true?"

"Yes, it is true. I am the son of her son. If her father the Haya chief had been told, would he have believed that one day his grandson and great-grandson would be men of great power?" Sawaya stood to his feet and brushed imaginary dust from his garment and hands.

"Be well, *Mama*. Remember—no story is ever finished. Not even yours." He gave her an intense stare with his one good eye, and then turned to walk down the path to the sandy street, and toward his government office.

"Thank you, Sawaya. Go with God," Ursula said. He nodded without looking back and disappeared behind the hedge.

Ursula pondered the story. Sawaya usually was a man of few words. There had to be a meaning to this story, but her brain was too addled by fever to grasp it.

Her thoughts were interrupted by a group of small boys who ran up the path shouting, "*Bwana Shabeli* returns! *Bwana Shabeli* is here!"

She stood and shaded her eyes from the setting sun. Pots clanged in the kitchen as the boys scrambled to prepare tea and food for a tired doctor coming home several days earlier than expected. In a few minutes she saw him—her own Fritz, who carried a bundle as he walked up the path with Kuyoni, followed by the mule cart. A man rode in the cart with the bundles of provisions and an old cow plodded along behind the cart.

She never took her eyes from Fritz's as he walked toward her. The cart creaked to a stop. Out of the corner of her eye she saw Kuyoni help an old Maasai man who stumbled as he got off. Fritz's blue eyes locked onto Ursula's as she took the bundle from him. It moved a little bit as she held it. Surprised, she looked down.

There in her arms lay a tiny newborn baby, weak and emaciated, crusted dirt around its eyes and mouth.

"*Mein Gott!* Fritzie, what is it?"

"A baby, *Liebchen*. What else could it be?"

"Of course it is! I can see that! But where…why…." She trembled as her greedy arms enfolded an infant once again.

"Can you care for her while I help this man? He has a wound that I must tend to. It may be too late, but I have to do what I can. The baby needs washing, and food…" but Ursula had seated herself again in the chair, released a breast, and offered it to the babe. The little black mouth fastened itself to her white breast, and she didn't hear him finish his sentence, "…until we can find some woman in town  to care for her." The tears rolled down her face as she crooned German lullabies to the little Maasai baby, feeling again the excruciating joy of giving a child suck.

Anderea brought a tin of hot water and two basins, and as Ursula caressed the face of the dirty baby Fritz cared for Mbae's foot. First he soaked it in a purple solution of permangenate crystals. Then he pierced the wound with a scalpel and let the pus flow out, and squeezed it until blood came too, then blood only. He set the foot to soak again before he poured iodine into the wound. Mbae flinched, but didn't cry out.

"We'll have to keep an eye on him.  He could get blood

poisoning, or gangrene. He'll stay with Kuyoni for awhile," he said as he finished bandaging Mbae's foot.

Fritz watched Ursula with unease as she finished feeding the child and prepared to wash it. "Use some permangenate in the water," he said. "I'm sure there's smallpox on her, and who knows what else. We'll see if Kuyoni can find some woman in town who'll be willing to nurse her until we can put her in the orphanage."

"Why can't I care for her? Milk is milk, and I have plenty."

"She's an African, Ursula, and if you keep her you'll become attached to her. She's not Marta. We'll have to give her back someday. No, don't even think of it."

"Fritz! Look!" She showed him the baby, fast asleep in Marta's blanket, her hand wrapped around Ursula's little finger. "I will not—" she flinched at the direct rebellion she voiced "—we must not give back what God has given to us.

"Over there," she motioned toward the three graves, "lie three German babies. Now God wants us to have this African baby. Don't take this from me—"

"Fine, Ursula. For now, we'll keep her. But someday—"

"I have already named her." She bent her head over the sleeping baby and whispered in her ear. "I've named her Rebeka. After Rebeka in the Holy Bible, who travelled to a far country to be the wife of Isaac."

"She didn't come that far, Ursula. Only a day's journey."

"Oh, it is far. From Maasai *manyatta* to German home. That is far, Fritz, very far. When she's grown you'll see how far it is."

"'That's what I am afraid of, *Liebchen*. When she is grown. What will become of her? You ask for a great heartache. No, she must go to the orphanage when she's weaned." Ursula didn't answer him. She held the baby in her arms and rocked back and forth, a look of peace on her face. *No story is ever finished,* Sawaya had said. He was right. There were more chapters to be told.

Fritz sipped the hot tea brought to them by Anderea and watched Ursula with the baby. "Ursula…" he said, then fell quiet, for the look she blazed at him was one he had rarely seen before, a look of fury and determination that sent a chill down his spine in spite of the afternoon heat, and then came the premonition, the same one he had when he took the baby from Mbae at El Engerot. He deliberately turned his thoughts away.

The late afternoon sun drifted downward into the horizon, silhouetting the roofs and trees of Arusha. Its fierceness gone now, the light painted the landscape a soft magenta as the sky turned tangerine. Mount Meru, to the northeast, glowed purple in the last light of the day.

He rose to his feet and stretched as Anderea carried a five-gallon tin of hot water into the bathroom from the kitchen. "I think I'll bathe before supper. I'll feel more human and you'll be able to stand my presence inside the house."

Ursula sat for a while as the twilight fell and the guinea fowl called from their nests in the trees. Women walked by in single file, large earthen jars of water balanced on their heads, and they curtsied in greeting as they passed. She looked at baby Rebeka as she slept in her arms and felt a vast peace envelop her. Life was hard here, but she had her Fritzie, and now a child to anchor her to the land. This one she would keep. Rebeka would not go to the orphanage with the other babies.

The sun slipped below the horizon, and in only a few minutes it was dark. The stars came out and she watched Orion rise from the plain that imprisoned him all day, released to hunt the constellations all night. To the south the Southern Cross outlined the purpose of her life. Ursula felt contentment as she listened to the usual night noises. Far away a hyena whooped. Dogs barked, and the men in the kitchen clattered pots. For this moment all was well in her world. She would keep Rebeka and raise her as long as she could. She glanced down as the child murmured and moved in her sleep. No one will take her from me, she determined, not thinking or caring about the cost.

CHAPTER TWO

# The Maji Maji Revolt, 1905

**Mpepo, the ten-year-old son of Kiwanga, the son of Mkwawa the great Huru chief, pressed his ear against the small hole in the back of his uncle's hut.** His heart pounded so hard he could barely hear the voices inside. He knew the strangers would beat him if they knew he listened to their secrets.

The five strangers had appeared just before sunset. They wore only loincloths and red armbands. They came from the south; they spoke in Swahili, the trade language, and their facial tattoos appeared grotesque to Mpepo, since the Huru did not decorate their faces—only their arms and chests. After the customary greetings, Mpepo was sent to call in other tribal leaders, and now twelve men sat squeezed together in Uncle's smoky hut, drinking the hot sweet tea that Mpepo brought to them before Uncle dismissed him. As he backed out of the hut, he caught his uncle's eye and a quick nod toward the back of the hut where both of them knew a small hole in the wall allowed eavesdropping.

Mpepo wrapped his cloth around himself to ward off the cool night air and hunkered down beneath the star-studded sky. Only a goat noticed him and trotted over. It stared at him as it chewed in a sideways jaw motion, barely distinguishable in the dark. He threw a small stick at it to make it go away. Someone coming from the hut to empty his bladder might see it staring at something and come to investigate.

For as long as he could remember, he had heard about his father and grandfather and their great battle against the Germans. His uncle would recite these stories as they sat around the fire, and then would say, "but tell no one, Mpepo. No one must know you are not my own son. Not yet."

"But why, Uncle?"

"Because there are those who would kill you if they knew. Your time of glory will come; your time will come."

Who would want to kill me? And why?"

"Because, as grandson of the great Mkwawa, you could be chief some day. Our present chief, Gurisa, is nothing but a German dog!" Uncle would always spit into the fire at this point of the story. "When the Germans come around, he gets down on all fours and licks their knees and whines for their approval. When they say *get us cattle and food,* he runs off and bites the people to get what the Germans want."

"Tell me again about my father and grandfather, Uncle."

"Your grandfather was the greatest chief of the Wahuru people. He was a large man with a loud voice, and his enemies quaked with fear. But his people loved him. During his time the rains did not fail and the people grew fat; women's breasts were plump with milk for their babies, and many of the young men became strong warriors.

"Mkwawa built a great city on the banks of the Sibiti River. Thousands of people lived there, safe from wild animals and enemies, behind a wall higher than a man can reach. When the hairy strangers with white skin demanded tribute, he refused, so they attacked with their guns and cannon. They shot over the wall from the surrounding hills and soon the houses burned to the ground. Mkwawa and two of his sons escaped. Your father died at the city entrance. That was the year you were born. I rescued you and your mother—my sister—and told everyone you were my son."

"And what happened to Grandfather?" Mpepo had heard it many times, but he never tired of hearing again.

"He ran away to a high hill. When he saw the city go up in flames, he wept. The Germans chased him through the land. They put out an edict saying that anyone caught giving him aid would be hanged. The Germans placed a new chief in charge, one who would give them what they wanted.

Your grandfather and uncles fled all the way to the Ruvuma River and crossed over into Mozambique. They were chased back into this country, and finally the Germans caught them and hanged them." Uncle always fell silent when he finished the story as though to say, *this is what happens when you try to resist those who are stronger.*

Now, Mpepo tried to make himself invisible against the mud-and-wattle back of the hut. His heart swelled with pride that his uncle would trust him and make him privy to this news. He heard Uncle offer the men beer, and heard it being poured into their calabashes. Someone coughed and cleared his throat.

"The Matumbe people have declared war on the Germans. Many tribes follow them."

Someone else took up the subject. "They marched on the cotton fields, pulled up plants, and shook them in the air. In the name of all African people, they declared war. They refuse to work any more in the fields. They do not reap the profits, and are forced to leave their families without a man to provide for them. Even you people here in Huruland are forced against your will to work six months every year for the German planters, and all for very little pay." A chorus of assenting grunts followed. Everyone in the country tired of forced labor on coffee and cotton estates.

"We have always been a peaceful people, living in harmony with those around us and with no one man telling us what we have to do. We do not go to war with others unless provoked by land- and slave-seeking tribes. But the Germans came. They put a stranger over us and forced us to work for five settlers who take what we grow, and we get nothing. They have forced us to live by strange laws, when once we had none. We see no end to the loads the Germans put on our backs. We are ready to rise up and do something."

"How are you going to fight against those who have guns?" It was Uncle who voiced the question.

"With magic—"

"Yes, Magic," someone else chimed in. "Special magic! About a year ago, a shaman named Kinjikitile fell into a trance. He was a prophet of the god *Bokero*, the god who lives in the trees on the banks of the Rufiji River. *Bokero* spoke through Kinjikitile by his spirit, called *Honga*. When *Honga* first possessed Kinjikitile, he fell on his stomach with his hands stretched out before him, and he crawled to a pool of water into which he threw himself. When he didn't reappear several men dived down to rescue him, but they couldn't find him. The next day he appeared out of the pool unhurt, his clothes dry, and he uttered strange prophecies."

"*Kumbe!*" one of the Huru leaders gasped. "That sounds like what the White Fathers teach us about a man named *Yesu*!"

"Yes. Some people say this Kinjikitile is the African *Yesu*."

"On with your story." Uncle was impatient. "What did he say to the people?"

"He said, first of all, that all tribes must unite to serve *Bokero* and *Honga*. He built a huge spirit-hut, large enough to hold many men. His first message was the oneness of the people; there should be no tribal or language barriers between them. People came from far distances to hear him. I was there, too. He took water from the pond where he had thrown himself and sprinkled droplets on us with the tail of a wildebeest." The other strangers grunted in assent.

Another voice took up the story. "I was among those who marched to the cotton field to uproot plants. Kinjikitile has given us small containers with water from the pool to wear on a string around our necks. We must wear them all the time. He said the water would make us strong and make the German's bullets turn to water so they don't hurt us."

"Also," chimed in another man, "we are not to wear European clothes, only a cloth and these armbands. The women have woven a new cloth design, called *The Eye of Bokero*. It is worn everywhere, even in Dar es Salaam, under the noses of the white people. They don't know it is the sign of war. We have brought a piece so your women can copy it."

The first man spoke again, his deep voice rumbling with passion. "We are taking the message to all tribes as fast as we can. Already we have won a victory." He went on to tell of how, after they declared war, the Arab *akida* arrived. Drum beats called neighbors who arrived en masse. They surrounded the *akida's* house, beating their drums and shaking dried millet stalks that they bound around their heads. When night fell, the *akida* fled. The rebellion had begun. The thousands of men were so elated by the victory that they marched on a nearby town, uprooted more cotton, and burned the Asian trading settlement. "Now the government is alerted, and all African men must join in. We need to make a joint attack on all missions and government *bomas* to force the white man out of our country!

"We will stay the night," he continued. "Tomorrow you must take us to see your chief to plan this attack. Already, the tribes around you are joining with us."

A heavy hand descended on Mpepo's shoulder, twisting him around. He cowered against the hut wall, his eyes wide with terror. The figure over him seemed so large, so black he could see little but the whites of the eyes, so threatening he thought he would die. He'd become so involved with what he heard from inside the hut, he didn't hear one of the men leave.

"What's a *shenzi toto* like you doing out here?"        .

Mpepo opened his mouth, but couldn't say anything. He shivered with his fear.

"Have you heard our talk, child?"

Mpepo shook his head, but reconsidered. It was obvious he had heard. He nodded.

The man shook him again. "You tell anyone, and I'll kill you! You hear? I've a mind to strangle you right here!" He put his hands around Mpepo's slender neck.

"I—I won't say anything!"

"I warn you! You'll be dead if you even whisper! Now go to your mother's hut!" He shook Mpepo again before releasing him to scamper away in the darkness.

The next day dawned serene and peaceful in contrast to the night before. Mpepo had tossed and turned as he battled his fear and vacillated between cowardice and bravery. Would there be a full-scale war? Would Uncle join these men in their cause? He tagged along as the visitors and Uncle set off toward the Huru chief's village, one more non-descript boy in a gaggle of small boys that followed out of curiosity as Uncle and the five strangers strode along the path that led to the chief's village. People stopped the group, curious about the strangers, to ask about their *shauri,* what big matter loomed in their flat existence. Most of them joined the group and soon it became a large cavalcade. The boys chattered with each other, speculating and sharing their misinformation. Mpepo pretended he knew as little as they and chatted along with them.

He had arranged for a friend to care for his goats. He promised to watch the other boy's goats one day, in return, but the lad was adamant about what he wanted. Mpepo had a ball, given to him by his teacher, Bwana Sh'miti, that Mpepo called a *tenisibali.* It was his dearest possession. It bounced with an amazing force like nothing any of the boys ever imagined and he was the envy of all his friends.

He'd been tempted to cut the ball open to find what was inside that made it bounce so well, but his teacher explained to him how extra air was forced inside to make a high pressure. "Like wind," Bwana Sh'miti said. "You know how, when wind blows against something, it will push it over if it's flimsy. But if it's strong, the wind has to go around. In the ball, it can't go around, so it spends all its time pushing against the inside."

This was a revelation to Mpepo. He had never thought of air as a substance that can push. All his life, he'd heard that wind was the spirits made angry. Now, since he had become a Christian and would soon be baptized, he learned that things his people called spirits were really physical things that he could touch or see, even things that were too tiny to see. Like water, his teacher said. If you boil it before drinking, it kills tiny bugs that make you sick. "It isn't spirits or curses that make people sick at all."

So Mpepo's ball represented a whole new world to him, a

world of knowledge that he wanted to suck up and understand. It was with great reluctance that he traded this valued ball for a day of following strangers to see what they wanted. Something inside spoke to his heart saying that this event would bring an unpleasant change in his life.

Mpepo was invisible in the crowd as they came to Chief Gurisa's compound. He wormed his way to his uncle's shadow to hear what was said.

Surprised at so large a group of visitors on an ordinary morning, Chief Gurisa stepped back inside his hut for a moment, then came out with his ceremonial lion's mane head wrap and his leopard skin cloak. One of his wives followed with his chair, made of ebony studded with ivory plugs and ivory rings around the legs and back. The soft hide of a zebra covered the seat.

When he finally seated himself and the ceremonial greetings were over, he gazed at the distant hills and asked the men the reason for their visit.

The visitors told him about the declaration of war, and Gurisa squirmed. Most of his wealth depended on the largesse of the German authorities. Gurisa laughed without mirth. "The countryside is swarming with prophets, buzzing like bees, who think they can conquer the Germans. I do not believe they can sting the white man."

The strangers bowed low. "Please let us tell you all," they said. After recounting all the victories they had through the spirit Honga and the magic water, the leader of the group said, "We are prepared to sprinkle water on your people right now. All your men who are here now, and you must call all your tribesmen— everyone who has reached circumcision age—to come and receive the water. It will protect them, by turning bullets into water. "

Gurisa turned and looked at the leader for the first time. "I don't believe it," he said. "Water turn bullets into water? Hah! I don't believe it."

"It's true! It's true!"

A scrawny, yellow dog got up from its place, stretched and yawned, and sought a new sleeping spot in deeper shade. "Sprinkle that dog," Gurisa said. Someone took the water and tossed a few drops over the dog. Gurisa then turned to one of his attendants who carried a rifle. "Shoot that dog," he said. The dog died immediately. Gurisa sneered.

"It only works on men," the leader protested. "Not dogs or any other animals."

"Fetch a slave from the fields," Gurisa demanded. Someone went out and brought a bewildered man, a slave bought from a neighboring tribe, a man who had killed another man over a woman.

The slave looked bewildered as the leader of the strangers stepped forward and ceremoniously flicked the wet wildebeest tail over him.

"Shoot him!" demanded Gurisa.

The attendant lifted his rifle and the man fell over immediately, thrashed a few minutes in agony, and died.

The strangers held a brief consultation before approaching the sneering chief who had risen to dismiss them. "Of course it didn't work with the slave," the leader said. "One must believe in the magic for it to work. He did not know the water was magic, so of course it didn't help him."

"Kinjikitile said," another stranger spoke up, "that it will work only on German bullets. These are not German bullets."

"Excellency," the leader stepped forward. "All the tribes around you have taken the water. They have pledged to attack not only the Germans, but also those who do not join us. If you do not, they will invade your country, kill your men, and take your women and children as slaves."

Gurisa sat down again and thought. Quiet filled the courtyard as the men and boys waited; the only sound came from that of shuffling feet, low coughs, and the buzz of flies around the bodies of the dog and man.

"All right! I will take the water," he said in a slow voice full of reluctance. Give all these men the water—" he swept his hand toward the gathering "—and then you men go out and bring every man here to get the water. We will see. We will see." He sighed, stood, and walked back into his hut.

The strangers spent the rest of the afternoon sprinkling the magic water over all the men and circumcised boys, and then filled small medicine bottles or tiny gourds to wear around their necks. The crowd soon swelled to thousands of men, some of whom began to beat drums and dance. Uncle whispered to Mpepo. "I cannot believe in this nonsense. I must return home. You stay around to see what they will do next and report back to me."

Mpepo nodded. When his uncle left, he wormed his way up near the strangers. Many in the crowd now drank beer as they bound red cloths around their arms. They cheered as the strangers incited them.

"We will burn the *bomas* and drive the German army away!"

"We will attack the mission stations and kill the people with the book of their god! We will burn down their churches and schools!"

The crowd yelled again.

"We will go tonight and show them whose god is strongest!

*Bokero* is God, and *Honga* is his spirit!" The people cheered.

Mpepo's heart pounded with fear. Would they really burn the mission? Would they kill the missionaries, his friends? He had come to love the kind men who took an interest in him. His teacher praised him, said he showed superior intellect. The gentleness of these people had impressed him. Mpepo didn't want them to die. But what could he, a small boy, do?

He edged away from the crowd. He found a stick and pretended to play a game to see how far he could lever a small stone into the air. He wanted to appear too young to understand or be interested in what was going on. He made his way slowly over a slight rise, and then, as soon as he no longer could see the chief's huts and the crowd around it, broke into a run.

He ran the three miles to the station as fast as he could and arrived at Bwana Sh'miti's gasping for breath. He pounded hard on the door until the man opened it.

"The men—the men—all the men—" he gasped, and pointed down the way he'd come. "They come—"

His teacher took his arm in a gentle grasp. "Calm down, Mpepo. There's no hurry. Sit here. Have a drink of water."

Mpepo took a big gulp of the water and then shook his head. "No time," he said. "You must send to all the *nzungus* to tell them that many, many men have massed and are coming to kill you!"

"Surely you joke," his teacher said. "How many men? We have guns to defend ourselves, if necessary."

"Hundreds and hundreds! Thousands! They have taken the magic water! The Maji Maji people have come! They have taken an oath to drive the Germans—all the *nzungus*—out of the country! They come now! I ran all the way to tell you, and they will kill me if they know I have warned you!"

The white teacher stood to his feet. Mpepo knew he had heard of the Maji Maji movement. Many people had whispered about the revolt going on in the south. His face became grim as he finally understood the message. He called to some of the African men who walked by toward their homes, and they scattered at a run to gather their wives and children and head for the hills. One ran to the other missionaries' homes to tell them to grab their guns, food, water, and run for their lives. "Come with me, Mpepo," Bwana Sh'miti said. "You aren't safe here. Come with us."

The small group of five missionaries gathered together for a quick prayer before they left. The three men had guns and packets of supplies, the women carried small satchels with bread, cheese, and papaya, and all carried canteens of water. Mpepo shouldered a heavy satchel containing the beginnings of a Bible translation into the Huru language, and the group set out on foot to the southeast, toward the river and beyond to Arusha, over a hundred miles away. They made about five miles before dark, and stopped on the banks of the Huru River. They built a small fire to heat some water for tea, but not before they saw the sky red with flames from the burning of their homes and church.

Someone started to sing a hymn. They sang through their tears, "A Mighty Fortress is Our God," the great Lutheran hymn.

"Come here, Mpepo." His teacher beckoned. Someone handed him a piece of bread and a drink of water. He felt shame that it was his countrymen who destroyed the work of these people. Because of their skin color the missionaries were seen, not as people of peace, but as emissaries of the hated European.

"Mpepo is an angel sent from God," Bwana Sh'miti announced as he put his arm around Mpepo. "He was sent to save us from that fire.

"Look at those flames, Mpepo. They are nothing compared to the flames of Hell." Mpepo, mesmerized, looked at the flames and then back into his teacher's eyes.

"God has spared us—and you, too—from suffering in both flames. He's spared you so you can come back someday and save your people from the flames of hell." He stared deep into Mpepo's eyes.

A warm feeling bloomed inside of Mpepo. A whole new world opened up to him; more than the rush of thoughts that followed his comprehension that physical things one can't see like wind and tiny bugs could be understood. That knowledge had whetted his appetite. Now he knew what he must do for the rest of his life. He felt lifted up to the top of trees. He felt joyful, strangely so, even though he didn't know what would happen to his mother and Uncle, and it no longer mattered that he would never see his *tenisibali* again. There was a reason for his life. Mpepo laughed and laughed, and soon his teacher laughed too. *Someday,* he thought as he munched on the bread, *I will make right what my people have done. I will build another church and lead the people to the true God.*

They forded the river the next day. After setting a lookout to watch for crocodiles, two men tied their shoes around their necks, took their wives on their backs, and waded out into the stream. One woman shrieked as her husband stepped into a hole that immersed him up to his shoulder and drenching her. Eventually they all made their way across, Mpepo on his teacher's back. The men turned their backs as the women removed their dresses and squeezed the water out. Mpepo peeked to see if their skin was as white under their clothes as the part that showed outside. To his surprise, it was even whiter.

It took four more days of travel in the heat and shivering under the stars at night before they stumbled into Arusha. Twice, African people had taken them in, fed them and given them fresh water to fill their canteens. They accepted it, gave thanks, and drank it though it was unboiled. Surely, they said, God would protect them from disease. No rebels had come after them. Though exhausted, no one became ill.

"This boy saved us," his teacher told everyone in Arusha. "Give him food and water first. Look, he's trembling with hunger."

"I'll look after him," Doctor Scheibel said. "He can work around the house, and he can go to school until this rebellion is over." He smiled at Mpepo and placed his hand on his shoulder. "We'll send for information about his mother, too."

Mpepo gazed at the stout man. What was it about these white people that it didn't shame them to show affection? Why, even the *daktari's* wife carried a black baby at her breast with the same care as she would her own child. In his village, people considered it weakness to show affection.

Mpepo was set to weed and hoe the vegetable garden. He often played with the baby as she sat on a blanket on the ground. Her skin shone with rich nourishment and she smiled at him with her big, black eyes. His thoughts turned to his mother as he wondered how she fared.

Rumors and stories drifted into town brought by refugees or the newspapers. The power of the water failed when an attack against the Anglican mission at Jakobi found the Anglicans praying as they cleaned their rifles. Gunfire erupted and several rebels were killed. The leaders of the movement declared that the men who died had somehow broken the taboos. A person could only be shot in the back. As long as they faced the enemy they would be impervious to the bullets. A man must not have relations with his wife the night before a raid. Certain foods could not be eaten. As more and more rebels died, more restrictions applied. The water was changed. In spite of continual failures, thousands from many tribes joined the movement.

In each village the leaders told the people, "Go and rob the white people. Take away their homes, their lands, and their women. They have robbed us first."

Then they asked, "Can you do it?"

"Yes, we can do it," the people chanted back. "We have the power of *maji* and it will turn the white man's bullets into water."

People were told to kill and eat their livestock; Bokero was coming and he would make everything new and bring peace.

In the middle of August, Uncle slipped into Arusha and found Mpepo. "They attacked Liwale," he said, as people gathered around him. "I followed at a distance to see what would happen. They came in from three directions; they set the thatched roofs ablaze with burning arrows and killed everyone inside. They ambushed German troops coming up from the coast and made them turn around and go back."

Five thousand men then danced all night to the war drums. At dawn they marched on the government offices at Mahenge, shaking their heads to make the millet stalks rattle. Two columns approached from separate sides. Uncle followed at a distance and climbed a tree to observe the battle.

Only ten German soldiers and twenty Africans in uniform, most of them Sudanese or Somalis, defended the town. The first line of attack fell to the ground when the soldiers fired, but the rest of the men pressed on. Two machine guns on the wall mowed down dozens more. Bewildered, the group broke and ran for cover, dragging their wounded with them.

"It sounded like they were rattling tin cans," Uncle said. "But it was bullets, and many men fell."

Over a thousand men came in from the east. Again the machine guns broke their ranks and they fled. Uncle observed many bodies lying in the dust. "The *maji* failed," Uncle said. "The European has superior strength. I was right all along. We can only win if we join the white man and learn his ways. Africa is doomed if we continue in this folly."

Later, when they were alone, Uncle told Mpepo his mother was safe. "No one bothers her because she is merely a woman," he said. "She still has chickens and several goats. Other boys take her goats to graze in exchange for eggs. She says you should stay here for now."

The news of the rebellion filled Arusha as the factions seesawed across the south of the country. Several times men appeared with the tiny medicine bottles filled with water and they were arrested on the spot and taken under guard to the nearest detention center. Fritz placed his hunting rifles close at hand and counted his ammunition.

"Do not worry, *Daktari*," Sawaya assured him with his crooked grin. "The government has placed troops between them and us. Besides, no one around here wants to rebel."

He was wrong. There were many among the Kamba and Chagga who resented the loss of fertile lands on the slopes of Kilimanjaro, given to Europeans for coffee plantations. The forced labor also caused disruption in the social order. Men were brought in from far away to spend their six required months on the plantations. The whispers they brought of the rebellion inflamed some of the more daring.

One night when the moon was barely a fingernail clipping in the sky, ten men crept into the hospital compound. Hansel and Gretel, the Scheibel's two dogs, began to bark and other dogs relayed the alarm. The men set tinder against the hospital wall and set it afire as people woke and lit their lanterns.

The flames shot up to the metal roof and destroyed one ward before the people put out the fire. Twelve patients escaped unharmed, but the loss of the ward meant rebuilding, and money was scarce. The armed forces stationed in Arusha caught the men responsible before dawn, and the next day they hanged them in the market place as an example.

In spite of their losses the Maji Maji Rebellion continued to spread. Desperation took hold of the people. It would be their only chance, they knew, to unite and throw off the shackles of the German. They found guns. They raided mission stations and small garrisons, looting and burning, killing and maiming, to the embarrassment of the government. After one attack, the German forces surprised five hundred young men taking the ritual oath. Overcome by enthusiasm, the young men charged the military, and before long two hundred Africans lay dead in the field.

This was the last great battle of the Maji Maji Rebellion. By the middle of 1906, the government finally crushed the will and spirit of the people. Doomed to failure from the beginning, the *maji* was ineffective against European rifles. Once and for all time the lesson showed them that old ways lost their power in confrontation with new ways.

The governor's submission policy consisted of seizing all food and destroying the crops. He refused to allow replanting until the whole district surrendered. "The people can just starve," he said, and the rumor of this sentence spread, adding salt to the wounds of the country. Only hunger and want brought about final submission. Famine covered the land. The Southern Highlands were almost depopulated. Close to three hundred thousand Africans died in the revolt. Only fifteen Europeans lost their lives, and fewer than four hundred African soldiers. Chaos reined everywhere. As chiefs were hanged, no one was left in leadership positions. Barbarized, the people did whatever they wanted. Status of aristocrats broke down and everyone became beggars.

When the few survivors returned to their villages, they found their fields taken over by the forest and wild animals occupying their gardens. Elephants and lions once again walked through the villages. People continued to die from famine, cold, sickness, and wild animals. Tsetse fly habitat spread, and with it sleeping sickness. The people lost everything: their spirit, their hope of regaining freedom, and their centuries-long war against nature.

In Arusha, the hospital filled with people dying of starvation. Children displayed bloated bellies from malnutrition. Women miscarried. Wounded, sick, dispirited men crowded the wards and dispensaries.

Mpepo went back to school while he waited for calm in Huruland. The way the government treated the African people puzzled him. The officials were so different from the ones who came to preach God's word. Could the victory not have been won without so cruelly depriving the masses of food? He was only ten, still a *toto,* an uncircumcised boy. But these thoughts ran around in his head with no answer like a dust whirlwind without direction.

## CHAPTER THREE

# Torino, Italy, 1905

**In the same year that Mpepo wakened to his destiny, and the same month that Rebeka was born, a man lay unconscious on the ground in Torino, Italy**. When Vittorio Fernaldi came to, his first impression was how much he hurt. His nose felt like a mountain of pain on his pounding head. Every bone in his body ached.

It was dark. Where the full moon had hung low in the sky when he left Professor Scalzi's residence, now only those few stars not veiled by clouds lent their meager light.

The next sensation was the smell and feel of decaying leaves and damp dirt as he moved his arms and legs and slowly pushed himself to a sitting position with a groan. He felt wetness on his upper lip; he touched his tongue to it and tasted blood. Then his memory rushed back.

It was Franco and Roberto who had jumped him as soon as he entered the Giardino Publico along the Riume Po. Even though they stood between him and the light of the moon, he recognized Franco by his distinctive triangular head that came to a point above his large ears and Roberto by his massive arms and smell of cheap tobacco. They had been his friends.

He began to shake. The river flowed past and paid him no heed as his memory returned. What was it they had said just before he lost consciousness?

*This is what happens to those who turn traitor, those who*

*leave Beni and his cause.*

Vito was only two weeks from finishing his law studies. His new wife, Therese, was large with child, and he wanted nothing more than to grow old and contented surrounded by family. He thought, as he rubbed his throbbing neck, how in this last year his accursed thirst for justice caused him to fall in with Beni's politics—and then out. Now he was here, broken and bleeding after midnight, on the path along the River Po. He longed for the end to his studies so he could go home.

*Home.* He thought longingly of the peaceful, sun-drenched valleys where he grew up surrounded by the majestic Alps near the border with France. Home—the little village of Chenneil in Valle d'Aosta, where four generations of his family had cultivated grapes for a fine wine known as Malvoisie. Its reputation brought orders from all over Italy.

Vito's grandfather, Count Riccardo Fernaldi, sent Vito to university in Torino to study finance to benefit the village and give him a place in the family business. When he finished his studies, he returned home to marry his childhood sweetheart, Therese. Almost as an afterthought, his grandfather decided he should return to Torino to read law. It was here that he caught the attention of his law professor, Eduardo Scalzi, who soon became his mentor.

A man of at least eighty years with white, unruly hair, incongruously pale blue eyes set deep in his dark, lined face, Professor Scalzi paced back and forth behind the lectern with singular fire as he taught his classes the rudiments of law, its evolution from the ancient days of the Greeks and Romans, through the precepts of English Common Law, and thence to the United States and the concept of equal rights to all citizens.

Late at night, as he lay in bed looking out the window of his cold, attic room at the starlit mountains surrounding the city, he pondered the evolution of law and order. Someday, he told Therese, all races—regardless of color or national origin—would be universally accepted as equal. He hoped he would live to see it.

In October of his last year, a printed flyer was handed to him as he passed from one class to another at midday. *All thinking men of Italy, Unite!* it said in bold letters across the top. *Come tonight to the café di Reale to hear about a new concept in government. Benito Mussolini*—this name in bold capital letters—*will tell us of a new system sweeping the world, a system of justice and fairness superior to present despotic regimes. Our friend Mussolini is leader of a new group of revolutionaries in Fiume. Come and hear how he proposes to change our world, and how you can help.*

That night, in the crowded, smoke-filled café, Vito became captivated by the words of Benito Mussolini. Beni, as he insisted on being called, was about the same age as Vito. He was pudgy, his round baby face pockmarked with acne scars. But his sharp mind and tongue were quick to respond to questions from the university students. He was on temporary leave from the army to tend to his dying mother, and swung by the university on his way back to his regiment.

"I attended University in Fiume for two years," he said, when someone asked for his credentials. "I learned all I needed to know, went back home, and supported my aging parents by teaching school. Then I went to Switzerland to study. Now I've come back to my country, joined the army, and will soon be printing a newspaper for the common man."

He and Vito became instant friends; Vito felt Beni's charismatic magnetism and the truth of what he said, and Beni heard that Vito was the school's top law student. "Together, we'll go far," he said.

Beni briefly outlined the history of their country to the gathered students. He showed how unification just twenty years previous had taken the control of the provinces from the hands of their people to those of the central government, especially the hands of the king. He traced for them the path of the taxes collected without mercy from the poor. He showed how the benefits from those taxes enriched the royal family's coffers without benefiting the local infrastructure. Most of the students nodded their heads and agreed enthusiastically with his assessment that Italy needed to join those countries that practiced an enlightened democracy.

"The Italian people are not ready for complete democracy as in American," Beni said. "Too many are illiterate and ignorant of the world around them. It behooves those of us who are educated to reorganize our government as proposed by the philosopher Hegel and others. Join me—and thousands of other university men—in forming a new political party for the benefit of our country!"

The cheers of the students showed that many were ready to join. During the next months the newly formed Socialist Society for the People met three times a week to discuss the tenets of socialism and communism as well as strategies for opposing the corrupt government. Some argued for violence, and others, Vito included, argued for education and grass roots reform.

Several times that winter Beni wrote to Vito, and a friendship was struck between the two men. "I admire your mind and abilities," Beni wrote one day, when he dropped by while on leave. "I want you in my inner group. When I'm through with my army duties, I hope to start a paper. You can run it for me and be my legal expert. What do you say, my friend?"

"I can't," Vito said. "I owe it to my grandfather to go home and use my education for the benefit of the village and the family. After all, he paid my fees. Besides, I have a wife, and a child on the way."

Beni scoffed. "It is just that paternalism that represents the ancient, reactionary ways of doing things. I propose doing away with royal families and nobles, including counts…" He backtracked, noticing Vito's distressed expression, "… I'm sure your grandfather is an exception, but by and large that class system practices injustice, treating people as children instead of equals."

Vito nodded. "Yes, perhaps you are right—"

"Perhaps?" Beni roared in sudden anger. "Of course I'm right! What have you not heard in all my speeches about the new socialism?" He smiled, changing mood. "I understand, Vito. Of course you are not so different from many—wanting to change the world but not your part of it. Am I right? It's always easy to see injustice in the world at large, but we acquire blinders when it comes to our own home.

"Maybe you *should* go, Vito. Go home, and see for yourself the petty things that are practiced in the name of God and King Victor Emanuele. Then your eyes will be opened. I will be waiting for you with open arms when you are ready to join me in bringing Italy into a new age. You have what it takes to be my right-hand-man. You are cool and calm. I need a man like that beside me."

However, his outburst of anger planted the seeds of doubt in Vito's mind.

Often that winter, during class, Vito saw Professor Scalzi gazing at him. One day, as he gathered his books and papers, his teacher said, "Vittorio, come to my house tonight for soup and bread. There is a matter I would like to discuss with you." Flattered, Vito consented. Professor Scalzi lived with his daughter in a small apartment between the University and the Academia Militaire near the Giardino Reale, not far from Vito's garret room where he lived with Therese.

"I have grown fond of you, Vittorio," the professor said as they finished dinner and his spinster daughter cleared away the dishes and refreshed their wine glasses. "Young men like you keep me teaching. My daughter would like me to leave and take a cottage in the country. But this atmosphere keeps me young.

"You are married," he said as he stroked his mustache. "I think I have seen your wife. Pretty woman, with black, wavy hair. Expecting a child. Yes?" Vito nodded.

"Ah, you have a family of your own to think about. Here, bring your wine and let's sit by the grate for a little while." The two men went into the small sitting room where Scalzi stirred the coals on the grate. They gave a rewarding hiss and burst into flames.

"I have heard some things about you, my son. You have been keeping company with Benito Mussolini and his cohorts, have you not? Now just a moment—" he raised a hand to silence Vito when he opened his mouth to speak, "—humor an old man, and let him have his say.

"Never let it be said that Eduardo Scalzi suggested a man not think for himself. But I wish to share with you the bit of wisdom I have gained over my long life." The light from the crackling flame in the fireplace played off his lined face and lit his pale eyes. "I have lived a long time and have seen new ways of thinking come and go. Some have merit, and some do not. Yet each leaves the world refreshed. But not everything that comes along is good. But not all is bad. Coming as I do, from seeing history made, I need to warn you about this Mussolini fellow.

"My information comes from friends in Fiume. I understand he ran to Switzerland three years ago to avoid the military. He also had a violent quarrel with the mayor of Fiume, when he begged for money on the streets and fell in with followers of Nietzsche, Hegel, and Karl Marx. I'm sure you have read their philosophies here in University." Vito nodded, his eyes not leaving Scalzi's face. "Switzerland kicked him out because of his revolutionary tendencies and sent him back home.

"He calls himself a Socialist. Vito, I am afraid of that man." Scalzi leaned forward and placed a few extra sticks on the fire, which immediately burst into fresh flame and warmth.

"Now I would not presume to say that all Socialists are bad; nor are their goals unworthy ones in most cases. I do not like communism, because it makes an arbitrary standard as to what constitutes too much or too little. It proposes to take away class, status, and wealth from those who have too much, to increase the class, status, and wealth of those who have too little. Perhaps a classless society is a good goal. But I believe that human nature will always classify itself.

"The Socialists, however, while having similar goals of redistributing status and wealth, usually work within the existing government to bring the common man equality with those whose class and status prevent them from understanding his need. This can be admirable. The lot of the common man is often to suffer in silence with no avenue of protest. Do you not agree?"

Vito agreed, and spoke up. "Yes, Professor. And Benito has struck a raw nerve. In my own hometown I have seen the agents of the King extort taxes from people who are not able to pay. One reason I have come to study law is because I am incensed by the injustice I see."

"Good," Scalzi said. "I'm glad you agree that something must be done. I would like to point out a different way.

"Are you acquainted with Immanuel Kant?"

"Yes, I read his theses in Philosophy class. Many of his ideas are based on the United States Constitution, are they not?"

"More likely both are based on a previous philosopher," Scalzi said. "I should think you would be tuned to his way of thinking. He speaks of a Universal Right, an external guide as to what is right for every man, and calls for each to exercise his right in the framework of every other man's right. This must start at the family level, then the town and province, and eventually the country. I believe we can save our world by starting a fire that begins from one small coal———" he tossed another stick on the fire, which reached out its arms and embraced it "—and then spread it across the country.

"And we need leaders—like you—who will start this at home and carry it to our nation's capital."

"That can take years. And in the meantime injustice is served."

"True. But any other way would cost too many lives in bloody uprisings. To take a man's life is to deprive him of his ultimate right, regardless of the rightness of the cause."

Far into the night, Vito and his professor discussed the many doctrines of revolution being bandied about in the new century. When Vito went home to his garret apartment he had new things to think about as he lay gazing at the stars beside the sleeping form of Therese. He turned over and studied her as she slept. He had loved her since they were ten years old. They played as children among the hills and the vineyards of their neighboring estates. He had kissed her on the hillside overlooking their village when they were fifteen. He was in love with everything about her—her teasing smile, her stare when angry, the cloud of dark hair like a halo around her heart-shaped face, her long straight nose that was so honest, her willowy grace even now as their child kicked in her belly. The winds of change were enticing, but he wanted only to spend his days with Therese, to bask in her warmth and enjoy her presence.

He drew away from his Socialist friends. When they approached him about his lack of enthusiasm for the cause, he replied that he needed to think some more about it. He continued his deepening friendship with Professor Scalzi through many late night talks.

These talks coupled with his withdrawal from the Socialists, resulted in his sitting on damp leaves after midnight in the park near his apartment, nursing a bloody nose, thankful to still be alive.

*How can I tell Therese?* He got to his feet and staggered home. He knew she would not say a word, only reach out and enfold him in her arms, kiss him, and tend to his wounds. He would tell her, of course, and she would say*, it doesn't matter. We will go home, far away from these bullies, and we will be happy.*

When Vito finished his studies and received his diploma two weeks later, that is what they did. For nine years life was just as he wanted it. Then Archduke Ferdinand of Austria was assassinated in Sarajevo, and Vito's whole life turned upside down and he became alienated from his country.

CHAPTER FOUR

# Tanga, Africa, 1910

**Rebeka was five when Fritz and Ursula returned to Germany for ten months to rest,** present their work to the Lutheran churches in Leipzig, and for Fritz to study new medical treatments. At the last minute, the mission disallowed Rebeka's passage money. "We do not believe it wise to take an African girl to Germany at this time," they wrote. "The people will understand your desire to minister to the Africans, but not the bringing of the girl into your home. We suggest you find someone to care for her while you're away."

Ursula frowned. "She is my daughter!" She slammed the letter down on the desk. "As much my daughter as if I bore her. How can I leave her? Whom will we leave her with?"

"I don't know, *Liebchen*. But it's stay here, or comply." Fritz, too, had grown fond of the quick-witted little girl who climbed into his lap at the end of the day and snuggled against his chest, who kissed his face all over and listened intently to every word.

Her command of languages stunned him. She not only understood and spoke their German, but also conversed with the kitchen help and Songea in Swahili. Several days a week Songea took her, at Fritz's insistence, to play with the children of Kuyoni, the Maasai man who had left his nomadic life and settled in town. Now she spoke Maa as well as she spoke German and Swahili, sometimes mixing the languages together.

Her play with homemade rag dolls consisted of bandaging

them, putting sticks to their mouths to take their temperature, and treating imagined symptoms. Their cloth faces were indelibly smeared with her medicinal concoctions. The strange premonitions of trouble that Fritz felt when he saved her had all but faded to the background.

They planned to leave her in Tanga with their good friends Ulrich and Giselle Hoffman, the mission administrator and his wife. They had two daughters close to Rebeka's age and Fritz and Ursula thought it the wisest course under the circumstances.

At first Rebeka was pleased at the idea of having sisters to play with, but when she realized that her parents would not be there with her, she dissolved into tears. As the steamship sailed out of port, Rebeka stood on the pier, solemn and resolute, only leaving when Auntie Giselle tugged at her hand.

She returned to the Hoffman's home and the guest room she had shared with her parents while they waited for the ship, but someone had changed the room and all her things were gone. She wandered into Margaret and Elspeth's room, thinking maybe someone moved them there, but there was no sign of her belongings. Feeling desolate and lost, she went to find Auntie Giselle who took her to the storeroom behind the dining room where a small cot stood, made up with sheets, a brown blanket, and a pillow.

"You will sleep here," Giselle said. "It isn't right for an African girl to live in the same room with my daughters."

The small room was hot and dusty. The only window was a tiny opening, barred and screened, up near the roof. The room smelled of flour and corn and other dried goods stored on shelves off the floor. Mixed in, and almost overpowering the smell of food, was the odor of kerosene. Several five-gallon tins of it stood against the wall. The household lanterns were kept here during the day and refilled as needed. On one shelf stood the vaporizing pump gun that held a mixture of kerosene and insecticide, a household staple to keep mosquitoes and other troublesome insects from becoming permanent residents.

"Let's get things straight right now," Auntie Giselle said. "I'm not your Auntie. You call me Frau Hoffman, and Uncle Ulrich is Herr Hoffman. Do you understand?"

Rebeka nodded her head.

"You may go into the girls' bedroom only if they invite you. I expect you to help around the house, though you're a bit small to be much use. If you don't have anything to do, you should go into the kitchen and talk to people of your own kind. I don't understand what Fritz and Ursula thought they were doing..." she rubbed her chin, "...we'll do what we can for you.

"Now, mind me, if I ever catch you getting into this food you'll be in big trouble. Understand?"

Rebeka nodded again, more slowly this time, never taking her eyes from Frau Hoffman's face, fighting back the tears.

The dam broke as soon as the door closed and Rebeka was alone in the dark, stifling room. She sat on the cot, her knees drawn to her chin, her arms wrapped around them, and rocked.

"Mama, Papa," she cried, rocking back and forth. She now understood that her parents had left her alone while they sailed away across a vast stretch of water. They might be gone a long time, maybe even forever. The waves of sorrow overwhelmed her. "Mama! Papa!" over and over she called their names into the dark room, her voice rising.

The door flew open and Frau Hoffman stood there, her face aflame, her nostrils flared, and her red hair escaping in damp tendrils on her forehead. Behind her stood her two daughters, wide-eyed and serious.

"That's enough, Rebeka," Frau Hoffman said. "There's no need to carry on as though someone died. They'll be back before you even know they're gone. No one is going to hurt you. Now, now." She laid a comforting hand on her head.

"Margaret," she turned to her eldest daughter. "Go to the kitchen and ask for a cup of tea for Rebeka."

Margaret returned with the tea and Frau Hoffman put a teaspoon of sugar into it—a real treat, since sugar was expensive. Rebeka calmed a little. Frau Hoffman took a medicine bottle from a high shelf and poured out a spoonful. "Here is a something that will calm you." The bitter-tasting liquid went into Rebeka's compliant mouth, washed down by mouthfuls of tea.

"Rest for awhile, now, "Frau Hoffman said, and Rebeka slumped down onto her pillow. The tears were gone, but sobs still wracked her body. Elspeth and Margaret both came over and patted her shoulders and Elspeth put her doll into Rebeka's arms. Elspeth gave her a tiny smile, turned, and followed her mother and sister out of the room.

Once again, it was dark in the tiny storeroom. Rebeka slept until hunger awakened her. The house was silent. She tiptoed out of the room and saw that night had come. A lantern, the wick turned down, stood in the middle of the table. Evidently the family had eaten dinner, because only one plate remained. On it were small heaps of food—a mixture of rice and beans with a side of red beets, all of it cold and unpleasant. She ate a few bites, all she could force down, and went into the living room where the family sat in the circle of light around the pressure lamp, the girls sprawled on the rug that covered the cement floor. Margaret did sums on a slate and Elspeth drew pictures on the back of an old letter.

"Well, look who's here," said Herr Hoffman. "We tried to

wake you for supper, but couldn't. We even came in and got the lanterns and you never moved. Come here, little girl," and he held out his hand. Rebeka ran over to him with a smile. "Uncle Ulrich—" she started, then saw Frau Hoffman's warning look, "—I mean, Herr Hoffman—"

"What's with the Herr Hoffman?" he said, setting her on his lap.

"It's only right," Frau Hoffman said. "After all, she's an African, and if the others hear her being familiar, they will be too and we'll lose the respect of the people." Her mouth settled in a grim line. "I never approved of the Scheibels taking her in, in the first place. But here she is, and we must do the best we can. And we will start right at the first to teach her what her place is." She talked as though Rebeka didn't understand her.

"And what is that place, Giselle?" Ulrich said.

"I don't really know for sure," she answered, staring at Rebeka who felt self-conscious. "She's a good girl and learns fast. But she's still an African, and a girl at that. What are they going to do when she grows up? How will she live? What African man will have her, a woman raised as a European? Tell me." She lifted her chin. "Whatever she does, she will have to learn a little humility. We might as well start teaching her now."

The months dragged on and on. Every now and then, when a ship from Germany docked, there would be a letter for her from her parents, a letter that would bring back the waves of sorrow. Rebeka slept in her hot little bed breathing kerosene fumes at night. Days were spent with Margaret and Elspeth or in the kitchen. Her job was to keep the kitchen floor swept clean, and as she wielded the long, homemade broom back and forth across the dusty concrete floor, she felt as though the broom controlled her. But she could relax and be herself with the kitchen help.

The atmosphere in the home strained as Frau Hoffman tried to find a way to teach Rebeka her place, while unable to define that place. She was often punished for infractions of the unwritten code set for her. Frau Hoffman's heavy hand, slapping and spanking, often sent her in tears to her room. Rebeka started to strip off her clothes and crouch naked in the corner. She began to spend her whole day naked, to run around the house and even play outside in the buff.

Frau Hoffman's lip curled when she saw this. "See," she would say, "I was right. She's just an African. And her behavior proves it. At least her clothes won't wear out."

There were times when Frau Hoffman acted kindly to Rebeka, giving her extra sweets and setting her example before her own daughters. But these were few and they confused the little girl. She never knew from one day to the next whether she would be in Frau Hoffman's good favor or not.

Rebecca wondered what was wrong with herself to bring such disapproval. Did God not love her, as he did the Hoffman's? Did dark skin make her more sinful? In her bath, she scrubbed and scrubbed. Maybe if her skin was white like Elspeth's and Margaret's, Frau Hoffman and God would love her more.

Yet Frau Hoffman had a weakness, too. She hated spiders. Rebecca knew from playing with her friends at Kuyoni's house that most spiders were funny little creatures. She knew which ones were good, and which ones would bite. At home, she kept spiders in little matchboxes and played with them. But Frau Hoffman shrieked when she found them taking up residence in corners of the house. She bustled about, her red hair berserk on her head, spraying insecticide about as though they all were in peril of their lives.

There were two things that brightened Rebeka's life. Margaret, who was eight and knew how to read, didn't have enough books to slake her thirst. She grew bored and decided to teach Rebeka and Elspeth to read. Every afternoon at three o'clock the three girls went outside and sat in the shade of a mango tree where Margaret drummed the alphabet and words into Elspeth and Rebeka. By the time Rebeka's parents returned she could decipher the words in books, discovering whole new worlds.

Sugar was the other pleasure in her life. When Giselle sent her to her room for small infractions of Frau Hoffman's strict code—little things like giggling on Sundays, not cleaning her plate at mealtime, kicking her chair, or talking back—Rebeka discovered the joy of passive rebellion by licking her finger and sticking it into the large can of sugar. She learned to lift the tight lid without making a sound, and when she felt vindicated enough by the sweetness that flowed down her throat and filled her stomach with comfort, she smoothed the surface of the sugar so no one would know. Whenever Frau Hoffman rebuked her, she smiled inside thinking of the stolen sugar.

Ursula and Fritz returned to find Rebeka taller, quieter, and reading books well beyond her age level. Frau Hoffman moved her into the guest room the day they arrived, and Rebeka didn't tell them about her place in the storeroom. Somehow she knew they wouldn't approve; maybe they would think she deserved it for being naughty. Weren't adults always right?

Before they left for home, while the adults gathered for tea in the living room and Elspeth and Margaret were in the kitchen, Rebeka ran out into the grass and found three large spiders that she captured in a cup. She carried them to the storeroom and gave them a new home in the sugar tin. She smiled to herself as she imagined Frau Hoffman's horror when she would find them.

"How was your time with the Hoffmans, *Liebchen?*" Ursula asked as they returned to Arusha from Tanga on a mule cart. "Did you miss us?"

One thing Rebeka had learned was the differences between herself and her parents. "I missed you, Mama," she said. "But I had fun, too. Margaret taught me how to read, and she gave me one of her books. When we get home I'll read it to you." She snuggled next to her mother, savoring her warmth. She'd survived the ten months; she felt ready to face the future.

**The future came two years later when the Maasai tribe came to claim her.** It was a beautiful day, the air washed clean by the first of the early rains. The earth drank in the water, and Rebeka had gone out to run and dance in the downpour, laughing and splashing as it fell on her face and soaked her clothes. When the clouds disappeared the sky seemed bluer and the trees greener with all the dust washed off the leaves.

She went inside to change her clothes and sit down at her little desk to study. She hated arithmetic, but knew she had to get the sums done before supper. Her mother would check the slate carefully to make sure there were no mistakes. Her parents were both at the hospital that day, leaving her alone in the house. Anderea and Yobi were in the kitchen. Songea's parents had accepted a bride price from a prominent chieftain and she now lived far away.

As Rebeka sat chewing the end of her slate pencil she heard an argument erupt in the kitchen, loud. She ran out to find two young Maasai *murani*, warriors, in an argument with the kitchen help.

Rebeka had seen many Maasai men. They came into Arusha to buy tobacco and beads, strutting with disdain as though they owned the streets. The young warriors coated their long hair with grease and red ochre, and braided it in hundreds of tiny braids laid out in intricate patterns around their heads and down their shoulders. They wore beaded ornaments around their necks and upper arms, and in their elongated earlobes. She secretly admired them. She knew from looking in the mirror that she had the same Maasai narrow face and high cheekbones, deep inset eyes, and narrow nose. The men looked so strong; their long legs strode purposefully with flexing muscles. The cloths they wore tied around their necks hid their bodies only from the front, their tight, round buttocks exposed for all to see. But now these young men frightened her.

As soon as she appeared at the kitchen to see what the argument was about, one of the men grabbed her arm and hissed at her in the Maa language.

"You! Maasai girl! You come with us!" and he started to drag her down the path. Anderea grabbed her other arm and she was pulled back and forth between them as they argued. Rebeka started to scream.

"She belongs to the *Daktari* and his wife," Anderea kept saying. "You must go to them to get permission. A child's father must give permission."

"He is not her father," the warrior hissed back. "She is a child of the Maasai and belongs with us. We have been sent by the elders to get her." Rebeka kept screaming, and before he could drag her away a small crowd gathered.

"Papa! Papa! Help me!" Rebeka cried when she saw Fritz running up the path. The young Maasai *muran* dropped her arm and stood, sullen yet defiant.

What's going on here?" demanded Fritz.

"They want me to go away with them," Rebeka clung to him and glared at the two men. "They…they want me to go live in their village."

Fritz closed his eyes in anguish. He knew what they wanted. "Go away," he spoke sharply. "She stays here with us. I will not permit her to be taken back to the village."

"She belongs with her people," one of the men muttered.

"Fritz shook his head. "She is now my daughter. She would have died if I had not rescued her eight years ago."

Ursula hurried her plump body along the path, her face a picture of distress. She put her arms around Rebeka and pulled her close. Fritz glared at the two warriors for several minutes and they glared back for a moment. They turned their hands palm out in defeated gestures, took their spears, and left as they came, swift and silent in their muscular gait. Rebeka trembled, wrapped in her mother's arms.

"Why…why do they want to take me, Mama?" she wailed, burying her head in her mothers waist. "I'm only a little girl!"

Ursula bit her lip. She knew she couldn't answer Rebeka. In fact, she had her own questions. "I don't know for sure, *Liebchen.* But we'll have to be careful from now on, won't we?"

Rebeka nodded, though she didn't really understand.

Supper was a quiet meal. Fritz and Ursula spoke only in monosyllables and Rebeka sensed their fear. It hurt her to think she caused it. She finished her reading by lantern light, said her prayers, and went to bed. She heard her parents speak in low voices in the living room, so she crept out to sit in the dark by the doorway to watch and listen.

"Ursula, *Liebchen*," she heard her father say. "We need to

face the fact that Rebeka is, and always will be, an African. Some day you and I will have to go back to Germany, or maybe we will die here—I don't know which—but we cannot always protect Rebeka."

"I know that, Fritzie. But what can we do now?"

"We must be sure to keep a watch over her," Fritz said. "I don't know what her future will be. This incident today is only the first in our fight to keep her from going back to the village. Sometimes I think it would have been better for her if I had never brought her here. Maybe we should have put her in the orphanage. I don't know." He shrugged. "Whatever we should have done, we didn't, and we have done what we have."

"Fritz! You don't really mean that! I know you love her as much as I do. You can't think it would have been better to let her die or go to the orphanage!"

"Of course I don't think that, Ursula. I just said that because when you take in a child, you never know what the consequences will be. Do you know why they came for her today?"

Ursula nodded. "How can I not know? That child, torn and near death last month…but why should they care about Rebeka?"

"Kuyoni warned me several months ago. He told me the tribe would come for her. What they do to their little girls is terrible, turning them over to their young men who await their circumcision rites. Civilized people find it unspeakable.

"But why Rebeka in particular, I don't know. They don't try to claim the little girls in the orphanage. I'll have to ask Kuyoni." Fritz ran his fingernail along a crack in the tabletop.

"That's why Kuyoni came to live in town," he continued. "Since he became a Christian he couldn't allow his daughter to go through that."

Silence followed. The clock ticked on its shelf. Rebeka, in

the dark hallway, bit her lip to keep from crying. Did Papa really wish they hadn't taken her in?

"What can we do?" her mother asked. "How can we protect her from such a life?"

"First, We must keep a watch over her. Someone of authority should be around all the time. If we can get through the next three or four years without another confrontation like today, she will be safe—for a while. But I think they'll come for her again. We must be prepared.

"I'll go to the *akida* tomorrow and see what we have to do to prove our claim on her. They will have to go to court if they want to take her. Why they would go to that trouble is beyond me. The Maasai women are valued so little. One little girl is as good as another.

"But we need to think about Rebeka's life. Now she's a little girl, but soon she'll grow to be a young woman, an African woman with an unusual background. Schooled, raised in a German home, and reading about the world. Do you know of any African woman who has what our daughter will have when she is grown?"

"No," Ursula said. "And there are precious few educated men other than those at the seminary. Even then, a wife with Rebeka's upbringing might be a problem."

"Here in Africa a woman is nothing unless she's married, and even then she's valued very little," Fritz said. "We should keep our eyes open for someone who would accept her."

"What do we do in the meantime?"

"I think one thing we should do is send her to the African girls' school. She'll be protected; yet will be with her own people. That might better prepare her for her future."

Rebeka crept back to her room, her ears and mind burning

with the thoughts planted by the overheard conversation. Questions rolled around in her mind far into the night before she fell asleep, so many questions, with no answers.

CHAPTER FIVE

# Valle d'Aosta, Italy 1905-1914

**When Therese gave birth to Antonio three weeks after she and Vito went home to Chenneil, Benito Mussolini sent a gift.** The child-sized maroon beret had a large *M* embroidered in front, and was far too large for anyone under the age of eight. A note came with the gift.

> *My dear Antonio, the note said. I welcome you to the world. I sincerely hope that when you grow up you will not be as unwilling as your father to join with me in the renewal of our wonderful country. Please tell your father I forgive him.*

Vito was not amused, and he threw away the beret. No man who resorted to thuggery would have his allegiance.

A more serious letter, sent to Vito, came a few days later.

> *We are facing strange times of indecision, my friend, and someone must do something. For nearly twenty-five years Italy has been a partner in the Triple Alliance with Germany and Austria, as you well know. If you have been reading the papers, you will know that on the one hand, we are at enmity with France over the fiasco in Tunisia. But on the other hand, Austria has broken promises made years ago by not releasing the Italian States in the Balkans to Italian sovereignty.*

*Many of us who study these political dilemmas feel war can scarcely be avoided. Italy must take a strong position! However, our esteemed King Emanuele has no backbone, and he allows the winds of opinion to blow him in every direction.*

*I believe we are on the verge of a revolution! Soon, as soon as I am finished with my military obligation, I will be publishing my own socialist newspaper, and you must read it to keep up on what is going on. Hundreds of men join with us every day. We will be able to change our world. I covet your good will and hope you will someday see that only the Socialist way will keep Italy from being trodden under foot by imperialists.*

Vito's response was a simple thank you for the gift and a short summary of his activities.

*The grapes this year are excellent, and we will have a good harvest. We see and hear little of what is going on in the rest of the world, and many of the people here would like to keep it that way. For centuries, little has affected the valleys of Valle d'Aosta, and I expect that little in the future will be of much concern. I do read the papers that come into town, though often weeks after publication.*

He heard nothing more from Benito. When 'Tonio was three, Therese gave birth to a daughter, whom they named after her mother. They called her Theresita, and as she grew she showed promise of looking just like her mother, with her curly black hair and large, gray eyes. As soon as she could walk the two children played among the vines on the warm hillside as Vito had done with his cousins the generation before.

In 1910, Vito's grandfather died at the great age of ninety, and his Uncle Dorian inherited the title of Count along with the castle. Dorian was a frail man of more than sixty years who depended on Vito and his father, and his own son Riccardo, to run the winery. His other child, a daughter, had married and moved away to Milan.

Vito's father, Augusto, provided the expertise bought by years of experimentation and practice. Vito and his cousin Riccardo marshaled the brawn of the many villagers hired for the hard work of tilling, weeding, and harvesting. Therese and Riccardo's wife Angelina managed the village women who worked in the winepress and bottling plant. Vito kept a watch over the money, and before long they were better off financially than most other wineries of the region. The village of Chenneil grew. More laborers came to work in the vineyards as the Fernaldi family bought neighboring fields. Vito also served as magistrate in the village—performing marriages, adjudicating disputes, and otherwise administering justice. Most of the people were inter-related and they took care of many of their own arguments.

Vito's cousin had not attended university, preferring to work with his hands in the fields. His two daughters, Marguerite and Serena, were a few years older than 'Tonio. The four children were as close as though they were brother and sisters.

Life was full of simple pleasures amid the sun-steeped mountains. The people laughed a lot, sang at weddings, and wept at funerals. There was always time to gather a group of men together to climb the snow-clad peaks of the Alps guarding their valley. People came from the south to see the famed mountains, and a small business blossomed as experienced men guided the novices up the difficult paths to the top where one could look down into France. The southerners bought bottles of wine with the Fernaldi label and took them home, and soon it was known all over Italy and served in the finest restaurants.

Vito seldom thought about Benito Mussolini. Therese was warm and loving, his children healthy and happy, and he kept his hands full with the business and the matters of the village.

The married men of the village gathered in the central piazza on Sunday evenings to smoke, play chess, and ogle the young women who paraded their finery. Here they discussed each other's daughters with earthy, lewd comments, sometimes wagering on which girl would be chosen by whose son. They also discussed politics. Newspapers were passed around until they were ragged; even those who couldn't read had to examine the print that carried the reports of the war in Libya, the shenanigans in Rome, and the unrest caused by the Socialists. Lists of casualties in Libya were especially noted, and when occasionally a local name made the list, the men would take off their caps and cross themselves.

The assassination of the Austrian Archduke in Sarajevo, in 1914, was only the official beginning of the war. For over forty years Austria and Russia had alternately pushed at the Balkan States and other nearby countries. They formed the *Dreikaiserbund* with Germany: The Three Emperors' League. Italy had associated with them, with the promise of the release of the small states at the head of the Adriatic Sea to Italy's rule. However, Austria refused to release these states, leading to disenchantment with the alliances.

The men of Chenneil were troubled by the news from the Balkans. "Austria has moved into the Balkans to administer them, along with those states we consider our own," Vito read to the congregated men. "Rome has sent an official protest. Here is what we have said to the Austrians. 'Since most of the people of these states are Italian-speaking, they are our possessions—

*Italia Irredenti*—unredeemed Italy.'"

"What can we do about it?" Giorgio said, tamping the tobacco in his pipe. Giorgio, the oldest man in the village was rumored to be almost one hundred years old, though no record of his birth existed. His hunched back and white hair that curled around his balding pate made him a unique figure in the village. Though he couldn't read, his keen intelligence coupled with the history he had witnessed through his many years earned him a strong voice in the weekly commentaries. Younger men listened to Giorgio, and even if they didn't agree with him, they would not voice opposition.

"So, what can Italy do?" he repeated, looking around as though someone would tell him. "Our country is weak right now. Our troubles with France in Africa keep us from speaking about this injustice. Only the men who write for newspapers dare to bait the King. I predict that nothing will be done. We will sit back and watch Austria, with the help of the other emperors, take the Balkans and threaten more of our territories."

Someone murmured a sound of disagreement, and Giorgio glared at him. "Let the people there decide their own destiny," he said as though no one had interrupted. "Let France and England make their objections."

Giorgio was right. Italy did nothing but sit back and complain. The Serbians struck back at the Austrians. France and England protested, and each year total war came closer and closer. Italy, along with Norway, Sweden, Denmark, Netherlands, Switzerland, and Spain, scrambled to declare neutrality in the fight that appeared imminent.

When Austria enticed Rome to join in with them in a coming war, promising the Balkan States as a reward, the villagers were incensed.

"Do they really think we should believe them?" thundered Giorgio. "Austria has never been our friend. God protect us if our King decides to join with them in their evil cause."

Then Balkan insurgents took the law into their own hands and fired a shot that caused the whole world to gasp. As the Archduke Franz Ferdinand of Austria rolled through the quiet Sunday streets of Sarajevo with his beloved wife Sophie, a man ran to his car and shot them both. Fighting broke out on nearly every front.

For nine months Italy maintained neutrality. But when Austria issued an ultimatum to Serbia to lay down their arms or be demolished, Italy took that as aggression.

Italy was scarcely prepared for war. Most of the small army was already occupied in Libya fighting insurgents and the French. The three thousand two hundred miles of Italian coastline were hard to defend, and she depended on foreign imports, especially from England. She bargained with Austria, and secretly with England, to see which side would bring the most benefits.

"Germany has advanced on France and Belgium," screamed the newspapers. "England, France, and Belgium have declared war on Germany and Austria!"

A week later came further news that the village men read with shaking hands. "Secret sources have revealed plans by Germany to wreak vengeance on Italy for not aligning with them! Rome is full of talk of joining the war!"

"We should remain neutral," Giorgio said. "Nothing can be gained by joining the war on either side. But we will, we will. Just wait and see. Devastation is come to our country." He refused to speak any more, just sat puffing on his pipe, as the younger men took up the discussion.

The Allies—England, France, and Belgium—fed propaganda

to the Italian people. Highly vocal factions of the whole political spectrum shook their fists in the market places and called for revenge against Austria and Germany. Since they controlled the press, they had the ear of the common man.

Even Mussolini, through his widely distributed newspaper *Avanti,* called for war. "Socialists of Italy, let us lay down our arguments with our government and join against our common aggressors. In this respect we can agree with those with whom we quarrel. Let us keep Italy intact, and later make the needed changes."

On April 26, 1915, Italy sided with Britain and France. The joint cause of all Italians was called *Sacro Egoismo*—Holy Selfishness.

By May 4 King Victor Emanuele III, unwilling to take the lead, deferred to his military leaders. "I am a parliamentary king," he declared, "not an emperor like Wilhelm and Franz Joseph. It is up to my ministers to make these decisions." A few weeks later he left by train for the front in North Italy vowing not to return to Rome until the war was over.

Rifles were thrust into the hands of young men from all over the country and they marched north to the Austrian border. The army in Africa and the Aegean islands came home. All these troops were grouped into four armies and arranged along the border under the command of the King, through General Luigi Cadorna.

The day before Vito left to fight for Italian sovereignty and dignity, he and Therese took their children to a hill overlooking the village for a picnic.

Therese packed a basket with bread, wine, cheese, and fruit and loaded it on the back of their donkey. The sun was warm for

May, and small flowers bloomed along the path. Puffy clouds dotted the blue sky. They spread a blanket on the ground and laid out the food. Therese's deft, sun-browned hands portioned out the food, and they sat around to eat and enjoy the quiet and the view.

The children soon finished and wandered off to explore their favorite haunts. The birds sang of new life with enthusiasm. War seemed far away. Vito beckoned Therese into his arms, and they lay back on the blanket, the sun hot on their faces. They kissed and caressed each other as the happy voices of the playing children echoed up to them. He pulled her skirt to her waist and moved on top of her, placing his finger on her mouth when she opened it to protest.

"Shhh. The children will be gone for a while. We haven't done this in the sunshine for many years."

Therese smiled and opened up to him. A butterfly danced over them, and a dove cooed from a nearby tree as they shared their love in intimacy.

Afterward, they talked about the war.

"Therese, I don't want to go. You know that, don't you?"

She nodded, too close to tears to say anything.

"I have to set an example to the others in the village. Oh, I am so afraid!" He buried his face in her hair, breathing in her scent. "If I don't come back…"

"Hush, don't even think it!" She laid a slender finger on his lips. "It's bad luck to even think it. You will come back. Keep saying to yourself, *I will come back, I will come back.*" She looked into his eyes, her own filled with terror at the thought of his not returning.

He kissed her again, and they held each other close until the children appeared laughing and talking about an eagle's nest they had seen. Life for all other creatures in the Alps would continue as it had before. As they gathered the picnic remains and left for their cottage, Vito turned to gaze at his family. The breeze mussed Theresita's braids, and her arms were full of gathered wildflowers. Her little mouth with a playful pout and laughing gray eyes were so much like her mother's it made his heart ache. Antonio, almost ten, already showed the awkward elbows and knees and large feet of future growth. A gentle boy, his mind was sharp. He must go to university some day, Vito thought.

Therese led the donkey, and he soaked into his memory the sight of her slender form, the simple dress she wore molded around her generous breasts, her quiet beauty and grace, her wavy black hair that hovered over her shoulders like a benediction. Her face still bore the rosy glow of love. They stood there, silent, looking back at him as he drank in the sight of the three most important people in his life, a sight he would take with him into battle to remind him why he went to war. He reached for Therese's hand; she took it with a smile, and he led her down the path toward home, tomorrow, and hard times ahead.

CHAPTER SIX

# German East Africa, 1914

**The news of the European conflict came as whispers on the breeze**; papers brought by ships were shared with others and considered as people hurried through their routines. Those events seemed so far away, so unconnected to the realities of disease, starvation, and death in Africa. To the African, it only meant that Europeans fought with one another as the tribes in Africa had fought among themselves. To the European, it meant looking with suspicion on others, and wondering how the war might affect their friendships. To the exporter of Africa's riches, it meant higher prices—along with higher insurance costs for shipping.

Fritz was in Dar es Salaam when the news of the war arrived. He had gone there to finalize Rebeka's official adoption papers, the ones he had started two years earlier. She was now legally his daughter, and if anyone tried to harm her, he now possessed the legal right to protect her.

It was July 30, 1914, and the bold print across the top of the Dar newspaper screamed:

**ENGLAND, FRANCE, AND BELGIUM DECLARE WAR ON GERMANY, AUSTRIA, AND RUSSIA!**

Wondering how this new development would affect his life's work, he hurried to the government offices to seek out information and let the governor know he was in town. Heinrich Schnee was now the governor and Fritz had a standing invitation to dine with him whenever he came to Dar es Salaam.

Traveling was easier now. He no longer had to make the five-day trip by mule cart from Arusha to Tanga, and thence by boat to Dar. The railroad, begun in 1891, finally reached Moshi, only 68 miles from Arusha. Now he only had to get to Moshi, and the rest was by train to Tanga, and then the ferry. And, since Sawaya Mawala had an old truck that he used to take merchandise to the rail terminal, he could ride with him in the cab.

Fritz found Governor Schnee in conference with his advisers and officials. Someone pulled out a chair for him.

"Doctor Scheibel," Schnee said. "I see you have the paper in your hands. What do you think of this war?"

"I am a man of peace," Fritz replied. "I can only pray that the war will not reach us here in Africa, and that it will not last long—" he rattled the paper clutched in his fist, "—but I'm afraid that with all these nations involved…. We've never seen a war like this before. I shudder to think of the devastation." He shook his head. "What do you hear from Berlin?"

Schnee stroked his long-handled mustache. "We have no official word. We are discussing the situation now, but I'm afraid our opinions are divided.

"Gentlemen," he turned to the group of men, continuing their previous conversation, "until I hear something firm from Berlin, we must be honorable and hold to the agreement reached by the 1885 Congo Act, that in the event of any war, all colonies are to remain neutral."

A murmur of voices followed his statement. Some, including Fritz, agreed, but another group, led by Paul von Lettow-Vorbeck, began to argue. Lettow-Vorbeck, much older than Schnee and nearing the end of his military career, commanded the Defense Force. His concern, as it became evident, was for Germany and her honor, not for Africa. He stood to his feet, tall and slim; his imposing military bearing crowned by a full head of silver hair reminded Fritz of an eagle surveying its prey.

"Governor, sir, I and others respectfully disagree. We have an excellent opportunity to divert the forces of the Allies by expanding the war to Africa. If they have to send troops and munitions here, we will have done well in draining away their strength. Already we have more manpower at our command that the British have in Kenya. The Portuguese in Mozambique have a small force, and the Belgians have not trained their African military for war. We have a distinct advantage here. In no time I—" he hesitated, "—we—can train additional troops for deployment against the British colonies. We must strike Kenya before they know we are even discussing it, while they are unready."

"It is exactly that, that troubles me," Schnee said. "We're surrounded by British, Belgian, and Portuguese colonies. We may have to fight on three fronts. And all of our shipping must sail past either Kenya or Mozambique. You know this, Paul, and you still think we must attack?"

"Yes," the military commander answered. "Of that I am certain." The group murmured again, with most of the men now arguing for a quick strike at Kenya.

Fritz shook his head and walked away. He knew Schnee; they were good friends. He was an intelligent man; able to listen to and understand both sides of an argument, but in the end he would not have the courage to stick to his initial decision. Several days later, as Fritz traveled home, he pondered the effect war would have on their lives. Money would be hard to come by. Food, they could grow. Old clothing could be mended, and new made from indigenous cotton cloth. Mail from home would be rare. Medicines would be in short supply. Maybe he should look into the uses of local herbs, employed by the Africans for centuries, on non-urgent cases. He determined to ignore the extra hardships and continue in his work, and the research he had begun on tropical diseases. With this resolve, Fritz arrived home, and the family celebrated Rebeka's official adoption with a cake.

**Mpepo, the grandson of Mkwawa, was now a young man of nineteen**. His broad shoulders, open honest face, and friendly disposition won him many friends and admiring glances from the girls. He had sailed through his schooling with ease. The mission teachers had long noted that teaching a syllabus replete with mathematical concepts and empirical thinking rarely earned more than frowns and dull looks from the students. Western lineal logic was foreign to a people steeped in circular thinking. But Mpepo showed superior intelligence and an ability to grasp the theories of both math and logic.

Knowledge of the world thrilled him. As he studied about the diverse cultures and economies of the globe and contrasted them with what he knew of his own tribe, he felt his people had been cheated of a precious heritage. What little awareness they had of other cultures they enclosed in the mysterious shrouds of tribal lore. He longed to share this new insight with the rest of his people.

"This boy should go to university," his teachers declared, but as yet few Africans from the German colony had dared enter a European university. Besides, Mpepo had other ideas.

His uncle still coached him from the background. "You are

Huru first, Mpepo," he said. "You are the grandson of Mkwawa who was the greatest chief of all Wahuru history. Your people count on you. Someday, when the time is right, you too will be a great chief. Your salvation lies in your people who wait for your return."

*Salvation*, Mpepo said to himself, though he kept his thoughts silent. *Salvation is in Jesus Christ.* He had long talks with his teachers and Dr. Scheibel, for whom he had a deep respect. Here was a foreign man, he thought, who would die for his adopted African daughter, a man who said he would not return to Germany until he could take her with him. Through their many talks Mpepo confirmed his desire to become a minister, and he entered the church seminary in Arusha. His uncle came to see him, his face clouded with anger.

"How can you be chief if you become a Christian?" he demanded. "Why are you turning your back on your people?"

"Because the old ways are no more," Mpepo said. "I cannot in good conscience condone the witchcraft a chief must practice to control his people. I will not call up spirits and consult them, or put curses on the disobedient. I will not enslave my enemies. I do not want to do those kinds of things. It would be a fine aspiration to be chief; I have always thought and dreamed about it. But I do not want it at the price I would have to pay.

"I can still serve our people, Uncle. As Mkwawa's grandson, I can bring Christianity and its benefits to my people, and they will listen to me. I will be their spiritual chief."

His uncle's face showed the struggle to keep his authority. "One other thing," he said, trying to save face. "You must think about marrying. I will line up some comely girls for you to make your choice."

"Uncle, There are many fine girls here in Arusha. I wish to

consider them first."

"Are they Wahuru?" The old man leaned forward intently. "Whoever you marry, she must be Wahuru. Or you can forget coming back to your land." He spat onto the ground to emphasize his point.

Mpepo didn't answer. He only gave his uncle a quick, shocked glance.

"Forget them," ordered his uncle. "One thing I will be as unbending about as you are about being a Christian. Whomever you marry, she must be Wahuru," and with that he turned and walked away.

Mpepo had barely begun his theological studies when the news of war in Europe came. The young men discussed it in their room at night.

"Why, when Europeans already have so much, do they go to war?" someone asked. "They don't enslave each other, as our people have done when we war. What are their reasons?"

"Perhaps they wish to expand their countries," Mpepo replied. "Even our chiefs want to have control over others, do they not? It is in the heart of man to seek power." He continued. "Also, there is the matter of money and products. If all the countries captured pay taxes to the victor, the victor becomes rich. And he will have access to all their goods without paying a tariff."

"True," said another student. "And when these big countries try to eat the little ones, other countries like England and France come in and say 'Stop it! Stop being a bully!' Like when we saw those thugs in the marketplace try to steal food from old lady Maranga's stall, and we made them stop." General laughter followed that recollection.

"Yet," said Mpepo as they quieted, "As members of the

German Empire, we are now considered the thugs. England and France are the ones trying to stop us from taking all those little countries. I do not like the side I am supposed to be on."

"Do you think we will have war here," someone asked.

Mpepo answered, "Do we not have three British colonies on either side of us with whom we have been friends for so long, but are now our enemies? Will you and I not be called to fight against our brothers in Kenya and Rhodesia?"

Everyone fell silent at that thought. As trainees to be ministers of the Gospel, they did not like war, or accept the fact that they themselves might have to take up a gun and shoot another person for a cause that was not their own. The group quickly scattered to finish their chores and studies before going to bed for the night.

As it turned out, the British started the fighting long before Schnee was ready for his own preemptive strike. A warship appeared one morning and shelled a communications center just outside of Dar es Salaam. The order came that Mpepo and his classmates must leave seminary and join the army. Protesters would be forced to be porters, the lowest rung on the military ladder. The missionaries' arguments that seminarians had always been considered exempt in the homeland had no effect. Lettow-Vorbeck was adamant. All able-bodied young men must serve.

On September 12, 1914, Mpepo and eleven other seminarians marched off toward Moshi, to be trained in strict German military discipline and warfare tactics.

**Rebeka didn't mind attending the girls' school where she made friends with other girls.** She stayed in the dormitory hut during the week, and went home for weekends. Three of the girls in her hut were also Maasai. One of them, Malia, the daughter of Kuyoni, had been her close friend since they were small children. Most of the girls came from aristocratic families who wanted their daughters to have an education, be kept from degrading tribal traditions, and perhaps gain a larger bride price when it came time to marry because of their education. Some of the girls were orphans, wards of the Lutheran mission.

Ursula had a harder time adapting to the change. Since Rebeka's infancy she had all but forgotten the difference in racial background. She caught herself several times about to remark on the pallid faces of other missionaries' children. Her love was so complete, and her acceptance of Rebeka as her own so absolute, that it hurt her to see Fritz champion her difference. Yet her intellect said he was right. Rebeka had no future other than in Africa, and she must be prepared.

The Arusha Girls' School compound was composed of a circle of five dormitory huts surrounded by a high fence. Each hut had a latrine behind it, and a four-room schoolhouse stood in the center of the dirt courtyard. Meals were prepared at each hut under the supervision of a hut-mother. Six girls and a mother, usually a widow, stayed in each hut. Security was provided for the protection of the girls at the school. Not only were they kept safe from wild animals that occasionally wandered into town, but also from the amorous attentions of young men.

Rebeka became africanized at the school. She learned to think like the other girls. She enjoyed the primitive act of kneeling in front of a grinding stone and seeing the coarse wheat turn into flour. She took her turn at the mortar, a hollowed out log standing upright into which corn was poured, then several girls stood around it and took turns thrusting a log pestle into it to mash the corn to make *ugali,* the staple corn meal mush. They frequently sang as they alternated pounding the corn with tapping the side of the log in time to their music. She learned to identify the herbs and greens that made the bland food tasty. The women taught the girls indigenous medical poultices.

Most of all, she learned the place of a woman in tribal society. She should never look into the eyes of an unrelated man, even if he spoke to her. Always curtsy when spoken to by an elder in public, even to her husband.

In spite of her many friends, Rebeka grew up feeling alone. European attitudes ingrained by the Scheibels clashed with the African way of thinking, and she constantly had to second-guess the reactions of the other girls. Even though she was a quick learner and soon picked up the idioms of speech and nuances of thought patterns, the two ways of thinking and doing things fought for dominance. She became quiet and introspective, an observer on the outside of everything.

Ursula went daily to the compound to check on her during the first year until Rebeka asked her to stop.

"The other girls tease me, Mama," she said. "They say you aren't really my mother, and that I think I'm better than they because I live with Europeans." Hurt, Ursula stopped coming by so frequently, often only seeing Rebeka on the weekends.

Since Fritz obtained the official adoption there were no more attempts to kidnap her. However he took no chances, and he came to the school on Friday evenings to walk her home and returned her to school on Monday mornings. She usually spent Saturdays with her father in the hospital learning to dress wounds and care for the children who were brought in with burns, fevers, and tropical diseases. On Sunday, they attended church, and Sunday afternoons were spent reading. The classics that Fritz and Ursula took to Africa with them so many years before became soiled and worn.

Then war came to them. Rebeka watched as Mpepo and the other seminarians marched away to fight. He had often come to talk to her father, and she would put her ear against the wall of her bedroom to hear what they said. She liked the questions he asked and learned things from her father's answers. Mpepo never spoke to her and she wondered if he even knew she existed. Her heart broke to see him go. She would miss him, and she resolved to pray every night that he would return.

## CHAPTER SEVEN

# North Italy

**Vito, along with the other men from Chenneil under the age of forty, joined the Alpini Brigade**. These special troops formed an elite branch of the armed forces, men who knew the Alps and how to conquer them. They were the experts who knew the snow and winds, how to find paths up the steep slopes, and the signs of imminent avalanche. They guided the terrified lowland soldiers expertly through the passes. When they marched through the tiny villages dotting the fertile valleys, they put on a brave front for the villagers who cheered them on. In their smart Tyrolean-style hats they strutted with cocky bravado, smiling at the children whose adoring eyes followed them, singing their theme song:

And the King he sends to tell us
That he can't get on no more,
And he needs us Alpini fellows
To go forward as before.

Therese and the other women stayed home to tend to the grapes and the wine. Cousin Riccardo, too, stayed behind since his ailing father was not able to take the reins of the business. The village was left in the hands of women, old men, and the very young. The war would be fought on many fronts, each citizen doing what he could to keep his country free of Austrian and German rule. Always, in the back of the people's minds, loomed the German threat to make Italy pay for not joining the

Triple Alliance.

The men marched to the nearest railroad town and rode north to the Austrian border. There they learned the fundamentals of warfare, and those who had never handled a rifle were taught the mechanics of cleaning and using them. Vito had hunted in his valley since his childhood so he already knew guns intimately. The overworked trainers made him captain over a battalion. The rifles they received were 1891 Mannlicher-Carcano carbine modified with a turnbolt action to hold a five-shot clip that automatically ejected when empty. Bayonets were secured to the ends of these rifles with a spring catch that snapped them either closed or open.

"What do we use these for," someone asked.

"In case we engage in hand-to-hand combat," Vito said. He shuddered to think of being that close to the enemy. How could he kill a man while looking into his eyes? Nonetheless, he trained his men to use them in the fields where bales of hay served as an unresisting enemy.

The Italian army faced the Austrians where the vast Isonzo River Valley sloped down to the Adriatic Sea that separated Italy from the Balkans and the rest of Eastern Europe. Ringed by snow-capped mountains that marked the border with Austria, this fertile plateau was watered by three great rivers that tumbled down the slopes and across the wide plain. On those stern mountains the harsh realities of warfare made men out of boys and agnostics out of men.

"There are three things you must do," Vito told recruits. "Let your hair grow long, grow a beard, and take to drinking wine. Those things will keep you warm."

Their first engagement proved typical of the ones to follow. Vito picked Luigi Longo, a lad from his village whom he felt had leadership capability, to be second in command. Their Alpini battalion, rifles and skis strapped to their packs and loaded down with ammunition and dry socks, wrestled cannons on mule carts up the steep slopes of the Alps. Range after range stood between them and the enemy. Men swore often when the paths narrowed and one wheel of their cart trembled over a precipice. They were hungry and cold. It was perpetual winter here in the mountains, and they froze their fingers and toes even in June.

They had been occupied thus for two weeks before they reached the border. Vito's men were exhausted. In a thick morning fog they found themselves on a summit.

"Level a place for the guns," Vito commanded. The men grumbled, preferring to start a fire and get something warm into their bellies.

But when Vito picked up a pickax and began to chop at the rocky terrain, they joined in, soon leveling a site large enough to place their cannons and aim them in different directions.

"Believe me, the enemy is out there somewhere. Just wait and see," Vito said.

The camaraderie among the men was high. The ordeal of the ascent forged bonds among them. In spite of their weariness, they joked and teased each other as they finally devoured a warm stew of indeterminate nature and drank coffee.

The fog began to lift. Patches of a distant valley lying almost at their feet appeared. Fog-strained sun surrounded them briefly, the cloud lifted, and they saw, a short distance away, another higher peak with enemy guns trained on them.

"To your stations," Vito yelled, and some of the men scrambled to the guns, the others to hide behind the rocks for protection. The Austrian cannons boomed first and two Italian cannons lay twisted and smoking, a half-dozen bodies of their comrades scattered around.

The men behind the rocks began to shoot their rifles at the enemy. The Austrian cannons roared again and bits of rock exploded. More of Vito's men lay dead.

"Retreat as you can! Cover for your comrades!" As some stepped up the barrage of rifle fire, others retreated. They retraced their steps away from the engagement as fast as they could, and the Austrians followed.

This became typical of their war as weeks turned into months, and months into years. The fight did not go well for the Italians. The Alpini would reach the top of one mountain and position their guns only to find the Austrians had already placed their own encampments nearby. Mules and men died wrestling carts of equipment up slopes never intended by God to be used for warfare. What they labored to bring up one slope, they soon took back down, only to push it all back up another. Peak after peak was lost to the Austrians.

Meanwhile, the other troops fought at the rivers with cannons, rifles, and mortars. The Isonzo River was lost, then the torrential Piave River became a momentary battlefront until Austrian troops stormed across it and pushed the Italian troops to the Tagliamente River. Back and forth the battle raged, with staggering casualties. Tens of thousands of Italian men lay dead or dying after each battle.

The trains that brought masses of increasingly younger men north reeked of male fear. They then turned around and went south, filled with the stench of the body fluids of the wounded and the smell of the dead being returned to their home villages and cities. In the summer, bodies were buried hastily on the battlefield.

Occasionally Vito received a package or letter from home,

sometimes with a sweet, or a new pair of socks or gloves. Once he found a scarf with a note from Therese.

*My dearest love, I wanted to make a scarlet scarf for you, but that would be too visible. You must be content with this drab brown, but think scarlet when you wear it. After you come home, you will have a red one to take its place.*

Later on he got a photo with another note.

*I am sorry I cannot include any sweet. What little we have goes to the children. I am sure you would agree. There is little food, since so much is taken for the soldiers at the front. We are pulling our belts tighter, and do not mind our food going to you men who fight so gallantly for our freedom. You would be proud of our Antonio. He has become a man, as you will see from this picture.*

The photo of the three of them showed Therese standing with her arm around Theresita, and on her left Antonio, straight and unsmiling. He looked taller than Vito remembered, and the jut of his jaw and determined look on his face made Vito's heart ache for his son's childhood cut short too soon. All three of them looked thinner than he remembered, but then so was he. He kissed the photo and kept it in his shirt pocket.

Each morning upon awakening Vito first crossed himself and thanked God for another day, took out the photo, and filled his mind with the sight of his family. He tried not to think too much about Therese. The dreams he could not control were enough to waken him with damp cheeks. The vision of his family on the hillside on his last day at home kept him going when he crouched in the wet and cold behind a rock, his rifle in his hand, waiting for the cold fog to lift so he could remove another enemy soldier from action.

The furloughs promised when they enlisted never occurred. The casualties were so high on the battlefield that General Cadorna cancelled all passes. The only way to go home was as one of the wounded or killed. Cadorna issued a command that deserters and those who retreated without orders be shot without mercy. Often Vito found himself at grim attention with his men watching as frightened young men, barely out of childhood, were blindfolded and shot as examples to the troops.

He himself refused to exercise that command. When Luigi, his second in command, received a letter from home telling him of his father's imminent death, he faced a decision. No furloughs were allowed for any reason.

"I will turn my back to you, Luigi." Vito turned away from his friend. "I do not see where you go, do I?"

Luigi stood there for a moment, but when Vito finally turned around again, he was gone. His disappearance would never be reported.

Several times King Victor Emanuele himself addressed the troops. Vito saw him for the first time and pitied him—a timid intellectual who alternated between his prayer book and the command headquarters. Everyone knew he was only a figurehead. Cadorna and the other generals were the ones who decided in the privacy of their war rooms where and how to fight. The king gave official, public sanction to their decisions.

From river to river, the Austrians and Germans drove the Italians deep into their own country. As they pushed the increasingly demoralized Italian troops back, the enemy burned the villages and fields that fed them. The blood of hundreds of thousands of men fertilized the now-untilled fields. Uncounted numbers of civilians died of starvation, or were shot trying to guard their stores of dwindling food. Old men willed themselves to die rather than face losing everything they had spent their lives to build, choosing to leave life behind and free what little they ate so a child could have more. It seemed as though the whole world went mad. Soon the Americans joined the fight in France and Belgium. The promised help from the British didn't come, and the Italian leaders secretly wondered if maybe they had joined the wrong side. Frequent pleas for help were ignored in London.

Vito learned this from Benito Mussolini, whom he met again at a reconnaissance in the main camp on the banks of the Tagliamento River. Returning from the command tent where he received his instructions to lead a new strategic assault, Vito ran into Beni standing outside.

"Vittorio, my friend!" Beni shouted as he ran to him and pumped his hand. "How are you? I have often wondered about you. Come. Let's go drink together, and tell me all about yourself!"

They spent an hour together catching up on each other's lives and families. Beni, too, had married. "But she is not much to my liking," he said. "Too pious for me. You know what I mean," and he punched Vito's arm lightly and laughed. "I find my pleasure in the girls who follow the camp. You should come with me; I can introduce you to some fine women who don't let their prayer books interfere with their fun."

"No, thank you." Vito said. "I prefer spending my leisure time in other pursuits."

"Well then, let us talk of Italy. Do you not see how cowardly our king is? Our country is on the brink of change. When this war is over, and it will be someday, believe me, and should we survive it, as I am sure we will, we must all work together to forge a new, stronger nation, one that no one will deign to push around. I still want you, Vito, by my side as an adviser. I value your intellect, your mind."

"Beni, you sent your men to beat me back in Turin."

Beni's eyes widened in fake innocence. "Those thugs took it on themselves! Now why would you think I could do such a thing to my trusted friend?"

Vito shrugged and changed the subject. "I can only think of the war right now; how we can win it and keep our families safe. Perhaps, after the war you can come to my home and visit. We will talk about these things then."

By now Beni was under the influence of the cheap wine. He put his arm around Vito's shoulders and whispered in a conspiratory manner. "I have a secret; I have been thinking. Do you know the Socialists in our country are not happy with me? They came out against this war, but I believed we had no choice. I am for Italy first, not the world organization of Socialists. I am coming to the opinion that while socialism and communism are partly right, they both employ too many people to make policy. Too many conflicting ideas can stalemate the progress of a government.

"I believe I am the man to guide our country. Even here in the army many men have come to me secretly to beg me to lead us to the greatness that is our heritage."

As the two men parted and returned to their separate posts, Vito thought about what Beni had said. He wondered if Italy would not fall into the hands of a despot if Beni had his way. If he, Vito, joined him and became a voice of reason, would that keep Italy on a saner course? He would think of that later.

Three years passed without the chance to go home. Vito's dreams of Therese and her warmth increased. He refused to visit the camp women because he knew they were poor substitutes, only degrading the love he had for his wife. He re-read the infrequent letters he received from home until the writing faded and the paper became smudged and disintegrated in his hands. His clothing became ragged. His men often had no ammunition and he had to order retreat. His heart hardened as he saw many of them leave in coffins or with arms or legs blown off, young men who had little on their chins to shave and who never had the chance to love a good woman. Now, in the mornings, Vito did not cross himself and thank God for another day. When a prayer came into his mind, it was for his family only. God seemed far away and silent. It seemed He did not care.

The Austrians, aided by the Germans, pushed the Italian army back across the Piave River again. General Cadorna felt a desperation that was evident to his troops, and his harshness increased. His frequent harangues included imagery of all Italian males sacrificing their lives in the attempt to keep the Huns off their land. At the height of their loss of spirit, just when it appeared that Italy was defeated, six French and five British divisions came to help. Cadorna retired and General Diaz, his replacement, lent a fresh spirit to the beleaguered Italian troops.

Elsewhere in Europe, the Germans and Austrians were being defeated. The Italian front was the only one where victory was on their side, and Italy's allies came to make sure that the aggressors would be defeated everywhere. The British marched up in sharp uniforms and cheerful demeanor, and those Italians who knew English were assigned to their regiments as guides and interpreters.

Vito was among them, having studied English at Torino University. His orders were to guide a battalion of the Northumberland Fusiliers across the River Po and through a valley to surround the enemy camped near a deserted village.

He knew this area well. It was only a short journey from home, and he longed to slip away and visit his family, but he didn't.

It was late September of 1917. Mornings were cold and foggy along the valleys and streams. Fresh snow dusted the tops of the mountains, a promise to the valleys below of another winter. By ten the sun came out and warmed the fields, making the earth steam in grateful release. Each evening the fog crept in again, blanketing the tents and men so they appeared as silhouettes beside the cook fires. After eating, they doused the fires, struck their tents, and crept forward in the dark and fog to a new position. They bivouacked in hidden locations during the day, sleeping and taking turns at watch, hoping the enemy troops remained ignorant of their movements.

One night about midnight they came upon an enemy outpost by surprise. Much to Vito's dismay the guard alerted the enemy and his men soon found themselves outnumbered. He and a score of men became separated from the main force and were driven into a narrow ravine from which there was no escape except through the enemy ranks waiting at the mouth of the small valley. The path into the ravine was littered with the bodies of their fellows.

The fog thickened as the dozen or so men remaining alive huddled, waiting for daylight, their hands in their armpits to keep warm. Scouts were sent out to find a way up and over the sides of the ravine, but there was no way out except the way they came in. The enemy soldiers gloated and waited because morning would bring another victory.

The British soldiers argued for making a sudden charge in the night; though many would die in the attempt, some would get through in the dark. As they argued back and forth, Vito listened, ready to agree that this was the only course of action left to them.

Just before ordering an assault on the opening of the ravine, a tinkling, bell-like sound came to their ears.

Looming out of the fog came a flock of sheep down the path from the head of the narrow valley, followed by a ghost-like shepherd, his hooded cloak drawn over his bent back and head, his shepherd's crook guiding his poorly-shod feet over the stony path.

At first taken aback by finding foreign soldiers in his ravine and unable to converse with them, he became alarmed. The lookout called for Vito to translate.

He was an old man, toothless, stooped, and slow of mind. He had a small hut up on the side of the ravine, he told Vito. Yes, he said, there was only the one way out. He had heard the sound of gunfire, and when it ceased he came down to see what damage had been done. He looked at Vito's feet as he said this, indicating silently that he looked for newer footgear. His sheep followed him, he said, because often in the wee hours of the morning he led them into the fields by the river to feed.

As he warmed up to Vito they talked together. The British listened but didn't comprehend their conversation. Vito had a bold idea. He discussed it with the shepherd, who listened, incredulous at first, then he nodded in excited agreement and laughed. As the soldiers watched, the shepherd removed his cloak and handed it to Vito, who gave him his much warmer army overcoat and a handful of money. Vito took the crook, put on the cloak, and immediately became indistinguishable from the shepherd's previous appearance. By the looks on their faces, he knew they expected him to perform a one-man escape and leave them to their fate. The shepherd disappeared up the path that he had come down. He left the sheep behind, which now crowded around Vito believing he was their shepherd from the smell of the cloak.

Vito first sent a scout to the mouth of the ravine to determine the placement of the enemy. After half an hour the scout returned to say that the camp was on the right side in a copse of trees. There was a guard on the left sitting on a rock, with three armed men resting behind him.

"All right, men," Vito said. "This is what I want you to do. Between here and there are a dozen or more bodies of your countrymen. As we reach them, you must take off their boots. They no longer need them, and you will." They gave him a puzzled look.

"You must first take off your coats, turn them inside out, and put them back on so the light-colored lining is on the outside. When we get close to the camp, you must put those boots on your hands and bend over, walking on both hands and feet—like the sheep." The men looked at the sheep milling around at their feet, the idea beginning to take shape.

"It's a wild plan," Vito said, "But it may work. I will be your shepherd. You will mingle with the sheep, and I will herd you all out of the ravine and past the guards. I believe, in this fog—" they all glanced around at the swirling mist of the pre-dawn hour, barely able to see each other, "—that most of us will get through before they realize what's happening. When they do catch on, stand and run. Most of you will be past the camp, and you know the way you came." The men laughed at the sheer ingenuity—and stupidity—of the plan, but knew their only other alternative was to go down to the grave in a gun battle.

"Also," Vito added, "Leave your packs behind. Strap your rifles across your bellies so they don't show, but where you can grab them when you need them."

Shaking their heads in disbelief, the men complied with

his directions. Vito adjusted the cloak, his own rifle hidden underneath, bent his back and shuffled along as the men camouflaged themselves as instructed. Most of them found boots to cover their hands, and they crept, mingled with the bewildered sheep, as they approached the enemy camp. Vito clucked and called to the sheep as Italian shepherds had done for centuries, making his voice sound cracked and old, not trying to hide his approach.

"Halt!" Shouted the guard, as sheep baa-ed past him. Vito shuffled to a stop in front of him.

"Who are you," the guard asked in German.

"I am simply an old man, a shepherd, taking his flock to the river," Vito answered in a quavering voice, and broken German. The sheep pushed on ahead of him through the mist.

"I should shoot you for your impertinence," the guard said. "Do you not know there is a war? That a battle has taken place here?"

"There is always war," Vito answered. "For centuries there has been war. I am an old man, and have seen much war. But people must eat, and sheep feed people, so I keep sheep. That is all I can do. I care not about war."

The guard looked hungrily at the sheep as they went past. "Give me a reason why I should not shoot you, old man," he said.

Vito put on the appearance of a frightened old man. "Please, I'll give you a sheep for your dinner tomorrow. In the afternoon, God willing, I'll give you another. You need me alive so I can keep the sheep alive. I'm no threat to you."

The guard scratched his chin and thought about it. "All right, old man. I agree you're no threat to me. Give me a sheep."

As Vito thrust an unwilling sheep into his hands, the guard

asked, "Did you see soldiers camped in the ravine there?"

"Yes," Vito said, "only about a dozen or so, up among the rocks. Britishers, I think." He shook his head. "Some of them are wounded, and they're hungry."

The guard laughed. "They won't be hungry long. By noon they will be stiff and cold on the ground. Go, old man. Get out of my sight before I change my mind and shoot you."

As Vito left to follow his flock one of his men stood to his feet too soon.

"*Ach*," the guard shouted and lifted his rifle and shot him. The soldier fell dead. The rest of the British soldiers quickly stood and raced away through the fog. The other guards sprang to their feet and began to shoot into the mist and the whole enemy camp came alive with surprised yells and gunfire.

"Run for your lives," shouted Vito as he flung off the cloak and began to run, then turned to shoot at the guards to cover for the men. As he disappeared into the swirling miasma, a feeling akin to utter joy came over him, something within his body blossomed and spread…a revelation of something he couldn't quite grasp…a thought of Therese…what was she trying to say? He listened but couldn't make it out. As the fog faded and utter blackness descended, he collapsed on the path. He didn't feel the hands that grabbed him, or the pain of being heaved over a shoulder, or the bumping as his carrier ran with the others into the trees by the river.

CHAPTER EIGHT

# German East Africa, 1916

When the English invaded the Kilimanjaro area in 1916, the
hospital wards in Arusha filled with the wounded. Troops
from Kenya marched through the streets, and no one had time to
ponder their own situation, least of all Fritz and Ursula who were
virtual prisoners of their work. Rebeka came home permanently
from the girls' school for her own protection.

She sat at her little desk on the porch, where she had sat when
only seven, reading and studying whatever Fritz could find to
turn into a school subject.

"I have no idea what you're going to need to know," he told
her. "But English is probably one of the things you should learn."
He found a grammar book and she added one more language to
her already impressive arsenal. She read history books and wrote
reports on the backs of old letters because paper was scarce. She
went to the hospital several times a week with her parents to
help with the children's' clinic.

Occasional newspapers brought some news, but most of
what they learned came through the troops of both countries
that seesawed through town. The war in Africa did not go well
for Germany. One by one, she lost her African colonies. Togo
fell first, a tiny little country taken in one surprise strike by the
French. Then Cameroon, a bleak land of fever and heat, fell

to the British. Next came German Southwest Africa where the governor was made prisoner before he knew what happened. That land, called by many *the beautiful, empty desert* became British territory, almost completing the British goal of contiguous colonies east to west and north to south in the African continent. All that remained for them to accomplish this was to capture German East Africa, the pearl of German overseas possessions.

Von Lettow-Vorbeck was a brilliant commander who had previously served in China putting down the Boxer Rebellion. He led his men on swift, guerrilla-like strikes, followed by retreats back into the central plains before the British could retaliate. This conserved both ammunition and men. They burned the fields and crops behind them to keep the Kenya troops from foraging as they pursued them. It didn't matter to Lettow-Vorbeck if the African peasants had nothing to eat either. "The natives be damned," he said. "There are more important things to be considered—like the honor of Germany."

He ordered heliograph stations to be built from Lake Victoria in the north to the Kilimanjaro area in the east, then west to Lake Tanganyika. The highest hills each had a station and a platform for a large mirror of polished brass. Morse code messages were passed from hilltop to hilltop, reflecting sunlight by day and lantern light by night without the need of telegraph wires.

Troops came and went like an ever-changing tide. Fritz and Ursula tended British wounded, then turned around and nursed German soldiers. Most of the wounded men were the African pawns of one country or the other. The empty seminary dormitory became another ward for the injured. General Jan Smuts came from South Africa where he had helped the British win the Boer War; now he commanded the Kenya African Rifles and the Kenya settlers' Legion of Frontiersmen.

"I am a man of peace," Fritz said when his loyalty was questioned. "My allegiance is to God first, and the African second. It matters not who the wounded and sick are. My duty is to them."

"Yet you are German third, are you not?" the British commander asked.

"Yes, of course. I am a citizen of Germany. I will return to Germany some day. But I do not ask the nationality of the man who needs my help. All men are my brothers. Do you have any medicines I can use?"

When the British saw that he treated all equally, they came to recognize his higher calling and trusted him. They found medical supplies for him as well as little luxuries like soap and cloth.

As if the problems of war were not enough, Fritz had new troubles at home. Ursula was not well. She tried to hide her swollen ankles from him, but he saw anyway and was troubled. He noticed her face was frequently flushed and bloated, though when he asked, she said she had been in the sun too long. She moved slower than she used to. She said she felt all right, but he knew she lied. He feared her heart was giving out. She had the classic symptoms of congestive heart failure, and there was little he could do except try to buy her time until the war ceased.

"Stay home with Rebeka today," he'd frequently say. "She needs help with her arithmetic." Ursula would demur a little, not too much, and then stay home. He noticed that, too. Whenever they obtained vitamins, he made sure she took some. Malaria medication came sporadically. The whole family suffered from frequent fevers.

**About a year after the war started**, the crisis between them and the Maasai over Rebeka deepened.

Rebeka was now nearly twelve years old. She came home from visiting Malia and her other school friends withdrawn and quieter than usual, her brow creased in thought, her eyes smoldering coals.

"What's the matter, Rebeka? Come here. Sit by me." Fritz placed his arm around her and drew her to a bench in the shade of a jacaranda tree. There had been a brief pause in the war around them, and Fritz had come home early from the hospital. Ursula rested in the house.

It was four-o'clock in the afternoon according to the sundial in the yard. The sun's gaze was less intense as it slipped toward the western horizon, and the Sunday traffic consisted mostly of people visiting one another. Children played on the dirt street that ran alongside the mission and hospital compound.

Rebeka was silent for a long time, wondering how to mention the subject she heard about years before when the kidnap attempt took place.

"My friends are talking about the cutting ceremony; they call it the womanhood rite."

Fritz froze. He knew the subject would come up some day, but with the war surrounding them he had forgotten about it.

"What about it?"

"Well, some of them are going to do it. The elders of their villages want them to do it along with the rest of the girls in their age group. Some of the girls ran off last week."

"Do you know what it is?"

"A little bit. We talked about it, and Malia's mother said it hurt and we shouldn't do it. I remember hearing you tell Mama that it was a bad thing. But the girls say that you can't be African without it." There was much more to it than that, but Rebeka couldn't frame it in words, least of all to her father.

"What about Malia? What does she say?"

"She says her father and mother don't want her to do it. But she says she wants to." Rebeka lifted her eyes to her father's. "The girls say that no African man will marry a girl who hasn't had it done."

"I think they're wrong on that," Fritz said. "But first I want to know what you think about it. Is it important to you?"

Rebeka shrugged. "I don't know. I think one way for a while, and then I think the other. I just don't know. But two women came to visit me this week when you and Mama were at the hospital. They said they are Maasai, that I am Maasai too, and I must go through the ceremony."

Fritz's stomach turned. "Why didn't you tell us, Rebeka? We need to know these things…when you have visitors."

She shrugged again. "They're coming back next week. Two of the girls from school are going to go with them—just slip out of the compound when no one is looking. They want me to go with them."

Fritz felt a chill of alarm. The Maasai hadn't given up. They still wanted Rebeka, body and soul.

"Rebeka," he said after a few moments to gather his thoughts, "I think you are grown up enough to understand what this is all about. In our country you would still be considered a little girl. But here in Africa you're nearly a woman. It's time we spoke plainly.

"From my experience in the hospital, circumcising girls is a bad practice. I can't begin to describe what it is to you. But tomorrow I want you to come with Mama and me to the hospital. You know we have maternity clinic on Mondays, and I want you to see for yourself what is done to girls. But I will say this about why I think it's a bad practice.

"First, the cutting of that part of the body can cause so much scar tissue that it's difficult for a woman to give birth to a baby." Rebeka was too embarrassed to look into her father's eyes." Sometimes the mother dies, and sometimes the baby dies because it can't get out into the air where it can breathe. This is sad.

"Secondly, this cutting away of flesh prevents a woman from enjoying many of the pleasures of being married. I know you don't understand this yet—" Rebeka ducked her head even further, "—but believe me, as a doctor, I know a little bit about a woman's body and how it functions."

"But what about later on, when I might want to get married? I want to marry when I grow up, Papa. But to whom? The girls say that not many men want a wife who is different."

"Perhaps it would be a barrier to some old village chief, Rebeka, or maybe some young warrior like the ones who tried to kidnap you. But would you really want to go and live in a filthy mud-and-dung hut with an ignorant tribal man? I hope for better things for you.

"There are some fine young men around the mission, some of them training to be schoolteachers, and others to be ordained. Right now they're off fighting in the war, but they are Christian men, and they will want Christian wives who haven't been tainted by the old tribal ways. I think perhaps one of them would be best for you, don't you think? We should start looking them over."

"Papa, I'm too young to think about one certain man." She smiled at her hands, dipping her head down so her father wouldn't see her embarrassment. For some reason she remembered Mpepo, the young seminarian that visited her father so often.

"No, Rebeka, you aren't too young. Mama and I are getting old. We may have to go back to Germany to stay in a few years when this war is over. We hope to see you settled before that happens."

On Monday, Fritz and Ursula took Rebeka with them to the maternity wards for the first time. Slender and tall for her age, and wearing a nurse's apron and head covering, she looked much older. The women never questioned her presence as her father examined the women's pregnancies and her mother took vital signs. Rebeka often accompanied her father on his rounds and consultations, but this was her first time in the maternity clinic. As Fritz examined the women, Rebeka could see the scars.

"Most of the time, when a girl is circumcised, all the soft flesh is cut away," her father explained to her in German, so the women would not understand what he said. "Only the birth canal remains. Sometimes, as you can see here, only the inner flesh is cut away, but still the scarring around the birth canal makes the skin as tough as leather."

Fritz kept up a running commentary as he examined the women, treating her as an adult nurse-trainee. "Now, Rebeka, if these women have their babies in the village, some of them will die, especially those with the toughest scars. If they come here to the hospital to give birth, I can cut the opening so the baby can come out, and then sew it up again."

"But why do they do this, Papa? What sense does it make?"

"I don't know for sure, *Liebchen*. Remember when that anthropologist visited us last year?" She nodded. "Well, he said he thought it was something started centuries ago and has been passed down until they don't remember why, except that they must do it. He said that originally it might have been because men had many wives, and they didn't want their wives demanding pleasure from them or looking elsewhere for it. They thought women were only supposed to have babies and help produce food. That's all. They are merely belongings, like their cattle. Too bad they still feel that way about women, and it's unfortunate that the women think they have to undergo this to be real women. Marriage is supposed to be about love and sharing, and it's a shame if a woman can't find pleasure in the marital act.

"I know this opens a whole new world for you, and you're still young. We'll talk more about all that later. Your mother can explain it to you."

Rebeka's eyes widened with alarm as her parents examined the women, spoke kindly to them and gave them what medication they needed, encouraging them to stay around to have their babies in the hospital. Before they were halfway through the clinic, she turned, ran to the latrine, and threw up. She sobbed as she finally understood what would happen to her friends—and herself—if she decided to go through with the ritual.

The two old Maasai women came to see the girls a few days later when Rebeka was visiting Malia. "Are you ready to become true women?" they demanded.

Rebeka reached for Malia's hand. "No. I don't want to go. I don't want to be cut."

"Do you know what can happen to a girl who does not consent? The elders can order her to be killed or her father's house to be burned, and she becomes an outcast! You must become Maasai women! Where will you go if you do not?" They spat on the ground to emphasize their anger, their elongated earlobes filled with strands of beaded wire swaying back and forth.

Rebeka swallowed hard, but remained adamant. "I don't know what will happen to me. But I will trust God to protect me. I have seen what happens to women who have this done to them.

If it means not being Maasai, then—" she hesitated, afraid, "—then so be it. I will be a nobody." Malia, heartened by Rebeka's stand, moved closer to her side and nodded, though she too was close to tears. She didn't want her father's house burned, but he had told her not to give in. The women left, muttering curses on them and the Europeans as they went.

Rebeka went home and wept. She felt bereft, alone, and alienated from her African heritage. She was nothing, nobody. She felt as though she stood alone in the dark between two houses; on one side the African house held busy families with laughing children, and on the other side her parents home, where they spoke and laughed about events so far in their past that Rebeka had no basis to understand their laughter. She didn't belong in either house. Everyone had something they could call themselves, but she was nobody. Just Rebeka.

**Mpepo and the other seminarians were trained together in an elite corps of troops,** mostly because their education and aristocratic status demanded they be given special treatment. In spite of their deep dislike for the Germans and their war, they knew protests would be useless. They were given rifles and trained in their use, taught to march and follow commands, and given squads to lead into battle. Within a few short weeks their bodies became hardened and strong and they were sent into battle, usually keeping close to the main army as von Lettow-Vorbeck fled south from the British, all the way to the Rufiji River delta.

One evening just after sunset a shout went up from the guard. Everyone grabbed his rifle to defend the camp. Out of the swamps came a rag-tag assortment of about twenty European sailors, yelling in German. The guards relaxed as the sailors approached, disheveled and bearded, their clothes in rags.

Mpepo stood near the command tent when von Lettow-Vorbeck came out to greet them.

"Where do you come from," he asked, surprised to see them here.

"We're from *The Konigsberg*," the lieutenant said. "We sank the British warship *Pegasus* out in the Indian Ocean nearly a year ago, but three monitors chased us up the Rufiji. We've been hiding out there for two hundred fifty-five days playing cat-and-mouse with them. We marked the days on the bulkhead. Last week we foundered in shallow water. They caught us and blew a hole in the side of the ship, but a few of us escaped."

"That's a long time. You will want to hear all the news—especially about the war."

"Yes. We presume it's still going on." The men huddled beside the tent, reaching for the food and coffee offered them with eager hands.

"Mmm, this coffee is good. We haven't had any for months. In fact, we ran out of food long ago and have been eating whatever we can steal or find growing along the riverbanks."

Von Lettow-Vorbeck ordered fresh uniforms to replace the filthy rags they wore. "You're welcome to join with us," he said. "I don't know what else you can do."

"With pleasure," the lieutenant said. "The ruins of the ship aren't far from here. It's in shallow water and mud. We can get the guns off with your men's help, and turn them into field artillery. There's a lot of ammunition, too."

With the addition of the guns and ammunition, the German army turned and made raids into Uganda, pestering the British and keeping them constantly wondering what would happen next. From Uganda they went east to Lake Victoria to disrupt

British shipping on the lake from Kenya to Uganda. They built crude boats and launched successful battles from the Port of Mwanza.

While the army was thus engaged, word came that the British made a daring raid on the barely defended coast, landing a ship at Tanga filled with troops from India. The untrained Indian soldiers immediately got lost, became disorganized, and ran away.

Von Lettow-Vorbeck laughed. "We'll make short work of them," he said, and ordered his men southeast to intercept the fleeing Indian army. He called Mpepo and several other squad leaders to the command tent.

"You and your men are to come behind the main army as it engages the enemy. Your job will be to see that no wounded enemy soldiers remain. The only prisoners taken are to be those we capture unharmed. Understand?"

Mpepo felt a chill run up his spine. He could do nothing but obey. He remembered the scenes from his childhood when the Germans put down the Maji Maji rebellion with so much cruelty. *God help us all*, he prayed silently as he stared straight ahead, saluted, turned, and went to take the orders to his men.

The German army on the coast raced in behind the fleeing Indians and took over their ship, capturing sixteen machine guns, hundreds of new rifles, and six hundred thousand rounds of ammunition. They flashed this information to the main army by heliograph.

Von Lettow-Vorbeck's army swept southeast to demolish the Indian army and to join up with the coastal forces and restock their ammunition. They ran into the fleeing Indian forces in Huruland and the battle took place in Mpepo's homeland valley.

It didn't last long. The German army, though outnumbered

eight to one, had superior leadership and their strict training won the battle over the fear and ineptitude of the Indians. Mpepo and his men followed those who fought, as ordered, to make sure all wounded Indians were dead. The men moved swiftly, trying not to think about what they did, bayoneting one after another.

*God, forgive me for what I do*, prayed Mpepo as he went along, repeating the prayer each time he plunged his bayonet into a man's heart, feeling the skin resist the point a moment, then feel it plunge straight through and into the equally resistant heart. He tried not to watch the light in the man's eyes fade.

He didn't know how many men he had killed when he came to one that made him hesitate. He was young—younger than Mpepo. His large brown eyes looked up at him, pleading, his hands folded as if in prayer. Mpepo saw a tiny cross on a chain around the man's neck. He hesitated, and then thrust his bayonet into the ground beside the man. The young man knelt before him, grabbed his ankles, and cried. Mpepo could no longer follow his own orders. He bowed his head and squeezed his eyes shut.

He didn't see an Indian behind a tree put the sight of his rifle on him. All he knew was a sudden rush of adrenalin, a sense of discovery…did he hear someone speak his name…was it God calling him…why was it getting so dark at midday…he felt so tired, he wanted to lie down on the ground and sleep.

When Mpepo came to, he saw his uncle as if in a reflection on water. Sounds were muffled and his body was wet with perspiration.

"Where am I?" he asked, then remembered the battle.

"You are in your own country, Mpepo," Uncle said. "You have been shot. Your friends brought you here to this village, where you have been for three days."

"I want water," Mpepo said. Someone brought him tepid water in a gourd, which he drank.

"We will take you to the hospital in Arusha," Uncle said. "We will carry you in a litter. We are just old men left in the village, but we have enough strength to get you there."

It took nearly a week. Mpepo, in frequent delirium, thrashed around in the basket-like litter in which the men carried him. He was near death when they finally arrived at the hospital.

By the light of lanterns, because there was no kerosene to run the electrical generator, Fritz operated on Mpepo's shoulder and removed the slug located just an inch from his heart. Rebeka stood beside him handing him his surgeon's tools. While Mpepo was under the ether she could look full into his face instead of averting her eyes as custom demanded, and she memorized every feature as she prayed.

"He'll live," Fritz said as the bullet clanked into the tin basin. "He's strong, and his body will fight off the infection. God be praised." He didn't see Rebeka's tears.

CHAPTER NINE

# Europe, 1918

**Vito floated in and out of consciousness for two weeks while the nurses and medics battled for his life**. The problem was not the bullet that lodged itself too close to his spine to remove in a field hospital, but the destruction it made as it bored through his body.

As he fled from the uproar at the Po River, he had turned to fire his rifle at the guards. But they fired too, and one bullet found his thigh muscle. Another entered his abdomen, missed his vital organs, but nicked his bowel on its way to where it now rested. Another millimeter, and he would never walk again.

The British soldiers had carried him back to their main camp at great risk to their own lives. Peritonitis was what he fought now. The medics repaired him as best they could, flushing out his body cavity with antiseptic, and he teetered back and forth on the edge of death. Occasionally he surfaced enough to see the bright lights and white shrouded figures hovering over him, and hearing, as if from far away, their muffled comments. Then the pain overcame him and he would swirl away into unconsciousness.

In his delirium he fell into a peaceful, hillside meadow overlooking his family home and winery. A warm breeze blew over him, and above him loomed the mountains that overshadowed his home village. His two children called to him with their happy voices—his daughter with her long dark braids and her arms full of wildflowers, and his son Antonio leading their donkey along the path toward him. Behind them walked Therese, her dark hair like a cloud about her face, her white teeth showing in a sweet smile, her sparkling eyes gazing upon him... his wonderful Therese...how he loved her...how could he ever have left her to go to war? In his dream he reached toward her to take her hand, but she turned away and disappeared.

His heart lurched with pain and he looked back toward his children, but they were gone also. Only a shadow remained as a dark cloud obscured the sun and a sudden chill came over him.

His eyes opened, and he saw the tent in which he lay. The door flap was open and lifted out, held up by poles. Late afternoon sunlight that slanted through the opening bathed everything in a golden glow. The outline of someone sitting at the foot of his cot startled him. His neighbor's son Luigi, his second-in-command who had deserted, sat there nervously twisting his hat in his hands, staring at him with intense eyes.

Vito felt lightheaded and disembodied. The lumps under the drab blanket must be his torso and arms and legs, all accounted for, but he could no more will them to move than he could climb a mountain right now.

"Vito...Captain," Luigi said, catching himself being too familiar. "Are you awake?"

*Of course I'm awake,* Vito thought, surprised he didn't say it aloud. "What?" he managed to croak.

"I must speak quickly and leave," Luigi said, "before they discover that I'm a deserter." He was in obvious distress. "Oh, it was so terrible! So terrible!!" He balled his hat in his hands, and straightened it out only to ball it up again. He said something so fast and mixed with gasping sobs that Vito couldn't pick it out. He struggled to stay conscious, his heart still beating painfully from his delirious dream.

What did Luigi say? Vito closed his eyes to concentrate…to understand…something about everyone dead…who was it… where…he fought off the darkness that wanted to swallow him again. He opened his eyes and saw that Luigi was gone, but the British medic bent over him, speaking to him. His understanding of English was enough to follow what the medic spoke, trying to tell him something important.

"Vito?  Vito Fernaldi?  Do you hear me?  Your friend Luigi has come from your home village with bad news. Did you hear him? Do you understand?"

Vito shook his head.

"Your wife and children…sneak attack by a ragtag army on the village and many dead…we are so sorry!  So sorry to have to tell you this way, at this time!"

*No-o-o-o!* came a cry from the shadowy corners and rebounded off the tent ceiling. Vito lapsed back into a dark, cold world of swirling evil shapes and feelings, and above all the noises and voices, someone was sobbing and sobbing, and saying over and over,  "Therese, Therese!"

Sometime later, he didn't know how long—minutes, or years—a cold cruel light slashed through the tortuous dark swirls, and he opened his eyes again. Everything appeared in sharp, unadorned focus. The fever was gone, the pain unfelt. A hard stone grew in the pit of his stomach. Every breath inhaled built up more armor plate on his soul, layer upon layer, to hide and protect him, each inhalation a piece of himself pulled back inside and hidden in deep recesses where nothing could ever hurt him again. He hated to exhale. It seemed as though each time he breathed out it released a vulnerable part of himself into his shattered world all over again. He lay on his cot mute, not eating, drinking, or sleeping, watching with unseeing eyes and numb mind as the sun faded and night came, and then early dawn seeped under the tent flap.

Whether he slept or not, he didn't know, but with the dawn came those who tended his physical injuries but were unable to touch the wound in his soul. He sat up and ate, able to feed himself for the first time since being shot. Someone carried him through the open tent flap and into a chair in the sun. He wouldn't speak. He refused to comprehend what was said around him, only noting that they spoke with the same infernal accent, always so polite and cheerful, so helpful, why didn't they just leave him alone and let him die?

Later that day they broke camp, and trucks roared in to take the wounded to the train bound for Genoa. Heavily sedated, Vittorio Fernaldi joined a score or so wounded British soldiers being sent to England. Someone had written on his papers: *This man is a British hero.* No one questioned out loud why an Italian soldier would be returned to England with other British wounded.

The news of his family's death added a deeper wound than the bullet in his body. He lost a quarter of his body weight. At one time he had been a robust and brawny man, always with a ready smile and hearty laugh for his comrades. Now, at thirty-eight years of age, he looked shriveled and old, a stern and broken man. He could barely take three steps to the toilet without help. The British sent him on a grey troop ship through the grey Mediterranean Sea and a continual grey rain, past that large grey rock they call Gibraltar, to a sanatorium in the grey south of England. Surgery removed the bullet from near his spine, but could not restore his soul. He spent the final days of the war wrapped in blankets, sitting in the occasional sun on the porch with other wounded men.

It was an old, large house, part of a feudal manor, turned over to the war office. The only son of Lord Cavendish of Kent had been killed in France. The broken-hearted parents donated the use of the house for convalescent soldiers. Built of granite blocks as were so many of the old houses, it faced a vast lawn that extended to the bluff overlooking the sea. On a clear day, the men could see the shores of France twenty-one miles away. They sat around wrought iron tables on the terrace playing cards and reading papers, or walking up and down the grounds with crutches or canes. Men cheered each other when these aids were tossed aside as they gained strength. Some had lost an arm or leg and would never be whole again. A few shivered in their beds, shell-shocked, whimpering at the slightest disturbance.

Vito began to walk. It became a passion to him. He walked slowly at first, and as he recovered, he walked faster, faster, as though he could outpace the demons that breathed right behind his shoulder. He limped, badly, but in a few weeks the limp diminished to a slight hesitation at each step, not enough to make anyone watching feel pity, and just enough to distinguish him from those who strode evenly through life.

He walked to the nearby village of Deal and bought a pipe and some expensive, rare tobacco. He seldom took part in the discussions and arguments that surrounded him, choosing rather to read the English papers, books, anything he could get his hands on to hone his language skills. He contemplated life from behind his invisible stone and steel fortress, and began to make cold and practical decisions.

Frequently, he pulled a well-worn letter from his pocket, reading and re-reading it even though he had it memorized, as though an unconscious hope burned inside him, that maybe he missed something, that what it said so plainly was not true after all.

> *My dear cousin Vito,* the letter read. It had been posted in Milan many weeks before. *Everything here in Valle d'Aosta, and our village in particular, has changed. You would hardly know it. Many people were killed when what we thought was the German and Austrian Army came through the valley. But they were our own people, soldiers who left their duty, unpaid, starving, and demoralized. They burned homes and businesses, including ours. Your parents, Therese, and the children have been given proper burial in the churchyard alongside our grandfather and great-grandfather. You may rest assured that they died quickly with little pain. They were shot in the back as they ran through the courtyard to take refuge in the wine cellars. I mourn them with you, though I admit that I thank God that my family was in Torino visiting Angela's parents.*
>
> *The vineyards were destroyed, and all the wine taken from the cellars. What the mobs did not drink, they smashed until the streets ran with wine. We are now as poor as the others who live in this valley. My father, the Count, is not well. I believe he lost his heart with the wine.*
>
> *My job is cut out for me; I must bring our livelihood back and replant the vineyards. It will be many years before we can be productive again, and all of us will have to feel our way like blind people.*
>
> *There is no reason for you to return unless you feel you must. It would be distressing for you, and there is little for you to do here. The people remaining have banded*

*together and are attempting to rebuild their lives, but I do not have enough for you to do. It should not be hard for you to find another place for yourself. Of course, if you want to return, I will help you all I can and you can work in the fields. But perhaps you should search for a different life.*

*My heart is broken, as is yours. Nothing can ever be the same again.*

*Angela and the girls greet you. I hope that someday we will meet again.*

*Your loving cousin, Riccardo*


Armistice Day, 1918. Church bells rang all over England, a clamor of joy not heard for a long time. Strangers congratulated each other on the streets. Peace and jubilation reigned all over Europe, even in Germany. Italy remained intact, for after the battle of the Po and with the help of the French and English, the enemy fled back into the mountains of their homeland. Germany and Austria sued for peace. All the soldiers laid down their arms and went home. Preachers thundered from their pulpits that war would be no more; swords were turned into ploughshares and pruning hooks; the lamb would now lie down with the lion. The newly formed League of Nations, composed of the wise men of every nation, would see to it. A new golden age dawned. The war to end all wars was over.

In Italy, Benito Mussolini took off his uniform and began screaming his way into the news. There were many ready to follow him. Life changed for everyone as machinery clanked and churned out peacetime goods and automobiles instead of weapons.

It was time to sort out the wounded. When an officer stopped by to talk, a sheaf of papers in his hand, Vito was ready for him.

Robin Smith was twenty-one, fresh-faced and handsome with blonde hair and the beginning of a faint mustache on his upper lip. He was privately a little put out because he spent his war years in London instead of being able to show his bravery on the battlefield, but nonetheless happy to be alive and intact. His directives gave him power over men his father's age. He sent some home to their families. Others who needed more medical care went to regional hospitals to finish recuperating. This sanitarium was to be used for the worst cases, the men who lost their minds in the trauma of battle. There were a few men like Vittorio Fernaldi, foreigners who got mixed in with the native sons.

Vito waved him into a seat, enthused for the first time since he arrived in England. "Put your papers away. I have a request of your government.

"I do not wish to return to Italy. I know, I know, it's highly irregular," he said as the officer started to protest. "But hear me out, and see if what I say makes better sense than sending me home. I have nothing to return to—no home, no family." Robin sat down to listen. Vito continued. " I can't go there and start my life over again. Italy will never be the same to me.

"I have a university degree in law, and finance. I owe a debt of gratitude to English doctors who saved my life, and I wish to become a citizen of this country. While convalescing here I've read many papers and books, and have studied your civil system. I'm satisfied that British laws best exemplify a code of fairness and justice, two long time passions of mine."

Robin sat back, a frown on his face. "That goes without

saying, old chap. Everyone knows we have set the standard for the world to follow. But become a *citizen*? I hardly bloody think so!"

"Why not? Your country is going to need her returned soldiers to rebuild your economy, and at the same time—" he waved a copy of a newspaper at the officer, "—you will need men to take over government functions in your new colonies. Here, it says that your leaders argue because you are stretching the limits of your resources to meet the needs of your expanding empire," and he pointed to a headline article.

## LEAGUE OF NATIONS TO MANDATE GERMAN-AFRICAN TERRITORIES TO BRITAIN!

Robin Smith didn't argue with him. He made a few notations on Vito's file, closed it and stood to his feet. "I will consult my superiors," he said. "But don't count on it. Be ready to leave in two weeks."

Two weeks went by with no word from the military office. Vito resigned himself to going back to Italy to pick up some sort of life, packed his meager belongings, and waited.

It was a rainy Sunday when Robin Smith returned. He arrived in a Rolls Royce limousine with a general and another officer who looked vaguely familiar to Vito, as he stood at the window of the conservatory, a warm fire in the fireplace behind him, and watched the three men get out of the vehicle and duck out of the rain into the entry of the building.

A bell sounded for assembly, and those men still in residence entered, some still on crutches, and gathered informally in the conservatory. Robin smiled in an extra-friendly way at Vito as the three visitors strode past him on their way to a spot just in front of the cheerful fireplace. It was then that Vito recognized the other man. He was the captain of the British group he led out of the ravine by the River Po, but he couldn't remember his name.

"Gentlemen," Robin Smith said to the assembled men. "I want to introduce General Pickering of the Italian Front. He commanded the British Forces there, and with the aide of the French and Italians, pushed back the last offense of the Austrians and Germans, thus terminating the whole war."

The assembled men applauded.

General Pickering took over. "I am here to announce an honor that is to be given to one of your number. Not only is this man a hero in the eyes of the British Government, but he is also an Italian. Vittorio Fernaldi, please step forward."

Surprised, Vito took several steps forward.

"Single-handedly, this man rescued a unit of British soldiers through an ingenious plan. These men escaped sure death at the hands of the enemy and rejoined the forces that had surrounded the combined German and Austrian Army. Through the knowledge they were able to give, the Allies won the last battle of the war.

"Captain Timothy Barker will now tell you the story of this escape." All through this announcement Robin Smith rocked back and forth on his heels, a smile on his face, as though he had discovered Vito all by himself. Captain Tim Barker stepped forward, looked Vito in the eyes, and told the whole story about the sheep, the fog, and the plan that saved the lives of all the men but one. He told how Vito himself was shot while trying to neutralize the guards, and how his men came back and carried him to safety.

When he finished, he gave Vito a big smile and stepped back beside Robin. Vito felt something behind his eyes prickle a bit, and his nose itched. General Pickering stepped forward again.

"In honor of his bravery, we are pleased to announce that Major Fernaldi has been nominated for a Victoria Cross. This will be presented to him in two weeks time at Buckingham Palace in London, by King George himself."

A stunned silence spread across the room. Someone shouted, "Hip-hip" and all the men burst out with a loud "Hurray!" They cheered three times, and took turns slapping a dazed Vito on the back, grabbing his arm, or otherwise expressing their best wishes. No one had told him until now that he had been promoted to Major. Tea arrived, and someone found bottles of wine for the celebration.

"Oh, by the way," Robin whispered to him. "They've accepted your request for citizenship. You're to come with me to London, old chap." He gave him a conspiratory wink.

Two weeks later Vito stood in the hall of Buckingham Palace with ten other men to receive his award. Robin had requisitioned a British Army uniform for him. "After all, you're an Englishman now, old boy. And you were on loan to the British Army at the time." Vito felt inadequate and ill at ease. What should he say to the King of England? He stood there, stiff and self-conscious.

An officer pinned a wide, red ribbon with a hook onto the left breast pocket of each man's uniform. He explained that the cross would be hung on the hook, and to stand still so the King could place it without dropping it.

Everyone stood at attention when the King came in accompanied by his generals. He was not a large man, rather dapper in appearance, with a thin face and a dark beard, but he carried an aura of authority beyond that of most men.

As each recipient stepped forward in turn, a brief description of his bravery was read. A general handed the small, heavy bronze cross to the king, who placed it over the hook. Each one was placed without incident.

When he came to Vito, he said, "For bravery under fire when you led a group of British soldiers past an enemy encampment, with no thought of your own safety, the British Empire wishes to award you this Victoria Cross." He lowered his voice and spoke directly to Vito. "We am pleased to award this decoration to an Italian. We understand you will soon be an Englishman. So we give you double congratulations."

After the ceremony the recipients received a case in which to keep the cross and a brief written history of the award.

The heavy cross was made of a curious, dark brown bronze. The four, equal-length legs of the cross splayed at the ends, much like a Maltese cross. In the middle stood the British lion atop the royal crown, and a curved motto below said *For Valour*. On the back was inscribed the date and details of the event that warranted the award. The bar from which it was suspended had Vito's name, rank, and regiment engraved on it.

The accompanying history told how Queen Victoria began awarding the decoration during the Crimean war of 1854. The first ones were made of mother of pearl, but at the war's end, they were cast from the melted-down bronze cascabels of two Russian cannons captured at Sebastopol. The etiquette of the cross was also included. It must be worn at all official occasions, and on the breast pocket of the uniform. It must never be worn during informal gatherings. It could be worn with a civilian suit if necessary. The recipient should use the initials "VC" after his name in official documents. Since it was an honor to receive one, the owner must use care to conduct the rest of his life with honor at all times. The award could be repealed if the owner proved to be unworthy in character.

For eighteen months Vito studied English law. He received his citizenship papers with little fanfare, just a small feeling of regret for Italy. But he had set his face and there was no turning back.

They also prepared him for Foreign Service in Africa where he could put his education to work. All Germany's holdings in Africa were put under the sponsorship of Britain. England already governed Uganda and Kenya, but there was a need for magistrates and commissioners at once throughout the newly acquired countries to facilitate a smooth transition from German rule.

On February 15, 1920, a steamship freighter, *The Cotswold,* sailed from Southampton, England, loaded with goods bound for Dar es Salaam. Vittorio was one of the passengers. He was 39 years old and ready to start a new life. His body was strong again, except for the limp that he knew he would carry the rest of his days, but his soul was permanently scarred by his loss. What remained intact was his passion for justice and truth.

## CHAPTER TEN

# German East Africa, 1917-1918

**Mpepo opened his eyes and stared at the ceiling of a small, dim room, and wondered where he was.** He barely remembered the terrible, painful trip to Arusha. He thought he remembered seeing *Daktari Shibeli* bending over him, an overwhelming pain, and vivid dreams of his mother. Writhing snakes and large vultures were in his dream; they attacked him and tried to eat his flesh as he pushed them away. Now they were gone, and the darkness around him felt cool and peaceful. He could hear chickens clucking outside, and from somewhere came the mournful call of a dove.

He lifted his head from the cot and looked around. He appeared to be in a food storage room, probably the *Daktari's*, judging from the goods that were there. A tiny, barred and screened window high up under the thatched eaves let in a small amount of light and air. An array of shelves against one wall held jars of preserved food. Several wooden barrels sat on skids above the earthen floor. A haunch of venison covered with a piece of burlap hung by a sisal rope from a roof pole. Two narrow strips of animal hide hung from the same pole, covered with a brown sticky-looking liquid and studded with trapped flies. *Clever,* he thought. *That keeps the flies off the meat. They must have dipped the strips in honey.* A small, gray lizard observed him from the wall next to his cot; its stomach throbbed as it breathed. He blew on it, and it scampered away. Several patches of spider eggs with tight, white, silk-like coverings dotted the walls. Spider webs festooned the beams and the shelves.

He started to sit up and grunted with a pain that shot through his shoulder, so he lay down again. *Why am I here, instead of in the hospital?* As though in answer to his question, the door opened with a loud creak, and the *Daktari's* African girl-child, Rebeka, came in. She carried a basket and a jug of water.

Her gaze caught his for a moment before she lowered her eyes in propriety and curtseyed. "Good morning, Mpepo," she said with a barely audible voice. "I see you are awake. I have brought you food and water."

She took a cloth from her basket, placed it on top of one of the barrels, and set out some biscuits, cheese, and a mango with a knife. She poured water from the jug into a gourd that sat beside the barrel. The light that came through the open door behind her silhouetted her graceful figure as she performed her duties, and Mpepo noticed that she looked more like a woman than a child.

"Where am I?"

"This is our storeroom. The British hold Arusha now," she answered, staring demurely at the floor. "Papa thought it best for you to be hidden away, to keep you from being taken prisoner."

"Thank you." Mpepo carefully rose on his uninjured elbow and looked with interest at the food. "Weren't you afraid of being seen?"

No, I always feed the chickens in the morning and collect the eggs. This morning I put the chicken feed on top of the cloth in the basket, your food underneath.

"There's a *cho* just behind the building." She looked toward the door and scuffed her foot against the floor, embarrassed. "Be careful; make sure no one sees you outside. I must go now," and she left as quietly as she came.

Each morning, Rebeka brought Mpepo food, usually a boiled egg, bread, and fruit. In the evenings one of the kitchen helpers brought a portion of food from the family dinner. Sometimes he got tea instead of only water.

Fritz Scheibel came with a lantern in the late evenings to examine Mpepo and give him books to read, and newspapers when they were available. As Mpepo got better, they talked longer. After several days, Fritz broached the topic of the war.

"How are things going?" Fritz asked. "We hear very little, except when someone from the army tells us."

Mpepo told him of the battle with the Indians. "Will God forgive me for what I did? For killing those wounded Indians?"

"There is nothing God cannot forgive, Mpepo. He sees the heart, and will forgive us if we ask. What is harder for us to accept is that he also forgives our enemies, if they repent." They fell silent for a few moments as they thought about the crimes of war. Then Fritz asked, "Have you seen how our other churches are doing?"

"They're struggling along, just as they do here. Every army that comes by loots people's homes. They put their empty tin trunks outside their houses to show they have nothing left to take.

"Most of the young men have been taken to fight in the war, and some of the older men are forced to be porters. There is little food, but the churches struggle along. It is worse for the CMS people."

"How so?" Fritz asked.

"The British missionaries have all been taken prisoner and are being held in the jail at Dodoma. All the teachers, pastors, deacons, and elders have been put in jail for being English-made Christians, or forced to be porters. Even Canon Petro Limo, the Anglican bishop, was made to carry loads for von Lettow-Vorbeck." Mpepo said the name of his general with distaste. "It is a terrible life, to be a porter. They get small wages, and the poorest of food. Many more porters die than we who fight. They die of cold, disease, and starvation. Sometimes the guards shoot them for trying to desert.

"In my country, the Wahuru people hate the Germans. Our own army stole their cattle, or left them hamstrung in the fields so the British wouldn't take them. Everywhere we go, we see hatred on the faces of the people. When we were up north by Victoria Nyanza, we found some villages that aided the British and we were forced to burn them to the ground and kill everyone. In another village, the chief met us, bowed, and gave our general gifts of food. But the villagers turned on him and burned his house in the night, and he had to come with us when we headed south to engage the Indian Army.

"I have seen tribes who were enemies sitting and talking to each other in their common hatred. If they thought they could, they would rise up and throw off the German yoke." Fritz winced, and Mpepo apologized. "I'm sorry, *Daktari.* I forgot you, too, are German. I don't think of you as such. You're a friend of the African."

"Thank you, Mpepo. Sometimes I forget I'm German, too.

"But I have seen enemies sit down and talk together—right here in Arusha. The Chagga leaders met with the Maasai elders and declared themselves blood brothers. Can you believe that? The Maasai have left their reservation and regained their former lands north to the border, and the Chagga have taken over the plantations of the Europeans who have gone off to fight."

"I don't know what will happen to this land," Mpepo said, his face downcast. "I almost pray that the English will win. Surely they will be better masters than the ones we have now. I'm sorry, *Daktari.*"

The two men sat silent for a while. A moth and several other flying insects danced around the kerosene lantern that sat on the floor. Somewhere out beyond the compound a hyena laughed. A *shienze,* a cicada-like bug, crept out of its hole in the ground and shrilled its continual, ear-splitting call for a mate. "I should find that creature and kill it," muttered Fritz, "or it will keep my wife awake all night."

Mpepo laughed.

"When this war is over, everyone must work together to rebuild the country," Fritz said. "People will have to learn to forgive in order to go on."

"That is strange, what you just said," Mpepo answered. "Up in Sukumaland, by the Lake, a pastor had his house and church burned by our own army, simply because he was CMS. He told his people they must forgive, and not hate, the Germans. That is hard to do. I know my heart is full of hatred."

"If you didn't have to struggle with forgiveness, how could you ever know what it is? Do you think everyone who forgives doesn't lie awake at night and fight off the hate?"

Mpepo said after a moment, "The people are dancing the forbidden dances again. Everywhere, even in the military camps, they dance the *beni.*"

Fritz raised his eyebrows. "Really!"

"Yes. They dance the secret message of unity against the European. The Europeans watch, laugh, and think us poor, wretched creatures trying to amuse ourselves. If they only knew!" He laughed. "Even the African soldiers in the British

Army dance the *beni.* "

In the silence that followed, Mpepo wondered if Fritz would ask if he had joined in the dance. During the Maji Maji Revolt, the dance spread the rebellion across the country under the noses of the unsuspecting German leaders. When the authorities finally caught on, that particular dance was banned, though others were started.

From ancient days, the dances were a form of secret society with vows and pledges, the dance itself being an expression of solidarity. Some were innocuous; one was only for women, and others for hunters or warriors. Each tribe had a special unity dance. All the missions—Protestant and Catholic alike—banned the dances, perhaps out of fear, but mostly out of distrust of the message. Yet they became a form of unspoken communication, similar to that of the drums that beat in the night, speaking a language that only the few understood. As if in response to his thoughts, Mpepo heard a drum throb in the distance.

"Our army is on the move again. I must rejoin them, or expect to lose my life for desertion." He winced as he moved his arm around in circles. "I think I am strong enough now. Thank you, *Daktari.*"

"It was only what one should do for a brother. May God protect you, my friend." Fritz picked up the lantern and left the storeroom and Mpepo in the dark.

Mpepo sneaked away that night, leaving behind on his cot a tiny silver box for Rebeka he had taken from a dead Indian, and a letter for his host.

*Asante, Daktari. I thank you for your thoughts for my safety. I hope someday to repay you for your kindness and the skill that saved my life. May Mungu continue to keep you safe and give you and your family peace.*

**The war, for the British, did not go well. Malaria, dysentery, and the tsetse fly affected their health**. Rain, mud, and the shortage of food and supplies that had to be hauled from Kenya contributed to the problem. The British troops, tired from the Boer War in South Africa, lost much of their effectiveness as they fell to tropical diseases. Mpepo saw his general smile with pleasure as he gloated over the news. He was now a member of the elite *askaris*, personal guards to von-Lettow-Vorbeck, and privy to all the incoming communications.

The problems that vexed the British worked in von Lettow-Vorbeck's favor. His troops, most of them African, were from that land and knew how to cope with the distractions. The sheer size of the country, the bush they could hide in, their knowledge of the land, and the availability of food from the reluctant, but unarmed, peasants aided them in conducting their lightning-like raids against the British. The heliograph communications system worked well as it signaled the positions of the enemy. They swooped in on encampments at night, machine-gunned the British as they slept, then slipped away before they could be caught. Von Lettow-Vorbeck's plan worked. The British set guards, but found them dead in the mornings, either knifed by the enemy or killed by lions.

Then the Germans learned that General Smuts sent his English and Indian troops out of the country to battle elsewhere. He brought in West African troops, more inured to the climate and diseases, to continue the war. Von Lettow-Vorbeck was dismayed when he found himself up against these crack troops that pushed him back to the south. To the Ruvuma River they went, across it into Mozambique, and still Smuts and his African soldiers pursued them. Von Lettow-Vorbeck led his army toward the coast, but the British army was there. They hurried back toward their homeland, and found that road blocked as well.

The German army lay encamped on the outskirts of Chambeshi in Rhodesia as the commanders plotted their next move. One evening, as the setting sun glinted gold against the hills and trees and a breeze with a promise of rain whispered through the foliage on the riverbank, an exhausted runner brought a message to the General. Mpepo saw von Lettow-Vorbeck take the note and read it. Then his shoulders slumped. He stood there for a moment, straightened up, and handed the note to his second-in-command who spoke to the waiting men.

"The war is over. Germany has surrendered."

A shudder of relief went over the mass of men. The news was whispered through the crowds and people smiled behind their hands, not showing their joy in front of their defeated leaders out of consideration, but happy nonetheless. Mpepo stood among them, head bowed, and thanked God for sparing him.

Twelve days later, the Germans surrendered to the British in Albercorn, Rhodesia. Led by Paul von Lettow-Vorbeck, the tired, dusty troops marched into the nearest town and laid down their arms in front of the British military compound. Traveling with them were over four hundred women, wives of the soldiers, who had tramped back and forth across the country with their men, cooking their meals and bearing their children, uncomplaining and loyal to the end.

They stood in the dusty street and watched as von Lettow-Vorbeck rode through their midst on a horse, his uniform freshly washed and ironed, straight in the saddle, as impeccable as though he rode to meet a king.

He rode up to the British General who waited with similar stance, surrounded by his colonels and captains. Sitting on his horse, Paul von Lettow-Vorbeck removed his sword and handed it, hilt first, to Smuts, who accepted it with dignity.

General Smuts said, "Paul, I would be honored if you would have dinner with me."

Paul looked at him for a moment, and said, "I thank you, sir, but no."

He rode away from the camp, conquered but unconquered, his dignity intact but his life in shambles. He had fought well, but not well enough, and he would fight no more. His brilliant career was over.

As soon as he was out of sight, a cheer rose from the men who had fought with him. It was a cheer of joy that the war was over, the cruel Germans would soon leave, and perhaps better masters would be installed.

## CHAPTER ELEVEN

# Aftermath: Tanganyika, 1918 – 1919

**Fritz and Ursula were not among the first group sent back to Germany**. During the first months after the end of the war the country fell into a stupor. No one knew who was in charge, yet the people were too tired, too poor, and too traumatized to care. Soldiers returned home to what remained of their families and gardens, with worthless money, ragged uniforms, and worn boots. Dissatisfied with their lack of employment, many either joined up as British *askaris*, or formed bands that traveled the land organizing dance societies. Food was scarce. As they had for millennia, the women took over the gardens and coaxed their crops to grow again. The birth rate dropped to dangerous levels as a result of poor nutrition.

Fritz knew his days in Africa were limited, and he became concerned as he pondered his family's future. There were days when Ursula, too ill to get out of bed, cried as Fritz or Rebeka stroked her hand or rubbed herbal liniment on her swollen legs. He sent runners to doctors in Kenya asking for medicines for Ursula's heart. And he searched for natural herbs to help her from the folklore he had compiled He brewed her teas that helped a little. Sometimes, in the evenings, she would get out of bed and sit in the rocker while Fritz read the papers to her and Rebeka. At times she would gaze at Rebeka, and he knew she felt the same concern he did over what would happen to her.

All German citizens were to be repatriated to their homeland. British government agents walked through the streets of Arusha with lists of names, and Rebeka's parents began to pack their few personal belongings, expecting at any moment to be told they would be included in the next busload to Moshi and on by rail to Tanga. All through the country, German citizens were rounded up, kept in a prison camp in Tabora, and then taken to Tanga or Dar es Salaam to get a ship. Even Governor Schnee and his family went home as prisoners with little more than a few trunks of belongings.

Fritz traveled to Dar es Salaam to talk to the British authorities. A new British governor had arrived to take Schnee's place, and he hoped to plead for permission to stay until the Swiss or Americans sent a replacement doctor. The Tanga hospital already lacked a doctor, and severe cases came by rail and truck to Arusha. Not only did the work call for a qualified doctor, but it required one who would be able to carry on the research that Fritz started on the causes and preventions of the tropical diseases that were so fatal—diseases like Black Water Fever that killed his three children. There was so much he must teach his replacement.

He ascended the broad steps and entered the Governor's mansion. Where once he could come and go at ease as a friend of the governor, now his presence was challenged. He stated who he was and waited in the foyer while the guard consulted with the new British Governor. After several minutes, the guard returned and ushered him into the inner office.

Governor Sir Cedric Darlington did not rise to shake his hand or even ask him to sit. A middle-aged English aristocrat, his tall, lean frame sat erect in his large chair. His grey hair was impeccably slicked back, and his trim mustache grew down by his mouth to his chin. After a few moments of reading some documents and scribbling his name on one, he looked up.

"What can I do for you?"

"I am Dr. Fritz Scheibel," Fritz said, aware of his thick German accent. "From the hospital at Arusha. I have here a letter from the American Lutheran Mission. I also have a request." Fritz opened an envelope, removed a letter, and placed it on the desk facing the governor. "In March of next year they will have a replacement doctor for me, but he will need to stay in Dar es Salaam for several months to learn Swahili."

"Ah, yes..." Governor Darlington scanned the letter.

"I would like your permission, sir, to remain in the country until this Dr. Johansen is available to take over the work. You see, sir—" Fritz moved a step closer to get across his point. "—there are too few doctors in the country to continue giving medical service. I must instruct this doctor in the research I have conducted—"

The governor waved his hand. "I've heard of you and your work, Dr. Scheibel. I'll take your request under—"

"Sir," Fritz interrupted. "Here also are letters from Jan Smuts and Lord Delamere." He placed the two letters of recommendation on the desk. He thanked God silently for the foresight when he'd asked the two generals for the letters when they had commended him for his blindness to the nationality of those he treated. The governor raised his eyebrows as he scanned them, then discreetly erased the look of surprise on his face.

"I see," he said. "Well, I'll see what I can do. I'll cancel the order to have you repatriated just now, until I make up my mind. You may go home and continue as before. You will hear from me in a few weeks."

**Rebeka sat with Malia in the dusty yard at Kuyoni's house on the edge of town.** The sun's heat intensified and they moved close to each other in the shade of the papaya tree, moving around it as the shade moved. Chickens scratched in the dirt looking for food. The square, mud brick house was a step up from being a hut. It had a grass-thatched roof, but windows allowed the air and light inside. Before the war, Kuyoni served as a go-between for the Maasai people in their dealings with the government, holding the quasi-governmental office of translator.

Malia's mother sat under the eave grinding grain into meal on her grindstone. The girls, now fourteen, chattered about school, other girls, and the recently ended war. Malia mended a seam on her school uniform with a makeshift needle, a long thorn pierced at the blunt end, and Rebeka watched.

"Do you ever feel as though you don't belong anywhere?" Rebeka asked, their conversation turning serious.

"Sometimes. But my father says there are many people like us who have given up tribal ways."

"It's harder for me, though."

Malia's silence felt like agreement. She finished her seam, folded the uniform, and put the thorn back in its matchbox.

"Watch this." She unwound a length of thread after checking over her shoulder to make sure her mother wasn't looking. She tied a kernel of corn to one end and tossed it toward the chickens. One of the chickens pounced on it and swallowed it, the thread hanging out of its mouth. Malia yanked on the end and the chicken squawked. It ran around on the end of the taut thread while the girls laughed at its antics, until finally the corn came back up from its gullet and the complaining chicken ran off behind the house.

"That chicken will never eat corn again," laughed Rebeka. "I know I wouldn't."

"It will. Chickens are too stupid to remember, unless you do it too many times."

"Let me try." Rebeka tossed the corn to another chicken, which eagerly grabbed it. "Its like fishing for chickens!"

"Girls! Stop that!" Malia's mother rebuked.

Malia put away the thread. They sat in the quiet for a while until her mother went into the hut.

"I have a secret," Malia said.

"What is it?"

"I think I'm to be married."

"What?" Rebeka turned and looked at her friend in shock. "Who? When?" She sank back against the tree trunk, speechless in wonder and jealousy.

When the Kenya troops came through a few months ago, after the war was over, one of their trackers spoke with my father. He's a Maasai man from Kenya. He came several times and had an evening meal with us."

"Did he talk to you? What's he like?"

"No, I didn't talk to him. But he kept looking at me when I served the food. My mother made me serve. I wondered why she did that, since she usually serves the men when we have guests. And later he had a long, private talk with my father.

"He seems real nice. He's not a *muran*. Mother says he's not a village man, but lives in Narok. He's training to be a game warden."

"Will you go live in the city?"

"We'll probably live in Narok Town or some place like that near the new game reserves in Kenya."

"What's his name?"

"Mandido."

Rebeka digested the information, already feeling a great loss. "Do you know for sure—about getting married, I mean?"

"No. I think my father would say if they had agreed on a dowry. But he said he'd come back soon. He said it loud when he shook my father's hand, I guess so I would hear. Yesterday, Father got a letter from him." She smoothed her wraparound cloth garment down over her thighs in smug satisfaction.

It seemed to Rebeka that the looming problem of a future was nearly solved for her friend. She would marry a man on the fringes of the tribe like herself, yet of the same ethnic group, have children, and live with contentment the rest of her days. Jealousy rose like a knot in Rebeka's throat. She jumped to her feet. "I have to go home now," she said, wanting to leave before the lump in her throat dissolved into tears.

"Please—be happy for me?" Malia grabbed her ankle.

"I am, really, Malia. But I worry about myself, that no one will want to marry me." Rebeka sat down again, wiping her eyes on the hem of her dress. "I love my parents, but they aren't really my parents. Sometimes I wish I had never been adopted by them."

"Why?" Malia's mouth gaped. This was the first time Rebeka voiced her dissatisfaction. "I've been jealous of you all my life. You have nice clothes, shoes—even if you like to go barefoot like me—books to read, lots of good things to eat, a comfortable bed! Why would you hate all that?"

"It's not that I hate it," Rebeka said. "I'm glad for it, especially the books. But it's…it's…I don't know how to say it. It's like being only half African. Any African man will imagine I think I'm better than him because I know so much more. He'll think I won't be content with whatever he provides me—and maybe I won't. I know I liked being in the school hut with the other girls. But I always got to go home on Saturday and Sunday. I don't know if I'd like it for the rest of my life." Both girls sat in silence thinking over what Rebeka just said.

"And—of course—no European man would even think of marrying an African girl. It's out of the question." They knew that some Europeans took African women secretly, because several light-colored children ran and played in the streets with the rest of the African children. Others belittled them and their mothers. No German ever acknowledged the paternity. Only the mixed-race Arabs were accepted because they had been around for centuries.

"I guess I'll just have to trust God, won't I?" Rebeka stood to her feet again to leave. That sounded too easy. Just trust God. Pull a blanket over the whole subject and hope it goes away. How would God—how *could* God—solve the insolvable? Malia walked her down the path to the street. As they parted, she placed her hand on Rebeka's arm in a gesture of sympathy.

Instead of going home, Rebeka turned and followed the road to where it left town and dipped over a hill toward Mount Meru. Afraid to wander far, she found a rock to sit on just out of sight of the last house. She wanted to think about her future. She knew that soon her parents would return to Germany. Mama was too ill to even dream about them staying in Africa. When it happened, Rebeka would be left alone.

She didn't really hate her upbringing. When she thought about the benefits, they far outweighed the problems. She loved Fritz and Ursula; sometimes she thought she loved them more than Malia loved her parents. It was too horrible to even contemplate any other life. She knew now what it would have been—being used as a plaything by teenage boys, being cut in a ritual rape by the women—her only allies—and married to some old man who probably already had a handful of wives. Scrounging to keep alive, having babies in a dirty hut, being sick, coping with flies— she shuddered to think of it. Yet, would it be so terrible if she never knew anything else? Were the Maasai women unhappy? They didn't appear to be when she saw them in the marketplace. If it was all she knew, then maybe she could manage. But she already knew more, and it would be impossible to cope.

The only alternative was to never marry, and that carried its own dishonor. For one, few decent African women remained unmarried. Those that dared to go against custom were snickered at in the marketplaces. Being an unmarried woman carried a strong social stigma, as though she were a prostitute. Even if Rebeka devoted herself to hospital work, she might always be suspect.

Yet this was her only option. Be a children's nurse or a teacher. She could say she dedicated her life to God and children. *That's it,* she thought. *Then, unless some man comes along who isn't afraid of my background, I'll have something I can do.* But in the back of her mind she mourned the possibility of never marrying, not knowing the companionship of a husband, and never having her own children. Rebeka wept. Several curious goats came over and watched her. When their herder came near to fetch them, she stopped crying, wiped her face, and went home.

**Mbae ole Kipchong strode down the road under the midday sun toward the cluster of Maasai *manyatta*s** near the seasonal watercourse that came out of the foothills of Meru. Following him at the proper distance of ten paces walked two old women, his wives, who argued between themselves about the Europeans and the girl child who lived with the *Daktari*. Occasionally one would spit on the ground to express her vehemence. Mbae said nothing, though he heard every word. It showed weakness for a man to enter women's discussions.

"We should go and take her by force," said one.

"And how do you propose to do that?" the other asked. "They have too many weapons to work magic against."

"If we organize a group of *murani* and go at night…"

"We'd have to have the blessing of the *laibon*."

"If our husband asked, he would give it. After all our husband is the *oloiboni*, the prophet and seer." She said this for Mbae's benefit. He heard and made a mental note of it, though the thought had already crossed his mind.

The sun beating down on them would exhaust a lesser people, but the Maasai, inured as they were by centuries of experience, knew how to pace themselves. They could go long periods of time without water. Shimmers of heat danced against the foothills, elongating the trees, forming a spirit lake between them and the hills. An eddy of wind whirled in the dust along the path and followed for a moment, then spun off into the grass where it whispered through the dry blades. Spiked mounds of clay baked in the sun; termites lived inside in cool comfort. The women stopped talking and followed their husband in silence as he continued on toward the village. Here lived an important chief of their clan with good bloodlines, and a powerful *laibon* shaman at his side. Mbae ole Kipchong had an offer to make this man, one he did not anticipate being refused.

**Mpepo threw himself into his studies at seminary. His eager mind soaked up all the knowledge he could.** He buried himself in studies of Biblical exegesis and doctrine, partially in an attempt to cleanse his conscience of guilt for his many murders during the war, and partially because he wanted to extend his love of God to his people.

He was twenty-four now, long past the time for marriage, but still he did not wish to face that choice. Each morning when he rose he prayed, *Please, God, bring me a wife who will be a help in my calling.* Other than this prayer, he did nothing to discover who it might be that God had in mind. At times the figure of a young girl came to him in his dreams—Rebeka, who lived with the doctor and his wife. When he woke, he would have a longing to see her again and look into her eyes, eyes that resembled a pool that reflected the sky. This feeling perplexed him because she was Maasai, not Huru. His uncle had warned him against marrying outside his tribe. He must put this girl out of his mind. Yet his dreams kept bringing her back.

Mpepo and the other seminarians held long discussions on the problem of evil. Many of the young men came from places that did not often observe the outside world. The only experience they had with European culture and people, previous to the war, came through the missionaries who preached and taught the people to read and write. Most of these white people were good. They cared for the sick and went out of their way to help the poor. Often they committed social errors by not understanding the way the tribes handled certain situations. The natives would laugh and forgive them for their ignorance. They saw that these white people believed in what they taught. It awed the tribes that people could be so good, and they came to represent Western culture.

Then came the war. Disillusionment hit hard as the observing natives saw that not all white men were good. Sometimes the missionaries suffered at the hands of the angry people, for they had come to represent the whole, and the people felt deceived.

Mpepo and his fellows saw white Germans fight their white

English brothers. Few had any idea why they wanted to kill each other. Even though their own history was full of making war against other tribes, they could see that this war was different. Whatever its reason, they knew this war would be disastrous to the people.

For the first time, the seminarians faced the discovery that white people had no more goodness than black people. Emulating the European did not bring righteousness. Following his laws and ways did not bring heaven to earth. They knew the evil of their own way of life. Now they understood that evil dwells in the hearts of all men, and in all ways of life. A new path to righteousness must be found and followed.

It became a time of maturity for everyone, not just the twelve seminarians. All the people searched for a way out of the morass around them. Some of them turned back to the old ways and placated the spirits with sacrifices and offerings of precious food and children. Others cloistered themselves in Islam, following the rigid laws with excruciating exactitude. Many others flocked to the churches, most of which had been left in the hands of African pastors when English missionaries fled the country during the German occupation. And now the German missionaries were being repatriated back to Europe. Strange cults arose instigated by those who had little training or teaching, cults that combined Christianity and paganism.

Mpepo and his classmates were fortunate, for as soon as the German teachers were sent home, Swiss and American Lutherans arrived to take over the school. The students felt pressured to learn and then lead their people in the villages. Mpepo never questioned his own calling. One more year of study, and he would be ready. His fervor and enthusiasm grew as he contemplated his future.

CHAPTER TWELVE

# An Italian in Africa, 1920

**Twenty-nine passengers boarded the steamship** *Cotswold*. Fifteen of these passengers were military men bound for Dar es Salaam, among them Major John Hampton, who shared a cabin with Vito Fernaldi. They had been introduced two weeks before at the Colonial Office, and John, who had spent the last year of the war in Kenya, assisted Vito with his outfit. The other passengers consisted of three married couples, four children, and two Anglican priests headed for Zanzibar.

The Nelsons, the parents of the four children, were missionaries with the Anglican Church Missionary Society going to Uganda. Richard, the husband and father, was a happy-go-lucky chap with an unruly shock of pale brown hair, which repeatedly fell down over his eyes even though he kept brushing it back. His wife, Angela, was round and blonde, with a continual contented smile. Even Vito in his moroseness was attracted to their easy-going manner. The children ranged in age from four years old to twelve; the older lad was a remarkable copy of his father. As the only children on board, they had the run of the ship and soon adopted everyone, including Vito, as honorary uncles and aunts.

The other travelers were all civil servants. One man was to be Aide to the new Governor of Tanganyika, and the other the

newly appointed District Commissioner for Arusha. Sir Cecil
Neville had been a career officer in the British army in India for
many years, then in Kenya during the war. He appeared to be
about fifty-five with thin, grey hair and a matching moustache
that hung down the sides of his mouth giving him a dour look that
his disposition did not share. He had, alongside Lord Delamere,
commanded His Majesty's troops against the Germans on the
Kenyan border with German East Africa. After the war he
received a knighthood. This would be his last posting before
retiring, he informed the others, and he hoped it would be an
easy assignment.

His wife Gertrude, who insisted that everyone call her Gertie,
was a striking woman. She stood almost as tall as her husband,
dressed fashionably, and kept her black hair pinned up in a cloud
over her brow. She might have been considered beautiful if her
nose had not resembled the beak of an eagle, yet it was so much
a part of her character and personality that, as Vito got to know
her, he thought of her as one of the most beautiful women he had
ever seen. From the moment she first entered the salon where the
passengers ate and visited together, he knew she was a woman
with presence. Ears inclined toward her to hear what she said,
which always seemed knowledgeable, witty, and never unkind.
Humor danced in her hazel eyes. Her husband, too, listened
to her, observing the reactions of others as if to ask, *am I not
fortunate to have such a wife?*

Here, thought Vito, is a man who has made his peace with a
woman stronger than himself, yet isn't intimidated by her.

The other couple, the McCrorys, seemed small and petty
compared to the Nevilles. Ian, a typical London bureaucrat, had
an unyielding, stern temperament. "The natives must be kept
in their place," he insisted at dinner the first evening as they

discussed the politics and social customs of Africa. "They're dirty and undisciplined. You must be careful not to allow them into your house until they're scrubbed and wearing clean clothing. And even then you have to watch them because they'll steal anything they get their hands on." He looked around as though it was his responsibility to instruct everyone in colonial protocol.

"Piffle!" exclaimed Gertie. "They're people, just like us, Ian. All they need is an opportunity to learn and water to keep clean, and they'll gladly learn civil ways. Besides, who's to say their ways aren't just as civil as ours? Cecil here—" and she turned to her husband, "—had a servant in Kenya who was more civilized and cultured than the average English foot soldier. He even read Shakespeare and Homer's Iliad.  His only sins were he was black, and he never learned to read until he was eighteen. Isn't that right, Cece?" and Cecil nodded agreement.

Ian did not take kindly to being contradicted. He stubbornly insisted that the African harbored no resemblance to the Englishman. Soon the dinner conversation became a lively debate between those who thought European customs superior and those who thought the Africans had a valid voice of their own. Mary, Ian's wife, sat silent and pale, a victim of seasickness and homesickness as the ship churned its way toward the Mediterranean Sea.

When Mary's seasickness overcame her at the end of dinner that first evening, Gertie whisked her away from the table, tut-tutting about how poorly she felt, too, and laid her on a couch against the salon wall. She called for a damp cloth for Mary, and was so attentive to her needs that soon the others fawned over Mary, befriending her because Gertie had done so. By the end of the week Mary had the bloom of acceptance on her cheek.

Vito, feeling an undercurrent of tension because he was Italian, didn't seek out anyone's company. He kept much to himself in the salon reading books, pamphlets, and directives from the Colonial Office about the people of Africa.

He read the memoirs of David Livingston and Henry Stanley, the travelogues of Richard Burton, Speke, and others who mapped Lake Victoria and discovered the source of the Nile. He perused accounts of how the Germans ruled their corner of Africa until they lost the recent war. He read about tribal customs and wars, African values, and their family systems. He thought about the mistakes that had been made by others, and studied legal decisions.

In the six weeks it would take to get to Dar es Salaam he would formulate a working plan as to how he would conduct his court. His instructions from the Colonial Office were to go with tribal law in every possible way, so long as basic laws of justice, fairness, and human rights were not broken. Every decision must come under the umbrella of Britannia.

After Gibraltar, came Genoa. Vito stood at the railing and watched the shores of Italy rise before him, his mind a turmoil of mixed feelings. He had said he would never set foot in Italy again, yet now there was a tug to at least take the opportunity to prowl the streets and speak his native tongue once more.

As the stevedores and dock workers swarmed around the ship shouting to one another and moving heavy cargo, he decided to go and buy a newspaper or two, ask about the feelings of the people, and maybe seek out a wine shop which might still have in its cellars a bottle or two of Fernaldi wine from before the war.

Genoa was built on rolling hills and cliffs overlooking the sea, a beautiful white city sparkling in the Riviera sun. A wide street fronted the wharves, flanked by an ancient stone wall, below which old boats waited on the sand for the next tide to take them out to the fishing grounds. Men mended their nets or scrambled over the sands carrying supplies, oblivious to the large steamship docked at the adjacent pier. On the other side of the street stood old, yellowed buildings—shops, offices, warehouses, *pensiones*, eating establishments—all catering to those who made their living off the sea. Most of the buildings were over four hundred years old. People of all nations streamed past, a motley assortment of sailors, office workers, businessmen, and sightseers. The scene had never changed through the centuries except for the garb of the people and the design of the ships.

Once his mind was made up, Vito was eager to explore the waterfront. He was the first one down the gangplank.

In a small shop, filled with dusty, pre-war items set beside newer radios and shoes, he found an old, used Neapolitan accordion, rich in sound and beautifully decorated with ivory and mother of pearl.

"I haven't played one of these since my college days," he exclaimed to the large, middle-aged woman who insisted he take books of music along for free.

"If you're going to Africa," she said, "You must take something of Italy with you." She pushed the old books into his hand. "Take them. No one wants the old songs anymore. They will remind you of your home."

With the accordion strap slung over his shoulder, Vito continued on his way through the shopping district across from the harbor. He entered three wine shops, asking if they had any old bottles of *Fernaldi Malvoisie* wine from Valle d'Aosta.

In the third shop, the wine merchant said, "I think so. I'll take a look," and he disappeared into his cellars. He was gone so long that Vito thought to leave, but the owner reappeared, cobwebs hanging from his brow, excitedly brandishing three dusty bottles with the eagle trademark.

Vito's heart skipped a beat. Wine created from the vineyards where he played as a child. He remembered the soulful process of distilling overseen and guarded by his family. Perhaps Therese herself had slapped the label on these bottles with her own hands. With reverence, he took them from the man. He would have paid anything for them, but the merchant waived the cost.

"A wine such as this has no price," he said. "This is a gift to you from your family and your country. Do not forget us."

Vito shook the man's hand, then they held each other in an enthusiastic Mediterranean embrace. "Thank you, my friend. But here, I'll buy a newspaper from you. I would like to know what's going on in my country."

"You will not be pleased," answered the merchant. "Many of the young become fascists and follow this Benito Mussolini. He has even wormed his way into the King's council chamber. Most of us older people do not understand his words. We think they will only cause trouble. We should go slow, accept change bit by bit."

"You're right," answered Vito. "I knew this Benito once, and I tremble for our country if his seeds of discontent take root. Perhaps we're in need of reform, but not his way. However, it is no longer my problem. I'll never live in Italy again. It's people like you who must make their voices heard."

The merchant lowered his eyes and studied the floor for a moment before replying. "It may be too late. The fascist goons in black shirts parade through the streets, watching who does not salute as they go by. All I want is to live in peace and provide for my family."

"*Bion giorno*," said Vito in farewell. "May God be with you," and he departed with the wine in a mesh string bag on the opposite shoulder from the accordion, the newspaper and music books clutched in his hands.

He could see John Hampton's curiosity when he returned. Why Vito! Are you a musician?" He noticed the wine bottles and his eyes grew big. "I thought you said you don't imbibe anymore. What're those for?"

Vito smiled. "Tonight, my friend, as we sail along the coast of my homeland, I will drink once again in farewell to the country of my birth. I'd be honored to have you join me."

As the sun set over the sparkling waves, spreading pink and gold colors over the hills of Italy, *The Cotswold* cast off her lines and sailed southeast down the coast toward Naples and the Straits of Messina. Vito and John sat along the railing, sipping the wonderful, sweet wine and watched Italy go by.

"I salute you, my former country," said Vito, raising his glass in the air toward land.

"This wine," he told John, in an unusual talkative mood brought on by two of the bottles, "was made by my family in Valle d'Aosta, in the north of Italy. For generations, my family perfected the wine from pinot grapes to make this sweet wine, famous throughout the country. It has even been served to the King. These are, perhaps, the last bottles in existence."

"Why do you say that?" said John, curious, hoping the wine would break through some of Vito's reserve. After a silence, Vito cleared his throat and began to speak.

He told of his idyllic home in the quaint village, and the silent Alps that towered over them. He spoke of his going to the University of Turin to study law and finance. He stumbled over the account of his marriage to his childhood sweetheart and the births of their children.

"Then," he concluded, tears dampening his cheeks for the first time in two years, "when the war was almost over and we fought that last major battle at the River Po, you British came to our rescue. I was wounded there. While I lay unconscious, fighting for my life, deserters from my own army rampaged through the countryside. It was mad, senseless, as they went berserk through villages—including my home village—burning and killing without thought."

He stood and leaned on the railing, trying to find his voice again. John stayed quiet, and Vito knew he did so out of respect for the emotion of the moment.

"They burned the vineyards and the winery, after smashing the bottles of wine in the streets. They shot my family–my parents, my wife, and my children. This is the first I've been able to talk about it."

Nothing further needed to be said. Vito sipped the last drops, then dropped the wineglass into the Mediterranean Sea. For the first time he had related his story, and for the last time tasted his wine—his sweet cup of bitterness—while the land of his birth slipped past him in final review. The remaining bottle would sit on a shelf as a reminder.

It took several days for Italy to slide out of sight behind them. During that time Vito stayed in his cabin or the salon either reading his books or becoming reacquainted with the accordion. The other passengers stood at the rail as the ship passed through the narrow Straits of Messina on a running tide, the plaintive strains of *O Sole Mio* in the background.

When Vito strode off the freighter in Dar es Salaam, he felt ready for the rest of his life. He was forty years old.

The humidity was close to unbearable. It felt like walking through soup. Everyone oozed perspiration, those with heavy clothing showing dark rings expanding from under their arms and around their waists. Most of the Europeans wore pith helmets. Even the women, modestly clothed, were uncomfortably damp. The smell of stale perspiration wafted by on the breeze mixed with the odor of spices, over-ripe fruit, and animal waste. The harbor was entirely land-locked, accessible only by a long winding channel. The city lay around it in a semi-circle, its profile punctuated by two steeples of Catholic and Lutheran churches. The Germans had outdone themselves in making this a contemporary city.

The wharf bustled with activity. Cranes groaned as they unloaded goods from the freighters. Stevedores chanted in unison as they pushed and heaved loads into place on flatbed trucks for upcountry delivery. The newly built Central Railway Line extended to the wharfs, and a steam engine labored by pulling carloads of rails and spikes. What the German's started, the British would finish.

Not far from the wharf they could see a large parkland with rows of palm trees. Vito soon learned that this was the grounds of the Governor's mansion, built by von Goetzen years before, now the home of Governor Sir Cedric Darlington. Vito and the Nevilles would be his guests before heading for Arusha.

They hired several rickshaws to carry them and their luggage to the mansion, which was an imposing, three-story structure, set in the middle of the park and accessed by a straight avenue shaded by large mango trees. The square, white-stuccoed building was encircled by a two-story verandah with a double tier of Moorish arches. Broad steps led to the first level that was composed entirely of government offices.

A wide marble stairway led to the second floor where vast rooms served as reception areas and the state dining room, as well as personal living and dining facilities for the governor. The center of this floor, the great hall, was open to the sky above. The walls were decorated with spears and shields, left behind by the previous German tenants. The upper level, narrower than the lower floors, held sleeping quarters. and opened onto verandahs to catch whatever breeze drifted over the roofs of the city and afforded a view of the beach and the many ships that transited the harbor. Here their hosts gave them rooms.

There were some curious structures on the grounds, and after tea Lady Darlington, a small middle-aged woman with dark hair and refined manners, treated Vito and the Nevilles to a guided tour.

"Schnee, the German governor for years, was an amateur botanist," she said. "He collected many different plants from all over the country and planted them here." Indeed, the park was like a botanist's dream. Paths ran among the plants—feathery palms, giant ferns, gorgeous shrubs with sweet or spicy smelling flowers—that were marked with little plaques giving their scientific names, where they came from, and included the year they were transplanted.

"And here is a real treat," she added as she motioned toward a stucco box-like structure on the beach. She unlocked and opened the doors, and they descended about ten steps before entering a large, one-room building with only high windows and skylights letting in the light from the setting sun. One side was open to the Indian Ocean, and glass panels allowed a glimpse of sea creatures.

"It seems that von Goetzen, who preceded Schnee, liked fish." The walls of the building were lined with vast aquariums, where colorful fish darted and octopi glared at them. Lady Darlington smiled in satisfaction at their astonishment. "He was an amateur ichthyologist, and he built these aquariums to hold both fresh and saltwater fish that are indigenous to the country. These over here are the varieties found only in Lake Victoria."

"Why are some of the aquariums empty?" Vito asked, his breath taken away by the idea of Germans engaged in peaceful activities while carrying on a brutal war.

"We have no one able to maintain them," she said. "We are offering the collection to various institutions in Europe and America, and some have already been shipped out. Collectors are here now from London who want to take the Lake Victoria collection."

"How do they transport them?" Gertie asked.

"Ships have holding tanks installed that are pumped full of the right kind of water for the fish. The specialists study the temperature and mineral content of the water—Von Goetzen kept good records of that—they then duplicate it. So far most of the fish have survived the journeys."

"Too bad you can't keep them."

"I agree. But the Home Office can't afford to send us the proper scientists to maintain the collection. It is better to get it dispersed to where the public can enjoy it and school children can learn." She ushered them from the building, leading them back through the park to the mansion.

Vito spent two weeks in Dar es Salaam waiting for the train to Tanga and then to Moshi, learning more about the people and the rudiments of Swahili. He prowled the narrow, crowded streets full of Arab vendors, Indian merchant stalls, and shops catering to Europeans. Donkeys brayed as they pulled loaded cartloads of fruits and vegetables. Graceful Arab women carried loads of goods on their heads, their felt slippers hushing their footsteps so that they moved as ghosts. He felt he had stepped back into ancient Baghdad, except that most of the people were black-skinned and dressed in a ragtag assortment of clothing.

Cecil often accompanied him, telling him what he would need to complete his equipment. Vito had already purchased a hunting rifle in London, but in one shop an Arab pressed on him an enormous old rifle, the silver-plating on the stock elaborately embossed with entwining snakes.

"For elephant," the man insisted. "470 Holland and Holland. Once owned by British explorer Burton."

"I doubt the pedigree," Cecil said. "But it's a good rifle, and well taken care of. How much?" he asked the shopkeeper.

The man did rapid calculations on a scrap of paper. "Two hundred pound. For you."

Vito put it back down. "I don't have that to spare, nor do I intend to hunt elephant."

"One hundred pound."

"Fifty," Cecil said. The man cringed.

"Seventy-five. You make me cry." The merchant wiped imaginary tears from his eyes.

"We'll take it," Cecil said. "Pay the man, Vito. You've bought yourself a fine collector's item here. If you don't want it, I'll bet you Lord Darlington would take it off your hands for a nice sum."

Among other things, Vito purchased kerosene lanterns and mosquito netting. The latter reminded him he needed a bed. Lady Darlington told him to be sure to buy mahogany or ebony, if he opted for wood. "Other woods get eaten by white ants," she added. "Iron is inferior because it rusts during the rainy seasons." In a dark, hot shop run by an old Indian tradesman, animal hides, chairs, tables, oriental samovars and dinnerware in piles everywhere, he found an amazing bed.

It was made of ebony with some of the white outer wood of the tree swirled around the heartwood of black and carved in intricate detail with a high-polished gloss. The posts at the head of the bed were two large, elongated elephants raised up on their hind legs, their trunks six feet up in the air and curved over to meet the trunk on the other side to form the holder for a mosquito netting. Their eyes and tusks were of inset ivory. Rising two feet above the mattress boards, the headboard was a curved piece of solid black ebony made of intricately carved lions on parade, each with the tail of the one in front of it in it's mouth, as Vito had seen carved into the ivory tusks for sale in the marketplace. Beneath the feet of the lions, inlaid ivory pieces resembled a stone pathway. The size of the lions decreased in size as they progressed from the right to the left. A matching piece was on the footboard, but the foot posts were carved to resemble impala horns, rising just short of the height of the head posts in order to hold the netting at the foot of the bed. It was one of those things a person finds once in a lifetime, a priceless item, and he would have paid anything to own it.

By now he had learned to bargain with the shopkeepers, and even though he got the price down to half the original asking price, he left behind nearly a month's pay. But he felt that buying this exotic African bed somehow planted him firmly in this his new country.

Just as he was leaving the shop, after arranging delivery by donkey cart to the Governor's mansion, the shopkeeper beckoned to him.

"Here," he said with a thick accent, lowering his voice though no one was around to hear. "I have treasure. Just for you." He took a small book bound in cracked leather out from under his makeshift counter. Vito looked at the cover and noticed that the leather was probably hand-tanned, the spine bound by a leather strip wound around and around to keep the covers together.

"Very old book. A gift. I cannot read." The pages, made of coarse paper glued together with a failing mucilage at the inner edge, were written by hand in ink, faded in places where moisture had gotten in and done its destruction. Tiny holes, made by silver fish, bored through the pages. It was written in Italian. Vito looked up at the man.

The Indian shrugged. "You take it. White man's book, maybe explorer from many years ago."

The title was written on the flyleaf in large, round letters of calligraphy, typical of nineteenth century writing.

*The Legend of the Lion*

*By Guillermo Venisi*

*1857*

Vito put the small book in his shirt pocket. That night, while waiting for sleep to come, he pulled it out to read by the light of the bare electric light bulb hanging over his bed.

CHAPTER THIRTEEN

# The Legend of the Lion By Guillermo Venisi

## Il dottore di Filosofia e la Storia L'università di Roma 1857

*I first came to Zanzibar in Anno Domini eighteen hundred forty-five by Commission of L'universita di Roma to document the diverse histories of the African peoples, their legends, myths, practices, and taboos. My first years were spent learning Swahili and the numerous dialects that would help me decipher the tales of the remote tribes. I also questioned the tribal peoples who made their way into this ancient city of trade. Many things I have seen and learned, from the brutal slave traffic to the exploitation of the riches of this land, have been documented in my previous writings.*

*Last year the English explorers Richard Burton and John Speke came to Zanzibar, thwarted by yellow fever in their pursuit of the elusive source of the Nile River. When they recovered enough to continue their travels they invited me to accompany them, and in June of this Year of Our Lord we set our faces to the north and west with over one-hundred-thirty men and thirty animals laden with beds, chairs, tents, blankets, mosquito nets, numerous instruments, fishing tackle, books, tools, umbrellas, firearms and ammunition, hatchets, knives, bullet moulds, and of course brandy. We also carried presents of cloth, brass wire, beads, and tools.*

*We had barely crossed the coastal bogs and marshes and begun the ascent of the Usugara Mountains when we discovered that the half-Arab caravan director was really a thief and he and many of the porters, angry at the physical abuse by Burton, deserted, taking with them over half of our stuff.*

*Both Burton and Speke were overcome by fevers. By day they barely kept their balance on their mules; by night they collapsed on their beds. Their mouths filled with sores and in their delirium they saw and fought off vicious beasts. My years in this country protected me with immunity from the usual ills that befell the Englishmen, or perhaps it was the brandy I kept in my personal luggage and drank almost as a religious rite each evening before taking to my cot. I was not completely spared, however, for I found the white ants eating my bedding, and pismire ants had mandibles strong enough and large enough to bring great pain when they bit me in the legs.*

*We made slow progress, but eventually came out on a vast plain of acacia trees with quantities of antelope and zebras that filled our cooking pots with rejuvenating meat.*

*We have camped for a while on the banks of the Pangani River several hundred miles inland from the coast. Here we wait for Burton and Speke to regain their strength before pushing north. The only Europeans to travel this far have been the intrepid*

*German missionaries Rebmann and Krapf.*

*While we tarry here arguments have arisen between the two leaders of this exploration. Mr. Speke is a prim and proper gentleman who despises both the African people and Richard Burton. He is willing to express his dislikes as often as he can, and I have found it to my benefit to keep out of the way of both of these men. Mr. Burton himself is critical of the people, though he enjoys the women in every way imaginable. I believe their dislike of the natives is an attribute of the English people in general, since they believe they are the modern Chosen of God. Even I, as a citizen of Rome, am relegated to an inferior place in their society.*

*To keep occupied while the two leaders recuperate, I have taken it upon myself to move amongst the native people and acquaint myself with their legends, dreams, and history. Not far from this camping spot lies a village of Masai people who are elusive in their dealings with expeditionary caravans such as ours, so much so that little is known of them. Burton and Speke have been warned against any commerce with them, since they are reputed to be fierce marauders with little respect for human life.*

*However, I have found these villagers to be peaceful and friendly as I move among them accompanied only by our new African caravan leader, Sidi Mubarak Bombay, who speaks enough of their tongue to translate for me. I also find that quantities of brass wire and beads win the loosening of their tongues.*

*I learned that they are in mourning for a great tribal leader, known as the Son of the One True Lion, who had ruled them for forty years. Their reputation for ferocious temperament came from his leadership as the tribe pressed outward on neighboring tribes in order to expand their territory and wealth, which is based solely on the raising of cattle. Their rapacious marauding and pillaging of cattle owned by their neighbors led to the legends of excessive strength and size. I enquired as to the stories of this great leader, and found this delightful tale underlying his reign. I also found that these people, rather than being weakened by his death, are strengthened by the prophecy that other leaders will arise in fulfillment of this legend. Whenever outsiders threaten the tribe again, they say, a descendant of the original One True Lion will appear. This leader will lead the Masai people back to their former strength. The recently deceased Son of the One True Lion effectively evaded the slave traders so that few, if any, of these people have ever been captured.*

*This is the tale as told by the village elders. I had heard coastal versions of this story, and I have set my hand to pulling all the accounts together into one. Those who knew told and retold their versions of the events until they became oral traditional tales repeated through the years.*

*At the dawn of the Masai people's history, a chief arose in a time of overwhelming pressure from people to the west. He had eyes of fire, as the eyes of the Lion. They called him the One True Lion. All men, Arabians and Africans alike, feared him.*

*It was a golden-eyed Arabian boy who gave birth to the legend nearly four hundred years ago....*

Vito settled back to read. He had read of the travels of Burton and Speke, and now to get a fellow Italian's view of them and the African people was a refreshing change. He, too, thought that many of the British were arrogant and conceited.

*The son of a rich Caliph and reared in the deserts of Araby in the dim days of history, Ali bin Said was a dissolute adolescent of less than pleasant disposition. In trouble with his family over the theft of camels, he was sent on a merchant's dhow to his uncle Hasan Al-Abu at Kilwa on the remote eastern coast of Africa. There, in a despotic sultanate, Hasan dealt in ivory, gold, exotic animal skins, and human slaves.*

*Adept with numbers and letters, Ali worked for his uncle keeping track of valuable materials, and to make sure that the traders and their porters were not overpaid. In fact his cunning often found ways to pay them little, and in return he received a larger share of the profits.*

*Several years after Ali arrived, his uncle sent him on his first slave-purchasing expedition. It was decided that at last he should see first hand this part of the business.*

*Through the centuries bargains were struck with the Africans along the Eastern Coast. Their willing participation, in trade with less sophisticated tribes and acting as porters on these expeditions, bought exemption for them and their kin from being sold to the many ships that berthed in the harbors. Indeed, the punishment for insubordination, crime, or simple lack of cooperation, was the sale of one's family. This kept the coastal people cooperative and minimized the number of Arabians needed to conduct the expeditions.*

*On this trip Ali would be second in command under Suleiman, an older, more experienced Arabian. Ali had heard the tales of a fierce inland tribe whom the slavers sidestepped because of their fierce reputation. The men were seven feet tall, the stories said. They wore lion skins as clothing and were orange in color. They carried spears so heavy that an ordinary man could barely lift one, much less throw it.*

*It was not part of Ali's plan, however, to show cowardice. His* goal—to succeed his uncle in his position as chief merchandiser of the sultanate—was worth all it might cost in bravery. He based his hopes on the fact that Hasan's only son was a weak young man with a penchant for too much strong drink. He wept often when he did not get his way, and showed no interest in marrying to perpetuate the family; instead he kept a harem of young boys. Hasan had several beautiful daughters, and Ali had his eye on Mariame. As Hasan's son-in-law, he would be in good position to succeed him. He set off with a resolve to conduct himself in a worthy manner. He would watch and learn.

The day they left was no different from any other along the tropical coast. The coastal winds were calm that time of year, the heat insufferable, and the air full of dank moisture from the swamps. Ali left with Suleiman the one-eyed Arabian, ten strong African slave hunters, and forty porters who carried their food, water, and trade goods on their heads.

For weeks they traveled through the mountains keeping well south of the plains populated by the Masai. As the men sat around the campfire at night, Ali listened in fascination to the tales told by the black porters of the few times they had stumbled across these people.

"Why are you so afraid of them?" he asked. "Are you not the bravest, most fearless people of all? Why, then, do you cringe in fear?"

Silence greeted his remarks. The fire popped and the green wood sang.

"Ah, Sahib!" protested one of the older men. "You do not know that it is not fear that keeps us from these people. We are more strong and clever than they. We have these wonderful swords you have given us from the smithies of Arabia. No, Sahib, it is not fear that keeps us from capturing them." He spat into *the fire.*

*"They are worthless as slaves. Many years ago, some were captured and brought to the coast. Out of twelve men, only four made it alive. And those four strong young men died before they could be sold to the ships. Two men lost their lives taking those twelve, and all for nothing. Others have told the same tale. They simply wish to die, and they do."*

*Ali worried this in his mind. He did not believe their tale.*

*Soon they traveled beyond the mountains and onto the high plains. The caravan wound its way far to the west. They came into hill country, and after stopping to trade for slaves in several large villages they looped east again for the return trip. The caravan was huge, laden with ivory and slaves, as they approached the final village that had grown along the route to the interior.*

*Here they filled their quota with twenty more slaves, five of whom were children. They struck their usual bargain, cheating the chief just enough to please themselves and leaving him confused by their arguments over the worthlessness of children. They now turned toward Kilwa with their booty.*

*The return trip of the caravan took longer than planned. Early rains swelled rivers to rushing torrents that delayed them. The captives had to be kept alive to get the best price in the coastal markets, and food must be found. Many times, out of boredom, Ali accompanied hunting forays to get wild game and to see some of the country.*

*On one of these trips he and his hunters were resting in the shade of a thorn tree. They had chased some antelope down out of the hills to the plain. The hunters were uneasy, since they knew this was close to Masai land. They waited for the sun to lower on the horizon before returning to the caravan.*

Ali climbed the tree to a low-slung limb to catch the breeze as it came off the grass. Thus he was first to see a small group of young men approach from a line of trees on their right. He slipped out of the tree and crouched in the grass, whispering the news to the men who became agitated. As the group approached, they could see that there were three young warriors and one girl who carried a load on her back. The warriors carried their spears in a casual manner, and they sauntered along glancing at the animal tracks in the dust.

Ali decided to attack. To the dismay of the Africans with him, he jumped up with a shout and waved his sword as the band came within a few yards. His companions now had no choice but to join in, so within a few minutes the four were disarmed and bound. Ali was jubilant. The only blood shed was a slash on the left shoulder of one of the African porters with him. None of the captives was injured, and they were all young and strong.

They were taller than most Africans, but not seven feet tall. The orange color was merely the ochre with which they covered themselves from head to toe. The warriors' hair, braided closely to their heads, was coated with a mixture of dust and grease, and their clothing was made from goatskins. The girl's head had been shaved. Their finely molded heads were angular with chiseled features and high cheekbones that gave them a solemn appearance. Their deep-set eyes were wild and inscrutable. None expressed fear, merely looked at their captors in silent arrogance. The girl was of special interest to Ali. She had barely reached her womanhood, yet she had the gaze of an old woman, her knowing eyes boring through his. There was something chilling, unearthly, about them.

The sun had now lost its fervor and they set off to rejoin the caravan. Little prodding was needed to get the new captives *moving. In silence they stretched their limbs and stepped along, their fearless eyes looking straight ahead. Even the girl followed in the same manner. A boiling resentment troubled Ali. African women were afraid of him. They bowed before him and scurried to do his bidding. This young woman disdained him, scorned him.*

*Suleiman was incensed when they returned with the captives. He shouted at Ali. "Do you know what you have done? These are worthless! Worthless! Even if they live until we reach the coast, they will die before they can be sold! Why are you such a fool?"*

*Ali had not expected to be berated in the presence of the African porters and the slaves. The new captives seemed to gloat. He fumed inside and despised Suleiman.*

*After they unloaded the venison and contained the new captives in leg irons, Suleiman turned away to supervise the portioning of the meat. Ali released the young girl from her brothers, threw her on the ground, and forced himself upon her.*

*She did not scream or fight. Instead she ignored him, studying the stars that appeared one by one in the evening sky, indifferent. Ali was furious. He would make her submit. He would not tolerate her insolence.*

*Night after night Ali continued to abuse the girl. But she continued to ignore him, never speaking. Her brothers never varied their expression from one of scorn as they refused all food other than water and meat. They never resisted or stumbled in their walk.*

*After several months the caravan made its way into the coastal area of the Indian Ocean. As they approached the city of Kilwa, they entered a populated area of many farms and villages. The convoy of captives looked around in fear, since these coastal people were different in looks and speech as well as the clothing they wore.*

*Mouth agape, the captives stumbled through the narrow streets of the city looking at the market places and hearing the cacophony of languages and music. Beautiful arched and domed buildings of glistening white coral towered several stories over clean streets paved with smooth stone. Carts lumbered everywhere; sedan chairs draped with multicolored curtains swayed by, each powered by the feet of four slaves. Men in white robes and turbans swept the streets of dirt and garbage. Never, in their wildest imagination, had they dreamed of such splendor. Yet they were marched and dragged past all these signs of opulence to the yards where slaves were kept.*

*These slave quarters were close to the wharves. They were nothing more than a rough stockade only partially roofed, surrounded by a dry moat filled with sharpened sticks that would pierce the bodies of anyone trying to pass through. The captives sat on the ground under the hot sun or rain, the men separated from the women to keep fighting from breaking out over the women. The stench from the lack of sanitation was overwhelming.*

*Ali appeared before his uncle with his report: One hundred and twenty five slaves, twenty tusks of ivory, ten live monkeys, and scores of bundles of exotic pelts of cheetah, lion, and leopard, and all well within cost.*

*"Ah!" said Uncle Hasan. "Very good, Ali! You have done well for your first trip. I have heard good things from Suleiman about your bravery. However, you showed your hot-headed youth in your decision to bring in the Masai captives."*

*As Ali started to protest, Hasan raised his hand to silence him. "You will see," he said, "time will show that this is a mistake.*

*But as nothing was paid, the lesson is free.*

*"Now go home and bathe and rest. I will send an invitation for a celebration dinner in your honor."*

*The invitation was long in coming, and as Ali paced back and forth in impatience he could not help remembering the slender young girl who treated him with so much scorn. He remembered her well-formed head; her chiseled features, her small full mouth, and deep-set black eyes. A perplexity at her remote insolence began to replace his anger.*

*The dinner invitation finally arrived. A heavy feast consisting of three kinds of game, three fowls, and three exotic fruits was served in three courses. Between each course, dancing slave girls and flutists provided entertainment. Mariame glanced coyly at Ali through her sheer veils, though he pretended to keep his gaze on the entertainers.*

*Uncle Hasan stood to make an announcement to all the guests. "My fine nephew Ali has shown himself to be a man. If he would have her, I would be honored to give him my daughter, Mariame, to be his wife. The wedding will take place one year from now!"*

*As the group cheered, Ali's elation was tempered by his dismay. He had proved himself a man, and wished to wed immediately. But he dared not challenge his uncle.*

*On his way home, on an impulse, he stopped at the slave quarters to get the girl. This was not unusual; young girls were often borrowed as domestics until the next slave ship came in, thus avoiding paying wages to a local resident.*

*Ali took her to his lavish home. He showered her with food and attention and called her Desert Flower. His anger was gone now, and if he had not been raised to believe that women were mere chattel, he would have understood his emotion. He bought her cloth to drape her body as she followed him to market to purchase food. He showed her how he ciphered, talking to her all the time. She never spoke to him or made any sound, nor did she smile. She was visibly with child, probably since the first day of capture. To save her child she now ate small portions.*

*When he went to the stockade to check on the captives, her brothers stared at him with hate, knowing what he had done to their sister. They ate next to nothing, the guard told him, and they were thin. They would not live long enough to be taken on a slave ship, he feared, since the winds that kept the ships from arriving continued in full force.*

*Desert Flower showed no emotion. She appeared more and more remote, and at times he thought her soul had already left her body, though she still lived. She only ate and bathed when he was away. She sat huddled on her cot, completely wrapped in herself. Many a time Ali struck her, hoping to hear her cry out. But she remained mute.*

*When her time arrived, only one brother remained alive. Late one night as Ali leaned over the outer wall of his house contemplating the stars and all the benefits of marriage to his cousin, a long drawn out scream pierced the darkness. Scream after scream piled up to the heavens as she tried to give birth. As a last resort the midwife took a knife and slashed open the birth canal. With a gush of blood a boy-child was born and Desert Flower died.*

*Trembling, Ali gathered the child into Desert Flower's garment and looked at him: a comely boy, the color of burnished copper, with tiny features now contorted in a wail. The loss of Desert Flower was painful. Never before had Ali cared for anyone but himself.*

*In the wee hours of the night Ali made his way to the stockade.*

*He slipped the sleepy guard a bribe and approached the one remaining brother. He unlocked his fetters and beckoned him to follow.*

*They went through quiet streets to the house. Ali took the baby boy, wrapped in his mother's garment, and pressed him into the arms of the captive. He gave him a bundle with bread and meat, a bladder of water, and trade goods for wet-nurses. He led him out of the city to the canoes along the beach, pointed toward the mainland where a track led over the mountains, and set his captive free. The young man understood and nodded his head. Turning, he got in a canoe and disappeared into the darkness.*

*He traveled from village to village, from wet-nurse to wet-nurse, until they reached the villages of the Masai people. It was a miracle that the baby boy survived.*

*In time this child, the grandson of a chief, grew until he too became clan chief. He warred with the coastal tribes and the Arabians. He unified all the clans under his leadership and led them up to the high plains at the foot of Kilimanjaro. Engai, their god, gave his approval by erupting fire from the volcano called el Doinyo Lengai, where he dwelt. The people called this man The One True Lion because of his burning amber eyes, his tawny skin, and the copper amulet with an inscribed lion's head that he wore. He brought order and led the clans in their pursuit of their god-given vocation of cattle herding. Under his leadership they warred with Bantu tribes from the west and from the north and succeeded in driving them away. During his years, the rains did not fail. When he was old, he disappeared up the mountain they call Kilimanjaro, and never returned.*

*Soon after his death, the legend and prophecy arose. When the Masai people are in trouble again, the elders whisper, a descendant of his will lead the people to freedom. Each generation of elders looks for a child with golden eyes. They keep careful track of the lineage of The One True Lion. The recently deceased Son of the One True Lion had eyes of amber like his forbear.*

*As for Ali, he did not live to take his uncle's position, or even to marry his cousin. The Portuguese swept up the coast of Africa making war with the sultans, subjugating those who would bow to them, and killing those who would not. Kilwa was destroyed by the Portuguese, built up again by the Arabians, and razed once more, never to deal in slaves and ivory again. Ali, along with his Uncle Hasan and his family, was hacked to death with an ax and his body dismembered, his head thrust on a spike in the city center.*

***Bombay, our native caravan leader, has told me with delight that many tribes of Africa have similar tales*** *and prophecies of great leaders from the past who will return in the future and lead their tribe to victory over their enemies. Perhaps these tales fuel the arrogance and latent disobedience of our porters. My vocation is merely to pass them on so Europeans who come after me will understand the hopes and dreams of the people of this Dark Continent. I would be delighted to look over the ramparts of heaven some day and see these black-skinned people receive the respect they are due.*

*Burton is well now, and Speke also. We will soon be underway again. Letters have been written and I will send this little missive back to Zanzibar with the post. I trust that you will find it amusing and will preserve it with the other findings I have sent. If I should not return, and you find it of no value, please give it to my son Willem.*

Very amusing, thought Vito as he closed the little book and laid it on his table.

## CHAPTER FOURTEEN

# A Pact in Huruland

**At twenty-five years of age, Mpepo exemplified superb African manhood.** He stood several inches taller than most of the other men of his tribe, with broad shoulders and defined muscles earned through hard labor. His open, honest face matched his friendly personality, and he preached with a fire and intensity that stirred the people. Those who heard him said he spoke milk and fire; the words came out of his mouth like milk, but they burned like fire in the hearts of the hearers. Young women and girls packed the pews and sighed, hoping he would notice them, and when he gave the invitation to come and receive *Yesu Cristo*, they made their way to the front in unprecedented numbers. His mentor, Pastor Luka, spoke to him about this.

"Mpepo, you must ignore what men say about your abilities. While God has given you a gift, be aware that pride is a dreadful stone that you will surely stumble over if you depend on your ability instead of God.

"Also, you should marry soon. It is not right for you to remain single. All your classmates have married, and some even have children. You leave the door open to temptation."

He was right, for Mpepo and his classmates were much older than other seminary students, their studies having been interrupted by the war. Those who returned came back with a mature edge produced by conflict and deprivation, as well as a sureness of what and why they believed. As Pastor Luka spoke of marriage, an image flitted across Mpepo's mind of Rebeka, the daughter of *Daktari Shibeli*. Indeed, when he preached, he noticed her slender form sitting on the women's side, her eyes fastened on him.

Something about her captivated him. Not only was she beautiful, she appeared to have a humble, modest spirit that attracted him. Yet he was afraid of her status as the daughter of *Daktari*—raised in a white man's home—as well as her being of the Maasai tribe.

"Yes, I know," he admitted to his mentor and teacher. "I will marry when I finish here. And you, my friend, will be the one to officiate."

Luka smiled. "I will be honored. Don't delay."

Fritz noticed Rebeka's rapt attentiveness in church whenever Mpepo preached, and he smiled. He saw her in the churchyard one Sunday, her head down in modesty as she answered a question from Mpepo who towered over her in a protective gesture. Yes, this might just solve the riddle of what to do with Rebeka. Perhaps he would make an African-style agreement with this man.

Mpepo's uncle came to visit every week. He and Mpepo had long talks together. He, too, emphasized the urgency of marriage. He was growing old now; his shaking hands frightened Mpepo, but his mind remained sharp and focused on his mission to prepare his nephew for Huru leadership. One week he came, his aging face animated.

"I have found a cousin of yours, Mpepo," he exclaimed. "I did not know...no one knew Mkwawa had another descendant! His name is Siferi, and you must come home to meet him."

"How did you find him, Uncle? How is it that we never heard of him?"

"He has just returned from Germany. He went there to university, to study, before the war, and just now came home. Other people hid him when he was a child because they knew the German's would kill him. Then he was sent to Europe. It is a long story, and you should hear it yourself from his mouth. When can you come and meet him?"

The next Friday, with classes over at noon, Mpepo hitched a ride on a sisal lorry going south, then walked several miles through the bush to his family village, arriving just after dusk. The deepening shadows distorted the trees and bushes making them resemble wild animals. He finished his walk with a half-jog, singing hymns to warn off predators. Every week, news filtered through the villages of someone taken by a man-eating lion or gored by a rampaging rhino while merely walking from one village to another after dark.

He arrived at his uncle's hut just as the evening meal was served. The first thing he noticed was a new, larger hut beside the one in which he grew up. Mpepo's mother and two younger women sat off to one side eating their meal together while Uncle and another man sat by the fire deep in conversation. Mpepo came out of the shadows with a hearty *Hodi.*

Uncle sprang up with joy when he saw Mpepo. "*Karibu,* welcome," he said, extending his hand in greeting. "We almost gave up on your coming. How was your trip?"

"Fine, Uncle." Mpepo looked with question at the other man, who most assuredly was his cousin, but waited for an introduction.

"This is your cousin, Siferi, the son of your father's brother."

Siferi rose and shook Mpepo's hand. He stood several inches shorter that Mpepo. His broad face and forehead wore a look of intelligent cunning, but it was his eyes that drew Mpepo's gaze. Their intensity reached out and gripped his soul. This was not a man to treat lightly.

Mpepo's mother hurried over with *ugali,* the traditional cornmeal mush, and a sour milk drink, insisting he sit down and eat. He soon learned the two attractive young women were Siferi's wife and her sister, Longea and Mbili. They lived in the new hut he had noticed when he arrived. Mbili dropped her gaze and in a soft voice insisted they remember to call her Damari, "the name I have taken since being baptized."

As Mpepo ate his belated meal the men talked about inconsequential matters—school, Mpepo's impending graduation, and his trip to the village. "I can stay tonight and tomorrow," he said, "but I must return on Sunday for school on Monday."

The meal over, the women drew closer to the fire to listen to the men talk. Uncle threw a few sticks on the fire, sending sparks upward and the light glowed on their faces and glinted in their eyes. The moon rose, and an owl hooted from a nearby tree. Siferi began to tell his story.

"Our fathers were brothers, sons of the renowned Mkwawa. That makes us cousins, almost brothers. I have heard many stories of Mkwawa. He made our people strong and built a big city. His soul was large with care for the Wahuru. He built that great city for them and circled it with a high wall for their protection. I have heard how he wept when the Germans destroyed it because he would not bend his knee to them and pay them tribute. You were a small child then, were you not?"

Mpepo nodded. "An infant at my mother's breast."

"In the fighting, your father was killed. I am sure you know of this from your mother. Her brother took her and you into his own hut and cared for you as his own son."

Mpepo nodded his head again. This much he knew. He had heard his grandfather and the two sons who escaped with him were killed several years later; that is all he knew.

"Our grandfather ran to the mountains in the south with his two remaining sons. Everywhere they went, the people cared for them, even if they were not of their tribe. His fame had spread all across the land. But the Germans pursued him, and they sent out an edict that anyone found giving him food and shelter would be killed. So they crossed the Ruvuma River into Mozambique.

"They lived there for a time, and my father married a woman who had followed them across the river. The authorities sent them back across the Ruvuma and I was born in a small village on the banks of the river. My mother died a few days after I was born, and my father gave me to the chief of that area, where I was raised.

"Soon after, the Germans found Mkwawa and his two sons and executed them." Siferi fell silent as the group remembered the stories of their bodies hanging from a tree in a marketplace, and that the Germans would not let anyone take the bodies down for three days.

"I was raised by the chief of the Matumbe people." He gazed at Mpepo as if to see if he knew who they might be, but the name didn't register. "They are the ones who started the Maji Maji revolt."

Ah, now he knew why the name sounded familiar. Old memories of atrocities and fanaticism rushed back into Mpepo's mind. He glanced with renewed interest at Siferi.

"While the chief raised me as his son, he made sure to tell me often that I was the grandson of the great Mkwawa. He sent me to mission school with instructions to learn all I could about the European, and when I excelled in learning—as I hear you did also—an opportunity came to go to Germany to study at a university. I learned much—some of it silliness, but most of it useful. I now have a paper awarding me with a degree in anthropology! All paid for by the German government! At least something good came from them." He grinned, and threw another stick on the fire.

"I had much fun teasing my fellow students. They all wanted to study me, and I filled their heads with imaginary tales.

"Now my studies are over, the hated Germans are gone, and it is time to come home to Huruland. Do you not think so?"

Uncle rose to his feet and stretched. "An old man needs his rest," he said. "I will go to my bed." The women rose, too, and slipped away to their sleeping mats. Siferi and Mpepo remained alone beside the fire.

Mpepo thought of the events culminating in this momentous meeting with his kinsman. A feeling of excitement ran through his body. Here was a bond with his past, his ancestry. Here, beside the fire of his home, sat a man who was a cousin, nay a brother even more than cousin, since they shared such a great grandfather. Already, his mind raced ahead to the future. What the two of them might accomplish together for the Wahuru— why maybe the people would accept Siferi as chief, and with himself as a preacher, together they might do so much...he looked up and saw Siferi watching him, as though he could read his thoughts.

"There's something I need to tell you, Mpepo. It is funny, really. My true name is Lusiferi."

Mpepo jerked out of his fantasy and looked at him in astonishment.

"I know. You are shocked that I would have the same name as

*Shetani.* Just before I came into this world, my mother went to church. The speaker gave a fine sermon on the Devil, and while she didn't understand all he said, she thought the name Lusiferi had a wonderful sound to it. Do you wonder that I have changed it to Siferi?" He made a comical face toward Mpepo, and then laughed. "I assure you, I am not the devil!"

Mpepo shivered in apprehension. Siferi's eyes glowed in the light of the fire with the same intensity as before. He shook his feelings off. After all, the man couldn't be blamed for the unfortunate name given by an ignorant mother, could he?

"What I want to talk to you about, Mpepo," Siferi continued, "is your future and mine. Together we can return our people to their former stature. Your uncle has brought the men together and they are considering asking me to be their chief. If they do, I will accept, provided you give me your blessing. As the elder cousin, you should be their first choice. But your uncle has said you have refused.

"The last chief of our people died in the war, and the acting leader is weak and inept. With you by my side, as a spiritual leader instead of a soothsayer, we can bring the people into a new age. Will you at least think about this?"

Mpepo was already ahead of him in thinking of the future. He saw a great Christian nation that would lead other tribes into the way of righteousness. He reached out and grasped the hand of his cousin for a long, hearty shake, unwilling to let go. Siferi's smile widened. Truly, they were brothers.

"I know you are a preacher of the Gospel," Siferi said, "But would you share a small cup of *pombe* to celebrate our new-found brotherhood? It is the way of our people to seal a pact."

Mpepo hesitated, but thought one small cup would not hurt, so he accepted the strong drink. He had not tasted *pombe* for years, and had forgotten the smooth fire it brought to his veins. As the two men continued talking quietly around the dying fire, he had another cup, and then another without really thinking about it, until he began to feel dizzy and decided he should go to bed.

He fell into a deep sleep full of dreams of preaching to receptive people, the warmth of acceptance, and even felt physical stirrings in his dreams. He awoke with a start, aware of warmth against his back. A goat must have wandered into the hut and lain down against him. But when the warm thing lying there placed an arm across his waist, he jerked completely awake. Turning, he discovered Damari lying naked against his body, her flesh against his.

"What are you doing?" he exclaimed in a horrified voice.

She said nothing. She made no move to leave. Mpepo felt his growing desire as her warmth reached out and enveloped him. He almost…. "No!" he said. "Leave me. Leave me now!" He snatched the blanket off of her, leaving her naked and exposed; though in the dark he couldn't see her well. Without a word, she rose, snatched up a cloth, arranged it around herself, and left his hut.

The men continued their discussion the next day. Uncle seemed more animated than he'd been for several years. "You are both my sons," he said with tears rolling down his cheeks. "You are the sons I never had; you are the promise for an old man. In you two sons lies the future of our people." He placed his hands on their heads and gave them his blessing, his voice rising in a quiver as he chanted an ancient proverb.

*"Blessed is the man whose sons rise up and are strong. They will tame the lion and teach the leopard gentleness. Truly, the*

*man who has such sons will die in peace, and all generations will call him wise."*

Damari went about her work without a glance at Mpepo. No one acted as though anything untoward happened, though he couldn't imagine everyone not hearing him order her out of his bed the night before. He wondered if he should bring the subject up, but maybe it was just a bad dream brought about by the pombe he drank. He resolved not to drink again.

The men of the village gathered for a *shauri*, a business meeting, to talk with the cousins. Mpepo felt an exhilarating rush; he found his destiny, his life's work. Truly, God was good. A feast followed the shauri, with chicken, roast goat, and lots of ugali. Children ran everywhere, and boys shouted and kicked around a homemade ball. Damari brought him a small bowl of ugali and gave him a direct, personal look right into his eyes. Her boldness startled him. What he saw there was a challenge. He remembered her warmth the night before and felt his desire rise again.

He wondered. She had said she was recently baptized, and that meant she was a Christian. Why would she have come to his bed? It was a puzzle.

That night he placed a stick against the hanging mat that separated his sleeping area from his uncle's. If she came again, the stick would fall and wake him and he could prevent her from coming closer. He knew he would not be able to resist her if she came into his bed again.

Mpepo was both relieved and disappointed when the night passed and dawn came and Damari had not come near him. He had prayed to God, *lead me not into temptation,* and God had answered. Now he knew what Pastor Luka meant about temptation. He would give serious thought to marriage as soon as possible, though as a penniless student he had no bride price to pay for a good woman. Maybe he could ask his uncle when the time came.

After an early morning meal of cold, dried cassava root and curdled milk, Siferi offered to walk Mpepo out to the road to hitch a ride to Arusha. The two men walked along discussing their homeland, the soil that needed good fertilizer, how they would train honest men to organize the people and teach them sanitation and other means to healthy living, the clinics and schools they would sponsor, and how they would implement all these plans.

"You know," Siferi said when at last they rested under a mango tree by the side of the road, waiting for a lorry to come along, "We are truly blood brothers as well as cousins. Do we not also think alike?  What do you think about Mbili...I mean Damari?" He turned to Mpepo with a knowing look.

"She came to your bed did she not?" He laughed at Mpepo's discomfiture, poking him in the ribs. "She is a pretty girl. Now you must marry her, since you have shamed her by having her in your bed. What will the people think when they hear about that?"

Mpepo gasped. He had not thought about that. Even though he had not touched her, no one would believe him. He gave Siferi a helpless look.

"You could do worse, my brother. No, you could do no better. Since she is my wife's sister, your marriage would make you my brother-in-law as well as brother. We will be doubly brothers.

"And our sons will be brothers, too, as well as cousins." He turned to Mpepo, his face beaming with pleasure. "Was not this a fine idea of mine?"

Mpepo sat, stunned. Siferi had sent his sister-in-law to entice him to sin. He felt trapped, strangled. He groped for a way out, but Siferi countered it before he could speak.

"Since Mbili's parents have both died, and her sister is her only family, that makes me her protector and guardian. You have no bride price, and I ask none. I ask only for your friendship and help, and allegiance to me as your chief. That is a bride price you can pay, is it not?" He held his hand out to Mpepo in the European way.

Mpepo took it cautiously. "I give you my friendship, Siferi. I will gladly acknowledge you as my chief, and help you as long as I live. But I must think and pray about marriage to Damari… Mbili as you keep calling her…before I can promise anything."

Siferi frowned. "Don't think too long, my brother. Stories travel fast between the villages."

A roar from the road interrupted them as a lorry, loaded with sisal bound for the railhead, ground its gears and labored its way toward them. Mpepo stood and waved it down, and after an animated conversation with the driver, took his place with a few other men atop the load. He waved to his cousin who waved back, a smug look on his face, and each went his separate way for the next few weeks.

Mpepo's last weeks at school were occupied with studying for his final exams. At night he dreamed of his future. Damari was in some of them, and Rebeka in others. In one dream, he saw himself sitting by a fire, with Damari on one side and Rebeka on the other. He awoke with a sense of loss. Since he was a Christian, he could have only one wife. How simple his choice would be otherwise. He pushed the thought out of his mind. After all, God's way was best, and he would follow it. He would tell Siferi that the decision to marry would be his alone. He wished he still had a father to arrange it for him as custom demanded.

CHAPTER FIFTEEN

# Arusha, Tanganyika, 1920

**When Vito arrived in Arusha, he was pleasantly surprised to find a small, viable town** where the basic buildings were well constructed of native stone, the streets were swept daily, and mature vegetation lent a feeling of tropical opulence. The Germans had settled in for the past thirty years, and the English took over the government buildings, moved into the abandoned German homes, and occupied the military barracks previously used by von Lettow-Vorbeck's troops.

There was one German family still in town, he was told—the doctor and his wife. They were on a temporary stay of repatriation until Americans came to take his place. The hospital complex was a neat, whitewashed row of wards shaded by large, colorful bougainvilleas. Pink oleanders, yellow frangipanis, and red hibiscus added more color. A generator roared all day and into the night in a shed behind the operating theater.

Vito's District Court was situated at the end of the long government building. It had high ceilings and windows on the three exposed outside walls, the front windows opening out onto a covered porch that ran the length of the office building. Inside, a half-wall divided the dais for the magistrate and other officials from the benches where observers sat and the tables from which the cases were presented. Most of the furniture remained from the German occupation; the British took over their use and added their touch, one of which was a portrait of King George V on the wall above the dais where Vito would sit in judgment over proceedings. Over all of this hung a ceiling fan and a single bare light bulb that added a small amount of illumination run by the government generator during the day.

Vito's office was next to the court with an interior adjoining door. It was a small room with the door and window facing out onto the same covered porch, but without the cross ventilation, since behind his office was a storeroom containing moldy, ant-eaten files left over from the defeated enemy.

Already waiting for him in his office when he arrived was a small Indian man meant to be his secretary and court clerk.

"Rajneesh Patel," he said in a perfect English accent, offering his hand "Graduated from Cambridge," he added when he saw Vito's look of surprise. Later, after they became good friends, he said, "an underdog in the empire—like you."

Vito spent the first weeks getting acquainted with his job, Rajneesh, the town, and its occupants. He bunked for a while in the barracks with the soldiers, but longed for a place of his own.

About a mile out of town was a plot of land on a knoll overlooking the road to Moshi and dominated by Mount Meru, a dormant volcanic cone that stared down on the town of Arusha. The plot belonged to an old man and his many goats. When Vito offered him money for the property, he gave it up without argument.

"I have no sons to inherit the land from me," he said, delighted to get the new currency that was now good in the three countries of British East Africa. "I will give my flocks to my sons-in-law and spend my last days in idleness."

The British, in their takeover from the Germans, determined that individual citizens should own no land in fee simple except for those estates that were already settled in the Mount Kilimanjaro area by Europeans. All land used by individuals for residences or farmsteads would be leased from the government for a period of time: fifty years for residences, and ninety-nine for business organizations. Much of Vito's work consisted of recording these leases as they came in. No one was summarily dispossessed of the property that they held before. They were simply required to come to court, pay the fees, and obtain their right to occupy the land. Part of Vito's directive was to see that no native rights to land were appropriated by European interests. Vito made sure that Rajneesh handled the case, and he brought in the old Chagga goat herder to witness that he sold the lease freely.

Vito's presence in town was officially accepted, but in general the British settlers and businessmen treated him with transparent courtesy. As an Italian, with an accent that contrasted with the clipped English of the other white people in town, he occupied the fringes of European society. The coldness shown him thawed as word got around that he had won a Victoria Cross, England's highest decoration of honor.

He was invited, a bit too heartily, into The Club, a former German residence situated on a field that the British turned into a cricket field. Occasionally he went there to talk to the other men who gathered around their Scotch and soda or beer and told their tales of safaris. It was here that he learned the rumors and political goings-on of the town and government. He always felt as though the men looked askance at him; whether because of his ancestry or because he wouldn't join them in drinks, he didn't know—or care. They soon learned not to ask him of the event that led to his Victoria Cross award because he refused to talk about it. That was part of his first life; his second life was just beginning. He was happy with his new place and intended to settle down and remain here the rest of his life. People soon forgot about the VC hidden amongst his belongings in his room.

It was at the Club that he heard more about Kilimanjaro, the snow-and glacier-capped mountain that loomed over the town of Moshi to the east, surveyed and determined to be the highest mountain on the African continent, one of the highest free-standing mountains in the world. He leaned forward to hear more.

"No one's ever climbed the lower peak," one man said. "Too bloody straight up and down. But I heard even a woman has climbed Kibo—the other peak."

"Blimey! It's that easy?" someone else said. "Who was it?"

"Some German artist's wife. Frau von Ruckteschell, I think. Not too bloody long ago—six or seven years ago."

"I hear there's a regular path up to the saddle between the two peaks. But many people don't make it the whole way. When it monsoons down here, it blizzards up there."

"I'm going to climb it one of these days," Vito said.

"You, my man?"

"Yes. I grew up in the Alps and climbed them as a child. If there's a mountain, I must climb it. But first I have to strengthen my leg."

"I hear a team is gearing up to climb it soon, so we can have our own flag flying at the top. You going to join them?"

"No. I like to climb alone," Vito said.

The others laughed and changed the subject, but Vito kept his resolve. He began walking again to strengthen his leg. He made short climbs up the slopes of Mt. Meru, the fifteen-thousand-foot high mountain that towered over the town, eventually reaching the peak on his fourth try. He lay awake at night thinking of ways to put together proper gear fit for climbing Kilimanjaro.

The mountain began to loom in his dreams, both at night and by day. Kilimanjaro became a personal challenge, an affront to him. He couldn't get on with his life as long as it remained unconquered. In his dreams it sang to him. In his life there was that part he called *Before Kilimanjaro.* This was his Italian life, and the war years. Now his future life waited as *After Kilimanjaro.* He couldn't get on with a life of value until he conquered it, as if it were a rite of passage, a test of his manhood. By day he imagined placing one foot ahead of the other until he reached the top. It was a rock of stumbling, and each day it loomed higher and higher in his mind, blocking out the air and light.

As he gained the strength he needed for an assault on the mountain, he built his house. He gathered stones from the riverbeds and engaged men who knew how to mortar them together to make a straight wall. He sat up at night and drew plans by the light of a kerosene lantern. The plan was for a five-room house with a short hallway in the middle to give separate access to each room. On the left in front would be a sitting room with a fireplace for the cool evenings during the rainy season; on the right would be the dining room. The back rooms would be two sleeping rooms with a washroom in between. The kitchen would be separated from the house by a walkway through the washroom door. This would keep the cooking heat out of the house and reduce the chance of fire in the grass roof.

Across the front of the house ranged a long verandah, shaded by the same roof as the house, with a half-wall protecting it from any animals that might wander by. Thus, the sitting room and the dining room would have air and light without the heat of sunlight.

He decided on a thatched roof rather than the tin roof that most Europeans chose for several reasons. One was the heat that tin roofs transferred, making the interior a virtual oven during the hottest season. Grass thatch, being eight to ten inches thick, absorbed the heat and provided insulation from the rays of the sun. The second reason was that it hushed the sound of the rain. The deluges that poured from the sky turned a tin roof into a continual drum roll that drowned out all conversation and thought. Thatch softened this roar and turned it into a pleasant rustle that soothed the ear. His third reason was simply esthetic. He liked the look of a heavy thatch over a whitewashed or stone building. To him it looked more like a home. He hung muslin between the walls under the thatch as a ceiling, negating one of the two disadvantages of thatch—resident insects that might drop down for a visit. Now the muslin caught these creatures and delivered them back again to their homes in the roof. The other disadvantage, its short life span, was easily taken care of by regular re-thatching every three or four years as needed.

Vito made several visits to Dar es Salaam and Tanga to get basic furniture: a desk, a rocking chair similar to one his mother had in his childhood home, and several dressers and cabinets. He found it satisfying to construct his own tables and chairs.

Nine months after his arrival, Vito moved into his new home. He placed the rocking chair on his porch and stared at Mt. Meru. To the right, Kilimanjaro challenged him from its distance. Sometimes he played his accordion, and small children came from everywhere to listen.

The British divided the country into twelve districts and placed a District Commissioner over each one. Arusha District was large, and Cecil Neville occupied the position of Commissioner. He and Gertie lived in a superb new house built of stone near the Club and the government building. A strong friendship grew between them and Vito.

Vito also found a friend in Rajneesh Patel. Raj, as he came to be called, lived in a poorer section of town because he was Indian. On the outside, his home was run down, undifferentiated from all the neighbors' houses, with unwhitened plaster walls and unremarkable windows and doors. Inside, it was another world.

Rich Persian carpets covered the cement floors. Ornate carvings of Hindu gods hung on the walls. An arched doorway led to the bedroom off the central living room that also doubled as the eating room, and inside could be seen a massive bedstead covered with a cloth richly embroidered in many bright colors. Raj's wife, Mahandra, a beautiful woman with dark eyes and gold studs in her nostrils, owned many silver and gold implements laid out on top of immaculate dresser cloths. Their two children, ages one and three, exhibited impeccable manners. Vito soon learned, as his visits became more frequent, that this was their usual demeanor, not put on just for him, and he enjoyed the gracefulness of Mahandra's movements as she served tea and ethnic sweets while he and Raj discussed politics in general and colonialism in particular.

Vito soon discovered a new passion. One Sunday afternoon Cecil and Gertie came by for a short visit after church. An Anglican church was under construction, and in the meantime those who felt compelled to attend services visited the Lutheran Church. The temperature was high that day, one hundred degrees Fahrenheit in the shade, and the humidity was almost as high since it had rained several times in the previous week. Gertie collapsed in the rocking chair, unpinned and removed her hat, and fanned herself with it. Cecil sat on the top step while Vito served them cool glasses of lemonade made with water from the clay jar in his dining room. The evaporation through the unglazed clay kept the water cooler than the surrounding air.

"I'm going hunting on Wednesday. Clear your calendar and come with me," Cecil said as Vito joined him on the step. "Its time you had some fun. There's nothing like a young eland or kongoni to take the place of stringy Maasai cow we find in the marketplace."

"Me? Go hunting? Why, I haven't—"

"You've got a perfectly good rifle. I saw it in your gear. Go get it and let me see it." Vito rose and went into the house to get the the rifle he'd bought in London.

"I've never shot it or even sighted it in," he told Cecil as he placed it in his hands. Cecil opened the breech and peered through the barrel, making satisfied murmurs.

"Nice," he said. "Go down to the barracks and tell the officer in charge I said you could sight it in at the military range. You do know how to—"

"Of course. I hunted all the time in the Alps…" Vito checked himself. He didn't want to go down that story path again. Cecil looked at him and raised an eyebrow, though he said nothing. Vito added, "It's been a few years. I'd love to go hunting with you. Wednesday it is."

"Gertie's coming too, aren't you Gertie?" Cecil turned to his wife who answered without looking surprised.

"Of course I'm coming! I've always enjoyed hunting with you, Cece, and if Vito doesn't mind having a woman along—"

Surprised, Vito said. "Not at all." Few women enjoyed hunting. Sometimes a female visitor from England or America went out with her men folk and did some token hunting, but for the most part it was a masculine sport. Somehow, it didn't surprise him that Gertie, with all her other accomplishments, savored the sport as much as her husband.

This was the beginning of many hunting trips he took with the Nevilles. He enjoyed sitting around the campfire discussing the recent war, philosophy, and even religion. Sometimes he hunted alone with only his helper, Mordecai Manola, an Arab-Chagga man with many talents including that of cooking. Most of the time they returned with either an eland or kongoni, or several impala or Thompson's Gazelles. He kept a few choice pieces of meat and distributed the rest to the hospital and orphanage. Mordecai Manola tanned the hides for him, which he threw over his bed and divan. He made several porch chairs with zebra skin seat and back.

Often his hunting trips took him near Kilimanjaro, where he sat by his evening fire and watched the iridescent glacier on the top fade into the navy blue night sky, or loom like a ghost if the moon was bright. He would light his pipe and gaze at it as though listening to its challenge. He made mental lists of all he needed to gather to make the assault against it. He needed to discover its secrets, conquer it, and live and die in peace.

One thing that bothered him was the presence of the German doctor. He often saw Fritz along the roads in town, his heavy-browed face sweating in the heat, his stocky frame walking as fast as he could or riding his bicycle, always in a hurry. Vito kept out of his way as much as he could. He thought he had good reason—it had been Germans against whom he had fought, and if they had not started the war, Therese and his family would still be alive. He wondered how the British put up with his presence.

But in a small town Vito couldn't avoid meeting him.

It was at a cricket match between the British soldiers and the civilians that Vito was introduced to Fritz.

"Pleased to make your acquaintance," Vito murmured. "Ma'am, likewise." He bowed courteously over Ursula's hand. She felt better that day, well enough to accompany her husband to the match. What Vito didn't expect was Fritz's friendliness.

Fritz's gaze pierced into his mind. "I don't believe I've seen you in church, have I?"

Vito shook his head. "I don't go to church. I don't believe in God." It was more than he wanted to say.

"Oh, really? We should have a talk about that some day. I'd be interested in knowing why." Fritz stepped too close to him and began a running commentary on the town, its history, the war, and much more than Vito was prepared to hear from this man with such a thick German accent he could barely understand what he said. He couldn't find a polite way to edge away, so was relieved when someone called for the doctor to be a judge in the match.

Another meeting came soon after when Vito cut his hand while making a chair, a cut that became infected and he had to go see the doctor. Fritz hailed him as an old friend, looked at the hand, and directed the young African girl at his side to soak it in a permanganate solution, and then drench it with iodine.

"My daughter Rebeka will help disinfect it. I'm afraid you'll need a couple of stitches. I'll be back in a little while." He hurried off to his next patient.

"You are his daughter? How—"

Rebeka laughed. "My parents died in a smallpox epidemic, and I've been with the Scheibels since I was a baby."

Vito brimmed with questions but politely refrained from

asking them. The girl knew English better than her father, and she seemed familiar with how to take care of his hand. When her father returned with the sutures, she disappeared to another part of the hospital. Vito wanted to ask about her, but Fritz started right away with a lecture.

"So. You say you don't believe in God. Right?" Vito nodded, and Fritz continued. "The question should be turned around. Does God believe in *you*?"

Vito gaped. Fritz added, "Of course He believes in you, the same way I believe in ants. I know the damage they can do to a house, to my books and papers, and what the fire ants can do to a body. But do they believe in me? I put out poison for them, I burn the streams of army ants when they come close to my home, and I soak the timbers of my house in oil to prevent them from eating my home down around my ears. But do they believe in me? I doubt it. Man is too big, too complex, for the ant to understand. He's grateful when I leave crumbs for him, and angry when I thwart his purposes. But he doesn't believe in me."

"Then where was God when, because of our war with you Germans, deserters raged through my town and killed my wife and children—shot them in the back as they ran away unarmed? Tell me, where was God then?" Vito's eyes flashed.

Fritz's eyes widened and his mouth gaped. He reached out and grasped Vito's arm in sympathy. "I am sorry my friend. That my country would cause such a—"

"I'm sorry for mentioning it," Vito withdrew his arm. "It was impolite of me. You had nothing to do with it."

"I am not one of that kind of people," Fritz said. He placed gauze over the stitched wound and rolled a bandage over that. "I am a man of God first, a doctor second. That I am German also is an unfortunate—for now—circumstance of my birth. I recognize no national boundaries. We are all God's children."

"If there is a God," Vito said as he put his arm in his coat sleeve and stood. Fritz smiled, unfazed.

"We will talk of this again, my friend. Come back in one week."

Vito's hand healed well and he didn't return. He pulled the stitches out himself. He didn't like the German doctor, and he didn't want to talk again about God.

CHAPTER SIXTEEN

# The Snatching: November, 1920

**For a month there seemed to be more that the usual number of young Maasai warriors in town.** They loitered around the shops that catered to the Africans, fingering goods, but buying little. Twice, several of them showed up after clinic hours at the Scheibel's home with trivial wounds and vague symptoms of illness. Fritz, being good-hearted, treated them and asked about their people, wondering if there might soon be a breakthrough in communication with these reclusive people. Each time, they looked around the compound with interest.

So it should have come as no surprise when, awakened one night by a sound, Fritz saw two *murani* standing over him and Ursula with spears at their throats. In the grey darkness he saw others take Rebeka, gagged and bound, through the house. The two warriors gagged both him and Ursula, tied them to the bedposts, and stood guard over them for nearly an hour before slipping out as quietly as they came.

Fritz struggled against his bonds without success. There was nothing he could do but look at Ursula and watch her sob, her tears running into her gag. He tried to communicate with his eyes. "Pray, Ursula, pray," he tried to tell her. Slowly, her tears dried and a look of mother rage came into her eyes. They stared at each other and he could see new strength taking hold.

"That's the way, *Liebchen*," he muttered unintelligibly into his rag, nodding his head. She nodded back. He closed his eyes and lifted his head toward the ceiling, indicating to her that prayer was in order. He opened his eyes a bit and saw that she looked up too. They spent the remaining hours in prayer until dawn.

Anderea arrived at sunup and found the front door open, and then found the doctor and his wife bound and gagged. He cut their bonds, and Fritz tended to Ursula, exclaiming over the raw marks on her wrists.

"Forget me, Fritzie! I can take care of myself! Go and get the authorities! Find Rebeka!"

"Yes, of course. Forgive me, *Liebchen*. My mind is so rattled." He pulled on some clothes and rushed off on his bicycle to the military barracks on the outskirts of the town.

Fritz pedaled as fast as his stocky, sixty-year old frame would allow. He passed bewildered people who wondered why the *Daktari* disregarded their greetings but shouted, "The Maasai have taken my daughter! I must find help to get her back!" He hadn't pedaled so hard for years, and now as he approached the barracks, he could hardly catch his breath.

"Sorry," said Captain Worthington at the barracks building. "We can't do anything without a court order. It would be interfering in a tribal matter."

"But it's urgent! They can't have gone far! Please!"

"She's a Maasai girl, isn't she? So they've merely come and taken what's theirs. Sorry, chap, it's the way it is. You'll have to see the magistrate."

"But...but..." Fritz sputtered in frustration. "Where can I find the magistrate? Doesn't he stay here with you?"

"Not any more. He moved into his own house months ago. But I think he's on a hunting trip with the D.C. I'm sorry, old man. You'll have to get a permit before we go rushing off to raid some Maasai village to find a girl."

Fritz left the barracks, desolate. It was still early, and the town started to come alive. Early risers pushed wheelbarrows down the street with empty containers in them for water from the river. A small boy herded a flock of goats to pasture. The birds began to sing. Everything was normal for a new day, but no day could be normal any more for Fritz. His heart pounded from both lack of breath and turmoil. It felt broken. The orphan girl who came into his life and wormed her way into his heart was gone, and he couldn't bear to think of what might happen to her. He thought of her innocence and her sweet smile. Surely, someone could help.

*God,* he prayed. *Protect her. Be a father to her right now.* Was there nothing else he could do, but just pray? Then he remembered Mpepo.

He pedaled as fast as he could down a side street to the seminary where he found Mpepo headed to an early class with a book under his arm.

"Good morning, *Daktari.* How is your family today?"

"Mpepo, something terrible has happened."  He said this quickly, wishing to avoid the customary long greetings."

"What is the matter?"

"Rebeka's been taken by the Maasai! They came in the night and took her from her bed, and tied up my wife and me. I need to find help!"

Mpepo's eyes grew big. "Surely the soldiers can pursue them and take her back."

"I have to have a court order before the soldiers will go and rescue her. The magistrate and the District Commissioner are both out of town on a hunting trip. No one knows for sure where they are; the captain thinks they went for buffalo up near Ngorongoro. I need someone to find them and get a letter from them ordering the soldiers to help."

"I can do that! It's the least I can do for you, *Daktari*. I know what this girl means to you. Come; let's go clear it with the headmaster."

An hour later, Mpepo had a satchel of food and a written message from Fritz explaining the urgency of his request. He stopped at the District Commissioner's house and found out from Gertie where she thought Cecil and Vito went on their hunting trip. He set off at a run toward the north. Fritz watched him go, feeling both frustration and relief that someone was willing to help.

*Godspeed, Mpepo,* he whispered to himself. *Be safe. Find them soon. God, please protect my daughter.*

In a matter of minutes the news that the Maasai had kidnapped Rebeka traveled all over the town. As Fritz went home, people came and walked with him to show their solidarity and concern.

"We'll ask around," some said. "We will see if anyone has news where they went. If we can, we'll get a rescue group together." Kuyoni came and accompanied him to his door.

"I think she was taken by the old man who gave her to you," he said. "Ole Kipchong. I knew—and should have told you—that someday he would come to take her back. He will think she no longer belongs to you, now that she is of marriageable age.

"It is best that you go to the D.C. to get her back. If you go alone, there may be bloodshed. But if you decide to go, my friend, I'll go with you."

Not everyone felt sympathy for Fritz and Ursula. "Too bad," some Europeans said over breakfast. "But she belongs with her people. The doctor should have expected something like this. They should have never taken her into their home in the first place. This is what comes of confusing the place of the natives."

Many Africans felt the same way. Some thought it time for Rebeka to become acquainted with her tribe. They resented her Europeanization. Only those in the church and close friends understood the trauma that Fritz and Ursula felt.

**The Maasai warriors traveled for over an hour before they stopped and took the gag from Rebeka's mouth.** Until now she had been slung over the shoulder of one of the warriors. Now they put her down and untied her feet so she could walk. All she had on was a sleeveless night shift that came to her knees, and she felt naked. They kept her wrists tied together with a rope tied around her waist. They made rude comments about her, not knowing she understood their language.

"She's too fat to be a good Maasai woman," commented one.

"An uncircumcised cow," spat another. "She's a barbarian. Why do the elders want her instead of one of our girls? I could name a few who would be good for the chief!" The warriors laughed.

"They want this one to make children," said the first. "They say she's the last descendant of *The One True Lion*. Too bad she isn't a decent Maasai woman. Her husband will have to beat her to teach her her proper place."

"And what place is that?" Rebeka asked, her eyes blazing with anger.

"*Kumbe*," muttered one. "She hears us." They fell silent.

They traveled toward Kilimanjaro for several hours. Rebeka

was faint with hunger and thirst, but the warriors pressed on as though they had no needs. Whenever they came near people, they gagged her to keep her from crying out and surrounded her to keep her out of sight. When they came to a river, they allowed her to bend down and drink, an awkward position since her hands were still tied together and she had to put her face into the river. One of the warriors made a lewd comment about her shift that rode up in back when she bent over. She lifted her head and glared at him.

Toward sundown they came to a *boma*, a kraal with a number of huts where they would spend the night. Rebeka was untied. Children came up and stared at her. Someone brought her a calabash of clotted milk, which she devoured. She didn't care where it came from or how clean the calabash was. She would die anyway, without food, and perhaps death would be preferable to whatever life lay ahead. She shuddered, not wanting to think about it.

That night she slept in one of the *manyatta*s. She had never been in one before, and had to bend over to go through the entrance. Just past the entrance, a dividing wall separated the sleeping quarters on the left from the living area, where she was led.

The dark and heat surrounded her like a blanket pulled over her head. The smell was sickening—a miasma of sour milk, smoke, and unwashed bodies. As her eyes adjusted to the windowless gloom, she saw a pile of goatskins in the flickering light of the dying fire. The woman who owned the hut pointed to the pile and told her that was where she would sleep.

Rebeka lay down on the goatskins, thankful to get off her feet and get some rest. She started to drift off to sleep, then began to itch. Fleas—or maybe lice—bit her all over. Scratching seemed to do no good.

For the first time in her life Rebeka prayed a personal prayer. This wasn't one from the prayer book, or a memorized one taught by her parents.

"God, please help me. I want you to be my God, same as you are for my parents. You do want to be my God, don't you? I don't know if you really want me; if I'm good enough. Help me to trust you. Just help me, God. I can't stand this. Amen."

As soon as she prayed, a cool feeling came over her body, soothing the itching and the insects stopped biting her. She slept until the first sign of daylight shone through the smoke hole in the top of the hut.

The old woman came for Rebeka just after dawn. The *murani* were waiting for her, and without food to eat or water to wash in, they set off again across the plains. This time they left her hands unbound.

They traveled for several hours, stopped, and one of the warriors untied a gourd from around his waist and lifted it to Rebeka's trembling lips. The water was tepid and it smelled rotten, but she drank it down. When she asked for food, he laughed at her.

"Maasai people don't sit around and eat all day, like the Chagga and Europeans," he said. "Maasai people know that food is precious. We only need to eat once a day, at night. That is why we are strong and healthy, and not fat and lazy like other people."

By the end of the second day, Rebeka's feet were bleeding. She wasn't used to traveling without sandals. A few of the warriors had sandals; others traveled barefoot, but no one thought to give her footwear. She was exhausted when they came to a larger settlement with several *bomas* near each other, crowded with many huts.

Children flocked out to greet them and stare with curiosity at Rebeka. Two old women came, decked in coils of wire around their necks, upper arms, and ankles. Rebeka recognized them as the women who had tried, years earlier, to get her and Malia to come for the female initiation rites and circumcision ceremony.

They each took an elbow and led her toward an old man who stood off to one side. As they approached, the children stood back in respect. The women called him *husband* and spoke so fast that Rebeka could hardly keep up with what they said, only that it was something about him being her uncle.

His name was Mbae ole Kipchong, he said. He told her he had been at her birth many years before, that *Engai* had preserved him all these years to protect her destiny. He had given her, he said, to the white man because there was no one left to care for her. Everyone in the village, including his wives, had left to escape the pox, and her mother died at her birth.

"Now *Engai* has brought you back. He has spoken, and there will be rejoicing in the clan." He indicated to his wives to take her to their huts and care for her. "I will tell the elders, and the man whose wife she is to be, that she has come."

Trembling, Rebeka followed the two old women. *Oh God, oh God, oh God, help me,* she prayed.

The women weren't unkind. They sat her down on a goatskin outside the entrance to the hut and gave her curdled milk. That was the entire evening meal. Rebeka ate until she was full, the women nodding their pleasure at her appetite. She knew that some Maasai ate little more than milk, sometimes mixed with blood from their cattle, and once in a while goat or sheep meat, but little else. Kuyoni and his family ate like his Chagga wife— *ugali* from grain, and meat and vegetables from the garden she hoed behind their house.

When Rebeka was shown a place to sleep in the hut, she sank with gratitude on the pile of skins and fell asleep immediately. She didn't notice the smells and lice.

On the third day of her captivity, Rebeka woke with a sense of fullness and quiet. For a moment she thought she was home, but when a goat wandered over and stared at her face, she realized where she was, and a sense of desolation swept over her. She cried for her parents for a few minutes. *God, do you know where I am? Are you too far away to help?* She wiped her eyes in a sudden fit of anger. *I will be strong,* she resolved. *My father will come for me, I know. I refuse to grovel before anyone—not ole Kipchong, or his wives, or this chief he thinks I'm to marry.*

The compound was alive with voices and the sounds of animals being taken out of the kraal to pasture, so Rebeka straightened her dirty shift and joined the women sitting in the early morning sunshine. They seemed glad to see her and began an inspection of her body.

Rebeka normally wore her hair clipped close, as did most African women. But the two women seemed displeased with it, and while the older one, Nareyu, rubbed rancid grease into her hair, the younger one, Wambui, went into the hut and brought out a handleless knife.

"Ow," Rebeka yelled as Wambui began to shave her head with the knife blade, and she ducked away.

"No, no! You must be shaved! Only barbarian women allow their hair to grow." The older woman held her head while Wambui shaved until her head was as bald as an egg, and shone, she imagined, like theirs did in the sun. Her scalp hurt as though she had scraped it with thorns.

The women had her stand and they removed her shift. She

stood naked before the crowd of women that had gathered while they rubbed the fat all over her body, exclaiming over her full breasts, saying they would give good nourishment to her children and make her husband happy, and also making fun of her soft skin and the fat under it.

She quickly clapped her hands over her genital area when the women came toward it with the knife. "No! No!" she cried, thinking they were going to cut her.

The women laughed. "Just the hair," one said. "There must be no hair."

"Then I'll do it," Rebeka said, taking the knife from them.

The women cackled as they watched her. Modesty was non-existent. "The cutting will come in four days. Full moon, in four nights." Rebeka gaped in horror. "See her? And her? And her?" they pointed out three pubescent girls watching the proceedings. "They will have the cutting too. Oh, there will be much celebrating.

"After a month to heal, you will be married."

*Oh God, please help me,* Rebeka thought. Then she said in as firm a tone as she could muster, "No cutting. I will not be cut."

The women laughed as though she had told a joke. "No cutting, no marriage. And there is already a marriage. The dowry has been paid." It was as simple as that.

When Rebeka sat again, naked and sore from the crude shaving, the women brought a cloth to wrap around under her armpits, and a beaded belt for her waist. Most of the women wore skins, but they said she should wear cloth because she was to be the wife of the chief. While one of Ole's wives held her head, the other pierced the tops of her ears, and inserted a large beaded wire hoop, about six inches in diameter, into the hole. There was little blood, and that they wiped away with a handful of dried leaves.

Wambui brought a wide, beaded collar of multiple strands of sinew laced together and beaded with a zigzag design in red, yellow, and green seed beads. They tied it around her neck with a length of sinew.

"This is the sign of your betrothal. You will wear it until you go to your husband's hut. Then you will wear your spousal collar and hang this one on the wall of your *manyatta* to remind you of your family. This is your mother's family design. Only you may wear it, and only until you marry. Your daughters will wear it during their betrothals." The collar covered her from shoulder to shoulder.

The girls who had observed the whole procedure, cheered and laughed. "Now you are almost a Maasai woman," one of the girls scheduled for the cutting ceremony said. "I will be married, too, after the cutting," and she displayed her own betrothal collar with pride.

"This will be a great celebration," Wambui continued. "We have prepared for a month for your arrival. Your mother's relatives will arrive the day before to celebrate with us." She sat down beside Rebeka. "I know you don't know about Maasai ways. Let me explain it to you.

"Europeans don't know anything." She spat on the ground. "They don't know what it is to be a woman. If you don't have the cutting, your husband may become ill and die, or his thing will fall off. And if you have a child, it will be an imbecile. You will be unclean and no one will want to be near you. You will have many mysterious illnesses. The spirits of your mother and father and all your ancestors will come back and haunt you. You must have the cutting and become a real Maasai woman."

"You said a dowry has already been paid. To whom? My

father did not receive any dowry."

Wambui laughed. "No, that European doctor is not your father, and you know it. Your real father is dead. He died before you were born. But Mbae is the brother of your mother's father, and in Maasai custom, that makes him your guardian. He has received ten cows and six goats from the chief. That is a good price for a girl who knows nothing of being Maasai. And he will receive more cows when you have your first child. You are an important woman. Your father was a chief, and you are the last descendant of *The One True Lion*. It is necessary that you have Maasai children."

Rebeka felt terrified, but she also felt a tiny pinprick of pride in being a Maasai woman. If it wasn't for the cutting and a marriage to some unknown man looming in her near future, she could almost enjoy the feeling of belonging somewhere. The women and girls laughed and joked, passed around gourds of beer, and spent the hours doing their beadwork, shaving their bodies of any vagrant hair they could find, and gossiping until late afternoon brought the small boys and the cattle back to the kraal. Then it was time to get up, get the gourds, and milk the cows before the calves got to them. Rebeka was introduced to milking, to great laughter at her ignorance as she tried in vain to squirt the milk with one hand into the narrow neck of the gourd she held in her other hand.

"Tomorrow," whispered Wambui, "you will meet chief Kulale ole Meoli, the man you are to marry, and his wives will teach you to build a *manyatta*—your own *manyatta*."

CHAPTER SEVENTEEN

# A *Manyatta* of her Own

**In the morning the women led Rebeka to a kraal close by, a large cluster of huts set apart from the rest**. Three women, one of them not much older than Rebeka and with a baby on her hip, came out and exchanged formal greetings. Several small children stared.

"This is Rebeka, the one who is to be your new sister," Wambui said.

"Welcome to your new home." They curtseyed to her. "We are happy to have you here. We have prepared a spot for your *manyatta*." They led her over to a spot beside the others where the ground was swept clean.

Two men approached. The younger woman whispered, "the tall one is our husband, Kulale ole Meoli. The other is Nakola, the *laibon*, the healer." All the women curtseyed and averted their gaze in deference as the men came near.

"*Engai* bring you peace," said the chief.

"And to you also," the women murmured.

"How are the children today?"

"Everyone is fine, thank you, husband."

"And you?"

"We are fine also."

"Good." He looked with interest at Rebeka. "And who is this who has come to visit?"

"This is Rebeka, the one who is betrothed to you, husband."

The women stood aside so Rebeka could curtsey and murmur her own greetings, which she did looking at the ground. Her stomach churned as she thought about marriage to this man. *He must be as old as my father,* she thought. She barely controlled a shudder. Had God heard her prayer? Would he send someone to rescue her, or would he abandon her to her fate? *Please, God. I haven't asked you for much. Please don't make me endure this.*

After exchanging a few pleasantries, the chief nodded his satisfaction and left with his medicine man, who had spent the whole time staring at Rebeka as though reading her thoughts. They held a low, but animated discussion as they walked away. Rebeka felt as though she had been considered and found wanting.

The young wife, whose name was Sialo, clapped her hands in glee. "Now we build your hut!" she handed her baby to one of the older women. "First we get sticks you need."

"I…I…don't know anything about building a hut," Rebeka said.

"I know. They told us all about you. You've been living with Europeans all your life, and don't know anything about being a Maasai woman. We'll teach you." She smiled and ducked into her own hut and emerged with a long knife in her hand.

The two young women exited the kraal through the space between the thorn bushes that the *murani* had opened for the cattle. They walked over to a thicket of trees in the distance. The heat was beginning to intensify. Sialo chattered about inconsequential things, and Rebeka barely heard her. Sialo pointed to a young tree and said, "There. That one has the best branches.

"First, you pick a sturdy branch about as long as a *murani*'s spear. Then you trim off all the side branches, like this," and she began to whack until a six-foot long branch was left denuded of its foliage. "You try it now."

Rebeka grabbed the panga and hit at a branch with little effect. She whacked at it several times, and only succeeded in fraying and weakening it until it hung down, limp. Her new friend began to laugh.

"You have to hold it this way…" she demonstrated a firm hold on both the branch and the knife "…and make swift, sharp slices." Rebeka finally got the idea, and before long they had a pile of sticks on the ground.

"That's enough for now. We'll take these back, and I'll show you how to get started after I feed my baby. This afternoon, after the heat has passed, we'll come out and get some more. But first, let's sit here and talk."

Sialo kept a firm hold of the knife. "Just in case a lion comes along." She laughed. "But if one does, we'll scream and the *murani* will come and rescue us. It is considered manly to kill a lion." They relaxed in the shade of the trees. Insects buzzed, and it was so quiet they could hear the faint rustle of a breeze in the dry grass. Rebeka looked out over the plain and wondered if she could run away. Which way was Arusha?

Sialo noticed her glance. "If you try to run to Arusha, the lions will get you. It's two days walking if you know the way, and where would you stay at night?"

With a sinking heart, Rebeka had to acknowledge the truth of what Sialo said.

"Do you think you will like our husband?" Sialo asked after a few moments.

Surprised by the question, Rebeka answered, "I…I don't know. I really didn't want to be here."

Her new friend laughed again. "Why? You are a lucky woman

to be chosen by our husband. He is a powerful and rich man. You have received great favor to be chosen as his wife. Do you know who you are, who your mother and father were?" She turned and looked at Rebeka.

"Not until Wambui told me a little. All I knew was that I was born at the time of the smallpox, and my mother died three days after I was born."

"You are the last descendant of *The One True Lion*. Your father was Njao, a good chief and the last of the lineage, until you were born. That's why Mbae ole Kipchong gave you to the white man to keep alive until now."

"What does that mean, I'm a descendant of *The One True Lion*? Lions have lion babies. Only people can have people children."

"You mean no one has told you?" Her new friend brightened. "Then I can tell you! I have heard the story since I was small.

"A long, long time ago there lived a strong Maasai chief who had great magical power. He had eyes like a lion's, and he could roar like one, too. They said his father was a great lion that killed many warriors before he died of old age. No one was able to kill him. His son brought all the clans together, and they traveled to the north to live in peace out of the path of the Arabs who came to take slaves. He fought them and chased them back to the sea, and after that the Arabs avoided the plains where our people lived.

"He came to be known as *The One True Lion*. It was predicted by the *oloiboni*, the seers who were Mbae Ole Kipchong's ancestors, that whenever an enemy threatens the Maasai people, a child of *the One True Lion* will appear again and lead his people out of danger. And we will know this man by his eyes, which will be the eyes of a lion.

"Since you are the only living descendant of *the One True Lion*, you could bear the one promised. The seers have prophesied that he will soon come, and they have chosen our husband, as the strongest man, to father this promised child and protect him until he is grown and able to pull the people together. The white man pushes us on all sides and tries to keep us from practicing our traditions. We need this leader to protect us and chase the white man away. And you are to be his mother. You are special. *Engai* smiles on you."

A sudden chill ran down Rebeka's spine as she heard this story. Everything that had happened to her in her short life now made sense. The day the *murani* tried to take her away when she was seven. Again, when Ole's wives came and tried to convince her and Malia to run away and be circumcised. She remembered her father saying how puzzled he was that they would pay so much attention to her. They had such little regard for women that she could hardly matter. Rebeka began to cry.

"I don't want to be special; I want to go home."
Sialo looked puzzled. "It is decreed," she said. "There is nothing you can do. It is a great honor to be so chosen."

Loaded with the sticks, they returned to the kraal. The young wife grabbed her baby and he nursed with a surprising fierceness. In spite of herself, Rebeka smiled. He was a cute little thing, and as he suckled he stared at Rebeka with a fixed gaze.

The oldest woman, Nyakeru, now took charge. She appeared beyond childbearing age. No small children clung to her as to the other women, and her breasts hung down to her waist like empty bags. Her lined face showed the years she had spent fighting for survival, her eyes bloodshot from too much exposure to smoke.

With a quiet firmness, she took over the building process. Rebeka couldn't see how the pile of sticks would form a hut.

Nyakeru began to dig shallow holes with a stick spaced about six inches apart indicating to Rebeka that she should do the same, all around the perimeter of the swept area in an oval shape, about six feet by eight feet. It was hard, tiring work, but the woman kept working so fast that soon all the holes were dug.

She then placed the heavy end of a branch in each hole, covered it with dirt, and tamped it down. Rebeka joined in until branches stuck up out of every hole, the narrow ends wobbling in the air.

"Now we tie the ends together," the old woman said, grabbing opposite ends of the sticks and twisting grass over them to keep them together. They went down the inside, tying opposite branches on the longer sides of the oval together, until they were all tied, making a bower about four feet high. The rest of the sticks were tied horizontally to these until a loosely woven cage-like structure appeared, leaving an opening in the front facing the yard between the huts. Several branches were set and tied around the entrance, framing it with a sort of entryway.

It was now late afternoon and the shadows lengthened. Rebeka's hands were scratched and bleeding and she was thirsty and exhausted. But she and Sialo went back again to the thicket, this time to cut smaller branches to weave in to fill the framework.

It was dark when the frame of the hut was finished. The wives inspected it with frowns on their faces, clucking over open spaces that still gaped. It was her first hut, and Rebeka felt proud of herself, though she still denied to herself that she was to live in it. They shook their heads, and without consulting her, decided that more branches would be needed the next day to fill in the spaces.

Morning came too soon. Rebeka's hands throbbed, and she groaned when she thought about cutting more branches for the framework. But this day it went easier. Before long she had enough to fill in the gaps, and soon the wives were nodding their heads in agreement. It was time to fill in the framework with clay.

There was no clay, and no water to mix with the dust to make mud. The three women led her into the outer yard where the cattle had spent the night and began to scrape up the fresh dung with their hands.

"Gather the soft dung," they instructed Rebeka. She hated putting her bare hands into it. She shuddered, but followed their instruction. They made a large pile of the soft dung.

They began to mix dirt with the dung, mixing it with their fingers into a dough-like mass. Once Rebeka got used to the smell, it wasn't too bad.  The women showed her how to take handfuls and apply them to the basket structure, smoothing it into the branches. They were so swift, that they covered a large area with the mixture of cow dung and dirt before she had barely started. The part they did was smooth. The part Rebeka did was ridged and uneven, and they had to go over it to smooth it out. They went out and gathered more dung from Mbae Kipchong's kraal, and by the end of the day the outside was all covered.

"Tomorrow we finish the inside," one said. "When you get up in the morning, bring a pile of dung from your kraal. That will save time." Rebeka rubbed her hands together to get rid of the drying mixture that clung to them. There was no water to wash in. When the cattle came back for the night, the women milked them with their dirty hands and offered it to Rebeka for her evening meal. It was that or nothing, and she was faint with hunger, so she drank it down.

The next day, Rebeka crawled inside her stifling, smelly hut, and plastered the walls in the near dark. The only light came through the low doorway and the smoke hole at the top of the roof. She did this job alone since it appeared the other women thought she knew how to complete the work.

It was the sixth day since her capture and the third in the village. Surely, someone should have come to rescue her by now. They were only a two-day journey from Arusha. Had she been abandoned? Would anyone care enough to come for her? She watered her plaster with her tears.

She also knew, now that the hut was built, that the cutting ceremony drew closer and closer. Would it be tomorrow, or the next day, or the day after? The moon was larger every night. Would she be strong enough to fight the women off?

The next morning, Rebeka crept out at dawn. The snow-capped mountain above her loomed out of the dark, catching the first rays of the sun as it rose into the hard, blue sky. She would have liked to sleep longer, but anxiety and apprehension came crashing in. She wanted to die. The rest of her life stretched out ahead of her, a bleak existence for sure. How would she cope? She should have stabbed herself with the knife yesterday.

Wambui greeted her again. "Today the relatives come," she said. "We get ready for the celebration tonight. Come and eat, and then we gather leaves and herbs for your healing, and pick the finest skins for your new home." Rebeka's heart sank. That meant tomorrow was the fateful day.

The three women wandered out over the plain surrounding the Maasai settlement. Wambui and Nareyu pointed out the various bushes and trees whose leaves were used for various ailments. One was for excessive bleeding. These leaves they picked and placed in leather pouches. Another induced strength and bravery, "for the warriors," they said, and laughed, "so they won't be afraid of lions." Another made one sleepy, and they placed some of these in the pouch also. They gathered armfuls of leaves from the tree where Rebeka and Sialo had harvested branches for her *manyatta*. These leaves gave off a sweet smell. "For your bed," the women said.

The sun was a quarter of the way across the sky when they returned to the kraal where a crowd of women began to gather. Songs and laughter greeted them, and strange women came over to see Rebeka, exclaiming over the fat under her skin, her soft hands unused to work, and other deficiencies. But yes, they all said, she looked beautiful in her mother's betrothal collar. They brought gifts of beaded jewelry: earrings, long strands of beads, a beaded belt, bracelets, coils of wire for her matrimonial collar, and other assorted gifts including soft goatskins and calf leather. They stood around until late afternoon, drinking beer and milk, and "eating the news," as they called gossiping. At dark, the festivities began.

A fire in the center of the *boma* crackled as they ate their evening meal. Soon the women of neighboring *bomas* came in, appearing out of the gloom like wraiths. The girls tied bells to their thighs. The warriors came, several at a time, ill at ease at first, but they soon relaxed and the whites of their eyes and their teeth flashed in the firelight as they drank the beer offered them.

When a dozen of the warriors were present, they began chanting and leaping up and down, a dance to see who could spring the highest. The girls sang as they watched, then began to join in with them, their collars flapping up and down as they jumped, the bells on their thighs jingling. Some of them moved their hips seductively as they danced.

One of the women, she couldn't tell who, nudged her to join in. When she resisted, all the older women laughed and pushed her into the ring. She tried to join in, but got tired and couldn't keep time with the rhythm. This only made the women laugh harder. "Dance! Dance!" they shouted. "This is the last dance of your girlhood!"

One of the warriors who had abducted her came over and smiled at her. He took her hand and showed her how to jump in time to the singing and chanting. For a moment or two, Rebeka let herself go. She could really enjoy this, she thought. Mama and Papa frowned on dancing, but this was fun. And if she could learn to be Maasai, she could even enjoy…she gasped at the thought of marrying the *muran* who stood before her. He was young, like her, and attractive, his muscles rippling under his brown velvet skin. But she was to marry an old man, a sedate, wrinkled old man who probably never smiled, and who already had three wives. And she had to be cut first. She lost her momentum and energy and collapsed onto the ground. The warrior smiled, turned, and went back to dance with another girl.

The celebration continued on into the night. Rebeka tried to hide the fear she felt clutching at her throat; a deep sob seemed to be stuck there like a wad of food. *Papa, Papa,* she thought. *Where are you? Don't you care about me? Please, God, do something. Don't turn your back on me.*

Morning burst in again, and no one came to rescue Rebeka. When she woke at dawn, she felt so dispirited that she didn't care any more what happened. Wambui greeted her again with a joyful greeting. "This is the greatest day of your life! The day you become a woman!

"Here. I have prepared a drink for you," she said. Surprised,

Rebeka looked over. A fragrant tea steamed in a calabash. What was this for? No one here made tea in the mornings. If anything was eaten, it was cold curdled milk or a bit of fresh milk from a cow before it went to the fields. Everyone scrounged for himself. She sniffed the tea.

"Drink it," smiled the woman. "It's for you. You are going to be a good Maasai woman."

Rebeka tasted it gingerly. It wasn't bad at all, a bit mint-like. Was it a reward? A peace offering of sorts? She drank it down, not noticing until afterward that no one else drank the tea, though they all stood around wrapped in their cloths and skins to keep the morning chill away. A relaxing warmth washed over her, and she leaned back against the side of the *manyatta* in the sun.

"That's good," the woman said, still smiling. "It will help you in the cutting. When the other girls are ready, we will have the ceremony. All the women will come to sing for you. It will help you be brave. We do it in the entrance to Nareyu's hut, since she is the eldest and closest to your mother."

The cutting. It was today, and the sedative tea meant she couldn't resist them. Rebeka tried to fight off the effects, and the women just laughed. She felt torn between two emotions, like two opposing storms unleashing their power on her body. She felt terror, fear, horror at the brutality of the cutting that would soon occur. Yet she felt sleepy, relaxed, calm. Maybe it didn't really matter. After all, every Maasai woman experienced this. They didn't seem to mind it. Perhaps it was of little consequence after all. She only wanted to sleep in the sun for now.

Rebeka's mind came alert when she heard one of the other girls cry out from one of the other *manyatta*s as the women sang around her. They would come for her soon. Wambui stroked her forehead as though she were a small child. The women came close, their shrill voices and laughter followed by their scrutiny of her.

"No!" she yelled, but they laughed at her discomfiture as they gathered around her.

"It is allowed, to scream," Wambui murmured in her ear as the others began to sing.

She pressed against Rebeka's shoulder to force her into a reclining position. She felt two women take hold of her legs. The women came closer, their friendly smiles turning to evil grins in her imagination. The terror that lurked near seized her, leapt into her in all its strength, possessed, and overcame her. The woman from the neighboring village who performed the ceremonial cutting came into view with her small knife. As Rebeka screamed with all her being, the screams piling up in layers, as it were, to the very gates of heaven. A roaring filled her ears, the edges of her vision grew dark, and she fainted.

CHAPTER EIGHTEEN

# Maasailand, 1921

**Hunting elephants is not a sport for the fainthearted, Vito decided.** After he and Cecil chased a rogue female for several days through the bush near the Ngorongoro Crater, he decided it wasn't a sport for him, either.

They had gone for buffalo. Each wanted a mounted head to preside over their dining room tables. The new government issued yearly permits for meat animals, providing the subsistence needs for most residents, with a lifetime limit on big game such as buffalo and elephant.

"Let's take our elephant guns, just in case," Cecil had said. "You never know if we might need them."

They set off in an army truck with six men—four to carry supplies, and two as gun handlers. Gertie didn't go along this time since she was recovering from a malarial attack.

They camped on the rim of the vast crater. The sunken area below them teemed with game of every description. It was here that Mpepo found them and informed them of Rebeka's kidnapping.

"Perfectly understandable, the tribe wanting her back," Cecil said. "But not that way. I'll vote for bringing her home and letting them address your court with their complaint."

"How did she get to be in Doctor Scheibel's household in the first place?" Vito asked, as he wrote out the order for her rescue.

Cecil shrugged. "I only heard through the gossip circuit. I never asked Fritz directly. Seems her mother died during that last bad smallpox epidemic, and Fritz happened to stop by looking for villagers to inoculate, just in time to save her life. So he took her in. I guess the tribe didn't know enough to protest the legal adoption a few years later."

"That could put a cloud on its legality." Vito pursed his lips. "Even if the Germans didn't think it important. I would have to take it into consideration if they come to court." He handed the note to Mpepo who, having eaten and refilled his water skin, took off at a trot toward Arusha.

The next day, three men came from a nearby village to tell of the rampaging, one-tusked elephant that killed a woman hoeing in her cornfield. It picked her up in its trunk and repeatedly threw her to the ground. It rooted up all the cornstalks in her garden and several adjacent ones, sending the women screaming to the village. When the men approached with arrows and spears, it attacked them, goring one of them through the thigh before running off. Several arrows dangled from its thick hide and blood flowed from two spear-holes.

Since no armed *askaris* were stationed nearby to chase and kill the wounded animal, Vito and Cecil decided to postpone their buffalo hunt and go after the wounded elephant before it did further damage. As government employees they could do this without the kill going on their permanent hunting list.

They followed the track of the elephant across the plains in the truck before having to abandon it when they came to a range of low, treed hills. As the elephant traveled it tore up gardens, stomped on huts, broke down barricades, and terrorized the villagers who, without guns, couldn't bring it down. By now they knew it was a female with a tusk broken off at the root causing a mighty toothache. At one point she joined with two other elephants and they ran amok through the forest tearing up trees and throwing them about.

After three days of trailing them Cecil and Vito finally caught up with them during a rare, peaceful feeding time. Cecil took the first shot—hitting her broadside—but he missed the heart.

The elephant turned, screamed, and ran at them, her ears flapping and her tail held straight out in anger. Vito put the next two shots into her chest as she raced toward them. She fell like a falling wall, sending up clouds of dust, and turned to her side. She lay still, breathing heavily, her small, bloodshot eyes filled with pain, as though knowing—just knowing—she had met her end. He reloaded and shot her directly between the eyes.

The other elephants came back and stood over her. They made soft mewling noises that sounded like weeping, as they stroked her body with their trunks. At one point, they placed their trunks under the dead elephant's abdomen and tried to help her to her feet. Whenever the men tried to approach, they turned on them, flapped their ears, lifted their trunks, and trumpeted.

There was nothing to be done except to crouch in the bushes, wait, and endure the insects drawn by their sweat. It seemed like hours as the dead elephant's companions tried to revive her. Toward sunset one elephant wandered over to the edge of the forest and waited, its back turned to the other. That one soon left the side of their dead friend and followed. Without sound they disappeared from view.

The two men avoided each other's eyes as they directed the Africans to start butchering the elephant. One man was sent to the nearest village to fetch the villagers to help, and long after sunset they worked under the light of several kerosene lanterns and the moon. When the job was done, they camped about a half-mile away to allow the hyenas and jackals room to clean up the remaining scraps. Within twenty-four hours, nothing but bleaching bones would be left of the magnificent animal.

They would forfeit the ivory to the government. "Probably end up in the Governor's home," grumbled Cecil as they settled into their camp. "But that's the law. By rights, I think, you should get it, Vito. You're the one who killed the elephant."

Vito shrugged. "I don't think I would want to see it sitting around my house. I don't think I'll ever forget the expression in her eyes as she died. Nor, I might add, the sight of her companions trying to help her." He pulled the blanket up to his chin and turned on his side. "My God, Cecil, they mourned over her just as a person would over a friend!"

The two men stared at the moon for a long time thinking about that. Cecil turned toward the fire and said, "Tomorrow we'll get our buffalo and go home."

**Three full days of heartache and frustration passed before Mpepo returned,** his clothing dirty and his body caked with sweat and dust, with an order signed by both Vito and Cecil. He handed the letter to Fritz with a smile of triumph.

"Success, *Daktari!*" Mpepo said, panting.

Fritz knew he had run for most of the three days. He envied the young man his youth and the strength in his limbs that enabled him to sustain that kind of endurance run. "Thank you, God," he breathed after opening the note and reading it.

*Go at once with a search party and bring back the daughter of Doctor Scheibel. Tell the Maasai people that if they have a problem they should use proper legal channels to solve it. The Crown is here to protect their interests in a fair manner. But evidence suggests that this girl is the legally adopted daughter of the Scheibel's, and until she reaches her majority or we decide otherwise, they have the control over her.*

"Go to the kitchen and eat, Mpepo. I owe you so much more than food. I'll take this to the Captain at the barracks. I'm going with them to get Rebeka."

"I will go, too. She is a friend, and I wish to see her safe. Will you ask if I can go?"

"You have your exams to take, Mpepo. You've studied too long to miss them. I can't let you do that for me."

"I will ask the headmaster. Maybe he will let me postpone them a few days. People are more important, *Daktari*. You have taught me that by your example."

"All right. But only if the headmaster agrees to postpone your exams. And you need rest, too. If the Captain wants to start tonight, we won't wait."

"I can be ready any time."

Mpepo went to eat, and Fritz left for the barracks.

Captain Worthington read the letter, folded it, and put it in his pocket. "We'll start out at first light. I'll round up four or five *askaris* to take with me. You want to go, too? Fine. Just promise you won't do anything foolish. Be here at five-thirty."

"Please, could you take British soldiers instead of *askaris*?"

The Captain frowned. "Why do you ask that? This isn't an insurrection."

"The Maasai will think the *askaris* are men of another tribe meddling in their affairs, Sir. They will be more inclined to ignore them. If you send white soldiers, they'll show more respect. Please, Sir. It is a serious thing that they plan to do to my daughter. It's much more than bringing her back into the tribe."

"Tell me, then." The Captain walked down the street with

Fritz, listening to him recount the story of the newborn baby he rescued, how he had kept Rebeka from being kidnapped when she was seven, and the custom of female circumcision just before marriage. The Captain had only been in Africa several months and had not heard of the female circumcision rite.

"Blimey! They do that to girls? How bloody awful." He stopped, realizing the dreadful pun he had just spoken. "Of course, Doctor. We'll use whites to rescue her. Wish I had known this before; maybe I would have gone ahead without the bloody note."

"May we take Kuyoni and Mpepo along too? Kuyoni was with me when I rescued Rebeka as a baby; he is Maasai and can translate. Mpepo has asked to come, I think he and Rebeka..." Fritz trailed off his sentence.

The Captain smiled. "Ah, I see," he said. "A young man with an interest in the girl. Of course. There'll be room in the troop truck."

Before six the next morning, the canvas-covered truck roared out of the barracks compound and down the road toward Moshi. Fritz and Kuyoni sat in front with the Captain.

Mpepo sat with the four British soldiers in back. The soldiers had only a rudimentary knowledge of Swahili, so conversation with them was useless. He sat watching the road and dust fall away behind them. When Fritz glanced back and saw him deep in thought, he wondered what was going through the man's mind. He wondered if this fine young man, a brilliant orator with a sharp mind, would be his son-in-law. *Yes, that would be good*, he thought. *A perfect solution. If they rescued Rebeka in time.*

Once they passed Mt. Meru and had traveled about halfway to Moshi, the truck swerved off the road onto a dirt track that led out over the plain to the west of Kilimanjaro. It was this track, not even a wagon trail back in 1905, that Fritz and Kuyoni followed when they set out on the smallpox vaccination program that brought Rebeka into Fritz's life. Nothing remained any more of el Engerot. The kraals were overgrown with small trees and the mud-and-dung *manyattas* had long been absorbed back into the earth, dissolved by the years of rain. They stopped at noon by a small river to eat and talk. The quiet pressed against their ears. Only the occasional buzz of a fly or the call of a guinea fowl disturbed the stillness.

"No Maasai villages around here," Captain Worthington said. "I asked last night in town, and rumor has it that most of them have gone north toward the Kenya border. They travel back and forth all the time. We'll have to hope they haven't crossed over into Kenya. If they have, we'll have to get permission to continue from the Kenya Patrol."

"There must be a few villages around here," Fritz said. "I see them in the hospital once in a while. The grass is green, and some may be herding their cows out here. Just last week I put stitches into a young *muran*'s arm."

"We'll go until nightfall. If we see anyone, we'll ask if they know where the villages are. If we don't run into anyone today, we'll go on tomorrow. We should hit the border by noon tomorrow, if we don't run into them before then," the captain said.

It was obvious to Fritz that the British only tolerated him. He could respect that. He tried to show them kindness whenever he could, and some of them came to respect him in return. He knew they wouldn't have to put up with him much longer. Dr. Johansen had been with him for ten months now and was ready to take over. Back on his desk was an order from the government that he hadn't shown yet to Ursula—it only came the day before—

telling them they had six weeks to leave the country and return to Germany. Six weeks to settle the matter of Rebeka—if they could find her. He hadn't shown it to Ursula, not with the tears of this fresh pain on her face. She mourned more for Rebeka than she ever did for her own babies.

The truck labored on in first or second gear as they made their own track across the grasslands, narrowly avoiding holes in the ground where anteaters had demolished termite hills and dug out the underground nests. Wild game ran away on each side of the truck. The soldiers joked about hunting on their trip back. Fritz could barely take the rocking back and forth of the cab. His back felt like a highway for elephants. A headache began between his eyes from the heat and bright sun.

About four o'clock, Kuyoni spotted a herd of cattle in the distance. Three *murani* guarded over them, tall and thin, standing like storks on one leg and leaning on their spears. The Captain twisted the wheel and drove over toward them. He and Kuyoni got out. The others watched from the truck, quiet.

The Captain sauntered over to the young men with Kuyoni at his side, as though he had nothing more to do than pass the time of day in trivia. He greeted them in a friendly manner in Swahili, and Fritz could see the young men, wary at first, relax and respond. The greetings continued for a while, then the Captain showed interest in their cattle and asked them questions about them. The *murani* seemed eager to recount the good features of their cows, pointing out their favorites and calling them by name. Ten minutes went by as the men talked.

Then the mood turned serious. "We are looking for a young girl who was taken against her will from a house in Arusha." The *murani* looked at each other and then at the ground. "The government takes this seriously. It is against British law." Kuyoni translated this into Maasai so they would have no problem understanding.

"Anyone who commits such a crime, or withholds knowledge about it will go to jail," the Captain added in amiable fashion. Rather than ask them directly if they had knowledge, or might have taken part in the raid, he said, "Maybe you can tell me where I can go to ask about such men who took this girl? Or maybe you know someone who could tell us where they might have taken her?"

The young men chattered among themselves. The Captain and Kuyoni pretended not to be listening. Finally, one of the warriors spoke up.

"We saw some men four days ago going north toward Kenya. They had a girl with them. There's a village about one finger of time from here; they might have gone there." He shrugged. "We don't know for sure."

"I think they do know," Kuyoni said when he and the Captain got back in the truck and it roared to life. "They are all of one clan, and they are related to each other. I think they know who the men were, their names, and where they went. The village they spoke of is probably their own village."

This was true, for when a short time later they came to a cluster of kraals, the village children who burst out to greet them told them that their herders were in the direction they had just come. The Captain used the same manner of questioning them, and after giving the mild threat of jail time to anyone withholding information, a woman stepped forward and said that yes, a young girl had been brought to her, and she had slept in her hut. She pointed further north.

"Big village that way. Chief's village—very big. They took girl up there. Her relatives are there. There is big celebration two nights from now."

Fritz's heart beat faster. Tomorrow, he thought, he might have his daughter back. Even if they had already mutilated her, he would take her back. He began rehearsing an alternate plan in his mind, a demand he would make of the government that Rebeka accompany him and Ursula to Germany. He would insist the government give her a passport as a German citizen. How fortunate that he had, so many years ago, taken the precaution of legally adopting her. Yes, that would be the best thing for Rebeka, maybe even better than marrying Mpepo. They could give her a real education.

The sun slanted across the earth as it prepared to sink beneath the far hills. It would be too difficult to continue over the plains after dark, so the men set up their tents not far from the village. In the morning, as they broke camp, children clustered around watching them, chattering in Maa and laughing as Captain Worthington got out his basin and soap and began to shave. Kuyoni spoke to them for a while, then came back with a frown on his face.

"What's the matter?" Fritz asked.

"The children say the girl wasn't taken north. They say she was taken back toward Mount Meru, on the north side."

The captain chimed in. "I hardly think the children know the meaning of going to jail if they give false information. I would trust the woman who said they went north." They had a spirited discussion for a few minutes before Kuyoni agreed that perhaps the woman might be more truthful. The truck roared to life and they set out toward the Kenya border.

About one-thirty they stopped by the river that marked the border. They had encountered no cattle herders since leaving the vicinity of the village. The soldiers discussed what to do, whether to cross the border boldly as some wanted, or wait for the Kenya Patrol to spot them and come over to see what they wanted.

Captain Worthington pulled out a map. Another river and a line of rocky hills lay between them and the border outpost about three miles to the north.

Kuyoni, would you run and ask their permission for us to cross?" He showed the outpost just up the river a few miles. It would be quicker for a runner to make the trip than to detour around the hills and cross the river by truck.

Kuyoni agreed, and set off at a trot. The rest of the group settled in the shade of a thorn tree and dozed. Fritz grew impatient and paced. The fifth day since Rebeka's kidnapping crawled at a glacial pace, and they appeared to be no closer to rescuing her than when they started. They should have sent Mpepo, Fritz thought. Kuyoni wasn't a young man, and six miles would be nothing for the younger man.

At four o'clock, Fritz spotted Kuyoni in the distance, his figure dancing in the shimmers of the afternoon heat as he ran back, appearing to be closer than he was. He arrived soon after, his face and body suffused with sweat, his lungs gasping for air. Fritz handed him the army canteen of water and he gulped quantities of it before wiping his mouth and getting his breath back.

"Yes," he panted, in answer to the captain's questioning look. "We can cross if we want." He stopped to pant a few times. "If we need their assistance, they will give it. But they told me something interesting. This morning—early—a group of women crossed the border there. They stopped to talk to the men, and told them they were going to a circumcision ceremony at Kuryok village. There is to be a celebration tomorrow night. It is for the daughter of their dead cousin. They were happy about it. I think that is where we want to go."

The captain had his map out again. "Where's this Kuryok?"

Kuyoni looked over the captain's shoulder at the map. "In this area north of Meru, somewhere near this river." The captain groaned. It was too far to make it this day.

"We'll go as far as we can before dark, another hour and a half," he said. "Tomorrow we'll start as early as possible. There's no road, only cattle and game tracks."

Fritz ground his fist in his other hand. They should have listened to the children that morning. They had wasted at least a day. He watched a hawk fly high and wished he could fly to Rebeka.

The truck whined and growled over the plains, most of the time in first gear as they wound around thickets of thorn trees, bumped through rodent burrows and beside termite hills, screamed through loose sand in dried up riverbeds, and stopped to have petrol nourishment poured down it's thirsty throat. They weren't making good time. It would have been faster to walk. Once in awhile, though, they hit an area of hardpan and they made decent time for a few minutes.

They stopped when sunset plunged the world into a deep darkness barely lit by the stars. The men pitched tents and built a fire by the headlights of the truck. To the young soldiers fresh from Britain, this was a wonderful, stress-free safari. They laughed and talked around the fire. Later, after most of them slept, the full moon rose large and orange through the dust and remaining heat shimmers of the day. Only Fritz, Mpepo, and Kuyoni saw it from their bedrolls. Only they understood the tension of Rebeka's situation.

At first light they were up. Fritz waited impatiently for the rest of the group to strike camp and get back on the truck. Their travel continued much as the day before—potholes, watercourses, thorn trees—and other unforeseen impediments to their progress.

"I wonder how far the women got yesterday, and where they stayed," Fritz said after a few hours on their ponderous journey west.

"Probably over there," the captain said, pointing toward a small group of kraals in the distance. As they approached, the ever-present children gathered to watch them bump up to the thorn enclosed *boma*. They appeared to be shyer than those in other villages. Fritz wondered if they had seen many Europeans before.

The captain and Kuyoni got out of the truck, as before, to talk to the people who showed up—a few *murani*, a couple of elders with shaved heads, and several women with shrill voices. They conducted a relaxed conversation with usual greetings, asked about their health and their cattle, complimented them on the fine healthy children that hid behind their mothers, and discussed the rains and the grass. The people thawed somewhat and became friendlier as time went by.

Again, the captain turned serious and asked more direct questions. "Some women from Kenya came through here last night. Did you happen to see them?" The women looked at each other, not speaking. The elders disappeared and the *murani* came in closer.

"Why would you ask about women? Have they broken a law?"

"Not at all," the captain said. "I only heard at the border that they are going to Kuryok for a celebration. They have done nothing wrong," he repeated to reassure them. "But we would like to know where Kuryok Village is located. That is all. Can you help us?"

One of the *murani* nodded and stepped forward, appearing to be eager to get in their good graces. "I can show you." One of the women turned on him and spoke sharply. He answered, just as sharply, and she turned away and walked back into the *boma*.

He drew a simple map in the dust with a stick. The mountain was a circle. His village was a mark; he stepped over it and pointed southwest, and made another mark. "Kuryok," he said.

The captain brought out his map and compared it with the simple one in the dirt. The *muran*'s eyes widened as he looked at a map for the first time. Captain Worthington pointed out Mt. Meru and the river they would have to cross to get to Kuryok. It didn't take long for the warrior to grasp the concept, and he pointed to a spot about ten miles from the river. Comparing it to the dust map he'd drawn, it was an accurate pinpoint. Only the major settlements were included on the map, since other villages moved every two or three years.

"How long to get there from here?" the captain asked.

"Walking as a warrior walks, one day's journey."

"It's just about eleven now," the captain said, looking at his pocket watch. "That would be about ten or more hours walking time. Must be about twenty-five miles, maybe less. We should make it by mid-afternoon if we don't have to detour."

They did need to detour. Just after noon they came to a shoulder of the mountain that stretched across the straight path to Kuryok. They stopped to pass around the rations for the noon meal, then followed around the base of the hill to resume their journey on the other side. Almost immediately, the truck lurched into a hole and a tire went flat. Valuable time went into changing it.

"We'll need to fix the flat as soon as possible," one of the soldiers said. He was the mechanic in charge of keeping the old truck in running condition. "We can wait until we start the return trip, but we don't have another spare and we may need it."

By four o'clock they were still several hours from the village. They came to the river that was marked on the map, now an almost-dried watercourse that still had a small, slow-moving stream in the middle, nothing the truck should not be able to cross. As they lumbered into it, one wheel dropped down into a pool deeper than expected, stalling their progress. For a while the gears whined and the other three wheels churned, only putting them deeper and deeper into the mud.

The captain tried rocking it back and forth to break it loose, but the engine overheated, and the radiator relief valve spewed a volcano of steam into the air.

The men sat in silence for a few moments, stunned. Then the captain let loose with a string of invectives. "Pardon me, Doctor Scheibel. I'm sure you understand."

Fritz said nothing. He understood. At that moment he thought he might use a few choice German words himself, but decided silence would be enough to underscore the captain's verbiage.

Captain Worthington opened his door and stood on the running board and called to his men. "Sit tight, men. We have to get the engine to cool. One of you come and pour some of this water—whatever it is—over the radiator to cool it. Use my cup. When I give the signal, you'll need to pile out and help get this heap of iron out of the river!" The men laughed and settled in to wait for the radiator to cool enough to start again.

Fritz felt frustration and fury rise within him. They didn't even know if they were going to the right village. The minutes seemed interminable. Only the wildlife moved; a few buzzards came and sat in the trees to watch them, perhaps hoping for a corpse to feed on. Insects buzzed in the stagnant mud. Flies came in the open windows and inspected their faces. A few Thompson's Gazelles with broad black and white stripes on their sides appeared, their tails flicking so fast they could barely see them. A mamba snake slithered through the muddy water. Fritz examined the banks and pools for crocodiles.

"All right, men!" Worthington shouted. "Out!" The men removed their shoes, rolled up their pant legs, and tumbled from the back of the lorry, eager to help rescue it from the quagmire. They kept their distance from where they last saw the snake. By now the radiator had cooled, so the mechanic filled it with the cleanest river water he could find. Captain Worthington jumped back in the driver's seat, and started the engine.

Once again he tried to free the wheels of the truck from the viscous mud that soon splattered the soldiers who, with Mpepo and Kuyoni, pushed from the rear. The slimy water swirled around the truck and came close to the running boards by the doors. Captain Worthington banged his fist on the steering wheel in frustration.

"If we cut branches from the trees and lay them in front of the wheels, maybe that will give us some purchase." Fritz had twenty-five more years experience traveling in Africa.

"Right. Men! Get your boots on and grab a panga! We need branches from those trees!" The captain joined them as they piled branches on the bank. Fritz, whose heart pounded too frantically for him to accompany them, sat in the cab and watched the evening shadows grow. The sun appeared to drop toward the horizon faster than usual.

There were only a few minutes of daylight left when enough

branches lay on the bank to warrant another attempt to free the lorry. The men, covered with too much sweat, dust, and mud to care how they looked, submerged the branches and wedged them under both the front and back wheels. As the lorry lurched forward a few feet, they lodged rocks behind the wheels to prevent them from rolling backward. They repositioned the branches and repeated the process. On the fourth round, within ten feet of the opposite bank, the front wheels slipped sideways off the branches and fell into an even deeper pool. This time the water topped the running boards and threatened to swirl inside the cab

By now the sun had disappeared with its light. The moon had not yet risen, and the darkness felt like ink around them. They could no longer see if crocodiles or snakes came too close. Only the headlights illuminated what stood directly in front of the lorry. "Pitch camp on the river bank!" the captain yelled. "We can't do any more until daylight!" The men scrambled for the tents and supplies and waded ashore as best they could in the dark, cursing when they sank into thigh-deep water. They pitched the tents about three hundred feet from the riverbed.

They sat around the fire eating their meager rations and drinking as little as possible of their dwindling water supply. Fritz couldn't eat. Anxiety burned in his chest, increasing in intensity when the moon rose, engorged and reddened by the dust and heat.

"Men, come close. We need to plan our strategy for the morning," the captain called.

Tired as they were, they knew they had to get the truck out of the river first thing, and that morning might bring an end to the chase around Maasailand. The captain outlined the basic plan. Kuyoni, who understood the customs of the people, explained what would be occurring at the village.

"All the elders will be at another *boma*," he said. "Only women stay close by. If what the villagers told us today is true, tonight they hold the celebration of girlhood. The girls and *murani* dance their last dance together tonight. Tomorrow, after sunrise, is when the ceremony takes place."

"We'll sleep until four," the captain said. "We'll not take time to eat, just take the tents down in a hurry and get that lorry out of the river. It will be starting to get light. We want to arrive as close to sunup as possible."

The moon still lit the world when they got up, took down their tents, and got in the truck. The sleepy men exchanged greetings with Fritz who had sat all night by the fire like a brooding gargoyle, his brow furrowed and caked with dust.

The men tackled the lorry with renewed strength and coaxed it a few feet closer to the bank. A promise of the coming day crept across the land, augmenting the moonlight and turning the dark shadows into bushes and trees. It increased and then burst into fingers of sunlight that stretched across the plains and touched the hills in the distance. As they shoved and pulled on a rope fastened to the front axle, they heard the roar of a vehicle and turned in surprise. District Commissioner Neville and District Magistrate Fernaldi were just as surprised to see the soldiers.

"We're headed back to Arusha with the remnants of an elephant," Cecil said as he gave a brief description of their chase. "We camped just a few miles north of here last night. What's all this about?" He motioned toward the lorry and the soldiers.

"We're going after the Scheibel girl," Captain Worthington said. "We've been chasing wild rumors all over Maasailand, but now we think we know where she is." He pointed it out on the map.

"We'll go with you," Cecil said and Vito nodded. "Maybe our presence will give you a little more authority. But first, let's get that lorry out of that pit."

They attached the rope to the back of the District Commissioner's vehicle. With all the men pushing the lorry and Cecil pulling with his lorry, it soon broke free and got traction on the riverbank.

As the men threw the tents and equipment into the back of the lorry, Captain Worthington and Fritz told the two hunters what they understood of the situation, and how they planned to confront the Maasai women at the village. In a hurry, since the sun had already risen, they raced for their vehicles.

"Let's go, men!" The Captain shouted. The soldiers scrambled into the lorry.

As they approached the village they hit an area of hardpan, the ground beaten level by the hoofs of the many cattle that made their way to and from the kraals. The captain shifted into second, then third, and they picked up speed. In the distance they could see the thornbush-enclosed kraals and several *murani* leading the cattle out; the warriors turned at the sound of the truck and stared in amazement as they roared up to the *boma* entrance, stopped in a jerk, and the soldiers jumped out with their guns ready.

Inside the *boma*, several groups of women turned to watch, speechless in wonder at the apparition of armed men running toward them through the opened gate. Some screamed and ran toward the chief's *boma* where the elders sat in the morning light.

Fritz stood by the truck. He saw clusters of women around several *manyatta*s. He surmised that several girls would be cut this morning, and tried to see which one held Rebeka. He watched the soldiers surround the women, holding their guns on them, the women terrified, unable to move. Beyond the lorry and jeep the *murani* came running, their spears ready for assault. Fritz's glance fell on the figure of a young girl lying in the doorway of one of the huts, appearing to be asleep—or maybe dead. *Rebeka!* A shout started in the back of his throat, but before he could even point toward her, a figure flashed past him. Mpepo had seen her too.

CHAPTER NINETEEN

# The Rescue

**The roaring sound filled Rebeka's ears as she floated back into consciousness**. In the instant that she saw the woman stand over her with a knife in her hands, the other women turned to stare behind them. Someone screamed; voices turned angry and confused. She tried to sit up and focus on what was happening, but someone bent over her, wrapped her cloth around her, and picked her up.

"No! No!" She thrashed and tried to get away, but the arms that held her were strong and male. Then she saw who it was who held her, and she fainted again.

Without thinking of the danger, Mpepo dashed forward to rescue Rebeka from the clutches of the women. To his mind, these were evil people. Even in their pagan ways, his own tribe did not perform such terrible acts on their girls, and they despised the Maasai for this horrible custom. His main thought was to get her out of their grasp and carry her to safety.

With a tenderness and care that he was unused to, he gathered her cloth around her to preserve her modesty in front of the soldiers, and picked her up from the ground. Her softness amazed him. He had never held a woman in his arms. He gazed down at her face and wondered about the mixture of feelings that came over him. Even the panic of the moment didn't keep him from feeling aroused as he covered her naked body with the cloth and held her close against his chest.

He controlled her struggling body until she recognized him and went limp. He murmured into her ear, "I am here, Rebeka. Do not be afraid. You are safe." She began to tremble as though overcome with a chill. All he could think about was her safety and taking her back to her home. He thought of her exquisite voice raised in a hymn in church, her joyous spirit and manner, her soft voice and good manners. Thank God, he thought, they had rescued her in time.

He only took a few steps. Three *murani*, their spears pointed at him, stood between him and the soldiers. Rebeka struggled to wake herself, clutching her cloth to her chest to cover her breasts. He stood her on her feet, holding his arms around her shoulders, and they faced the *murani* together.

"Put down your spears!" The captain shouted, and two soldiers came over, their guns pointed at the warriors. Slowly, they lowered their spears, but they didn't turn away.

"Stand back," one of the soldiers said and pushed one of the warriors out of the way with the barrel of his rifle.

Mpepo, holding Rebeka's elbows, guided her forward until she gave a little cry and ran to her father.

Fritz took Rebeka into his arms, amazed at her transformed appearance. Though wrapped only in a short native cloth that threatened to come undone, she didn't seem as naked as she would have if a dress had slipped. With the colorful beaded collar, her shaved head, and the huge hoops in her ears, she seemed no longer a black German girl, but an African woman. It was as if the sixteen years in his home were wiped away and all his and Ursula's teaching and training disappeared.

"Papa, you came for me. I knew you would. I prayed, and you came." She closed her eyes again, though her trembling continued.

Fritz led her to the truck cab and placed her on the seat. "Here are some clothes, Rebeka. I'll help you put them on." He pulled out a dusty knapsack from under the seat and opened it. "We'll be leaving as soon as we can."

Captain Worthington and Cecil Neville conducted a heated discussion with the women and the threatening *murani*. By now, Mbae ole Kipchong and several other elders had arrived, adding their demands to the melee. Rebeka managed to pull on the simple dress Fritz had brought, with his help, though it caught on the ear hoops. She pulled her beaded betrothal collar on top of the dress and removed the cloth that she wore. Fritz climbed in and held her in his lap again as though she were a little girl. Her shaking soon subsided and he got out and joined the captain and Kuyoni.

When matters turned ugly, Kuyoni had a sinking feeling that perhaps this marked the end of his career as a go-between for the Maasai tribe and the government. Raiding a circumcision rite—as much as he detested that practice—and arguing with the women and *murani*, and now the elders, would not sit well with the Maasai people. He had to be the interpreter, so all the government words came through him as though they came from him.

Mutual respect and trust between the two entities were a fragile state of affairs that took years to build. The Germans had damaged it by trying to set boundaries for the nomadic tribe. They further destroyed it during the war. For the past three years, the British had set a standard of excellence in their relations with the Maasai, and Kuyoni had rejoiced to see dignity and respect restored. But now—he hated to think of the repercussions.

Kuyoni wasn't afraid when he, the captain, and the District Commissioner stood unarmed in front of the angry women. Even when the *murani* rushed over, posturing with their spears, and the elders ran over from their *boma*, he knew that the soldiers stood with their rifles ready.

One old woman with a knife in her hand approached them, shouting invectives that made the British wince, even though they didn't understand them. Kuyoni did. The other women chimed in.

"We have come for Rebeka, the daughter of the German *Daktari*. By law, she is considered his daughter and he has control over her—not you, the tribe that gave her birth. He has a paper that says she is his daughter."

The old woman shouted and shook her knife at them.

"Drop that knife!" The captain's voice took on an edge. Kuyoni didn't need to translate. She dropped her hand to her side, still gripping the knife.

"I said—drop the knife on the ground!" It thudded to the ground. By then, Mpepo had picked up the girl, the *murani* had backed off, and Fritz took her to the truck.

"Very good. Now let's talk this thing through," Cecil said.

"I understand that you feel that Rebeka is your property, since she was born of Maasai parents. But when she was a baby she was given to the *Daktari*. Is that not right?"

The old woman nodded and pointed to Mbae ole Kipchong, who strode forward and began to talk.

"She was only loaned to the *Daktari*. There was no other way to save her life. I told him, and that man was standing beside him—" he pointed to Kuyoni "—that some day we would come to take her back. She is the last descendant of—" he paused a moment "—of a great chief, so she is important to the Maasai people." He glared at Kuyoni as he translated this statement. The chief came and stood beside him in a sign of solidarity, his back straight, his dignity and demeanor showing his position.

"I understand." Cecil tried to sound reasonable. "Now, if you have a problem with our taking her back, there are legal ways to protest. We are not Germans. We are British, and British law allows anyone who feels wronged to come and take it before a court of law. We try to respect the rights of African people, but we do follow laws of justice and right, as I know you do.

"Taking the girl in the middle of the night is not the way to do right. That act makes it thievery—a serious offense." Cecil knew that thievery was one of the most detested crimes among the Maasai, though they turned a blind eye to raiding cattle from other tribes.

"We will take the girl back to Arusha with us. You are free to come to our court and speak your case. Our judge, who stands here with me—" he motioned toward Vito "—is one who is impartial to all parties involved."

The people were still angry, but there was nothing they could do. Rebeka was already in the lorry. Their angry looks and gestures turned to a discontented murmur as the captain and his soldiers backed up. The *murani* thrust their spears into the ground beside them at a word from Mbae and their chief.

Mbae stood straight before them, seemingly unafraid of the soldiers and their rifles. "I gave the girl once before to the white *Daktari,* and I give her again, but only for a little while. The Europeans do not understand the customs of our people. The girl belongs with her people. She is Maasai.

"If indeed the white man promises justice, then we will come to your *boma* to see what you mean by that word." He motioned to his people to fall back, speaking in a low voice of authority.

They backed away.

"Blimey, we did all this for just a little African girl!" one of the soldiers protested as they came to the truck. "I thought it was a *white* girl they kidnapped."

Fritz glared at him. "In as much as ye have done it unto the least of these, ye have done it unto me," he quoted from Scripture. The soldier ducked his head in silent embarrassment.

They sped away as fast as Captain Worthington could drive, leaving the people in the Maasai *boma* barely visible through the dust raised by the truck. Cecil and Fritz followed in their vehicle in case they should break down again. Kuyoni had given up his place in front to Rebeka and had joined the soldiers in the back. They were all tired and longed for a bath. The tension was over.

"We can head west and pick up the Namanga Road," the captain said. "It shouldn't take long. I saw on the map it isn't more than ten miles from here. Then we'll head home and be there by night. Not bad, after three days getting here, right?" He looked with interest at Rebeka.

"So this is the girl. Rebeka," she turned and looked at him. "When you feel up to it, you'll need to give us an account, for the record. You understand?"

She nodded.

Fritz held her close again. "You're home soon with friends, *Liebchen*," he said. "Away from those awful people."

"Papa, they weren't awful people." She frowned as she pulled away and looked him in the eye. "What they were going to do would have been awful. But they're nice people, and I feel as though they are my friends.

"Isn't that funny?" she looked at him with a question on her face.

Tears sprang to Fritz's eyes and he pulled her back to him. "We'll talk about this later," he said. He also had to tell her about the order to go back to Germany, but he'd save that for another time.

**"She's a beautiful girl," Vito commented to Cecil as they followed the dust plume from the lorry at a distance.** "What a terrible situation to be in. Caught between two cultures."

"Yes," Cecil agreed. "I've seen it happen before. Goodhearted people think they're helping by taking in orphans and raising them in European homes, then—blam!—the poor children don't fit anywhere when they're grown. Like trying to tame a wild animal."

"People aren't animals, though," mused Vito. "They have intelligence and adaptability. If we continue to have influence in this land, we have to learn how to guide them into the modern world. And do it in a way that doesn't make them copies of us, a way that preserves the best of what they have of their customs."

"You might not feel that way if you knew what they were going to do to that poor girl," Cecil said, and he explained to Vito the custom of female circumcision. "Imagine how one of our women would react to that," he said. "Rebeka has been raised as a white girl, so this must have been a terrible shock to her."

The two men fell silent. Vito reflected on the ramifications of colonial involvement in Africa. He felt troubled and perplexed by the jumbled feelings that Rebeka stirred in the depths of his long-cold heart. Was it a premonition, a sense of foreboding, or what?

CHAPTER TWENTY

# Unwelcome Choices

**Ursula stood on the verandah of her home watching the military truck labor into the yard** carrying Fritz and Rebeka, the two people who were her life. She had been feeling better for several days. Maybe it was the cooler weather, or perhaps the tension of thinking about Rebeka poured extra strength into her limbs. For days she had fretted, her mind fixed on her love for her adopted daughter and the realities that faced them all. After Fritz left, she had gone to the hospital to work and found the order to return to Germany on his desk.

She had lived for two things. The first was to serve God with her whole being. She had done this with single-mindedness. It had been a good life in spite of the many hardships, the worst of which were the three headstones under the bougainvillea. She had grown up in poverty as a peasant girl, so never considered the absence of personal wealth or prestige as much of a loss. Her training as a nurse had been paid for by the local overlord, in the days when Germany was composed of many feudal states. The work she had done here with women and children, especially the orphans, would go on long after she breathed her last. All around her she saw those children who would have been killed if she hadn't rescued them, now finding their place as contributing adults. This made her happy and fulfilled. In spite of the pain, her life was a gift she offered to God.

Second, Ursula lived to please her husband. Fritz was so

good to her that this had not been a hardship. The only time she ever pitted her will against his was the day when he brought the infant Rebeka home. But he must have seen the wisdom of her choice, because he never again said they should give her up. Rebeka had been good for both of them.

Yes, Ursula decided, it was time to go home to Germany. The church would find them a little house in Leipzig, and maybe Fritz could work at the hospital and continue some of his studies in tropical diseases. She knew her body's limitations. With her weakened heart there was little more she could do here. Yet now she dared to question God.

"If only Rebeka…" She kept repeating this out loud without finishing the sentence. *If only Rebeka* what? What did she really want for this dark daughter, the girl-woman with depths of soul Ursula could never fathom, her child of Africa? Oh, she wanted to take her with them, to enjoy her quiet, comforting presence, as they grew older and drifted off toward death. What a comfort that would be. Rebeka's quick mind should soon adapt to her new surroundings.

But, as Fritz kept pointing out, was that course best for her?

"What will she do in Germany, *Liebchen*? How will she make a living? Her education here will be worthless there. She won't find a husband there. Soon we'll be gone, and who then will care for her?"

His arguments had silenced her. He was right. They must think of what was best for Rebeka, not what they wanted. Fritz brought up their long-ago disagreement.

"I knew, when we took her in, that someday we would have this difficult choice. We've prepared her for life in Africa. Therefore, she must be left here—in God's hands."

*In God's hands. In God's hands.* The words ran continually

through Ursula's mind. So easy to say, so hard to do—or even believe. It seemed as though all the platitudes they had voiced through the years were really ways of avoiding the hard choices one must make in life. For the first time Ursula questioned her faith in a God who presented no choices in this most painful difficulty of all.

Now, leaning against the roof post on the verandah, she watched the two people she loved more fiercely than anything in this world climb, weary and dusty, from the cab of the truck.

Fritz had removed the wire hoops from Rebeka's ears, but she still wore the beaded collar over her dress. Ursula gasped at her shaved head that accented her stark, Maasai beauty. It was as though a strange woman stood before her, dark impenetrable eyes full of pain staring into her own blue eyes, no smile of joy. She opened her arms, and Rebeka ran into them, sobbing on her ample bosom, becoming her little girl again. She saw the holes in her ears, clotted with blood, and shuddered. What had they done to her little girl?

Fritz came in behind Rebeka and reached his arms around the two of them, wordless, not caring who saw. He rocked them back and forth for a long moment and then released them. He opened his mouth and closed it, unable to speak his feelings, shook his head, and went to the kitchen to order bath water.

"Mama! Mama!" Rebeka cried as Ursula held her close.

"Did they hurt you, Rebeka?" She was afraid to ask the question.

Rebeka shook her head. "Almost. But Papa got there just in time. Oh, Mama! I have so much to tell you, but now I just want a bath and some sleep!"

It was later, while Rebeka slept, that Fritz told her what happened. If they had arrived one minute later,  what a terrible difference would have been made in their daughter's life.

"There's no question now, *Liebchen*. Tomorrow I will go to Dar and request a passport for Rebeka. We'll take her with us. You were right after all. She needs to be with us. We can't run the risk of this happening to her again."

"But—you said—what will she *do* in Germany, Fritz? You know we talked about this before, and…"

"The matter is settled, Ursula. The girl is going with us. Now be a good girl, and pack some things for my trip. While I'm gone, you can start packing our things for going home."

**Mpepo's grades on his final exams reflected his lack of study, but he did pass**. One of the seminary's best students, he had hoped to graduate with perfect scores. As he leaned back on his cot at night and thought about things, he imagined that God did not put particular approval on good grades over good deeds, and he felt a deep satisfaction that what he had done to help save the Scheibel's girl was, indeed, a good thing. He kept seeing her lying naked on the ground in the doorway of the Maasai *manyatta*. He remembered the warmth of her body next to his as he picked her up and carried her to her father. He wondered if the tenderness he felt toward her, different from the physical longings he had at the same time, was a flaw in himself. He knew men were to desire their wives, yet few men he knew showed tenderness toward them. Except *Daktari*. People laughed behind his back about his weakness in the presence of his wife, and how he catered to her wishes.

Mpepo knew his thoughts should not dwell on the girl, but he couldn't help it. He wanted her very much, he decided, and as soon as he could consult with his mentor, he would speak to *Daktari* and ask to marry Rebeka. Cheered by this thought he rose from his bed in the morning and went to find Pastor Luka, only to hear that he had gone into the countryside to visit relatives and would not be back for three days.

The day Luka returned was the day of celebration for the first graduating class of the Lutheran Seminary, the day when they received their ordination and challenge to go out and serve God. Everyone's friends and relatives came to congratulate them, including Siferi with his wife and sister-in-law, Damari.

As he sat on the platform listening to Luka's solemn speech, he glanced toward Rebeka who sat near the front on the women's side. She met his gaze for one bold moment, ignited his loins with fire, and then dropped her gaze in modesty. He knew now that she felt for him what he felt for her. He glanced over to his kinfolk, and there sat Damari, gazing at him with a wistful expression, immediately averting her face when she noticed him looking. Again his loins stirred, and he wondered about his responses to these two women—he, who had never even considered a woman more than in passing pleasure, to now want two women and have them want him too.

After the service and during the feasting time Siferi drew him aside.

"Next week, my cousin, there is to be a big celebration in Huru country. I will be made chief of all the tribe, and the D.C. will be there. There will be a feast, dancing, *futuboli* games, and speeches. I want you by my side."

"Congratulations!" Mpepo grasped his hand and arm. "I am so happy. Our grandfather would be proud."

"I want you by my side as my brother, cousin." Siferi didn't give up. "I want you betrothed to Mbili—I mean Damari. If you are not, I do not want you there at all." His intense look pierced Mpepo like a poisoned arrow. His expression hardened as he continued.

"If you decide not to follow my advice, then I do not want to see you in Huru country again. I will take Damari as my second wife. She is beautiful and obedient, and will live up to her real name, *Mbili*—second."

His face softened as he added, "Just a joke, my friend. Though I might think about that if you do not marry her. Do the right thing, and come to the celebration next week."

**The three days that her father was gone were hard for Rebeka.** How would she find the words to tell her parents that she did not want to go to Germany with them? Whenever her mind idled, she found herself remembering Mpepo—his strong arms around her, his body smell, his voice as he said *I'm here, Rebeka. You will be all right now.*

She knew her mother watched her carefully, interpreting her silence as pain, so she emptied her mind of Mpepo and resumed her usual humming as she went about her daily duties.

She found solitude in the storeroom where he had recuperated from his war wound. She sat on the barrel where she had laid out his meals and thought of him. Here, where no prying eyes watched, she remembered his face when she first studied it while her father removed the bullets. She went over and over in her mind the sensation of being held in his arms, his strong, deep voice, the rigid muscles on his chest. She remembered another storeroom long ago, in Tanga, where in punishment she sat among the barrels of food and tins of kerosene, where she found solace in the sugar tin, dipping her finger into the stolen sweet. Sitting here thinking about Mpepo was like stealing the sugar, she thought. It was a private pleasure that thrilled her whole body, not just her mouth.

"What are you doing in the store room?" her mother asked.

"Taking stock of supplies," she replied.

"They don't matter. Whatever is left when we leave, we'll give to someone else." Ursula looked reproachful, as though Rebeka were avoiding her by going into the storeroom.

After that, Rebeka was careful to go there only when Ursula rested in bed. When her father returned, she would tell them both that she planned to stay in Africa. It was time to take charge of her own life.

The day before her father came back, Malia came to tell her that Mbae and his wives were seen in town. This time the chief accompanied them along with three *murani* and a Maasai man from Kenya who wore a European suit.

At the seminary graduation service she stared at Mpepo until he turned to look at her. Defying custom, she continued her gaze, trying to communicate to him her anguish before lowering her eyelids in modesty.

**Mbae ole Kipchong stood by the courthouse door waiting for the magistrate** to return from a trip to Moshi. Even though he and his counselor had already spoken to the Indian clerk and registered their complaint, he didn't want to miss the judge's arrival.

When the soldiers came and took Rebeka away, the men of the tribe had met at the chief's *boma*. One of the men had recently visited relatives in Narok, Kenya, and he said he knew someone in a government position there who would help interpret if they decided to go to the courts.

"The English are fair," he said. "My friend understands English laws and ways. Why do we not send for him, and he can go with you to Arusha to see the judge?"

Two *murani* were dispatched immediately to find this man. Now his group waited in town for the magistrate. Mbae would make sure that justice prevailed.

He stood by the door, his right foot resting on his left knee, leaning on his spear. His wives huddled in the shadow of the building, moving only as the sun in its circuit took the shade from one side and deposited it on another. Waiting was something they knew about.

CHAPTER TWENTY ONE

# A Maasai in His Majesty's Court

**The early morning dawned as fresh and sweet as an innocent child**. The sun reached its golden fingers across the sleepy town, playfully poking them in the windows and waking the residents. Vito locked his door at 7:00 a.m. and stood on his verandah breathing in the cool air. The dew sparkled on the grass, and the lingering scent of night jasmine filled him with pleasure. He glanced toward his mountain. Kilimanjaro reflected the morning sun and looked as if it smiled at him.

"Soon," Vito murmured aloud. "I have killed an elephant, and you are next. So stop taunting me." He'd been having similar conversations with the mountain for some months. Now he knew he was ready. His bad leg was barely stiff from the hike during the hunt—not nearly as sore as the shoulder that took the kick of the rifle.

He strode down the dusty street toward his office and exchanged cheerful greetings with several workmen still yawning from recent sleep. A small boy herded a flock of goats toward the edge of town. Sleepy guard dogs stretched and yawned in their yards and gave half-hearted barks as he walked by. He passed a group of school children on their way to class, singing as they went. They stopped and the small girls curtseyed, chorusing their greetings. The boys presented their heads to him so he could put his hand on each one.

"What are you learning today?" Vito asked.

The children laughed, embarrassed. One boy said, "We are learning our vowels. *Ah—eh—ee—aw—oo*!" and they all ran off like little antelope, laughing and repeating the vowels.

Vito smiled and continued to his office.

The door was unlocked, which meant that Rajneesh was already there. As he entered, he glanced over to the courthouse door where a grizzled Maasai man stood, his impassive face staring out into the street. Where had he recently seen this man? Two women huddled in blankets against the side of the building.

"What's going on, Raj?" he motioned over in the direction of the court.

"The Maasai nation takes on the British Empire," Rajneesh said with a laugh. "They came in two days ago, filed suit, and have been waiting right there ever since. Here are the documents, all filled out. They have a counselor from Kenya—not a real barrister, but someone who understands the law and can interpret."

"What in heaven's name…" Vito sat in his chair and read the paper Rajneesh handed him, written in a poor imitation of a legal document.

*Whereas Njao, the head chief of el Engerot Clan, died during great pox epidemic in 1905 leaving only baby girl as issue; and whereas the German Doctor Scheibel did remove her from her tribe and try to call his own; and whereas said Doctor Scheibel defied the efforts of the Clan to restore her to her people; and whereas the British soldiers did present guns for the return of this girl to notorious doctor: therefore the el Engerot Clan does*

*bring suit against the British Government and Doctor Scheibel to have the girl repossessed and put back to her people and to seek compensation for the acts above.*
*Signed,*
*XXXX*
*Known to me to be Mbae ole Kipchong, girl's closest man relative, uncle of her mother.*
*R'sp'ly yrs,*
*Mr. Willemi Engare*

"Is that the uncle standing out there?"

Rajneesh nodded.

"Well, we asked for it. Cecil told them that if they wanted, they could bring their case to court." Vito sighed. "What else is on the calendar?"

"Just two cases. A man beat his wife and put her in hospital. He says she was spending his money. And there's a man in jail for stealing. He was caught crawling out the window with the goods. Says he's innocent, of course."

"Let them stew in jail for a few days. We'll tackle this one first; see what comes of it."

As he spoke the doorway darkened and Mbae entered, followed by his wives and a man who rubbed his hands together in a nervous gesture. Mbae began to speak rapid-fire Maa to Vito, his wives nodding in agreement. Before the man, whom Vito decided must be the barrister replica from Kenya, could interpret, something leathery and dark landed on the desktop in front of him.

Startled, Vito looked at it a few seconds before he realized it was the old man's foot; it was so dry and dusty it resembled elephant skin. A long, hardened scar ran down the instep. He wondered how an old man could have such agility to be able to lift his leg and foot in that swift, effortless motion.

"Wait–wait—wait—" Vito waved his hands in the air, trying to shut off the verbiage spewing from the old man's mouth.

"What is this man saying?" he turned to the Kenyan who answered in careful English.

"He says, sir, that he was near dead from a wound to his foot, and not in his head, when the Bwana Doctor took the child of his dead niece. He would have kept the girl himself, but was not in his head. He…."

"Save the details for court. Please ask him to leave my office. As soon as I can notify the proper defendants and have them present, we will hear your case. Then will be the time to tell your story. Rajneesh will notify you when the case is to be heard."

"Yes, sir." The Kenyan bobbed his head in an obsequious gesture. "Mr. Kipchong only wished to give reasons for desire for justice." He translated to ole Kipchong, and they left.

Vito wrote a letter to Fritz and Ursula Scheibel detailing the case and asking them to present themselves, with Rebeka, to court at a date convenient to them. He also wrote to Cecil asking that he also be present as the District Commissioner. He got answers by runners that afternoon.

*Dear Sir;*

*I am unable to attend court any time within the next two weeks as I have been unexpectedly called to a meeting with the Governor in Dar es Salaam. I trust that you will represent the British Government in an exemplary manner. Perhaps Captain Worthington can be an additional witness as to why and how the military became involved. Please accept my regrets.*

*Cecil Neville*

*District Commission, Arusha, Tanganyika*

And a letter from Fritz:

*Sir, I can be in court any time since my duties at the hospital are now limited. My wife is not well, but she will try to attend also. We are shocked that the Maasai tribe would go to this length to try to take our daughter from us. I have obtained a passport for her, and she is to go to Germany with us within the month.*

*We have all her papers in order to show that she is our legal daughter and have no doubt that the court will rule in our favor.*

*Respectfully,*

*Dr. Fritz Scheibel*

Thursday brought a hot muggy blanket of humid air that settled like a pall of gloom over Arusha. Kilimanjaro was barely visible when Vito strode down the street to the government offices; it's glacial head shone like a white smudge above its mantle of cloud. Vito was barely aware of it, forgetting, almost as soon as the thought struck him, that if he didn't tackle the mountain in the next month he would have to wait until after the rains.

He entered his office and reread the documents while Rajneesh seated the litigants and defendants in the courtroom. At five minutes to nine, he went to the closet and took out the black robe hanging there, noting the ravages made by white ants eating the wood of the wardrobe. One sleeve of the garment had a few holes in it where it had touched the wooden back of the closet and encountered the voracious appetite of the tiny creatures. He made a mental note to find someone to patch the sleeve.

Exactly at nine a discreet knock on the private door to his office told him that everyone was ready. As he opened the door, he heard Rajneesh say, "All rise." Even Mbae ole Kipchong, followed by his wives, stood to his feet after the Kenyan kicked him and motioned him to his feet.

Vito strode to his spot at a table set on a raised platform about twelve inches above the floor. Rajneesh stood at one end of this table ready to record the proceedings in shorthand. Behind them, the British symbol of a lion on a shield hung on the wall; above it presided a painting of King George V.

On Vito's left, below the platform, stood a table where ole Kipchong stood beside his counselor. His wives stood in front of a brick bench behind him, and behind them stood three *murani*. Rajneesh had taken their spears from them and set the weapons outside by the door. On Vito's right were Fritz and Ursula with Rebeka, who wore a scarf to cover her shaved head. Behind them sat Kuyoni and a few observers, there to give support by their presence, as well as Captain Worthington from the military barracks.

Vito stared a moment at Rebeka. *I wonder if she understands the national import of these proceedings,* he thought. When she glanced at him and he saw the fear in her eyes, he realized that the import went far beyond setting a precedent in colonial law and practice and touched the very existence of a human being. He again felt the premonition he had first felt after her rescue. What was it about this girl?

"Please be seated," intoned Rajneesh.

"Since English is a second language to some, but not all, and many mother languages are represented, I have ordered that the proceedings be done in Swahili. Does anyone here object?" Vito said. When no objection was raised, he added, "Mr. Patel, please make note of this fact.

"Also, I would like to make clear to all parties that the intent

254 Where Lions Still Roar

of the British Colonial Office in its presence here in Tanganyika is to allow the chiefs to preside over civil matters such as this. In this particular case, where the chief is adversely affected, and where the British Government is a respondent, I have deemed it more equitable to hear the case myself in order to bring an impartial judgment. Do you all understand this?" Everyone murmured assent.

Vito nodded to the Kenyan. "Mr. Engare, you may state your case and introduce your witnesses."

Willemi Engare stood to his feet, perspiration beading on his brow, his tie askew. He cleared his throat and began speaking.

"Mr. Kipchong, my patron, represents the el Engerot Clan in their wish to restore the Maasai girl, known to the people in the room as Rebeka, to her rightful people. Mr. Kipchong is the girl's only living relative, being uncle to her mother who died at birthing.

Mr. Kipchong will speak words to the court of how, when he was close to death, he gave the child to the doctor to keep alive. He did not want to give her forever. When he tried to take her back, the doctor resisted him.

Mr. Kipchong will also tell that he arranged marriage for the girl with Kulale ole Mioli, chief of the clan, so she would be cared for. He has received cattle in the arrangement. He took back only what was rightfully his when he took the girl to her ancestral village.

Mr. Kipchong's wives will tell how the soldiers frightened the women with guns pointed at them. They were afraid of being shot and killed. The soldiers stole the girl away from her rightful place, and the clan demands that she be given back to them and payment made for the food prepared for the feasts and the gifts given to the girl."

He spoke to Mbae, who rose and limped to the witness chair placed at the other end of Vito's table opposite to Rajneesh.

Mbae's testimony was torturous. Mr. Engare had to first state his question in Swahili, then translate it to Maa, then translate his answer back to Swahili. At times, the old man rambled on and on, to the point where his counselor couldn't keep up in translating.

"Mr. Engare, please advise your client to keep his answers short. No one here has a month to hear all he has to say," Vito said.

It took about ninety minutes to hear and translate all of Mbae's testimony. Vito read off his summary of main points.

"My understanding of Mr. Kipchong's testimony is the following: After both of her parents died in the smallpox epidemic, Mr. Kipchong asked Dr. Scheibel to care for Rebeka because he thought he was dying and wouldn't be able to care for her himself. His wives had moved on with the surviving villagers, and he knew there wasn't time to find someone else. He never intended for Dr. Scheibel to keep her past weaning. Is that right?"

Mr. Engare nodded.

"He sent his *murani* to get her when she reached the proper age to be introduced into village life, and they were repelled by Dr. Scheibel. He sent his wives to convince her to come to her people. None of those efforts were successful, so he sent *murani* to take her by force."

Mr. Engare looked doubtful, then nodded again.

"A marriage was arranged with the chief, Kulale ole Mioli. In fact, cattle were transferred and, in the minds of the people, the marriage has already taken place. Tribal law says that is when a marriage is confirmed. Is that right?"

"Yes," Mr. Engare said.

"We'll leave until later the legality or illegality of the marriage and military incursion into the village to retake the girl by force. Right now I want to visit the rights of the plaintiff as opposed to those of Dr. Scheibel, as to guardianship of the girl Rebeka." Vito glanced at Rebeka and saw her, head down, hands clasped in her lap. She turned her head slightly to hide her tears from her mother and wiped at her cheeks.

"I have a few questions I would like to ask Mr. Kipchong." Vito turned back to the counselor.

"First, why did he not make it clear to Dr. Scheibel that the intent was only to keep the baby alive until someone else could care for her?"

Every eye turned to Mbae as Mr. Engare translated the question.

Mbae pointed at Kuyoni and said, "I told *him* who she was and that we would want her back." Eyes turned to Kuyoni. Mr. Engare made a notation.

"Second," Vito said, "why didn't he come himself to take her back? Why did he send people to coerce her?"

Mbae sat straighter in his chair. "I am an important man in my village. When I speak, people do my bidding. When someone else has what we own, we go and take it back."

"So that's why your *murani* came in the night, tied up the doctor and his wife, and carried off the girl? We call that kidnapping, and it is considered a crime to take someone from their home against their will."

"It is the Maasai way. The village is her rightful home."

"As to the marriage—did the girl consent to be married to this chief?"

Mbae hedged, then said, "It is the Maasai way. I am her uncle, and I consented. That is all that is required. She is a woman and cannot decide such things."

"Mr. Engare, may I ask you a personal question? Where did you go to school?"

Mr. Engare looked puzzled a moment and then answered with a look of pride. "I finished fourth form at the Colonial School for Tribal Leaders in Nairobi."

"How did you happen to go there?"

"My clan in Narok paid for me to go; they said I should be their eyes and ears in the white man's ways."

"I see. Did you learn about British laws there, about marriage and divorce, and that a marriage cannot be considered legal unless both parties consent?"

"Yes, your honor, I did learn such things. But they are clearly British laws, and not African laws. I also know that the government in Kenya acknowledges tribal law. I believe it is the same in Tanganyika."

Vito said nothing, though he knew that Mr. Engare was correct. His instructions included the directive that colonial powers were trustees, not owners. He was to administer justice with primary concern for the welfare and benefit of the indigenous people, and in most cases to follow tribal law unless the rights of one of the parties were threatened.

"Dr. Scheibel, do you have anything to ask Mr. Kipchong before I release him from the witness chair?"

Fritz lumbered to his feet. He looked hurt and distressed. "No, your honor, but I would like to mention one thing. I saved this man's life. He surely would have died from his infected foot if I had not intervened." He turned to Mbae. "And this is how you repay me?" He shook his head and sat down.

The old man said nothing in answer. When it became obvious

to Vito that nothing further would be asked, he dismissed him.

Mbae's first wife, Nareyu, was called to the chair. She related in her shrill voice the story of how the soldiers came and, with guns pointed at her and the other women, forced them to give up the girl. She pantomimed the frightening effect this had on them. "*Eeeya*! We had great feast prepared," she said. "Relatives came from far away in Kenya. They brought gifts, and food. Now we have eaten sorrow, and they all went home disappointed." No one had any questions, so she returned to her chair behind her husband.

"Mr. Engare, do you have any further witnesses?"

"I do, your honor. I would like to call that man." He pointed to Kuyoni who reacted in surprise, then came and sat in the chair with a quick, nervous glance toward Fritz.

"Mr. Kuyoni, were you with the doctor when he came to el Engerot?"

"Yes, I was."

"When Mr. Kipchong gave the child to the doctor, did he tell you who the girl was?"

Kuyoni was silent for a moment, then said, "yes."

"Did you tell the doctor?"

"No. Well, I told him she was descendant of an important person, that is all."

"Did you tell him that the Maasai people would want her back someday?"

Kuyoni shrugged. "I don't know. Maybe I did. I think I said something. I don't remember what."

"Yet Mr. Kipchong told you these things, did he not?"

"Yes."

"No more questions, your honor."

"Doctor Scheibel?" Vito turned to Fritz, who shook his head, a look of defeat on his face. Ursula's face was ashen, her eyes wide with apprehension. He couldn't see Rebeka's, but he guessed she still wept. Kuyoni stood to leave, but Vito interrupted him.

"Wait! Wait! I have a question to ask of this witness.

"Mr. Kuyoni, from whom is this girl descended, beside the chief who was her father? Why would you not tell your friend, the doctor, about this?"

Mbae and the Kenyan counselor exchanged glances as Kuyoni responded, hesitant in manner.

"There is an old Maasai fable of a great chief many years ago who came to be called *The One True Lion*. They say he was the son of a lion, because he had eyes the color of a lion's eyes and was mighty in battle. I know it is not possible for a woman to mate with a lion and produce offspring. It is only a fable. That is why I did not tell it to my friend."

"Do you believe this so-called fable?"

Kuyoni shrugged. "They say that a son of this *One True Lion* will come some day and lead the people. I do not know if he will come or not. I only know it is not possible for a lion to father a man."

Vito's interest was piqued. He remembered the little leather book on the shelf at home, the one given to him by the Indian merchant in Dar es Salaam when he first arrived in the country. "How does this relate to Rebeka?"

"Mr. Kipchong told me that she remained as the only living descendant of that man. Her father was a chief, but he could not be the great one to come because his eyes were not the right color. Mr. Kipchong said that she could be the mother of the promised great leader who will restore the Maasai people to their former place in the land."

"I see. So then, according to this legend, this girl—" Vito

pointed to Rebeka, who sat head down, frozen, "—is more than a simple, ordinary Maasai girl. She is the only one who could bring the Maasai redeemer, as he might be called, into the world."

"I would not call him a redeemer," Kuyoni answered stiffly. "I am a Christian. There is only one Redeemer, and that is...."

"Nevertheless," Vito broke in, "to the Maasai he will be a redeemer. Right?"

"Yes."

"Hmmm." Vito considered the complications. He glanced at Rebeka and felt sorry for her. There were too many weighty matters resting on her small shoulders. To his government, the matter consisted of setting the precedent of meddling in tribal affairs. To the Maasai, their hopes for the future rested in Rebeka's fulfillment of the prophecy. To Rebeka, the innocent victim caught in the middle of the whole mess, the case concerned her life.

"We will stop for our noon meal," Vito said. "Please be back in your seats at two this afternoon. Dr. Scheibel, you may defend your position at that time."

CHAPTER TWENTY TWO

# The Defense

**By two o'clock, the air was heavy with moisture, an omen of the weighty situation facing them**. Though no clouds were visible, it felt as though it might rain. Storm birds flew over the fields and the heat pressed down on man and beast. Yet the rains were not due for nearly a month.

Ursula could hardly draw her breath. She tried to rise from her bed, but Fritz persuaded her to stay home and rest.

"There's nothing further we can do, *Liebchen*. All I can do this afternoon is present our adoption papers. It's in God's hands, now. We must bow to his will."

"That's what I am afraid of, Fritzie. And what are we to do if God does not do what we think he should? Are we to smile and let them lead Rebeka off like a goat to be slaughtered for dinner?"

Fritz didn't answer. He leaned down and kissed her. He put on his helmet, picked his folder off the table, and called to Rebeka to follow him.

The participants in the case straggled into the courtroom. The overhead fan only stirred the soup of heat and body odors. Fritz arranged his papers on the table in front of him and waited for Vito to come to court and open the proceedings. Several lizards posed on the walls in silent attentiveness. Through the open windows came the afternoon marketplace sounds, vociferous conversations, laughter, children playing in the schoolyard, and the occasional bleating of a goat or braying of a donkey.

"Doctor Scheibel, you may come to the witness chair," Vito said when everyone settled into their seats. "You may now present your side of the case."

Fritz came forward and sat in the witness chair. He began to speak, turning from Vito to ole Kipchong and back as he spoke. He told of his trip to the villages when he found el Engerot deserted except for the old man and the baby. He went on to describe how Ursula took the baby and nursed her, loved her as only a mother can love. How they schooled her, nursed her through illnesses, taught her to work in the hospital.

"We have done no less than any other parents would do for their child. Except for the color of her skin, Rebeka is a German girl. She speaks German as her first language. She also speaks four other languages—Swahili, Chagga, English, and Maa. She has read books about other lands. It would be a bad decision to make her return to where her future will consist of making mud-and-dung huts and milking cows.

"I have here," Fritz said as he pulled out the adoption papers and handed them to Vito, "a declaration making Rebeka my adopted daughter. Here also is a passport in her name as Rebeka Scheibel. Our intentions are to take her to Germany with us in four weeks."

Vito frowned over the documents, saw that they appeared in order, and handed them to Mr. Engare who didn't seem to know what he held. He read them slowly, then handed them back to Fritz.

"Mr. Engare, do you have any questions to ask?"

"Yes, your honor." He smiled as he made a few notations. "Doctor, did you know the names of the girl's father and mother?"

"No. I was not told. The mother was dead in the hut from smallpox."

"Did you ask if her father was still living, or not?"

"No, but my understanding was that the child had no one to care for her. That is why I took her home. She would have died with no one to nurse her."

"So you did not ask then—or later—as to any relatives who might want the child?"

"That's right," Fritz answered, frowning.

"Why did you wait seven years to get the adoption papers?" Mr. Engare had noticed the date on the papers. Fritz thought he asked the question in a triumphant tone, as though he found a fault on which to pounce.

"I was busy with the hospital, and didn't think it necessary, until several *murani* came to try to take her away by force. I couldn't let them take her because I know what they do with little girls. They didn't say a relative sent them, simply that she belonged in the village with her people."

Mr. Engare frowned and asked, "Did Mr. Kuyoni ever say to you that Mr. Kipchong would some day want her back?"

Fritz twisted his brow trying to remember. "Not directly. He only mentioned that the tribe might want her back because she was descended from a famous chief. I knew nothing about this so-called *One True Lion*."

"Did you ask the girl if she wanted to be your child?"

Fritz looked surprised. "No, of course not. I did it to keep her safe. A father does not ask his child, 'may I keep you from harm?' He does what he has to in order to make it more difficult for others to hurt her."

Vito interjected a question of his own. "Dr. Scheibel, when you had these adoption documents drawn up, what did you tell the authorities about her family?"

Fritz choked. What had he said? He wracked his brain trying to remember. "I believe I said that her parents might be both dead, that I didn't know who they were. That was good enough for them."

"They didn't require you to ask about the whereabouts of any living relatives?" Vito asked.

"No, they did not."

Vito frowned. Now Fritz saw his house of paperwork come tumbling down. He glanced apologetically at Rebeka. Mr. Engare jumped to his feet with another question.

"Sir, have you not at times rescued a child through your orphanage, and then later the parents came forward—maybe several weeks or months, or even a year later—and said, '*Asante*, you have saved my child, and now I want her back,' do you not give her over to them?"

"Yes." Fritz's face had a pained expression.

"Ah," Mr. Engare said with triumph in his voice, "yet Mr. Kipchong sent emissaries, not once, but two times to get his niece back to her family and her people, and both times you turned them away!"

Fritz couldn't answer.

"No further questions, your honor," Mr. Engare said, and sat down.

"You may step down, Doctor," Vito said with kindness in his voice. "We would like to have Rebeka speak, if she wishes." He looked toward her and waited for her hesitant nod. Fritz pressed her hand and looked into her eyes to give her strength.

Rebeka sat down in the witness chair and tried to stop the trembling of her hands by clasping them in her lap. She turned, and fastened her eyes on Vito. There was something about this strange man with a big nose who wasn't either German or English that she trusted.

At his prodding, she told of being taken in the night, the two-day trek across the land to the village, about finding out that ole Kipchong was her mother's uncle, and about building the matrimonial hut.

"What did they tell you about the proposed marriage?" Vito asked.

Without tearing her gaze from him, she answered, "They said that cows had already been traded, and there was no way out of it. They said I had to undergo the womanhood rite, the cutting, before the wedding feast."

"Did they ask you if you wanted to be married to the man you met?"

"No. They said it was already decided."

"Do you want to be married to him?" Vito's gaze bored into hers.

"No. He is old, and already has three wives. I told them I didn't want to marry him, but they just laughed. They said I should be happy to marry a chief."

"This womanhood ceremony—were you willing to undergo it?

At this, Rebeka's lowered her gaze to her hands. Mr. Engare looked embarrassed. "No," she whispered. "I—I didn't want it to happen. I don't want to talk about it—here." She looked at her father, who stood to his feet.

"Sir—your honor, can we speak about that in private—later?"

"If you wish," Vito answered, "Though I already know a good bit about it.

"Mr. Engare, do you have any questions for this witness? No?

Rebeka you may step down. I would like to ask Mr. Kipchong a further question."

When ole Kipchong came back to the witness chair, Vito said, "I would like to address the matter of marriage customs. Is it always customary to arrange a marriage for a girl without her consent?"

Through several questions and answers, Vito got a sketch of Maasai arrangements. Often, a girl and a man flirted with each other with their eyes before a marriage was arranged, always initiated by the man. If several men wanted the girl, then the number and health of the offered livestock came into the decision. The girl was not consulted at all. It made things more pleasant, though, if she liked the arrangement.

"Why do you buy and sell girls this way?"

An angry look crossed Mbae's face. He straightened in the chair and said in a perturbed voice, "We do not buy and sell. The nature of a marriage is that families are bound together. The cattle given are to show good will, a promise that now the two families will defend each other and work together. They are to compensate for the loss of a child."

"What happens if a girl does not want to be married to the man who has given cattle for her?" Vito asked.

"She has no choice."

"What I mean, is, what if she runs away and refuses to be the wife of the man? Say he has a bad reputation. Maybe he beats his wives, or is an idiot or something."

"It is the work of the family to make her be his wife. But…" ole Kipchong stroked his chin, reluctant to answer. "But sometimes, when a bad decision has been made by her father, he can give the cattle back. He will have lost honor, and his daughter will always be known as willful. It will be difficult for her to make another marriage."

"I see," Vito said. "I see it becomes a matter of personal honor for a man to continue with a marriage arrangement for his daughter even if she does not want it, to the point of forcing her. In an extreme case, given a rebellious daughter, he can give the cattle back and negotiate a marriage with another man. Right?" Ole Kipchong nodded.

The clock on the wall showed four o'clock. It had been a long time since Vito craved a drink of something stronger than tea or coffee, but now he did. Anything, to get his mind on something else. Up to this time his job had been fairly easy; right and wrong were easily distinguished one from the other. But this case. . . he shook his head.

"We will adjourn until Monday morning at eight o'clock. I have other matters to attend to tomorrow, and I want to speak in private with you and your wife, Doctor Scheibel, and you too, Rebeka. If necessary, with Mr. Kipchong also. Please be available to come to my office when I ask. I will sum up the case and make my decision on Monday." He pounded his gavel, stood to his feet, and exited the courtroom.

Instead of going to the club and getting a drink, though, Vito stayed at his desk until seven o'clock going through his books concerning colonial law practices in India and Kenya to find some sort of precedent for this case. Rajneesh left him there, going home with a sympathetic shake of the head.

Hours later, Vito rubbed his tired eyes. The only precedent he found was the banning, in India, of *suttee,* the custom in which wives were expected to throw themselves on their husband's funeral pyre. The only clear deduction he could make was the illegality of the adoption papers based on Fritz's wrongful assumption that Rebeka had no living relatives. He had therefore obtained a passport for the girl on a false premise. But given that the girl was not legally adopted, did that give the tribe the right to force her to undergo circumcision and arrange a distasteful marriage for her? And who was he, Vittorio Fernaldi, to decide such a matter?

The lantern flickered as moths fluttered around it. In the corner, a cricket began to sing. Outside, an owl hooted. Vito went home to a cold dinner and his bed.

On Friday morning, he heard the tabled cases. The man who beat his wife was fined twelve shillings, because that was what he had in his pocket, and then sent home. "It is not right to beat your wife," Vito told him.

With an impassive face, the man replied, "If a man has a donkey or mule that does not behave, he beats it until it does. It is the same with a wife."

"No," said Vito. "It is not the same. A wife is a person. One does not beat people to make them do what they should. One finds other ways of persuading them. You treat them nice when they do well, and ask them to stop when they don't. It works that way in English families. Englishmen don't beat their wives—" he remembered a case not too long before, when an Englishman had done just that when drunk, so he added "—and if they do, they are severely punished."

The man walked away with an amused expression. Vito sighed. It would take several generations for the people to accept new ways, he thought.

The second case was a little easier. Even though the thief pled not guilty, having been caught with the stolen goods in his hands was enough evidence to convict him.

"I went to sleep in my bed," the man lied, wide-eyed with

false innocence. "When I woke up, I stood in the street and the police had their hands on me, and someone had placed these items in my hands."

Vito sentenced him to a month in jail. As the police took the prisoner to jail, his wife wailed and beat her chest with sorrow. "Ay-ee! Ay-ee!" she mourned, as though he were dead, and followed him down the street.

Around three o'clock, Vito decided to go and talk with the Scheibels.

Rebeka, weeding the vegetable garden, saw him coming down the street and ran to tell her parents. Ursula sat in her rocking chair on the porch in a flowing caftan, fanning herself. Her swollen legs rested on a stool, and when she struggled to rise to her feet, Vito told her to remain seated. Fritz left his desk inside the house and joined them on the verandah.

The discussion turned to the court case, and Vito sighed before speaking. "It appears to me that the initial adoption was not legal. There's no way around it. Questions should have been asked that weren't; a search should have been made for relatives.

"Yet, on the other hand, the British Government has, in the recent past, turned a blind eye to violations of law by previous governments unless, of course, a flagrant abuse of someone's rights have taken place. I don't see that Rebeka being brought up in your home has been such a violation, unless she feels it has been." He looked at Rebeka, who shook her head.

"The British consider a girl of sixteen who is not yet married to be a child. If I rule that she is not your child legally, then she might have to be put under the care of her uncle, Mr. Kipchong. And we know where that will lead."

Fritz put his arm around his wife's shoulders. "We have faith in God," he said. "We trust that he will lead you to do the right thing, not just for us, but for Rebeka."

Vito winced. Why did the man have to keep bringing God into the picture? "That's all well and good," he said. "But in the end, it will be the wisdom of man that decides the case, not that of God."

"I disagree." Fritz's chin jutted out with German stubbornness. "It is God who has man's mind in his hands. I have faith in God."

"Faith," said Vito, deciding to argue. "Saying you have faith is like throwing a bucket of paint into a mud hole. It changes its color, but it's still mud and just as impassable. To say 'I trust God to work things out' is to excuse yourself from the task of making it work."

"To the contrary," Fritz said. "Faith is a dependence on a strength outside yourself. Faith believes this strength will add to natural strength, flow through your veins to accomplish the task that needs doing. It is the cement in that bucket of paint that mixes with the mud and makes it passable."

"I say that faith is like having a cloth tied over your eyes," Vito argued, "and waiting to be led about by someone else. Faith makes you blind."

"Not so, my friend. Being *without* faith is like being blind, or in the dark. You can't see anything. You have to touch things to understand them and to avoid bumping into them. You don't know—unless you hear or smell them—when others enter the room. You can't see the sunrise or sunset. You don't even know that it's the sun that's warming the world and your skin. You have to take others' word for it that there is, indeed, a sun.

"You see—faith is like light. You can't touch it, smell it, or actually see it except as it shines on things. Sometimes you can't even see where it comes from. But it illuminates everything. You don't even think much about the light itself—just what it shows you."

"Yet the sun—and its light—is physical and can be understood by the human mind," Vito said. "A man of reason doesn't see light and shout, 'a miracle of God!' He studies it. He doesn't have to believe in God to understand its properties. I told you before, I don't believe in God."

Rebeka sat by with wide eyes, looking back and forth between her father and Vito.

"Of course you don't believe in God," Fritz said. "You are blinded to him. I assure you, he exists. Faith has opened my eyes, and he is there. Without faith, you can't see anything. You feel things with your hands and describe them as best you can, but often they are not what you think.

"That's what faith does for a man. It reveals the whole. One can see faith at work everywhere, just as light shines on everything and brings out true colors and shapes."

Vito scowled. "Some would argue with you about faith being light," he said. "I still say that faith blinds people to reality."

"Do you think I am blind to reality, Mr. Fernaldi?" Fritz said, his voice incredulous. "Do you think the work I have done in building this hospital, my research in diseases, has all been the work of a blinded man? I would say I am very aware of reality. I would be in Europe working in a hospital with a large salary if I didn't have faith."

"What about the situation you are in now?" Vito said. "What does your faith show you about that? You're concerned about Rebeka's future, are you not? In fact, I see you as distraught with worry as any father would be who has no faith."

Fritz smiled. "Ah, you see that I am also human! I have allowed my eyes to be covered by the seriousness of the situation. Just because I have faith, doesn't mean I don't have human emotions and reactions.

"She is my daughter, as true a daughter as any that could come from my loins. I have great concern for her future, as any father would have. I see her walking toward the rim of a crater, and I can't see what is over the edge. Of course I'm concerned, but I also trust that God will provide a way for her, give her a special grace to endure whatever she must endure, and a way for me to rest my worries for her."

"Please, " Ursula reached out her hand to her husband. "Please, may we not argue at a time like this? It's Rebeka's future we speak of here. She is my life. I would die for her if I had to." She turned to Vito. "Please, sir, keep her best interests in mind."

"Forgive me, *Liebchen*," Fritz said. "And you, sir. I didn't mean to get into a sermon about what is important to me. We are here to speak of Rebeka."

"I would like to speak to Rebeka alone, if I may," Vito said. Fritz and Ursula agreed, and Vito and Rebeka walked out into the yard and sat on the terrace. The sun settled toward the horizon like a warrior king mellowing in late life, spreading a gentler, more benevolent strength to his subjects. The edges of the few clouds snagged on the top of Kilimanjaro turned gold and pink. A cool breeze picked up and ruffled Vito's hair.

"Rebeka," said Vito, "What I said about you still being a child in the eyes of the law is true. But after what you have been through, as well as in the eyes of the Africans, you are a woman. With thoughts and feelings of your own. I want to know how you feel about all this."

Surprised, Rebeka stared at him. "No one has ever asked me that. Everyone thinks they know what is best for me."

Vito was just as surprised at her vehement answer. He stared back into her eyes, realizing that here before him was a mature woman, born a hundred years too soon, full of intelligence and wisdom. There would be no easy answers for her. "Tell me," he said. His respect for her deepened.

"Whether I am their child or not, it doesn't matter. I am who I am." Rebeka started pouring out her thoughts and feelings, for the first time feeling free to speak without reproach. "I never was their child. I never felt that I was. I love them and they love me, but from the beginning I sensed the differences, even before I noticed the color of my skin.

"I am an African woman who has been raised as a white woman. Yet my parents took care to see that I knew what it would be like to live as an African when they sent me to the boarding school for girls. I know how white people think. I also know how African people think. I am somewhere in between. The two parts of me fight each other.

"I don't want to go to Germany to live. I'll cry when they leave, because they have been my family. But I don't want to go where people will stare because of my skin. I'm sure there are others like me somewhere. I'd like to find them and talk to them, to see how they manage while walking two paths at once. It's not knowing what will happen to me now that has me worried."

"Do you want to go with your uncle back to the village and be a Maasai woman?" Vito asked.

"No. As my father said in court yesterday, it would not be right to take someone who has an education like mine and force them to go live a life like that. I don't want it. But I don't know what I can do if I stay in Africa."

"Maybe you could go to Kenya, to Nairobi or somewhere, and work in a hospital," Vito suggested. "Maybe there you would find someone like yourself to marry."

Rebeka shrugged. "If I have to," she said, and he could tell she didn't want to. "What I really want is to stay here and work with children in the hospital and orphanage. Arusha is my home. But I know I don't want to go to the village."

"Believe me, Rebeka, I'll do everything possible to keep that from happening to you. But you understand I have to follow the law, don't you?" She nodded and looked down.

"I need to talk to you about something else, Rebeka, about the womanhood rite—the circumcision. I've been informed about it, so you don't have to describe it to me. What did the women tell you about having to undergo it?"

"They said I had to have it done," Rebeka said. "They said I could not be married without it." She shuddered, just thinking about it. "They say—but it's not true—that a woman who doesn't have it done will have idiot children, and her husband's—thing— will fall off. They said I was unclean without it." She closed her eyes in embarrassment and lowered her head.

"I see."

"I've worked with my parents in the hospital and have seen many women having their babies. The Maasai women, in particular, have a hard time because they are cut so much. My father says sometimes the baby dies because it can't come out, and sometimes the mother dies because she rips herself apart trying to give birth. I don't want that to happen to me. Please, can you make it so I don't have to endure that?"

"I will do everything I can. You have my promise."

Just then, Fritz came out of the house. "Mr. Fernaldi, sir, please excuse me. I've thought of something else I would like to mention. May I speak to you alone?"

"Of course. That's all I wanted to ask you, Rebeka. Do you

have anything else you want to say?"

Rebeka shook her head and left for the house. Fritz sat down beside Vito on the bench.

"Something you said yesterday, in your discussion with Mr. Kipchong about marriage, has finally seeped through this thick brain of mine. He said that if cattle were returned to the spurned suitor, the marriage would be annulled, and that someone else could come in and make an offer for the girl's hand in marriage."

"Yes, I remember," Vito said, wondering where this was going.

"There's a young man, just graduated from the seminary, who appears to be taken with Rebeka—and she with him. He's a fine person, a Christian, and he would make a good match for her. If there was some way…" Fritz faltered, then continued. "I don't have much money, but what I have I would pledge through the court so he could purchase cattle to give the old man for her hand. That is, of course, if you decide she isn't legally my daughter. I wouldn't ask for anything in return from him except a promise of good treatment."

Vito felt relieved. That might solve the whole problem. "Who is he? Should you—or I—go speak to him?"

"His name is Mpepo. He's staying at Pastor Luka's house over on Sokoine Street next to the church while he serves his six-month training period. He came with us on the rescue trip, and he's the one who ran and picked her up from the *manyatta* and brought her to me. I think you should speak to him, since you carry the weight of the law."

**The next morning, Vito found Mpepo in the church office** writing notes for a sermon the next day. He'd seen the muscular young African around town and a glimpse of his actions at Rebeka's rescue, and was impressed. He would make a good match for Rebeka. Yet he still had misgivings.

The two men had a long talk about Rebeka and her situation, the arranged marriage, her parents leaving, and her future. Mpepo agreed that he found the girl attractive, but said he had no cattle of his own, much less the money to purchase them.

"If you should want to marry her, it can be arranged and no one will know where the cattle came from," Vito said. "No repayment will be required. It will be a gift." He saw Mpepo's chin jut out slightly, and added, "however, if you feel the need to repay, something can be arranged. I understand that a man wants to know he has done his duty in a proper manner."

"I would like to consider this," Mpepo said. "When do you need my answer?"

"Monday morning. Be in my courtroom Monday at eight o'clock. I expect that your answer will be yes?"

"I will seek God's will."

"Go ahead." Vito sighed, and decided not to argue with him. "She is a prize that is dropped into your hands without having to fight for her. There are not many women with her strengths in the world. If I were you…" But Vito knew he wasn't, so he left Mpepo staring out the window instead of at his notes. Yet Vito still had that itch of premonition that things were falling into place too tidily, that it would take much more to find a solution to this case.

## CHAPTER TWENTY THREE

# His Majesty's Court, Arusha

**Vito spent Saturday evening and all day Sunday in his office drafting his decision** and typing it in English on the ancient typewriter with a crooked *m* key. He knew this ruling would become the law of the land until either overturned, or until new decisions were made on other similar cases. After a night of troubled sleep, he felt old and exhausted when he opened court at eight o'clock Monday morning.

Mbae ole Kipchong strode down the street just before eight. He felt confident that justice would be done this day, and that he and his wives would take Rebeka and go home to the interrupted wedding celebration. Mr. Engare had assured him this was the only decision that could be made. He was tired of staying with town Maasai. They ate the wrong foods and wore European clothes—he was sure their shirts and trousers made them itch and smell.

His counselor walked beside him toward the court. His two wives, wrapped in their best cloths and bedecked in coils of brass wire and beaded ornaments, followed at the proper ten paces, the three *murani* behind them. Those they passed on the street noticed the cavalcade, as did the residents coming out of their homes. Ole Kipchong knew everyone in town talked of this case and would do so for years to come. He felt vindicated.

Fritz rose from his knees and reached for his helmet. He had refused breakfast, choosing instead to spend the time praying. Rebeka and Ursula waited for him. Ursula insisted that on this day of decision she would attend court. He worried about her, but she refused to reconsider. He had sent a boy to ask for the bicycle *takisi,* a rickshaw-type conveyance, to be at his house to save her the dusty walk.

After he helped Ursula into the *takisi,* he got on his own bicycle, and with a demure Rebeka seated on the back, pedaled to court in time to help Ursula down from the *takisi* and into the courtroom.

All this took his mind off the proceedings, but when he finally sat down at their table, staring at Mbae ole Kipchong with his triumphant, arrogant face, the turmoil began again. Now he went over the plan he had in his mind, in case God didn't come through for him.

If the judge decided against them, he would ask for a few days to say goodbye to Rebeka, smuggle her to Moshi on Sawaya's lorry, and on to Tanga by rail. He and Ursula would join her and all three of them would sail back to Germany. He already had the passports and tickets. Sympathy would be on his side, and he was sure he could count on the court to not send anyone after them until it was too late. He congratulated himself on his plan. Either way, he would win.

Rebeka, oblivious to Fritz's plan, went into court wondering who she would be when it was over. Would she come out as ole Kipchong's niece, bride of Chief Kulale ole Mioli? Or would she remain the daughter of Fritz and Ursula Scheibel, and go to Germany with them, a slightly better future? All her efforts to take charge of her own destiny ended in futility. There was nothing she could do except take whatever came with whatever grace she could muster.

She sat beside her mother as they waited for the judge and stared at ole Kipchong and his wives—her uncle and aunts in the flesh. True, she thought, they had a kinship. She felt herself to be Maasai under her skin. Then she thought of the impending circumcision and marriage, and shuddered. Not *that* Maasai.

She looked at her father and wondered how he could be so calm. She looked at Ursula, who vigorously fanned herself, sweat beaded on her brow, and it wasn't even hot yet. Her mother had gained so much weight even though she ate so little. The teas her father brewed for her did little good anymore. He had told Rebeka it was her heart that didn't work right, and her body accumulated fluids. In Germany they would find doctors who could perhaps put her body right again. Rebeka hoped so.  But now it was her case that took everyone's attention. Just then, Vito came into the room. For the first time, Rebeka noticed the holes in the sleeve of his robe.

"All stand," intoned Rajneesh. They all stood, waiting for Vito to sit.

"I will read the decision in English," Vito said, after everyone sat down. He looked around, and noticed that everyone except Mpepo was present. He wondered where he was, and hoped that he would show up soon.

"This decision will go into the judicial files for the future, so it must be rendered in English. Mr. Engare, if you wish to translate word for word to your client, indicate so now. Otherwise I will pause at each point so you can summarize for him."

Mr. Engare said he would summarize to save time.

"All right then." Vito cleared his throat and began reading his decision.

Mpepo waited until the last minute to go to court. He didn't want to be seen traveling the same path and in the same direction as the others. He didn't want to have to explain why he attended. If someone asked, he would have to tell him he was ordered to do so. He entered the door as Vito began to read his decision. He slipped in and sat down on a bench against the back wall.

All night he had paced in his room, mulling the implications of the sermon he had preached on Sunday morning. His subject had been *Doing the Will of God,* in which he pressed on his listeners the importance of seeking God's will and following it, no matter what the cost. One must avoid evil and only do that which was good.

But later that night he saw the good and possible evil in each decision he faced.

On the one hand, if God had called him—as he believed—to be an emissary to his own Huru people, then his cousin Siferi opened the way. Hand in hand with the chief, he would have a status he might not obtain otherwise. And Damari, a beautiful Christian girl who pulled at his heart, waited to make his life complete. Together they could do so much.

On the other hand, Rebeka was the one he really longed for. Every time he thought of her, his flesh agreed. She, too, owned a beauty that went beyond the average African girl. Her intelligence rose far above Damari's. And as the magistrate said to him on Saturday, she was a prize being handed to him on a plate, and he alone could rescue her from a terrible destiny. Yet if he chose her, a Maasai girl, then he would not be able to go home to Huruland, and that was the stumbling block to this choice.

His thoughts roared like thunder all night, and when the roosters announced the early morning, he made his decision. He washed, dressed with care, and walked into the courtroom a few minutes late.

Vito noticed Mpepo slip into the rear bench and sighed with relief. Everything appeared to be going according to his plan. He cleared his throat and began to read his decision.

"When the League of Nations mandated to England the right to administer the former German East Africa, it was with reluctance that the Colonial Office took over this country, and called it Tanganyika to give it a new identity. This country is not a colony, as is Kenya." Vito looked at Mr. Engare who simply sat with his eyes fastened on him. "It is a territory, and the British government is here as a trustee.

"Even now there are debates within the Colonial Office and Parliament as to whether the colonies and mandates should be overseen with direct rule or indirect rule; whether the policies should be ones of assimilation of the people into western society, or peaceful preservation of ancient tribal customs, societies, and laws. Here in Tanganyika, the rule of law leans to the side of indirect rule and preservation.

"However, there is no question as to the reason for Britain being here. We are here to preserve peace—peace between Tanganyika and her bordering countries, and peace between the many tribes that make up the country. We are here to bring education and medicine, to find intelligent men and women who will one day be leaders of their people and find a place for Tanganyika in the world community. This policy will eventually cause the indigenous customs, societies, and laws to change as the leaders learn what other people in the world consider right.

"Therefore, at times we must make arbitrary decisions as to what is right and wrong in the way things are done. We tread carefully here, since our intent is to encourage chiefs and other leaders to form the policies and make the decisions in the villages.

"My decision here is not to address the right or wrong of Maasai marriage customs, or the way the people conduct their day-to-day lives. It is emphasized that this decision is only for this particular case and others like it, the case of so-named Rebeka Scheibel, Mr. Ole Kipchong and the wrongs he believes are done to him, and Dr. Scheibel and his wife who have raised this girl as their daughter. I will outline the major points of the suit filed by Mr. Kipchong and Mr. Engare, and address each in turn:

> One. He alleges that the British Government wronged Mr. Kipchong and his family by sending soldiers with guns to abduct Rebeka from their village and the intended circumcision and wedding ceremony.

> Two. He alleges that Dr. Scheibel received adoption papers calling Rebeka his daughter under false pretenses, and therefore put his guardianship of her into question. Who then, is her legal guardian—Dr. Scheibel or Mr. Kipchong?

> Three. He alleges that he and his village have the right to kidnap Rebeka and force her to undergo the circumcision ceremony and subsequent wedding to a man she does not care to marry.

On the first point: first of all, I find that the decision to send soldiers to return Rebeka to the Scheibel household was based on the knowledge held at that time. Those who made the decision were aware that Dr. Scheibel held adoption documents received from the German administration. For all intents and purposes, she was his daughter, and those sent by the village did not follow proper procedures to bring their claim.

Secondly, the *murani* who came in the night came like evildoers, like burglars. They tied and gagged the doctor and his sick wife. The manner of this seizure was against the law of the English as well as tribal law.

Therefore, the soldiers did no wrong. Since she was taken by force, the soldiers expected to be resisted with force when they came to take her back. Hence the use of guns.

That is my ruling on the first point of the suit. I give my apologies to Mr. Kipchong's wives that the soldiers felt it necessary to frighten them in order to do their duty.

On the second point, I am forced to decide that Rebeka is not the legal daughter of Dr. and Mrs. Scheibel."

Rebeka froze. Ursula gasped and jerked in her chair. Fritz stared at Vito, his heavy brows in a frown, his mouth in a straight line. He sat erect as though ready to jump to his feet.

"Through an oversight on either Dr. Scheibel's part or the part of the German government, no inquiries were made about any living relatives the girl might have. Without their consent, no legal adoption could be made. According to tribal law, the girls paternal and maternal relatives have the responsibility of caring for orphaned children." Mr. Engare translated this to ole Kipchong, his wives leaning forward to hear the translation.

"However," Vito continued, raising his voice over the courtroom murmur, "I also find that Dr. Scheibel did not operate in bad faith when he got those documents. His intent was to protect Rebeka from undue harm. His intentions were kind and well meaning.

"Considerable amounts of money were spent on her education, food and clothing, as well as medical care and instruction in the hospital. She attended the mission boarding school to help her adapt to African ways. Therefore, before I will allow Mr. Kipchong to assume his legal authority as guardian, I will require him to pay to Dr. Scheibel the sum of ten thousand shillings to reimburse him for his expenses. Until then, she must be a ward of the court."

The murmur grew louder. Ole Kipchong argued with his counselor, and others whispered to each other. Vito waited a few moments, then brought the court to order again.

"I have yet to cover the third point, that of the right of Mr. Kipchong to force his niece, Rebeka, to undergo a circumcision and marriage without her consent—in fact in the face of her passionate disagreement.

"This is the hardest decision to make, since the government mandate is to protect the customs of the indigenous people while instructing them in preparation for international awareness.

"It is here that the policy of Individual Rights must be followed. Britain, along with most nations, holds that a fundamental respect of the rights of the individual is central to a peaceful society. The government will not permit slavery or forced indenture, even if it is customary. We do not tolerate bogus trials of supposed witches. We do not sanction murder of deformed babies, or of anyone. The taking of goods without permission is against all laws, both European and tribal. Nor will we knowingly allow young women, who by nature of their gender are powerless, to be forced into acts that deprive their right to full enjoyment of their gender. We consider this a ritualized rape.

Nor should they be forced into a life-long association with anyone in a marriage of which they do not approve. If young women willingly accept these customs, that is one thing. But if they should seek escape, the court must give them sanctuary.

"Therefore, I have decided that in this case Mr. Kipchong must return to Chief Kulale ole Mioli the cattle and other property he has received for the hand of Rebeka in marriage. He is free to offer her to another suitor, preferably one of her approval. The District Commissioner will return next week, and he will give a final review of this ruling. I believe he will concur. If Mr. Kipchong so desires, he may take this to Dar es Salaam for review by the High Judiciary.

"So that Mr. Kipchong does not further feel shamed, there is one in this court who is prepared to offer him a price half again higher than that accepted from the chief."

Vito looked over at Mpepo and everyone followed his gaze. Mpepo sat stunned at everyone's open-mouthed gape. He hadn't anticipated that it would be like this. The words he wanted to say flew from his mind.

Ursula could barely keep up with the decision by Judge Fernaldi. Her understanding of English wasn't as good as her husband's, and her mind went blank when he said they were not the legal parents of Rebeka. All she could think was, *they are taking away my daughter.*

To intensify her confusion, the increasing heat of the day weighed down on her, and she could barely catch her breath. Her heart hammered inside of her, and though she took deep breaths, it felt like a bird struggling to escape.

When the judge announced that someone present offered a higher price for Rebeka's hand than the chief had offered, she turned along with everyone else to see. A feeling of relief washed over her when she saw Mpepo. His eyes met and locked onto Rebeka's. She turned to her daughter and saw the joy on her face. A vast relief washed over her.

She glanced back to Mpepo. On her other side, Fritz had reached out to hold her hand, and he squeezed it. *He knew,* Ursula thought, *Fritz knew this might happen, but he didn't tell me so I wouldn't raise my hopes.*

As she watched, she saw a glazed look come over Mpepo's face and he shifted his gaze away from Rebeka and turned it to the judge. He gave an imperceptible shake of his head, got to his feet, and walked out the door.

Ursula saw her daughter—the daughter of her heart—open her mouth in astonishment, a look in her eyes like that of a wounded gazelle. Her heart beat harder, a sharp stabbing pain this time, the bird pecking its way out of her rib cage.

She turned to the judge who stared at her. Behind the judge stood a stranger, his body in shadow, but a shaft of light that came through the window illuminated his face. No one saw him come in; she wondered how, while watching Mpepo leave the room, she didn't see the stranger come in.

He placed his hand on Vito's shoulder, and his glance at her thrilled her.

*I understand!* The realization burst into her mind like a blindfold being removed from her eyes. *Oh, yes! I understand! The judge is in God's hands!*

She stood to her feet and pointed at the man. "Fritzie, look!" she said. "An angel from God!" She choked, and could say nothing more. A burst of joy flooded her as she understood. As she stood transfixed by knowledge, the joy slowly receded and she slumped to the floor.

Vito watched Ursula as she saw Mpepo leave. He understood

her love for Rebeka. He saw her face flush as she tried to comprehend what was happening. He saw her struggle to her feet, transfixed by joy. She pointed toward him and cried out, "Fritzie, look! An angel from God!"

His plan crumpled even as Ursula crumpled to the floor and the courtroom erupted in pandemonium. He joined Fritz and Rebeka as they knelt over her. Fritz tried to find her pulse. Rebeka wailed, "Mama! Mama!" Everyone else just stood around, mesmerized, wondering what to do or say.

Fritz stood slowly to his feet. "My wife—" he covered his face with his hands, "My wife—is dead." He knelt again and put his arms around Rebeka and wept.

Vito went back to his table and banged his gavel several times to get the attention of the room. "We will take ten days to give the family time to take care of the matter at hand and grieve. Come back a week from Thursday at two o'clock for the disposition of the case.

Had Ursula called him an *angel?* He hurried from the room so no one would see his tears.

CHAPTER TWENTY FOUR

# Plans Laid to Rest

**Right after he left the courtroom, Mpepo went to his bedroom at Pastor Luka's home to gather some things and leave for Huruland.** He would get a ride with a lorry going north. But before he could leave, someone pounded on the door, calling his name. The magistrate was angry.

"What have you done?" Vito fumed. "You walked out on the best woman ever offered to you. You humiliated me, you spit on the doctor's offer, you told me—"

"I only told you I would seek God's will," Mpepo said. "And I did. All night. I cannot marry Rebeka and go to my people in Huruland. They do not like Maasai people, and I could not take a Maasai wife. My calling is higher than a choice of wife."

"So your almighty God says that, to keep your promise to him, it's all right to throw a defenseless girl into a den of lions."

Mpepo flinched. "I do not wish that. I pray for another solution to her problem. But it is God's problem, not mine."

"Well, your God better solve it, because I'm fresh out of ideas. And now, on top of it all, her mother—the doctor's wife—has died in the courtroom. It seems that God is punishing Rebeka for crimes she has not committed."

Mpepo started. "I didn't know. I left...."

"Yes, you left before it happened. Go on now; go to your beloved people! Others will try to solve the problems caused by your decision!" Vito, red with anger and with clenched fists, left the room. Mpepo almost wished he had felt the pain of a blow. But the spear had been cast, and he must follow through.

He left on the first lorry out of town. He mulled over the events that occurred in the courtroom. While he mourned the death of the doctor's wife, he couldn't avoid the feeling inside that he had made the right decision. He was anxious to get home where the celebration of his cousin's chieftainship would take place. He wanted to get home in time to arrange his betrothal to Damari. He had decided, and now he felt free of the weight that had burdened him for the past weeks.

Luka had told him, "Long before you were faced with the choice of a wife, Mpepo, you knew God wanted you to go to your people. Your choice must be made with that in mind." It took Luka, an outside observer and a man whom he respected, to set things in their proper order.

The betrothal arrangements were easily made. His mother was happy with his choice; she had worried about him bringing home a stranger she might not like. Damari was ecstatic. Her smiles could not be contained and her eyes glowed with love whenever he spoke with her. He knew she could make him happy. And Siferi kept punching him on the shoulder and calling him brother.

The celebration the next day took place with marching *askaris* in full uniform demonstrating their rifle skills with volleys that sent children scurrying for their mothers. Dancers came on the field in native regalia to honor their new chief. The women came out and danced in a line, chanting the glories of their new chief. Siferi glowed with obvious pride. Afterward, came *futuboli* games and races for children before the women served the feast and the *pombe* flowed. It was dark when Siferi stood to make his speech.

Mpepo kept this first disagreement with Siferi to himself. Surely, with all he had to drink, the man did not know what he said. He lifted his fist into the air and shouted, "Give me your sons to educate, your daughters to learn! We will send them to the best schools and teach them the ways of the white man! We will then fill the posts of government and take the leadership of our country! The Huru people will become known as the *People of Uhuru*, Freedom! Everyone will flock to us and bow at our feet because we are the people who will bring freedom and strength!" Mpepo gaped at him.

Then Siferi shouted, "My cousin—and soon to be my brother as well—will be the spiritual leader of our people. My first decree is that everyone must put away their spirit objects and be baptized as a Christian!" He whispered to Mpepo, "Isn't that a good idea of mine, brother?" He raised his voice and continued to the people, "As soon as he has finished his apprenticeship in Arusha, my cousin will come and build us a church. Everyone must come and spend one day a week building this church. God will notice this, and bless us and make us strong! No other religion will be allowed in our land!"

Mpepo scowled. This was not the way Christianity worked. He decided he must have a talk with his cousin when he was sober.

**Rebeka, her heart filled with sorrow, moved quietly about her duties.** Her father was a broken man. He sat in his chair, his face impassive, not moving or noticing those who gathered in the room in silence to offer him unspoken comfort. He reminded Rebeka of the granite faces she often imagined on the hills. There was one in particular that had shadows that smiled in the morning and frowned in the evening. She often thought up stories about people of long ago who remained in perpetual guard over those who traveled the plains below. Now she imagined her father as one of these unmoving faces.

The second day after the funeral, a cough in the yard brought her to the doorway. Surprised, she saw Nareyu and Wambui, ole Kipchong's wives.

"We have come to eat sorrow with you," Nareyu said.

Wambui added, "And to pour oil on your troubled spirit."

Touched, Rebeka said, "Come, sit with me in the shade." She led them to the shady side of the house and they sat cross-legged in silence. Several more Maasai women came in from the street and joined them, until eight of them gathered around Rebeka, wrapped in a silent sisterhood of grief.

Anderea brought sweet tea made with milk. The women drank it in silence. After about an hour Nareyu stood to her feet and said, "We will go now. May you have peace in spite of your loss."

When they left, closing the gate behind them, Rebeka ran to her room and had a healing cry into her pillow. Their surprising kindness gave her comfort. They helped her find within herself a well of strength, enough to see her through the desert of trouble that lay ahead.

The next day Fritz came back to life and said, "Rebeka, we should sort through your mother's things before I leave. Anything you want you can keep. The rest we can give away."

There was little of anything more than sentimental value. A brush and comb, an ivory hair ornament her father had found in the bazaars of Dar es Salaam, Ursula's Bible, a few items of clothing Rebeka could wear, such as a red sweater that still held Ursula's scent. Fritz gave her some photographs to keep, pictures of happier days when she clung to Ursula's skirts or mugged for the camera. In these, her healthy mother smiled at the photographer. Rebeka took the meager pile to her room, and when she returned, she saw her father standing in front of the storage chest, his back to her, his shoulders heaving in silent sobs. He held Ursula's underthings in his hands. Rebeka watched a moment, then slipped past the doorway. How he had loved her mother. A stab of pain went through her. Would anyone ever love her?

**Mbae ole Kipchong's eye twitched when he was angry, as it did now.** He could still the twitching by placing his hand on it, but as soon as he put his hand down, it started twitching again. He strode around the dusty kraal where he and his retinue stayed trying to figure out what to do.

There were three stumbling blocks, as he saw them. First, ten thousand shillings was an impossible sum. If all the Maasai sold all their cattle, they would hardly gather that much money. It was a ridiculous amount. That much money did not exist in his world. He would disregard this ruling and just take the girl again at the first opportunity. After all, the judge had ruled that he, Mbae ole Kipchong, was her legal guardian, whatever that meant. Anyone with sense could tell she belonged with him.

Second, he would have to give back the cattle he received from Chief ole Mioli. He had become attached to them, but this could be done. Maybe he could do it in the dark of night so no one would see and mock him. But he wondered what to do about the two calves that were born after he received their mothers. Must he give the calves back, too? He would have to take that matter to the men at the *boma* to decide. And lose even more esteem. But it could be done discreetly.

The third matter puzzled him, and that was the legend. The

entire world seemed bent against its fulfillment. If he must publicly give back the cattle and be humiliated in order to see it come to fruition, then he would submit. The legend said *The Expected One* would be a descendant of *The One True Lion*. He would lead his people, the Maasai, to their destined greatness. With Rebeka as the only living descendant, she had to mother either the One, or one who would give birth to him. Somehow, she must become a mother to pass it on. Chief ole Mioli might have to be pacified, passing him over so late in the betrothal, but ole Kipchong had no problem with submitting several names to Rebeka for her choice. But if she turned down the most prestigious man in the tribe, who would she accept?

He mulled over these things and called in vain on the spirits to illuminate him. He decided to call a convocation of all the *oloibonik,* all the Maasai seers. Perhaps their concerted efforts would bring light to the difficulties at hand. Ole Kipchong called his three *murani* over for a talk. When they were through, the young warriors set off at a jog toward the villages around Kilimanjaro.

Several days before the participants were to return to court, twelve men sat in a circle under the thorn tree by the kraal pondering the future of the tribe.

**The lower slopes of Kilimanjaro contained a heavy rain forest with little undergrowth,** and Vito found it easy to climb. Propelled by his anger, he ascended the slopes with his pack on his back at a speed that made him breathe hard and expel the resentment he felt toward Mpepo. Exhilaration replaced it as he relaxed and enjoyed the steady ascent. He felt his lungs expand to inhale more air as he climbed. He was thankful for the years in the Alps that developed them so well.

The trees around him were mostly cedar with date palms, figs and some wild olives. Torrents of ice-cold water tumbled down deep gorges. The well-trod path from Marangu pointed the way up to the summit.  For the past twenty years, expeditions from all over Europe came to climb the mountain. Once a path emerged, the others found it easy to make it more indelible. Just the month before, a large British team had made the ascent and planted the British flag on the summit. Vito had a copy of their notes with him to help him on his way.

He thought about Ursula Scheibel's funeral that took place the day after she died. The Lutheran church, crammed with people from all over the area, witnessed to her life. Vito had been amazed to see the many people she had rescued from death when they were babies. The orphanage children sang a song in her memory. This quiet woman had lived a meaningful life, and Vito felt shamed by her selflessness.

He had glanced around and not seen Mpepo. He asked about him and was told that he had gone to his cousin's inauguration as chief of the Huru nation. When Vito strode out of the church, he knew that in the nine days remaining before court convened again he must leave town to rid himself of anger. What better thing to do than climb the mountain that taunted him each morning? His pack had been ready for months. All he had to do was get his things, pack some food and water, tell Rajneesh and Mordecai, his house man, where he would be, and find some conveyance to take him to Moshi and on to Marangu.

At least a dozen men accosted him in the tiny town of Marangu to ask for the job of guide. "No," he answered each. He needed to do this alone. The climb would return him to his roots in the Alps, where from the age of fifteen he climbed, alone, some of the most perilous peaks. It would take his mind off the problem at hand, and the cooler air offered an escape from the heat.

After spending the night in Marangu, he traversed the forest area. This year the government had declared it a National Forest Reserve to keep people from stripping the trees off the slopes for firewood. By afternoon the path took on a serious climb and he had to pause often to catch his breath. He stopped frequently to gaze at the unusual trees that towered above him or to hide beneath one when the misty air turned to rain. By late afternoon he came to Bismark Hut built by the German Kilimanjaro Club. He felt thankful for the pieces of firewood left by previous climbers. There was a distinct evening chill.

He slept soundly, and when he rose in the morning he dressed quickly because it was cold and the fire had gone out. His breath formed vapor in front of his face, something he hadn't experienced since leaving Europe. His anger had left him now and his mind was sharp and clear as he climbed upward. While there seemed to be no explanation, Mpepo had chosen against Rebeka, and now Vito needed another plan to protect her.

*Rebeka,* he thought. *How much pain can one young woman endure?* In one short afternoon she lost her identity, the man she loved, and her mother. He needed to study the ramifications and possible results of his decision. It dismayed him to realize he was no longer an impartial judge.

He left the forest early in the day and came to an area where clumps of giant heather grew. The morning mist dissipated and allowed the sun to break through. After about a mile, he came onto rocky ground with clumps of grass. The high altitude forced him to walk with slow steps and make frequent stops to catch his breath and admire the view.

Immediately below him the slopes were blanketed in a thick cloud. But beyond that he saw the sun-drenched plains, Mt.

Meru, and the towns of Moshi and Arusha. Peace and quiet seeped into his soul. He lifted his face to the sun, closed his eyes, and savored the moment. The last time he had climbed a snow-capped mountain, he struggled with guns and ammunition to fight the Austrians in the Alps with a battalion of Italian soldiers. He tried not to remember those days.

He arrived early at the second cabin and hesitated, wondering if he should continue past it. But his notes said there was nowhere else to stay until the cave at the saddle. From there, the instructions said, it would be possible to make a one-day dash for the peak and back to the cave. So he made camp and lit a small fire with the few sticks of olive wood he had brought with him. Perhaps some uninterrupted thinking time would be in order.

First of all, he thought, as he drank a cup of hot tea, regardless of his ruling, the Maasai people would do as they pleased. They were not noted for their willingness to abide by the law. Even though they were restrained from taking Rebeka until they paid for her upkeep, they might do again what they had done before—kidnap her. He thought it likely that they'd attempt that when Fritz left for Germany. This time, the law might not be able to rescue her. The tribe could force her to undergo the circumcision rite and the marriage before she could be freed, and though threats would fly, they would be too late.

If she were a ward of the court, he could send her to Kenya, to the hospital in Nairobi where she could enter formal training as a nurse. This course appealed to him. But Maasailand reached to the outskirts of that city, and with no one to protect her, she would be even more vulnerable there.

There was also the loss of face Mbae ole Kipchong must be experiencing. One thing Vito had learned during his year in

Africa was that *face*, that ethereal element that preserved respect and dignity, was all-important to the people. There must be some way he could save face for the man, as he had tried by arranging a marriage between Rebeka and Mpepo.

The legend was another matter. He dismissed it from the case. All people had legends—mysterious promises—that kept people dreaming around their fires, elusive prophecies that constantly danced out of reach. Without them, groups and clans disintegrated. He would not sacrifice the girl for such a legend.

Vito fell asleep soon after dark and dreamed he sat in a courtroom where everyone stared at him, waiting for him to perform some sort of magic trick. He dreamed he walked across a glacier carrying Rebeka away from the Austrian army. He whispered to her, *don't be frightened, Rebeka. I'll take care of you. I promised your mother*. He kissed her, and she turned into Therese. He hadn't dreamed of Therese for several years and when he woke he shivered in the pre-dawn cold, wondering about the dream and the feelings stirring through his body, feelings that had been dead so long.

The climb to the desert-like saddle took longer than expected. The altitude bothered him more than he thought it would. He stayed in the cave, called *The House of God* by the Chagga people, for two nights to get acclimated to the altitude. He sorted out the items in his pack. Since it should only take one day to get to the peak and back, he left most of his food and extra clothing behind, keeping only the ice-climbing equipment, the scarf Therese had knitted for him during the war, a little food, and a canteen of water.

Early the next day he set out for the peak that loomed over the crater. It wasn't long before he encountered the snow-covered glacier, so he pulled his axe and crampons out of his pack. He had made the crampons out of building nails studded in leather straps to slip over his boots. He continued his climb upward.

He stood on the rim of the crater and felt the awe every climber before must have felt. To be alone on the top of the African continent with only the wind for a companion made him feel small and insignificant. Nearly two miles across and five hundred feet deep on the south side, the extinct crater held another, smaller cone that also had a small crater. He climbed around to the highest point, on the maps named *Kaiser Wilhelm Spitze.* He didn't linger long. At over nineteen thousand feet, he felt faint and dizzy and knew he should descend as rapidly as possible. To make matters worse, a mass of clouds billowed upward from the blanket around the base and he knew it would be dangerous to remain on the glacier.

It was his rapid descent that caused him to fall. The storm blew upward with blizzard conditions and he could barely see his way. One of his leather crampon straps broke and came off. He slipped and tried to catch himself with the axe, but it twisted out of his grasp and clattered down across the ice and out of sight. He fell and wrenched his knee, his leg twisted behind him.

He knew there was a cave nearby just below the glacier—he'd seen it on his way up to the peak—so he peered through the snow and crawled along until he found it. When the wind swept the snow off the glacier and into the cave where he tried to hide from it, he knew he was in great danger. For the first time he thought of possible death.

He shivered as he drew his inadequate coat around his shoulders and hunched down to wait for either his own death or that of the wind—whichever came first—though he anticipated the former if the storm didn't soon blow over. His fingers and feet were already numb with the bitter cold. He fumbled as he took off his knapsack and removed the final packet of dried goat meat, a canteen of water that appeared to be frozen, a pair of dry socks, matches, and a single candle. His injured knee was now swollen and stretched the fabric of his trousers so tight he could barely bend his leg. He was thankful for the cold that numbed the pain a little.

The swirling clouds and snow hid the setting sun and made the cave dark. *Might as well light the candle*, he thought. It would be stupid to die without tapping that small source of heat. His fingers shook and stumbled over each other as he tried, and failed, to strike a match, and each fell in turn onto the cave floor. He couldn't feel the stones as he swept his fingers across them to try to find the lost matches. He only sensed them as they vibrated through his muscles up his arm. Finally, peering through the gloom, he sighted a match, brought his two hands together to pick it up and placed the stem end in his mouth. He picked up the matchbox the same way and passed the match end over the emery coating. When it burst into flame, he dropped the box and lifted the candle, which he managed to grasp between his stiff fingers. He held it to the flame until the wick caught and dropped the match before it burned his nose. The warmth gave momentary comfort to his face. He cupped his hands around the candle flame as best he could to warm them.

The first sensation of heat pained him as it prickled its way up his arms to his shoulders. Rather than a comfort, the awareness of cold only heightened and he began to shiver even more. This time he knew it was his body's last attempt to warm itself. He remembered his first solo climb twenty-seven years before, when he was fifteen.

A similar storm had pinned him near the summit of Mont Blanc. Then he had been better equipped, with adequate clothing, food, and an extra woolen blanket. Death never came near, nor did it enter his mind. Instead, after three days, he emerged victorious though less cocky. But this time his circumstances differed.

His gear for Africa did not include mountain climbing equipment. Canvas safari jackets and leather boots were the heaviest clothing he possessed, though his one sweater of Scottish wool fit nicely beneath the jacket, and he wore two pair of trousers over silk pajamas and three pairs of socks. His gloves and hat were home made from several layers of cotton cloth with an outer shell of tanned antelope skin and stuffed with kapok.

He shifted his body against the side of the cave and fastened the candle by its drippings to a flat stone and held the frozen canteen of water over the flickering flame to thaw as much as he could before the candle burned out. He sipped the drops of melted ice and ate the final piece of dried goat meat.

As he chewed the dried meat, he noticed some stones close to the entrance and decided to creep forward and pile them in an effort to keep out the cold and snow. He brought the candle with him, shielding the flame with his hand, and he started to stack the stones into a semblance of a windbreak. He pulled some more stones out from the side of the cave, and as he finished stacking them into a windbreak, the candlelight glinted on something in the dust.

He reached forward and grabbed it. It trailed a brass wire fastener that caught on something. A few tugs broke it loose and brought to the surface some old bone fragments. He paused, then began to push the dirt away from the area, discovering more bone fragments and part of a skull that crumbled as he unearthed it. The item in his hand was made of brass pounded flat and augured with a hole for the wire. In the center of the medallion was a large stone, and as he rubbed the encrusted dirt off it and turned it toward the candle, he could see the stone was yellow in color, surrounded with crude etchings of the face of a lion.

A chill ran down his back as he remembered the little leather book the Indian merchant had given him back in Dar es Salaam when he first arrived in Africa. *The Legend of the Lion.* How had it ended? Of course, he remembered now. *The One True Lion* climbed the White Mountain of God and never returned. Perhaps part of the legend was true, after all. He put the medallion in his pocket and went back to his place against the cave wall. He settled back to allow sleep—or death—come to claim him. He harbored only one regret in his mind. *Rebeka, forgive me.* Someone else would make the final disposition of her case pending in the Arusha District Court.

Instead of sleep or death enveloping him in soft, silent arms, he drifted in a dark world somewhere in between, not a delirium of fever but one of hypothermia. In this unnatural state, he observed a parade of people walk through the cave, some of whom he hadn't seen for many years.

His parents led the way, with his grandparents. They came by him and touched him in sympathy.

"Vittorio," his father said, "every generation that lives strives to leave something of itself behind. You are what your mother and I left for the future—your mind, your passion for justice. Don't desert it now. Make sure what you leave behind is only good."

His mother kissed his cheek and smiled. His grandparents tousled his hair as though he were still a small boy. They all walked on and disappeared out the mouth of the cave.

His college friends came next, drinking beer and grinning. Along with them his former friend Benito Mussolini, who raised his mug in salute as he passed by, as though to say, *Vito, you should have stayed with me. I would have made you famous. You wouldn't be dying here in this god-forsaken place.*

Cecil and Gertie Neville followed. Gertie said: *No, Vito, you shouldn't have stayed with him. You are who you are—a man of strength. We are your true friends now, and we have complete confidence in you. You will survive this.*

When everyone passed out the cave entrance and Vito felt alone again, he heard a sound and turned. Therese came and sat close, putting her head on his shoulder. He could smell her hair and feel her warmth—his beloved Therese with her black hair a cloud around her face. A sob rose in his throat as he felt himself become vulnerable again. Antonio and Theresita, quiet for a change, sat nearby and observed him with sober expressions. 'Tonio held his white cat in his arms, and 'Sita twisted her long braid, looking at him as though ready to ask a question. Behind them he saw Rebeka, hovering in the shadows, her eyes wide with terror. *Please don't die,* was her silent message. *You have to help me.*

"Vittorio," Therese said. She had always called him that, never Vito as his friends did. "Vittorio, listen to me. You will not die. Remember, though, that death is always a breath away, and after that there is God. You may have mislaid your faith, but you haven't lost it entirely. God is here, waiting for you to come back.

"Remember, Vittorio, that God does not care about a person's outward appearance, but what is in the heart. You shouldn't, either."

She reached out and beckoned to Rebeka who stepped forward. She took her hand and brought her over. "Sit here with us, Rebeka," she said.

Therese reached into his pocket and drew out the medallion.

She handed it to Rebeka, who looked at it with a puzzled expression, then handed it back to Vito. Therese placed Rebeka's hand on his injured knee and he felt warmth suffuse his whole leg. Then, with a smile, Therese stood, took the hands of the children, and they vanished. He felt no pain at their disappearance, only gratitude for that moment with them. They were from another life, from a book now closed and put away. But he had no idea what her words meant.

Rebeka exclaimed over his swollen knee. She bent over and kissed it, took his scarf—the one Therese had made for him four years previously—and wrapped it around the knee. The look of terror was gone from her face. She stood to her feet and followed the others.

He must have slept then, because he woke with warm sunshine streaming through the partially blocked mouth of the cave. He no longer felt cold. He moved his leg carefully, and felt little pain. The swelling was almost gone. He marveled at the scarf wound around the knee. Did Rebeka do it, or did he in his delirium? The candle had died into a lump of misshapen wax on the stone. He rose to his feet with difficulty, his joints complaining, and tested his injured leg. If he kept his foot facing straight forward he could step without too much pain. Maybe he would find a staff along the way to lean on. He limped out of the cave with the euophoria of a man given a second chance to live.

During his descent of the mountain to Marangu, Vito had plenty of time to think over what occurred. He found a sturdy pole just below the saddle and used it as a staff. In spite of the pain and difficulty in walking, he marveled at how little the wrenched knee hindered his movements. He hardly noticed his surroundings as he descended, his mind preoccupied with trying to understand the meaning of the events in the cave. Had he hallucinated? Or was it a dream? He couldn't tell for sure. The medallion and the skeleton were real. So was the candle; it was there in the morning. Someone, probably he himself, had wound the scarf around his knee. He pulled the medallion out of his pocket. In the sunlight he could tell that the stone was amber, set in the etched lion's face where an eye should be, gleaming at him with a surreal intelligence.

Why had Therese brought Rebeka to him? Why had she taken the medallion from his pocket and handed it to her? Was he supposed to give it to Rebeka when he returned, maybe because it was her ancestor he took it from, there in the cave? What did Therese mean by what she said? *Remember, Vittorio, God does not care about a person's outward appearance, but what is in the heart. You shouldn't, either.* Why did she think he needed to be reminded of that? He had never paid much attention to a person's nationality in determining justice.

Vito was halfway down the mountain, mulling these things over and over in his mind, when a thought struck him and he stopped on the path, astonished by the idea. Did Therese mean for him to take Rebeka into his home as a—?

*Surely not! The English community won't stand for that! No, she'll be my ward, like a daughter to keep me company.* The thought of someone around the house to talk to gladdened him. Rebeka was so much more than any woman on the streets of Arusha. She had a rare intelligence, even compared to European women. She had been raised as a European. In his dream—or hallucination—she had brought healing to his injured knee. After she kissed it and wrapped Therese's scarf around it—he paused, thinking of the significance of that—it began to heal. *She will be my daughter*, he thought Would she bring healing to other parts of his life, to wounds that he didn't want healed until now?  He would wait and see how it played out in the courtroom on Thursday.

When Vito got home on Wednesday afternoon, he called Mordecai to his living room and held a long discussion with him. He gave Mordecai a wad of bills and sent him out of the city.

CHAPTER TWENTY FIVE

# Saved by a Butterfly

**The courtroom filled up fast on Thursday afternoon. The sky was overcast, and a wind blew through the streets sending dust eddies whirling.** The leaves of trees turned underside up, predicting rain. Men clutched their hats, and women their skirts, as they hurried along. The children enjoyed the skin-tingling breeze and danced in the wind.

Fritz and Rebeka held hands, deciding to walk to court this time rather than ride Fritz's bicycle. They wanted the time to calm themselves, not knowing what would happen this day. Kuyoni came and walked with them, as did a few other friends. Mpepo was nowhere to be seen.

Mbae ole Kipchong came with his usual attendants, increased by the eleven *oloibonik* who came to hear what the court decided and, if necessary, to protest. These Maasai took over most of the benches in the room and the *murani* had to stand along the back and in the corners. Mr. Engare held his papers in a neat pile. There was nothing further to be argued.

Ole Kipchong felt remorse over the death of the white doctor's wife. He had sent his wives to eat sorrow with Rebeka because he wanted her to know that her people were not enemies. He still held out hope that she would return with them to their village. He felt comforted by the presence of his eleven *oloiboni* brothers behind him, many of them related to him by blood.

Vito was several minutes late, and when he entered the

crowd was restless. Rajneesh had them stand as usual. The new attendees were a little puzzled by it all, but they shuffled to their feet at a word from Engare. Then they all sat and quieted; even the lizards on the wall froze in place as though waiting to hear the summation of the case. The fan barely circulated the thick, humid air.

Vito glanced around at each person. Fritz seemed to have aged ten years in the ten days since he buried his wife. Even his hair appeared whiter and thinner and his jowls sagged, giving him a tired expression. Rebeka had aged, too, though she looked more poignant, more beautiful. She still wore a scarf to cover her shaved head. Vito made eye contact with her and held her gaze, trying to communicate hope. She must have understood something because she suddenly looked away.

"In the event anyone has forgotten the points made ten days ago," Vito said to the crowd, "I will read them over." He read the statement in English again as he had before. Mr. Engare translated in a loud voice so all the Maasai would understand.

Just before finishing, Vito saw a flicker of movement in the doorway and glanced over. Mordecai was there, a grin on his face. He put both hands, fingers outspread, up in the air and then held up his right hand. Vito nodded, and Mordecai disappeared. It happened so fast that few people saw it.

Vito finished his summation, and then added, "Mr. Kipchong has been ordered to give back the cattle Chief ole Mioli paid for Rebeka. There is still an offer to Mr. Kipchong for her, fifteen head of cattle, half again as much as the Chief gave."

An electric atmosphere struck the room. Loud whispers buzzed as people looked at each other. Word had gotten out that Mpepo had refused to take Rebeka as his wife. No one had heard of another suitor. Vito glanced at Rebeka, who looked puzzled.

Fritz's face couldn't be read. He had already borne too much to show emotion.

Vito brought the court to order. "The offer is mine. The cattle are at my friend Mordecai Mayala's house. Mr. Kipchong is free to examine them today. If he agrees they are fine cattle, the matter is settled. Rebeka will become my ward."

It took a few minutes for the statement to sink in. Vito saw incredulity overcome confusion as everyone grasped that he, a European, was offering to buy Rebeka, an African girl—an unheard of situation. Rebeka's look of astonishment turned to dismay as she gasped and put both her hands over her face. Fritz was the last to get his meaning.

"As I climbed down from the peak of Kilimanjaro," Vito continued, "I took shelter from a storm in a cave. There, under a pile of rocks, I found this." He took out the medallion and offered it to Mr. Engare to show to Mbae.

Awed, Mbae reached out a finger and touched the amber lion's eye, then slumped back into his seat. The men behind him stood to get a glimpse and then began a buzz of conversation. Mr. Engare returned the medallion to Vito. Ole Kipchong stood to his feet, about to say something, when a sonorous voice came from behind him speaking Maa in a singsong voice. He turned and saw Sitanga, the youngest *oloiboni* and the son of his sister, get to his feet, his eyes fixed on something beyond the corrugated tin roof. It was obvious the man had a message from the spirits. *Finally*, ole Kipchong thought, *Engai speaks to us.*

"I have seen *The One True Lion* standing on the mountain," the *oloiboni* said. "He is large, and his voice is terrible, like the sound of a mighty river rushing over rocks during the time of the rains. As he roars, I see many butterflies burst from the ground and fly in the sunlight among the trees and grasses. The whiteness of their wings blinds my eyes, but not the eyes of the lion.

"As I watch I see a large butterfly land on his nose. He opens his mouth and swallows it, and its brightness shines through his face from within, his skin becomes like brass, and he grows bigger. Another butterfly lands on his nose, and he swallows it and becomes brighter and more golden in color and larger in size until he is larger and stronger than all other lions. Then his roar fills the land and even the trees bow down before him."

He finished and sat down. Everyone was quiet. Kuyoni whispered the translation in a low voice to Fritz, but Vito interrupted. "Mr. Kuyoni, please translate loud enough for all of us to hear." Neither Vito nor Fritz understood the communication, though they saw Mbae conferring with his colleagues, all of them nodding their heads and grunting assent.

Ole Kipchong stood and waited for the court to quiet. He said something to Mr. Engare, and sat down. Mr. Engare cleared his throat and said in a trembling voice, "Mr. Kipchong accepts the offer of the Bwana judge because the judge holds the sacred amulet of *The One True Lion*." As though to underscore his statement, a brilliant flash of lightning lit the darkening room and the rain poured down onto the metal roof, drowning out the surprised gasps and conversations of the people in the room.

As soon as Vito banged his gavel dismissing court, Rebeka was out the door and running home in the rain, her hands over her face, running to hide before everyone knew her shame. To be sold again like a commodity in the marketplace was more than she could bear. The judge, the one person whom she trusted besides her father, betrayed her trust by dictating her future without consulting her. Yet she wondered, as she threw herself, soaked with rain, onto her bed in her darkened room, what choice did she have anyway? What choice had she ever had? Her father came through the door and sat on the foot of her bed.

"*Liebchen,*" he said, "don't be so dismayed. He'll be here this evening to talk to you. He must have a plan; he would not tread so hard on your soul. He has done what he must to keep you from being forced to marry the Maasai chief." Fritz rubbed her calf as he talked, his sorrow etched on his face in deepened lines, his mouth turned down at the corners.

"Oh, Papa, it is all too much for me to bear." She dissolved into tears again. Fritz reached for her, and she crept into his arms and sobbed. "I wish I had never been born," she wailed. "I've lost everything—my home, Mama, you will be gone in two weeks, and I hoped Mpepo…" She wept even harder. "Even my friend Malia will soon be married and gone to Kenya. I have no one, no one!" Fritz could do nothing but stroke her head and make sympathetic murmurs.

**As soon as the rain stopped, Mbae ole Kipchong walked with Vito out of town to Mordecai Mayala's kraal** where he sheltered the thirteen cows and two young bulls he had purchased at Vito's direction from local Chagga tribesmen. It took much of Vito's savings, but he had ordered Mordecai to buy the best ones he could find. The bulls were young and strong, and ole Kipchong admired them. They would bring new bloodlines to the scrawny Maasai herds. He forced himself to show no emotion so no one would detect his excitement. But the thought of bragging about driving a hard bargain blossomed in the back of his mind. He examined the cattle carefully and made the appropriate grunts. He would have no further argument with himself over returning the two calves born to the cattle given him by the chief. When he finished, he turned to the people who waited for his response. "The cattle are fine," he said. "I accept them."

He turned to Vito and said, "*Engai* has spoken. I accept his word. The promise will be fulfilled through you. My family is now your family." He reached out his hand to Vito's and brushed his fingers across his palm in a Maasai handshake.

Later, as he drove his new cattle toward his home village, he consulted with his nephew Sitanga who walked beside him. "I have fulfilled my destiny. I have a roaring in my bones and sleep with difficulty. It is time I took my last walk on the plains.

"I place in your hands the sacred duty of keeping watch over the lineage of *the One True Lion*." For the rest of the trip he recounted the saga and the names of the ancestors, insisting that Sitanga repeat it all back until he had it memorized. They knew without speaking the meaning of the message Sitanga had received and imparted to the crowd at the courthouse.

Their mutual grandfather had a dream, long before the white man came to their land, of colorful butterflies that filled the land. *The butterflies will change everything,* the dream went, *but be patient. The changes will only make the Maasai stronger.* They both believed the Europeans were these butterflies.

**Vito returned home, changed his clothes, and ate the dinner Mordecai had prepared.** Afterward, he took the lantern and walked through town to the Scheibel home, followed by the watchful gaze of those inhabitants who lived along the road. News traveled fast through the town. The rain had brought the night insects out of their burrows and they shrilled with glee in the cool, cleansed air. Fritz ushered him into the living room and called Rebeka from her room.

She came after a few minutes, her face swollen from crying. *The poor girl, what have I done?* Vito thought. Fritz stood to leave the room, but Vito insisted he stay. "What I have to talk about is for both of your ears," he said.

"I need to explain what I did, Rebeka. I had to do it so the Maasai won't attempt another kidnapping. When your father leaves, you will be alone. If you're unattached, they can easily take you as they did before, and this time there would be little I—or anyone else—could do about it. They might ignore my ruling that they would have to first pay back the cost of your keep and education.

"Remember when they said in court that they consider you married when the cattle are transferred?"

She nodded.

"Well, they have accepted the cattle. They may think I have offered a bride price for you. But as I stated in court, I will take you as a ward. Let them think I am offering to marry you."

Rebeka clapped her hands over her mouth, her eyes big. "Did you say *ward?*"

"Yes. You know what a ward is, don't you? What did you think I—oh!" He was embarrassed. "You thought I said *wife?*"

Rebeka nodded.

Vito smiled. The similarity of the words wasn't unintentional. He'd intended for the Maasai to take it that way, but thought she'd hear the right word. "I'm sure everyone else in the courtroom made the same mistake. I don't care what they think. Let them talk."

"But why would you want them to—"

"To insure that they won't come after you again. Isn't that what you want?"

She nodded.

"The government accepts African customs as legally valid. But that's between Africans. You are African, but I'm not. I don't fall under those customs. Legally, then, we aren't married. But I am your guardian now until you reach legal maturity.

"I see we have three choices, and I'll do whatever you want. The first is, I can release you to go to Germany with your father. You've already said you don't want to go, but that option is still open.

"Second, you can go to Nairobi to study medicine at the hospital there. After that, you could stay there or come back here, whatever you want, and we can discuss then what you want to do next. We'll look into that option later.

"Third, you can move into my guest room and live with me as my ward, my daughter. That will be fine with me. In fact, I'd prefer that course of action. You've been through too much in the past weeks to make sudden decisions. If you choose that, then you'll be fully protected by me. You can continue working at the hospital here if you want, and wait until you're ready to marry or go to Nairobi.

"We'll walk that path when the time comes. I'm sure it would put the Maasai into an uproar. People will talk, of course, but they'll talk anyway."

"But why don't you care what people say?" Rebeka asked, overcome by the thought and fully aware of how the arrangement would be viewed by others. "You're a European. Europeans don't marry African girls—or pretend to—nor would they want others to think they do."

"I had a dream on the mountain," Vito said, and told her of his hallucination—or dream—where Therese, his dead wife came, and how she brought Rebeka to him. He told her how she had kissed his knee and made it start to heal.

"I think you're supposed to be part of my life, sort of a daughter. What people think doesn't bother me," Vito said. "If God looks on the heart, Rebeka—If indeed there is a God as your father says there is—" he glanced at Fritz "—we must see things the way he does and not care about the color of a person's skin. You don't have to decide your future now. The time your father has remaining should be just for you two to spend together. Think about each of these options before you." Rebeka nodded, her eyes clear. "I'll come back each evening, and we can talk some more," Vito said as he stood to his feet.

"Oh! I nearly forgot!" He reached into his pocket and drew out the medallion. "I think this belongs to you."

Rebeka drew back. "I don't want it. It has an evil spirit, and I don't want to touch it."

Vito replaced it in his pocket. "All right. I'll keep it for now. But it's part of your heritage. Someday, if you want it, I'll give it to you."

Fritz followed him out the door and they stood in the street talking. "I understand what you have done," he said. "I never knew…well, when I took her as a baby I had a premonition that difficulties would come because of it, but all this…" he shook his head. "You know, Ursula always said it would be over her dead body that they would take her, and now—" he clenched his teeth.

"Thank you," he finally said. "It's a great thing you have done for her. You'll be criticized for it."

"I know," Vito said. "But as an Italian, I'm an underdog anyway. Opinions don't lessen loneliness. I only now realize how lonely I've become, how much I long to have someone to talk to. It would be nice to have Rebeka around the house, but I won't force her choice."

"It would bring comfort to my heart," Fritz said, "to know that she's safe. But I guess it's really in God's hands, isn't it?" He looked pointedly at Vito, who sighed.

"Yes, Fritz. It really is in God's hands. Maybe I'll come around to your views yet." He reached out and took Fritz's hand. "When I first met you, I couldn't stand you because you were my enemy. But now..." he shrugged. "I find that good people come in all races and nationalities."

As Vito walked away, he wondered about what he was doing. He felt raw and vulnerable, and judicially compromised. His life seemed to be taking an unexpected turn and he could no longer control it. Nor did he want to.

## CHAPTER TWENTY SIX

# Transitions

**Because he lived his life serving others, Fritz had had little inclination to amass much more than necessities** and a few books for intellectual stimulation. Rebeka moved a bed, Ursula's treadle sewing machine, and her childhood desk into Vito's guest room. She also kept a large trunk of towels and bedding, and some doilies her mother had crocheted. The rest of the furniture would be left for Dr. Johansen who would move into the house when his wife and children arrived from America. At the last minute, she decided to keep the tiny rocking chair her father had brought from Germany when she was six.

Each evening, when night shadows had thoroughly chased away any remnants of sunlight, Vito would walk the road to Fritz's house for supper and to help go through books and papers. He and Rebeka took each book and noted the title and author on a piece of paper, then paged through them to see if any were too badly damaged to keep. They made three piles: one to be discarded, one for Rebeka to keep, and another to be donated to the hospital or church. Fritz kept nothing for himself but his Bible.

Fritz opened up as he never had before, in long reminiscences of his youth in Germany. Little work would get done as Vito and Rebeka listened wide-eyed to stories Rebeka had never heard. In their minds, they imagined a young Ursula and her poor beginnings. They could almost see the young, enthusiastic couple set their faces toward Kilimanjaro, not for the mountain, but for the people who lived in its shadow. In a halting voice, Fritz told of the babies they lost to disease, and then of the baby he found in a deserted village and took home to a grieving wife.

"I know God had his hand on the child," Fritz said. "She became a source of joy to us. I've worried much over her future, but here she is, beautiful and grown, and I must continue trusting God to guide her." He opened another book.

"Look at this!" Tiny silverfish raced from the sudden light. The pages were riddled with holes, some larger than others, and the edges were nibbled away. Dust and shards of paper fell out onto the tabletop. 'This old anatomy textbook will be of no use to anyone. It's outdated, anyway." He set it on the discard pile and brushed the dust and paper fragments into a waste can.

"That reminds me," Vito said. "Before you leave, you should write down everything Rebeka has studied so I can write to the hospital in Nairobi. I want to find out what they require of students."

Rebeka sat back in her chair and stared at him. Before she could say anything, her father responded.

"That's a wonderful idea! I've thought the same thing. You must send her there. Please look into it."

"Then it's agreed," Vito said. "I'll write letters first thing tomorrow."

Rebeka frowned, wondering just who had decided what without asking her. A feeling of anger rose in her mind and she stared at Vito, and then her father. Why was it that men always made decisions for women? She shut the book she held in her hand and slammed it down on the table.

"Why don't you ask me first if that's what I want to do?" She stood to her feet and went outside, letting the screen door slam behind her. Anger filled her body and ran down her arms to her clenched fists. Then grief joined the anger in a torrent she could not contain.

The moon, a sliver lying on its back just above the trees, cast sinister shadows across the yard. She felt as though her life hung on that moon; at any moment it would slip off into oblivion. She ran, her hand over her mouth to keep the storm of emotion inside, to the far end of the yard where she could sit on the platform that held the water tank.

A well of black emptiness bubbled up through her as she cried. So many losses. So many more to come. She cried for her mother and her soft bosom where she had wept out her little childhood griefs. She cried for her father who would leave her forever, the father who had tenderly brought her to his home and taught her so much. She cried for her life, stigmatized by the trial, torn between two worlds, her future stretching out before her like the dark, deserted road to town. She cried until she had no tears left, only dry shuddering sobs as she shivered in the dark.

The screen door opened and closed. She watched as Vito walked the other direction toward the street, his lantern in his hand. *He left early tonight. He must be angry.* She needed him now. She needed help finding a new place in the world. Until recent events, she had borrowed her identity from her parents. In all her nearly seventeen years she had been neither African nor European; she was simply Rebeka Scheibel, the loved daughter of Ursula and Fritz Scheibel. They had set an example for her of steadfast resolve and faithfulness to God and their calling. All she knew had been filtered through them. Things would be different now.

She heard the screen door open again, and soon a comforting

hand gripped her shoulder. "Papa!" She buried her face in his chest giving one last shuddering sigh.

"*Liebchen*," Fritz said, stroking his hand over her hair. "He meant no harm. He wants to help. I told him you're not ready yet to make decisions."

"Is he angry with me?"

"No, my dear, he's only angry with himself for being insensitive."

"Papa, I wish I could go with you to Germany, I could take care of you the rest of your life. And you would keep me safe."

"You made the right decision to stay, *Liebchen*. This is your country. You belong here. You would not be happy in Germany. Taking you there would be like capturing a beautiful impala and putting it in a zoo for people to stare at. It would be even worse for a person like you to go to Germany where people would not know how to treat you.

"I will miss you." He kissed her forehead. "It's strange. When you were small, I wanted you to need me. I wanted to guide and teach you how to live, and protect you.

"But now that you're grown, and I am old, I find that it's I who need you. Everything is reversed and confusing. I wonder if it is that way with other fathers. I'm not afraid for you anymore. I have confidence in you." He patted her back. "But I'm afraid for myself. I have less self-confidence. Your life is before you, full of promise; my life is behind me.

"Are you finished crying?"

Rebeka shivered, the heat of her anger and grief had drained away; exhaustion took its place. "I feel better now, Papa. I want to go inside and go to bed."

Father and daughter, their arms around each other in mutual empathy, went inside where the lantern glowed and made the room warm.

In the days that followed, Rebeka discovered a new feeling of peace that replaced the distress of the days since the trial. People still treated her as though she had become leprous. The African women in the marketplace smirked with knowing expressions and whispered among themselves.

The white English, who had always ignored her, now looked askance at her. Vito said it would pass; he had explained to them that she was his ward, not his wife, that he had paid the price to keep the Maasai from claiming her again, but she still felt their animosity. She tried to keep away from people as much as possible. Only Cecil and Gertie Neville seemed to care.

Even at church, those who had been her friends seemed to force their friendliness as though unable to figure out how to treat her. She saw a desert of loneliness stretch out before her. As she went about her duties during the day, preparing for her father's departure and cleaning the house for the new owner, she reached into her soul and found a vast quantity of self-respect and self-sufficiency that she never knew existed. It came to her, that all her life she had been alone, even with her parents. She had searched in vain for a place of belonging. Now she found it within herself. *Solitude,* she decided, *is not the same thing as loneliness. Solitude is my place in life. I will make the most of it and not allow myself to be lonely.*

The day before Fritz left Arusha, they both moved out of the house and into Vito's home. Their final dinner together was spent in more reminiscing, only this time it was Rebeka who told about incidents in her childhood. Laughter and sweet tears mixed together, especially when the stories included Ursula.

Even Vito, who had seldom laughed since the end of the war, joined in.

Fritz was amazed when he heard for the first time what Rebeka told them about the ten months with the Hoffman family in Tanga, when he and Ursula went to Germany. Tears formed as she told how she ran around naked, and how Giselle had treated her. Both men laughed when she recounted her revenge with stolen sugar and the planted spiders.

They stayed up long into the night, only retiring when the lantern flickered signaling the need for more kerosene.

Early the next morning, before breakfast, Fritz went to the four graves under the bougainvillea. He laid oleander flowers on each grave.

*Peter,* he whispered, remembering the laughing, freckle-faced boy. *The son of my youth. How I've missed you.* He went to the next one. *Katherine.* He remembered her quiet manner, her sweet round face and blond hair, so much like Ursula. *Marta.* The baby, too small to really know her, but she had begun to smile at him before she died. It had been too long since he last thought of them.

The last grave, larger and fresher than the others, took his attention. *Ursula, my love, my love.* He knelt beside the grave and bowed his head. *I will see you again, my Liebchen. Wait for me; it won't be long.*

Sawaya was to come right after breakfast to take him in his freight lorry to Moshi to catch the train to Tanga, and this last hour the three of them had together weighed heavy with unspoken thoughts, though everything had already been said. The minutes ticked ominously up to the roar of Sawaya's lorry at the gate, then they plummeted forward too fast until all Rebeka had was a quickly receding view of her father's arm waving at her through the open window. Soon she was waving at nothing but the faint hum of the lorry as it disappeared over the hill and down to the river crossing.

A peace filled Rebeka's soul as she turned to go into the house and face the rest of her life.

Vito had offered to stay with her this day, but she told him no, she wanted to be alone. Solitude would be her friend from now on, and she would draw strength from it.

The days and weeks clicked by in routine order: Vito at his office and the court, and sometimes at the Club, and Rebeka at the hospital and in the house. They avoided the subject of the future and Nairobi. She took charge of the evening meal, eager to try her hand at the domestic skills passed on by her German mother. After dinner, she would join Vito in the living room where she studied. At times she would lift her head from her book and ask a question. He had argued with her about her African habit of looking at the floor when speaking to him, so now her intense, dark brown eyes fastened on his.

She spent her days at the hospital with Dr. Johansen and his wife. She helped him understand Fritz's notes on his research on tropical diseases. Paul Johansen was a tall, thin, blond-haired doctor from Midwest America, who had spent several years working with American Indians in the west. When he saw that Rebeka knew English quite well, he became open and friendly. He told her of some of the heartaches he and his wife, Mattie, had while working with tuberculosis patients. He was quite ready, he said, to do battle with different sets of heartaches. He didn't look down on Rebeka, like the British people did, and they became good friends.

One day, Vito told her he had written to Nairobi and had

received the entrance requirements for their school.

"This is just an option," he said. "You don't have to follow through. It's good to know what you will be able to do." They compared the requirements to the list her father had drawn up. She lacked enough—especially in mathematics—that it would take a long time to get it all. In addition, all they offered their African applicants was a dresser's certificate.

"I'll help you," Vito said. "I studied mathematics in college. Show me your book."

"You went to college?" She dug out her arithmetic book and handed it to him. "Of course! After all, you had to learn to be magistrate. Tell me about your life before you came to Africa."

The smile on his face receded, replaced by a stony look. Rebeka wondered what griefs lay just under the surface. For the first time she was curious about his life. Everyone had his own private grief.

"Another time," he said, taking the book and opening it. "How far did you get?"

In the next week, she spent her spare time studying mathematics, a subject she had always hated. But under Vito's tutelage, she began to understand the sense in it. He showed her how the whole universe was built on mathematical symmetry; he showed her the linear concepts intrinsic in the science, as well as the shortcomings. For the first time she appreciated the discipline it imposed on everything.

The most painful part of her life was seeing Mpepo at church on Sundays. He was finishing up his six-month apprenticeship under Pastor Luka, and while they avoided each other, each time she saw him a sharp stab of pain pierced her. She stopped going to church.

One day he paid an unexpected visit.

"*Hodi,*" he called from the front gate. Rebeka glanced out the screen door and saw him, head down, as though examining something on the ground.

"*Karibu,* come in," she answered, her heart pounding. *Why was he here?* Mpepo came up the path and stood at the bottom of the steps leading to the verandah. "May I offer you some tea?" she said, her heart pounding and her hands clammy.

Mpepo nodded and sat down on the lower step. Rebeka went through the house to the separate kitchen in the back yard and returned with two cups of tea in her trembling hands. Her hand brushed his, sending a shock wave up her arm. He drank the tea in silence. She didn't know what to say; it was customary to exchange banal greetings, but the blood pounded in her head and kept her from thinking straight.

"Would you like to come here and sit?" She indicated the other chair on the verandah.

He shook his head. "No, it would not be proper." After a moment, he said, "I have come to say I am sorry that you have lost your mother—the woman who raised you. She was a good woman."

"Thank you," Rebeka said, wondering why it had taken him so long to offer his sympathy. "I miss her very much."

Mpepo cleared his throat as though something was stuck there. "I have done you great wrong. It is a shame that I must carry the rest of my life. That day, in the courtroom…" He shook his head. "I was blinded by what I thought God wanted me to do. Sometimes it seems that God offers us two paths to follow, both of which seem right, and we let our own wishes and desires choose for us. I think I have made a mistake."

Rebeka remained silent. There was nothing she could say.

Several women passing on the street stared. She knew they would gossip about her visitor and imply that more went on between them, and she was glad he had chosen to sit on the bottom step so far away from her.

"I should have said *yes, I will marry Rebeka* that day. That would have been the right thing to do. Instead, I think I have fallen into the trap of the devil himself. I chose to follow my cousin who is himself in the clutches of *Shetani*." He paused and scuffed his toe in the dirt. "I have married his sister-in-law, and tied myself to his plans."

His words were like a knife-thrust to Rebeka's heart, where hope had momentarily reared its head. Word of his marriage had not reached her.

"I thought I would have a better opportunity to preach to my people and see them come to God. Instead, I am bound to Siferi's plan and message. Also, I find that I must come to you and make things right before God can use me."

He cleared his throat; the confession was obviously hard. "Believe me when I say that I have always had a great affection for you." His voice shook and his forehead beaded with perspiration. "The white man calls it *love*—" he used the English word "—and the African does not even have a word for this feeling, or admit to ever experiencing it. Even if a man feels it, he views it as weakness. I should have recognized it as a gift from God. Rebeka, I am feeling wretched! Especially now that it is too late to make amends." He stared at the ground, his face a picture of defeat mixed with pain.

The tears rolled in silence down Rebeka's cheeks as she mourned what could have been hers, but now no longer was within her reach. Mpepo was gone—forever. He had married Damari. Another woman enjoyed his presence every night.

Mpepo cleared his throat and continued, his voice husky. "I have to believe that God does not cast us aside when we make wrong choices—or when others make wrong choices for us. I believe that if we recognize these things as within his knowledge, that he will continue to bless us. That is for you as well as for me, Rebeka." He looked her in the face for the first time.

"I need to hear from you that you forgive me."

Rebeka understood how hard it was for him to admit his error. She knew that African men did not easily admit to mistakes and ask for forgiveness, especially from a woman. Deep within her, somewhere in the pit of her stomach, a clenched fist began to release its hold. Slowly at first, then with increasing speed, a ball of pain rose into her throat. It was hard to say it, but when she found the strength and voiced the words, *I forgive you, Mpepo*, the ball of pain burst out of her and vanished like a bubble, leaving behind it a feeling of release and joy. For the first time in her life she understood the healing power of forgiveness.

Mpepo stood to his feet, and she knew by the look of peace on his face that she had released his pain as well as her own.

"This is the last time I will ever see you, Rebeka," he said, his voice trembling. "I leave for Huruland tomorrow. I will think of you all my life."

Rebeka got to her feet, too. "And I you, Mpepo," she said, and they stood there with locked gaze until he turned away and walked down the street.

"Mpepo?"

He turned and looked back.

"Do you really think God allows us to make wrong choices when we don't know they are wrong, when we really want to do the right thing?"

Mpepo thought a moment, then shrugged. "Perhaps not. The

years will show us." Rebeka went into the house and wept, not out of bitterness or pain this time, but tears of release. She wiped her eyes and prepared the evening meal.

**The next day Rebeka found Dr. Johansen in his tiny office going over government paperwork.** He smiled broadly and invited her in.

"I would like to ask your advice," she said, sitting in the chair beside his desk. "I need to decide what I should do; whether I should stay here and keep doing what I am doing—" she hastily added, "I really enjoy it. I am not unhappy here—but Mr. Fernaldi wishes me to go to Nairobi to study medicine. I lack too much schoolwork to be able to do that now. I don't know which way to turn."

Dr. Johansen gazed at her with a thoughtful wrinkle of his brow. "That is one, good option for you. You have the ability to finish what you need in the way of book knowledge. The Nairobi hospital has a good training school, but they send white applicants to England. You have the background to go to England, but I don't know any school in England that will accept an African girl."

Rebeka winced. "But I don't—"

"Of course, that's wrong of them. American schools might take you in. Unless you want to settle for what Nairobi offers?"

"I really don't want to leave. I feel safe in Arusha because it has always been my home." Maybe she *should* have gone to Germany with her father. She knew German far better than English. "But I might think about Nairobi. America and England are too far away."

Dr. Johansen leaned back in his chair and put his hands behind his head. "There is another option to consider.

"I am constantly amazed at how your father set up this hospital. The workers are efficient, everything is in order, and the research he has done is far advanced, probably ahead of what Nairobi has to offer. And I've seen you at work. How long have you worked around here?"

"Since I was about twelve. Of course, I didn't work all the time. I helped on weekends and only with the children."

"I don't think Nairobi can teach you anything. Let me look into things. Bring me a list of what you've studied so far. I think I can set up a special course right here, and give you whatever you need."

He brought his hands back to the desk and straightened up. "I've been thinking about starting a training school. I can use you as my first student. What do you think about that?"

Rebeka brightened. This felt promising. Dr. Johansen looked out the window.

"I just had another idea, to go along with the first one. You're Maasai, aren't you?"

Rebeka nodded, wondering.

"The Maasai avoid medical care; they reject it, actually, except in life-threatening cases. You can be the bridge between medicine and your people—especially the women. If you can go into the villages and talk to them—why you could be the break-through I've been looking for!" He got out of his chair and paced back and forth, his excitement evident before he caught himself.

"But it is your life, and your decision, Rebeka. Go home and talk it over with your guardian. Pray and ask God's direction. It will come to you in time. You are young; you have the time to wait."

Rebeka felt his excitement catch a small flame in her mind.

This was something she could do. She could start with her aunts. Since her father had left, she felt an overwhelming urge to open the door of friendship with them. Even if this school failed, she would still have them.

## CHAPTER TWENTY SEVEN

# A New Church, a New Home

**For the first three months, Mpepo preached in the shade of a large fig tree in the center of the village**. Siferi came each Sunday with his wife and retinue. He brought a folding chair for himself while everyone else sat on the ground. Mpepo made sure not to water down his message for Siferi's sake. In fact, many times his message was directed right at Siferi who never gave any indication that he noticed.

Their first argument was over the building of a church. Siferi wanted to conscript the people to spend one day each week on the construction. In return, they would get the promise of forgiveness of their sins.

"You can't do that," Mpepo objected. "Only God can forgive sins; you can't buy forgiveness."

"The Church used to do that all the time," Siferi said. "How do you think they built all those huge churches in Europe many years ago? Do you think the people will come and build just for the love of it, when they have gardens to hoe?"

"I wish to do it my way," Mpepo said. "I won't allow you to put the name of the church on such a promise."

Siferi shrugged. "I was only trying to help you. Do it your way then. You'll see that no one will want to build for nothing."

But Siferi was wrong. When Mpepo spoke to the people,

they listened. Already, a number of converts spoke of the need for a building for the rainy season. The men banded together and brought dirt and straw for bricks, mixed them with water with their bare feet, then formed bricks to dry in the sun. Siferi glowered when he saw that Mpepo's way worked.

When the crude church finally had its roof of straw, and mud brick pews placed inside, Mpepo went in daily to pray. The rift between him and Siferi widened as Siferi realized that Mpepo wasn't going to be subservient. Mpepo knew he had to move his hut when, as he prayed one day, he felt someone slip in and kneel beside him. He looked over and saw Damari with tears in her eyes.

"My sister screamed at me again," she said.

Mpepo nodded. The two sisters were arguing in the same proportion as he and Siferi argued. "I know. I am sorry. I think we should build a new hut here by the church. I will be able to see who goes in and out. And it will be closer when we have meetings. What do you think?"

Damari's eyes brightened as she nodded.

"All right, we have decided." Mpepo reached his arm around her and smiled at her. She was a good, obedient wife and would soon be a mother. He couldn't have done better than to marry her.

Soon after they had married, she had whispered to him as they lay side by side at night, when no one else could hear, "I am sorry I came to you that night long ago. You were right to send me away, even though I felt shamed. It was wrong of me to listen to what Siferi told me, but he said if I didn't—"

"Shhh," Mpepo had said, "we will forget about it. I understand, and I don't think any less of you for it. Neither does God. You were torn between what you knew to be right according to God, and our people's custom. I do not fault you."

Since then she had been happy and relaxed. *No,* he thought, as he took in her large, wide-spaced eyes and round face—so different from Rebeka's, yet so beautiful and dear—*I couldn't have done better.*

He remembered Rebeka's last remark. *Do you really think God allows us to make wrong choices when we don't know they are wrong, when we really want to do the right thing?* Perhaps she was right. And if he stayed true to what he believed, he would continue here as long as his cousin didn't interfere. Maybe someday Siferi would see the truth.

**Vito came home early one day**. Mordecai had gone to his wife's village for a week and Rebeka had taken the day off to do the laundry and to sweep and dust the house, usually Mordecai's duties. Vito couldn't find her. He went to the kitchen, but no one was there. The laundry tub was put away. A few things remained on the clothesline. He walked through the house again, and this time went into his bedroom.

Rebeka stood at his clothes chest with her back to the door. He knew she heard him come in, but she didn't turn around. He went over to see what held her attention, and saw in her hand the old photo of Therese and his children, the picture that he had kept in his pocket during the war.

"That was my wife," he said. "And my children."

He took Rebeka by the shoulders and turned her around. She looked stricken, and he put his arms around her to comfort her, and he held her close for an awkward moment.

"I didn't know," she said. "I didn't mean to pry...the picture was right there...I only wanted to put away your clean clothes."

"I know," he said. "It's all right. Come, its time I told you about my life before I came to Africa. You have every right to know." He led her into the living room where they sat side by side.

Holding the photo in his hand, he told her about Therese and his children. He told her about the Austrian army, and how renegades had killed his family. The shadows deepened as the sun dipped toward the horizon, but they didn't notice. Except for the one time he had opened up on the *Cotswold* to Major Hammond, he had never talked about this part of his life. He told her about the murders—executions, he called them—of his defenseless family, of the years of bitterness and pain, his defiance toward God for allowing it to happen. He explained how he had disliked Fritz and Ursula because their being German reminded him of the war.

"So you see," he concluded, "you and I both have the pain of loss in our past. Now we can understand each other."

Rebeka nodded. "Yet, even so, you didn't give up, did you?"

"I wanted to," he said. "But I couldn't. You'll find, too, that loss can turn your life in a whole new direction.

"Your mother said something once. She said, *no story is ever finished.* She said it when you were kidnapped, before your rescue. She was beside herself with grief, but at the same time she knew it would not be over for you, no matter how it turned out."

"Yes," Rebeka said, "She told me that, when Baby Marta died, Sawaya came and told her a story about his grandparents, and then he said that at the end. Mama told me I should always remember those words—no matter what happens, the story isn't ended."

Vito stood, stretched, and went to light the lanterns. Rebeka left to gather together a light meal of cold sandwiches since the wood-burning stove was cold. She started the paraffin camp stove for tea, and they sat at the table together eating in companionable silence.

"I've been thinking," Rebeka said. "About what I'm supposed to be thinking about."

Vito's heart lurched. She would tell him she would go to Nairobi, he thought. In the six months she'd been living under his roof he'd become used to having her around, and now that he had bared his life to her, he didn't want her to go away.

"I know you want me to go to Nairobi, but I don't want to."

A feeling of relief left Vito weak. He wondered why he felt this way, and why he wanted to reach out and take her hand. Perhaps he shouldn't have hugged her earlier. After all, she wasn't really his daughter, and the closeness had awakened something in him.

"Arusha is my home," Rebeka continued. "I want to stay here. Dr. Johansen said he could teach me whatever I could learn in Nairobi. He is going to start a school. But—" she paused and looked down at the table, "—you might not want me to stay here any more. Maybe I can find another place to live…."

"Nonsense. This is your home. What would the Maasai do if they think you're no longer my wife?" It was the wrong thing to say. He felt Rebeka freeze.

He looked into her eyes and held her gaze. *No*, he thought. *I can't even think it. But it's true. I want her.* There was a hungry, intense look in her eyes, too. She was now Rebeka, the woman. Rebeka, who no longer appeared black in his eyes. His heart began to beat faster; he wanted to share the rest of his life with her; he wanted to—dare he even think it—make her his wife in spite of what the world would say. He closed his eyes. Surely she didn't feel what he felt.

Before he opened his eyes, Rebeka was on her feet and clearing away the dishes, taking them out the back door to the kitchen. She stayed out there for a long time. He wondered if he should follow her, if he should say something, or act as if nothing happened. How could he go on living with her with these feelings? He lit his pipe and went to the living room to read, but couldn't concentrate on the page.

"Rebeka, we need to talk about this," he said when she came back from the kitchen.

She paused in the hall leading to her room and looked at him with haunted eyes. "I am tired. I don't want to talk now." She disappeared into her bedroom.

Later, as he lay in bed, he thrashed through his feelings. His life in Italy had receded into a misty past, as though it were someone else's life he had only read about. It had been a long time since he had thought about it, until Rebeka found the photo, and he waited for the pain to return. *Therese,* he prodded his thoughts. Nothing happened. *Antonio. Theresita.* All he felt was a sweet nostalgia. No pain or feeling of loss. He only felt gratitude, thankfulness for the sweet memories to hold close to his heart. He felt enriched for having shared them with Rebeka.

*Rebeka.* Now she was an integral part of his life. He had only intended to bring her in as a ward, a daughter of sorts, to guide and send out equipped for life. But she was so much more now. He ached for her, as he heard her turn on her cot in her room.

*God.* Why had God intruded into his thoughts? Was there really a God, who having seen him suffer, now rewarded him with a new opportunity to love again? In the cave, when he had hallucinated Therese, what was it she had said?

*Vittorio, listen to me. You will not die. Remember, though, that death is always a breath away, and after that there is God. You may have mislaid your faith, but you haven't lost it entirely. God is here, waiting for you to come back.*

*Yes. God is here. Rebeka will lead me back.* He turned over and went to sleep.

Lying on her bed in the dark, Rebeka felt her skin tingle. All of her senses were heightened. She could hear Vito in the living room moving around in his creaky chair. She heard him get up and wind the clock, lock the doors, and go into his room. It seemed she could hear things she'd never heard before, like his breathing, and his tossing and turning in his bed. Her skin felt as though it was on fire. She could feel every hair on her head.

When he had found her in his room looking at the photograph, and taken her in his arms, she had felt his warmth and the beating of his heart, and she thought of him as a man, not a guardian. She had loved Mpepo, but she didn't remember feeling this way about him. Now that Vito had shared his past with her, she felt overwhelmed by the flood of feelings. *How can I stay here with these thoughts? Where can I go to get away from them? This situation is impossible.*

How could this be—that she would feel so strongly for a man of another race, another culture, another era? This feeling was more powerful than anything she had felt in her life, like a flooding river that tore out the trees along its bank, swept up unsuspecting cattle and wildlife, and carried them to the sea.

There were things she must do in the morning. She couldn't stay here like this. And she needed to talk to her aunts in the village.

**"I can't believe you'd get your heart so involved with her,**

**old man,"** Cecil **exclaimed** when Vito went to talk to him the next day. "But, I guess you've jolly well got yourself into a pickle, what with the Africans believing you have already married her."

"But I haven't," Vito said. "I could never take her as a wife without it being legal."

"Of course it's not legal as far as the Crown is concerned. Most of the whites think she's your concubine, in spite of what you told them." Cecil shook his head. "Never had to face this before, you being white and her being African—and getting married all properly."

"Would you—I mean I want it legal and all and have a certificate—you could do it for us, couldn't you? If Rebeka wants it, I mean. I haven't asked...."

Cecil shook his head. "I don't like it. It's too bloody improper."

"Oh, Cece!" Gertie interrupted. "And what will they do if you don't? Live in sin? If they want to marry, why not?"

"Well, I'll think about it," Cecil grumped. "What a bloody mess you've got yourself into. You should have sent her away somewhere right off."

Gertie glared at him. "Cecil Montgomery Neville, if you refuse when you're asked, I don't believe I'll speak to you again!"

Cecil gave a hesitant laugh, as though he wasn't sure if she really meant it. "I said I would think about it. We'll see. Maybe the girl will want to do something else and we won't have to worry about public opinion and all that."

**Rebeka asked Dr. Johansen about night duty.**

"Why would you want to work nights?" he asked.

"I like to work when there are fewer people around," she

answered. "I want to be there for the night emergencies, like babies. They always seem to want to be born at night. I'd like to try it and see how I like it."

He looked at her thoughtfully. "I think I can arrange it," he said. "Filomena would rather be home with her own family in the evenings. And Miss Hesston is in charge at night. She can handle most anything that comes up."

Rebeka told Vito about her new hours at dinner that night. "I'll be working from 9:00 until 6:00 in the morning," she said. "I'll get home just before you leave for work, and I can sleep during the day and get up in time to cook dinner and clean up before I leave."

"But I'll hardly get to see you," Vito said, looking perplexed.

*That's the idea,* Rebeka thought, but she said, "I want to see what it's like to work at night. It is a whole different hospital then, and I want to experience it." She stared at the table, not wanting to look into his eyes for fear he would guess her real reason.

"I supposed we will at least have Sundays."

"My days off will be Monday and Tuesday." She continued looking at the table, not wanting to see the hurt in his eyes. He sat still, and she was afraid if she looked up she would break.

"Very well." His tone was cold. He stood and left to go to his desk in the living room.

Rebeka swallowed hard. It would be difficult, but she had to do something to kill her feelings. This was the only possible solution.

On Monday morning, when she came home from the hospital and he was on his way out the door, Rebeka told Vito she was going away for her two days off.

"Where are you going?" He frowned at her, looking worried.

"I'm going to visit my aunts in the village. Mbae ole Kipchong's wives. They are all I have left of my family."

"I don't think you should go there. What if they—"

"They won't hurt me. After all, they still think I'm your..." she avoided the word *wife*. She only wanted to remind him that he was the one who had placed her in this awkward situation. She refused to think about how she really felt.

He passed her without saying a word and strode down the street. She knew he was angry by the set of his shoulders.

Rebeka spent all her days off with Wambui and Nareyu. She caught a ride on a merchandise or government lorry each time and soon became known to the truck drivers. They dropped her off where the road turned toward the border, just two miles from the village. The women were always happy to see her, and so was Mbae, who now spent his days sitting in the sun wrapped in a blanket. Since he was the senior *oloiboni,* the village men came to consult with him. The wives and Rebeka would go to the other side of the *boma* for their woman-talk.

A bond grew between them, one that had been planted before the fateful day of circumcision. They never talked about that day. Instead they satisfied her curiosity with stories of her mother and father. She listened to the Maasai legends and wove them into her soul. They taught her their art of beading and helped her make ornaments to wear. As the weeks grew into months, she felt a change coming over her, a settling, as though she could now comfortably straddle both cultures.

It was then she decided to bring up what Dr. Johansen had

suggested. "I would like to do something to help my village," she said one day, after greeting her aunts and then following them to a seat in the shade of the *manyatta*.

Nareyu stared off into the distance. Her bloodshot eyes had begun to cloud with cataracts, and she could no longer see the beads that Wambui deftly strung together. "We thought you had taken on the white man's ways of thinking along with his clothes," she said. "The white man thinks that he stands alone."

"Why do you say that? What do you mean?"

Nareyu picked up a piece of kindling, a brittle stick, from a small pile by the hut. She snapped it in half with one hand. "One person, standing alone, cannot be strong enough. Even an old woman can snap him in half.

"The white man thinks he is enough—alone—to be a village. He has no village, even when he lives in towns. He builds strong houses, then crawls inside and closes his door. Everything he does is for himself. You think Arusha is your village? It is a place full of strong houses, but no family, no real village." She clamped her mouth shut.

Wambui looked up from her work. "We knew, afterward, that you had too many white man's thoughts to be ole Meoli's wife. Nareyu and I have been like sisters since I married Mbae. That is because we think like real Maasai.

"Maasai know what it is to be a village. The person is nothing. Strength is in the people. A bundle of sticks cannot be broken. You cannot break a village. You think this is our village?" She pointed at the cluster of *manyatta*s and the circle of thorns around the cattle yard. "No, it is not. The village is the people; it is our family and clan. We have moved many times since you were born, though we have never gone back to the place of death. But wherever we go, we are el Engerot, and the clan lives on in the many, not the one."

The women fell silent. Rebeka tumbled the new thoughts around in her mind. Never mind that she lived in the white man's town of Arusha. She was Maasai; she was a piece of el Engerot. She wasn't alone. She wasn't only one person, but a part of a village.

Yet she was Rebeka. She was herself, complete in her new-found solitude. And she was stronger than the twig Nareyu had broken with a flick of her fingers. She was a staff, like the one Nareyu walked with, strong and straight and too thick to break.

"Perhaps," she said when the silence had stretched out past the time to break it, "perhaps a person can be both alone, complete in herself, and still be a part of the village. That is why I want to help el Engerot. I am of this village. And I am of the European. I can bring the good of the white man to the village and still keep its unity.

"I can bring good things to you." She motioned toward Nareyu. "Your eyes. I know the *daktari* can help you see as you did years ago. How many other women and men are there who can no longer see the leaves on the trees? If only the clan would see that they can remain Maasai and still accept the help."

Nareyu blinked but didn't say anything. Wambui looked back and forth between her and Rebeka. "Maybe," she said. "We will discuss it with the others. Perhaps *Engai* sent you to Arusha for a reason."

It was a start, Rebeka thought. She was young. The years stretched out before her. She had a purpose in life, after all.

A week later, as Rebeka prepared to leave for the village again, Vito knocked on her bedroom door.

"I would like to ask a favor," he said. Next week, on your

days off, would you please not go to the village? I have some important things to discuss with you."

"Like what? Can we talk about it now?"

"I'd rather wait until we have time to sit together and talk. Would you do this for me?" He could have simply told her to stay home, but she was no longer his charge. She was the woman he wanted to marry.

"Yes, I will do that. But if I get news that Mbae is about to die, I want to be able to go to be with his wives. I told you he is ill."

Vito nodded. "If you must go to be with him, then go. But this is important to me."

Rebeka nodded, a question in her eyes. He knew she would wonder the whole week. Maybe she would think that he wanted her to live somewhere else, or go to Nairobi, or maybe he had thought of another choice for her life. Let her trouble about it, he decided. After all, he didn't even know yet how he would frame his question.

During the following week, he felt her eyes on him in wonder, but he didn't say anything to her other than the usual pleasantries they exchanged. He rehearsed and discarded what he would say. When he and Therese married, there were no questions and answers. They knew from when they were small that they would marry. This time, near-insurmountable difficulties threatened him.

When Rebeka came home from the hospital Monday morning, as he prepared to go to work, he said, "I'll be back about three. Let's take a picnic up the road and watch the sunset. I can borrow Sawaya's small lorry. It will be fun.

Rebeka nodded, a surprised look on her face.

He left right away, knowing she watched him walk down the

road. A knot of anxiety gripped his stomach all day.

Rebeka had a basket with bread and sliced meat from the kongoni roast left over from Sunday, a calabash with cottage cheese she had learned to make from Ursula, two mangos, and a canteen of water to make tea. The camp stove was on the steps. Vito arrived exactly at three in Sawaya Mayala's old truck and lurched to a stop with a puff of smoke from the exhaust. His boyish grin made her smile, too. They loaded the food into the truck, and he had to crank it again to make it start. They set off toward Mount Meru to a place where the road wound along the lower slope, giving a wonderful view west over the plains.

They stopped and laid out the picnic blanket on a knoll. Neither spoke. The sun had lost its fervor and spread its benevolent golden light over the hills and valleys. Several small clouds overhead picked up the color. The guinea fowl and doves began to nest in the trees with clucks and calls to each other. Several rock coneys stuck their heads up out of their niches between the stones and watched them. They could hear the grunts of the wildebeests as they moved across the plain. It would soon rain again, bringing precious nourishment to all creatures that called Africa home. The quiet was almost palpable.

Rebeka made the sandwiches and handed one to Vito and they ate in companionable silence. Vito felt so at peace that he all but forgot why he had brought her here. They finished their picnic supper and sipped their tea as the sun began to slip below the horizon. He knew he couldn't put it off any longer. But he forgot the words he had rehearsed for several days.

Finally, he blurted it out. "Rebeka, this has to stop."

"What? What has to stop?"

"You know what I mean."

He knew that she knew, but she said, "You mean the picnic? Do you want to go home now? The sun hasn't gone down."

He leaned toward her. "Rebeka why are you trying to avoid me?"

She glanced down. "I don't know what you—"

"You know perfectly well. You deliberately busy yourself when I'm around. And I think I know why. Don't I?" He put his hand under her chin and lifted her head. "Look at me, Rebeka."

Her fathomless brown eyes looked into his blue ones, and he saw them moisten. He decided to spare her further embarrassment.

"Rebeka, I want you to be my wife." Her eyes widened, but he plowed on. "Ever since I found you that day with Therese's picture, I have loved you. No, it might have been before that.

"And I know you feel the same way, and that's why you want to work nights and spend your spare time with the village women. Am I not right?"

Rebeka shook her head. Then she nodded. "Yes," she whispered. "But those feelings are wrong. They're impossible. I can't be your wife; it just isn't done. It isn't right. I tried so hard to stop the feelings."

"Why is it wrong, if we both love each other?"

"Because…because…"

"Because I'm European and you're African?" It lay out in the open, a problem with no solution. She nodded.

"There's no law against it. I checked. I also found that there are several other marriages, in Kenya, of white men and African women. There is no reason we can't think about it, is there?"

She shook her head, then seemed to change her mind and nodded.

"We can't. What about the curse on me?"

"What curse? What do you mean?"

"I mean the legend. The fulfillment rests on me, and it feels like a curse. It might be simpler if I were just an ordinary person, but now my people have their hopes pinned on me; I have a purpose that goes beyond what I want."

"Perhaps the legend is wrong. Maybe it's just that—a nice story to tell around the campfire, the wishful dreaming of old men. I seem to think your happiness is more important than a legend.

"Besides, if the legend meant all that much to you, you would have gone ahead and married that old chief."

He looked at her reproachfully and she looked down.

"You don't have to answer me now. I want you to think about it. Will you?"

She nodded.

"We'll talk some more about it, soon," he said.

"I had a dream," Rebeka said.

"What about?"

"I dreamed I was on a path at night with no light and no moon. There were two houses, one on either side of the path. I was frightened because a hyena laughed close by, and I heard a lion cough.

"I went to one house, but the door was locked. I looked in the window, and inside Mama and Papa sat around a lantern. Papa read a book to Mama; it was an adventure story, and I wanted to hear it better. I called to them, but they didn't hear me. Mama was hemming my red dress. When I was nine years old, she made that red dress for me. I knocked on the door, but they didn't hear me.

"I crossed the road and went to the other house. There, the women of the village sat around a fire telling stories about my mother. I tried to creep closer to hear, and they smiled at me, but didn't invite me into their home. I had to stay outside in the dark. I felt lonely and afraid. There were no other houses." She fell silent.

"Rebeka, look at me," Vito said. "There is another house. You simply have to open your eyes and you will see it. The door is standing open for you. That is where you belong."

Her eyes filled with tears again as she gathered up the remains of their picnic.

**A few days later, Rebeka came into the living room where Vito sat, pipe in mouth, reading.** As soon as she entered, he closed his book and put down his pipe, and stood to his feet. His eyes were intense and his brow puckered.

"Rebeka…" he said, and reached out and enclosed her in his arms.

She closed her eyes and relaxed against his chest and breathed in his warmth. She could feel his heart beat, and she felt his face against her head.

"I'm asking you again. Will you be my wife? Are you ready to give me an answer?"

"Yes," she said. "The answer is yes. It's you who has the most to lose, not me."

"Both of us have everything to gain," he said. They held each other close. He tightened his arms around her. "After we get married, Rebeka, I want you with me every day of the rest of my life. No more of this working at night."

Cecil performed the wedding ceremony in Vito's living room. Gertie and Mordecai were the witnesses. Vito had wanted to take Rebeka to Dar es Salaam for a honeymoon, forgetting that no hotel would allow the two of them to be in the same room, if even in the same hotel.

"No," Rebeka said. "I want to stay here. That is all I want. To sleep next to you in your wonderful bed, and talk and talk and talk."

Vito took down his one remaining bottle of Fernaldi wine and they shared it that night. Rebeka wore her birth-mother's betrothal collar. It was a sharing of their different pasts, a celebration of their joined future.

Each morning, as she made their bed and rubbed an oiled dust-cloth over the contours of the black ebony and white ivory bed, she marveled at its magnificent symbolism. If man could create such a work of art, what might God do with her life?

Her mother and Sawaya were right. No story is ever finished.

# POSTSCRIPT

**The late afternoon sun struggles to keep its hold on the plains, clutching the hills and trees with its long golden fingers.** The animals lift their heads from the grass to bask in the last warm rays. Night draws near, casting long dark shadows as its grip overcomes the day. The *murani* drive their cattle homeward, the clouds of dust turning to gold along the edges.

A lean, old man walks slowly away from the village, aided by a long staff. He moves as though in pain, his back bent with age. He wears only a loincloth. Mbae ole Kipchong, after bidding his wives goodbye, takes his final walk as custom dictates. He has lived to an age long beyond the years of most elders. It is time to die. Not everything has turned out as expected, but the legend of *The One True Lion* remains alive. Sitanga now holds its guardianship.

He reaches a pile of rocks and sits with his back against a large boulder, far enough from the village so no one will hear his death-cries. He watches the sky turn a deep blue and the stars burn holes through it, like sparks burning through cloth. Soon the sky sings with stars, a final chorus of joy and eternity, as they have since the time of the First Maasai.

When the lionesses come, slinking through the dark without a sound, they encounter no resistance. He feels one grip his throat and the other rake a hot trail across his abdomen. He wills his lifeblood to them. As the stars fade from his vision he knows that by morning there will be nothing left of him but a few scattered bones and a memory for his wives to mourn. This is the way of his people.

The second book in this series is

# Rogue Lioness

You can find more information about all the books in this series at the author's Web site:

www.joycebakerporte.com

# GLOSSARY

**Akida:** Government agent in charge of a town, as an unelected mayor, appointed by the German colonial government, often an Arab or other non-local man.

**Allah:** The Islamic term for God.

**Ayah:** A female childcare provider, usually an African or Indian.

**Bantu:** A large group of African peoples covering many tribes. Most of the people across the mid-section of Africa are Bantu.

**Beni:** A dance with a message of rebellion. It spread throughout German East Africa with its blatant message. When the Germans learned its meaning, they banned it.

**Blackwater Fever:** Later discovered not to be a separate disease, but the stage of malaria just before death when the kidneys disintegrate and fill the urine with black blood.

**Boma:** A place of judgment, either under a tree where the elders meet to make decisions, or the seat of the colonial governments. There is a town named Boma, perhaps originally where people came together from afar to decide district matters.

**Bwana:** A term of respect for a man of authority, literally "lord" or "master." It became a term for any man of European descent, whether he deserved it or not. Now it is used for any man of authority.

**Chagga:** The Bantu tribe living in the vicinity of Kilimanjaro and

Arusha, often in historic conflict with the Maasai herdsmen.

**Dawa:**  Magic.  Sometimes used for ingested magical potions. Eventually used as a term for medicine, since the people, when first introduced to modern medicine, attributed its effects to magic.

**Dresser:**  A medical assistant.

**Engai:**  The Maasai term for God.

**Female Circumcision:** A rite of passage for girls that takes different forms in different tribes. The Maasai practice what is called Pharonic Circumcision—the complete removal of the clitoris and inner and outer labia. Some tribes only remove the clitoris and inner labia. A small number of tribes do not practice female circumcision at all.

**Groundnuts:**  Peanuts.

**Hodi:**  A word of greeting usually outside the door of the visited house.  Because many African houses do not have doors on which to knock, it is considered polite to speak this word to indicate a guest has appeared.

**Kamba**: A tribe neighboring the Maasai.

**Kanzu:**  A long, white, ankle-length, skirted garment worn by men, particularly of Muslim origin.

**Kraal:**  An enclosure for cattle, sheep, and goats, also called a boma.  Sometimes huts were built inside the kraal.

**Maasai:**  A Nilotic tribe of people who are strict pastoralists. They occupy the often-dry plains of northeastern Tanzania and southwestern Kenya. They herd cattle and do not plant gardens.

**Manyatta:** A Maasai hut or cluster of huts. They are domed structures of sticks covered with mud and dung, about four to five feet high, with a small doorway that one must stoop to enter. There are no windows, only a hole in the top for smoke to escape.

**Maji:** water. **Maji moto:** hot water.

**Maji Maji:** The term used for a massive rebellion against the Germans in 1905. Those in rebellion thought that sprinkling themselves with magic water would protect them from the German bullets, turning the bullets themselves into water.

**Malaria:** A recurring fever caused by infection of the spleen. The anopheles mosquito that is prevalent in Africa is the carrier.

**Mama:** Mother. Also the proper term of respect for a married woman.

**Mshenzi:** A barbarian. A term of extreme disrespect, and one that will often produce an angry response if used loosely.

**Mungu:** The Swahili term for God. Tribal names for God are closely related in sound.

**Muran:** A Maasai warrior. Usually a young man between the ages of 15, when circumcision took place, and 25, when he married and took a wife. The plural is **Murani.**

**Ndio:** Swahili for Yes.

**Nilotic:** A subgroup of African types. Several tribes of east Africa are Nilotic in origin. These people came originally from the Nile region of North Africa, migrating south possibly as the Sahara Desert expanded into their space. Most of the other tribes in East Africa are **Bantu**.

**Pesi pesi:** Fast, in Swahili. A repeated word emphasized its meaning. Thus, this would mean very fast.

**Rinderpest:** A cattle disease that began in India, spread to Ethiopia, then down to middle Africa. In 1900-1905, it wiped out ninety percent of the domesticated cattle and affected the wildlife – like buffalo – that are related to cattle.

**Shienze:** A cicada-like insect that lives in holes in the ground. It makes ear-piercing mate-calling noise at night when it comes out of the ground just after the rains.

**Swahili:** The term used for the coastal people of East Africa and the language they spoke. The people are often a mixture of African and Arab ancestry. The language holds many Arabic and Portuguese terms. These people were more aware of the world at large centuries before the interior people were. **Swahili** has been used as the trade language of East Africa for two centuries, becoming the universal language today.

Lightning Source UK Ltd
Milton Keynes UK
UKOW01f1634041016

284440UK00002B/440/P